# THE LON HUNT

## Richard Zappa

### A Jo Crowder Crime Thriller

ALKIRA
PUBLISHING

*Lion Hunt*
Richard Zappa
Copyright © 2023
Published by Alkira Publishing, Australia
ABN: 32736122056
http://www.alkirapublishing.com



Paperback ISBN: 978-1-922329-63-9
Hardcover ISBN: 978-1-922329-66-0

For all of you who read my novels


**Also by Richard Zappa**
*Identical Misfortune*
*The Easter Murders*
*Double Indemnity*


*No person is so bad as to be beyond redemption.*
**—Mahatma Gandhi**

# PROLOGUE

## Chiapas, Mexico

## 1985

An imminent rising sun had reduced the night to a thin smokiness. The air was still and steamy, the usual pre-dawn prelude to a day during the dry season that made the subtropical climate in the valleys of the mountainous regions of southeastern Mexico only slightly bearable.

The morning's dense, humid warmth mutated into sweltering heat under a blistering sun by early afternoon. By then most of the work in the fields had to be done. If not, it was best to return in the early evening, when the sun had dipped below the tree line of the Sierra Madre mountains to the west.

For Diego, his chores began when the pre-dawn light was just beginning to shine through. He toted water from the communal well in buckets that dangled from the ends of a yoke that rested on broad shoulders. Twelve years old, the boy looked sixteen. He stood two inches taller and weighed ten pounds more than his best friends, Carlos and Raul, who were two years older. It was preordained, a genetic reality—his papa was called *El Gigante* by the villagers.

He too would grow to be a giant.

When he was seven years old, his father and pregnant mother emigrated from Guatemala and settled in Pueblo en las Montañas—the "Village in the Mountains." A year later, he was working alongside his father, clearing the woodlands and farming the fields of beans and maize. His father brought their produce to the village square tethered to a wooden cart until he could afford a mule to pull it, and he didn't leave until every last bean and ear of corn was sold or bartered for things the family needed.

Most of the acreage, however, was reserved for another crop—a staple of the peasant farmers who lived in and around the village. The crop had been called many things, but most often the *flor de alegria*—the "flower of joy." Its botanical name was *papaver somniferum*. It flourished in dry, warm climates, like where Diego and his friends lived.

Cultivating and harvesting the crop followed a regimen unique to farming. About three months after the seeds were planted, bright-colored flowers bloomed at the top of greenish tubular stems. When the petals fell away, an egg-shaped seed pod full of an opaque milky sap was exposed. The sap was extracted by slitting the pod vertically in parallel strokes with a curved knife. As the sap oozed out, it turned darker and darker, forming a brown gum. The farmer then collected the gum with a *cuchillo para raspar*—a scraping knife—and bundled it into bricks and wrapped the bricks in leaves.

Like numerous other farms in and around the mountain villages of the region, the two hectares of land Diego's father farmed on, the seeds he planted, and his equipment and tools, were supplied by the man known as El Lobo—The Wolf— including the four-room adobe building they lived in, the ramshackle outhouse behind it, and the kerosene that fueled their lamps.

The pesos Diego's father and the other farmers were paid for cultivating the flower of joy were infinitesimal compared to what El Lobo was paid in U.S. dollars after the bricks were refined in a laboratory and the final product emerged—a fluffy, white powder. By the time the powder passed through a multi-layered distribution chain and was peddled on the streets of every major city in the United States at ten to twenty-five dollars for one-tenth of a gram, its value ballooned exponentially, providing hundreds of millions of dollars of annual income for El Lobo.

A good fifteen-minute hike through rugged woodlands from Diego's home brought him to the well. He always walked the dirt road back, rather than through the forest, so as not to spill the water he carried. Water was the most precious commodity during the dry season when the cisterns were as dry as noonday desert sand.

Diego's mind wandered as he walked the dusty, uneven road and deftly navigated through a mogul field of ruts, bumps, and holes. Though still an adolescent, he had the worries of a young man who had little in life to look forward to. His father had worked hard every day of his life and had not much to show for it. He owned nothing. He could barely support his family with what he received for his crops and what El Lobo paid him. He was as poor then as he was when he arrived in Mexico five years ago.

Was he destined to be a peasant farmer like his father, and have his life controlled by the *pandillas* and *sicarios*—the gangs and hitmen—who worked for the cartels? The grim prospect followed him like a shadow. Poverty, crime, and violence were the reasons his parents left Guatemala. To what end? They were just as poor and had only found even more violence and crime in Mexico.

The cartels and gangs had a stranglehold on Mexico for more than forty years. They followed no rules other than ones they made for themselves. They acted with reckless and ruthless abandon. Diego had heard the men in the village gossip about the kidnappings, rapes, murders, beheadings, and indiscriminate killings. The cartels killed for lots of reasons … and for no reason at all. No one was safe, least of all the peasant farmers who were shackled to their farms and depended on the cartel to protect them. For Diego's father and so many others, the price of protection was a life of servitude.

The unfairness of it all didn't just sadden Diego, it angered him. His melancholy festered deep within him like an open sore. To block it out, he forced himself to think of pleasant things. This time he thought of Ceci, and he smiled for the first time that day. It was her birthday. Five years old and pretty like his mama. The same mane of curly black hair. The same inquisitive, soup-spoon, chestnut-brown eyes under lush, dark eyebrows. The same delicate mouth and nose and caramel complexion. The same perfectly straight, bright white teeth that seemed to sparkle whenever she smiled.

Diego had spent the better part of his free time during the past week carving a figurine out of a piece of pine oak. He'd whittled it with the *cuchillo* he used to collect the gum from the opium poppies. A set of wings protruded from the back of the statuette. He'd painted it with liquid squeezed from berries that grew wild in the fields.

Ceci was waiting for him by the door when he returned. She greeted him with a broad, toothy grin. Seeing her in her favorite white cotton dress with a flower in her hair brought a smile to his face so broad he felt like the ends of his mouth had stretched to his ears. The melancholia he'd felt evaporated like the misty dew always did when the sun came out after an afternoon rain shower. He was relaxed and at peace with himself … at least for a while.

"Good morning, little angel," he cried out in English as he approached. He squatted to place the buckets on the ground, then knelt in front of his sister. His mother insisted the family speak in English as much as possible. "When you go north and are in America, you will need to speak like the others," she reminded them over and over again. But Diego knew his mama's plan for them was wishful thinking. His papa could never save enough money to pay a coyote to smuggle them across the border, and refusing to farm the poppies for El Lobo was a lethal option.

Ceci lunged at Diego with open arms that were thin and soft and wrapped them tightly around his neck. The squeeze she gave him went straight to his heart. "*Te quiero*, Diego," she whispered softly in his ear.

"In English, Ceci," he gently admonished.

"I love you," she repeated, her sweet breath warm on Diego's neck.

He'd always responded the same way. "And I love you, Ceci, with all my heart."

The little girl stepped back to look at her brother. Her lower lip momentarily protruded into a sulky pout. The sweet smile soon returned, and this time she took her time and enunciated each word in perfect English. "And … I … love

… you … with … all … my … heart."

Diego stroked his sister's hair and kissed her tenderly on the cheek. "I make something special for you, Ceci," he said, purposefully exaggerating the excitement in his voice. He lifted the buckets of water to the bench beside the door and reached behind it where he had put the doll he'd carved. The bench, like much of the furniture in the house, was made by his father, Manuel. Only a tattered couch and the kitchen table and chairs were acquired elsewhere. His father had bought them from a villager who moved back to Nicaragua after her husband was killed by a bullet meant for someone else—the collateral damage from a gunfight between the paid hitmen of rival cartels.

A wide-eyed Ceci took the doll from her brother and held it tight to her boney chest. "Keep her close to you, *Hermanita,*" Diego said to his little sister. "She is an angel like you and will keep you safe."

By then the sun had risen but still hung low on the eastern horizon. The smell of gruel and coffee pierced the dense, stagnant air like a whiff of freshly cut flowers. Diego's stomach growled like a hungry feral cat. Breakfast seldom varied—eggs, if the hens were in a cooperative mood, gruel made from oats and flour, tortillas, and one or two glasses of hot *atole*, a drink made with corn mesa and sweetened with cinnamon.

But today his mother had also made something special for Ceci's birthday—*pan dulce*, a sweet bread that she'd serve at breakfast and dinner. She hadn't made it since *El Triduo Pascual*, the holy days of Easter week.

Manuel was seated drinking coffee when Diego and Ceci joined him at the table. Gabriella, Diego's mother, had their plates of food in front of them. She extinguished the kerosene lamps and sat. Eating began only after hands were held, heads bowed, and the morning prayers were recited in Spanish and English.

The custom among peasant farmers was for the family to eat their meals in silence. Ceci picked at the food on her plate. In contrast, Diego ate like a wolf. He had a weekly routine to follow between morning and evening meals—fetching water from the well and collecting it from the cistern, cutting wood to fuel the stove, working in the fields, attending the mission school in the afternoon, and going to the chapel in the village for mass on Sundays. His routine, like breakfast, rarely varied.

The sameness of how they lived frustrated Diego, though it didn't seem to bother his father, who had sold his life … and soul … to El Lobo when he was conscripted to farm poppies for the cartel. But Diego knew his father had no choice. He'd come to the village with only a few pesos in his pocket. The cartel offered him a job, a home, protection from *mala gente*, the bad people who terrorized outsiders—mostly immigrants, like him, who were on their own in a new country without any family or friends to help them. Desperate people did desperate things. Out of desperation, he agreed to farm for the cartel.

When the meal was eaten, Diego's mother rose to clear the table. Manuel, droopy-eyed, raised his hand and spoke haltingly in a mixture of English and Spanish. "Gabriella … sit, *por favor*. I have something to tell you. A very bad thing happen yesterday." His sigh was long and heavy. "Carlos—his papa was shot dead by *sicarios* from the Santana cartel."

"*Dios mio*," Gabriella shrieked. Aghast, she covered her wide-open mouth with her hands. It was as though all the air had been sucked out of the room. The sudden outburst startled Ceci, who slid off her chair and went to be hugged by her mother.

Manuel drank from his cup, which shook in his hand and

caused some coffee to drip on his chin. He wiped it away with the back of his hand.

Diego sensed his father had more bad news to tell them. "What else, Papa? What else?" He'd heard the stories—*sicarios* killing farmers and their families when they refused to work for the cartel or failed to turn over all of their opium bricks. They were expendable. There were plenty of poor immigrants to coerce into service.

Manuel's face sagged, and his cheeks became puffy and his eyes glossy. "Carlos's mama, sister, and brother … all dead." His face reddened into anger. "*Los bastardos* hung all of them from trees and slit their throats."

"*Dios bendigo sus almos,*" Gabriella cried out in horror, covering Ceci's ears with her hands. Diego had wished his mama's plea—for God to bless their souls—had been an earlier prayer to have saved their lives.

Diego knew his father had a good reason for telling everyone, including Ceci, about what had happened to Carlos's family. Once the shock of the news of the slaughter receded, they'd all understand the seriousness of their predicament. "But what of Carlos, Papa?" Diego asked, a knot somehow finding space to form in a full stomach.

Manuel frowned. "He would have been among the dead if he had not been with Raul."

With Ceci cradled in her arms, Gabriella rocked back and forth in her chair. She removed a *rosario* from the pocket of her peasant dress, held the crucifix snugly in the palm of her hand with her thumb and finger on the first bead, and began to pray. "*En el nombre del Padre y el Hijo y del Espiritu Santo. Amen.*" She prayed aloud until her sobbing snuffed out her words.

Diego knew his mama would complete the prayers of the

rosary in a hushed tone, as she'd done every Sunday in the chapel for as long as he could remember, always after mass while kneeling at the foot of the statue of the Virgin Mary.

Manuel rose from his chair and walked over to Gabriella. He stood behind her and put a pair of large, calloused hands on her delicate shoulders. His gentle embrace had a calming effect on her. She stopped rocking, and her sobbing subsided. But silent tears still streamed down her face, and they glistened in the morning sunlight that beamed through the screen-less kitchen window. He kissed the top of her head, stroked Ceci's cheek with the back of his hand, and turned to face his son. "*Hijo, ven conmigo,*" he said in a stern, husky voice.

Diego, always the obedient son, followed his father into his parents' bedroom. At five feet four inches tall and a hundred and thirty-five pounds, he was almost the size of the average adult Guatemalan man. He was called *El Alto*—The Tall One—by the boys in the village. He'd certainly grow as tall as his father.

Diego had also inherited his father's rugged good looks— dark, deeply set eyes the size of grapes, pronounced cheek bones, and a strong chiseled jawline. Sensing the importance of the private meeting, he closed the door behind him. Diego stood facing his father and fixed his eyes on Manuel's desperate, haggard face when he spoke.

"Diego, I fear we are in danger. I was with Carlos's papa when Santana's men approach us in the village a week ago and tell us to no longer give our bricks to El Lobo. They promise to pay us more for them and protect us if El Lobo's men come after us. They tell us they will be back for our bricks this week.

"When they left us, we talk about what to do and agree we are better off staying with El Lobo. Like me, Carlos's papa gives his bricks to El Lobo, and his family is slaughtered because of it."

Diego's heart thundered in his chest. "You think the *sicarios* come for us too, Papa?"

"*Si, hijo.* I tell El Lobo's men we need their protection, but no men returned yesterday to kill the *sicarios* … and they murder Carlos's family." He paused and squeezed his eyes shut in disgust. "And they are not here to protect us this day." Manuel put his hands on his son's shoulders. His vice-like grip signaled to Diego that Papa was about to reveal his plan.

"I want you to take mama and Ceci to your uncle's house in the next village." He raised an eyebrow. "Do you know how to get there?"

"*Si*, Papa," he answered attentively. "I brought him food Mama made for him when he was sick."

"Keep to the woodlands," his father cautioned. "If you need to walk the road, watch for Santana's men. Their jeeps, they are black like their souls. After El Lobo's men pay me today for our bricks, I come to you."

"Are we coming back, Papa?" Diego asked warily. He'd heard the stories—the cartels torching the homes of farmers who didn't turn over all their opium to them, often with their families in them.

The furrows in his father's brow deepened. "It is too dangerous to return, Diego. If El Lobo's men kill the *sicarios*, Santana will fight back and send others. If there is a war between the cartels, our village and others who farm for El Lobo will be caught in the middle."

Manuel went over to a chest in the room, opened it and reached for a wooden box. Diego knew what was in it. His father opened the lid, removed his revolver, and loaded it with six bullets. He handed the gun to Diego. "Last year I show you how to use it. Remember to hold it in both hands. Point it at the chest and ..."

"I know," Diego interrupted excitedly. "Take a deep breath, let it out slowly, and ..." He paused long enough to follow his father's instructions. He pointed the gun at the center of the open window in the bedroom. His mouth twisted into a crooked smile. "And slowly press the trigger," he continued, shouting out "bang" as he pretended to fire the gun.

"Manuel, come quickly," Gabriella shouted from the kitchen. "Some *hombres* are outside."

Manuel darted from the room and went to the window with Diego on his heels. He was tall enough to look over his father's shoulder and see a black jeep parked in front of the house. Two men stood beside it, smoking cigarettes and talking to each other in a voice too low for him to hear.

His father raised his eyes to the top of their sockets. "*Hijos de perra*," he cursed under his breath. Diego knew then that his papa had recognized the men as the "sons of bitches" who'd confronted him and Carlos's father in the village.

Gabriella cowered in a corner of the room with Ceci pulled tightly into her, their faces portraits of terror. Diego stood anxiously behind his father with the gun still in his hand.

Manuel turned to face his son. "Take Mama and Ceci and leave through the bedroom window. You know what to do."

"Take the gun, Papa," Diego pleaded, offering it to him with an outstretched hand.

"No. You may need it to protect Mama and Ceci. Now, *vamos!*"

Diego's jaw clenched. He knew not to argue with his father, and time was too valuable to waste. He tucked the gun into his waistband. "Come quickly, Mama," he demanded in a voice as deep and stern as his father's had been.

His mother hurried into the bedroom with Ceci, her

brother's figurine clutched in a white-knuckled grip. Gabriella climbed out first. Diego helped Ceci through the opening and into his mother's arms. He followed next.

Diego knelt in front of Ceci, with his back to her. "Climb on, Ceci. You know, like when I let you ride me like a horse." His sister put her arms around her brother's neck and gripped the wrist that held the figurine with her free hand.

With Ceci on his back, Diego and Gabriella raced into the forest.

Diego stopped about a hundred yards into the woodlands when he could no longer see the house. He knelt, and Ceci got off his back.

"Now, listen to me, Mama, and do exactly what I tell you to do. Go to the well and wait nearby where you cannot be seen from the road. If I am not there in fifteen minutes, you and Ceci go to Uncle's house. Stay off the road as much as possible."

"Diego, what are you going to do?" Gabriella's voice trembled as she spoke.

Diego's eyes widened, and he rubbed his chin with the back of a hand. "I am going back for Papa," he answered in a tone whose matter-of-factness didn't quite hide excitement.

Gabriella's stare fixed on the gun in her son's waistband. Tears streamed down her cheeks, and Ceci soon followed her lead. "Diego, I do not want to lose you too," she pleaded with him out of desperation.

Ceci dashed to her brother's side and flung her arms around his waist. "Come with us, Diego. Please come with us," she begged through her sobbing. Diego felt her body shivering when he drew her closer. He bent over and kissed the top of her head.

After a moment of sweet reflection, he stood erect again

and squared his shoulders. "Mama, Ceci, do as I say," he demanded. "Papa needs me. You will be safe if you stay off the road." He pulled Ceci away from him, and she went to her mother, who grabbed her by the hand. He glared sternly at his mother. "Now, *vamos!*" He was as resolute as his father had been.

Diego watched as his mother and sister scampered off in the direction of the well. His eyes were moist and swollen—he might never see them again. He watched them race with purpose in their stride, and long enough to see them safely out of view. He took a deep breath and let it out slowly. Then, with his father's revolver in his hand, he ran as fast as he could to the back of the house.

Hunched over, he gulped in air to catch his breath. He heard his father pleading from the front of the house to spare his wife and children. It sickened him to hear his father degraded and humiliated that way. His body went limp, but only for a moment. His muscles soon stiffened with resolve again.

He cleared his head of images of his father pleading for mercy and formulated a plan. It was safer to confront his adversaries from inside the house. He climbed into the bedroom and dashed to the kitchen. With his back against a wall, he sidestepped to the kitchen window. The door was ajar and chairs were upended—Santana's men had been in the house and had seen that it was empty.

He'd have the element of surprise in his favor.

Diego peered through the window and saw his father on the ground in front of the *sicarios* with his hands and feet bound with duct tape. One end of a rope was in a noose around his neck; the other end was tied to the back of the jeep.

He had a good view of his father, who was looking in his direction. He lay there defenseless, his face a bloody pulp.

The sight of it made him momentarily sick to his stomach. Bile formed in his throat, and he thought he might vomit. When the nausea passed, something roiled up in him that he'd felt only once before. His blood boiled as it coursed through his arteries and veins. He was hot in his core, but he wasn't sweating. His heart raced, but he wasn't scared or nervous. His palms were dry around the handle of the gun that was pressed tightly to his chest with the barrel pointed up.

The first time Diego had felt rage was a half year ago in the village. After Sunday mass, his mother remained in the chapel to pray. The rest of the family waited in the park. While his father was talking to another farmer with Diego by his side, Ceci wandered off and out of sight. He'd learned afterward she had been chasing a butterfly when she was confronted by a boy several years older than Diego and known for being a bully. He'd lured Ceci into a passageway behind the chapel and wanted to touch her under her dress. She resisted, and the boy pushed her to the ground.

When Diego noticed his sister was gone, he went to look for her and found her lying on the ground, crying. Her dress was torn, and she was rubbing her shoulder. The boy who had assaulted her stood over her, taunting her and calling her *mi pequeña perra*—"my little bitch."

Diego had felt the same rage then, when he'd beaten the boy with his fists until his nose and jaw were broken, his eyes blackened, and his face battered so badly he lost consciousness. Had his father not intervened and pulled his son off the boy, Diego would have beaten the young thug to death.

Santana's men had their backs to the house, their rifles shouldered. They took turns kicking Diego's father in the stomach and head. They laughed and mocked him, saying that, after they dragged his dead body through the village, they'd come back and rape his pretty wife and kill her and his children.

Diego had flashbacks of Mama smiling at him when he'd left to fetch the water that morning, of Ceci hugging him when he'd returned, and of Papa talking man to man to him in the bedroom when he'd been given the gun and entrusted with the lives of his family.

He walked very calmly to the front door and stepped into the opening. He felt Papa's penetrating stare through the slits of his swollen eyes. He gripped the revolver firmly in his hands and pointed it at the middle of the back of one of the men. He alone would decide whether two men would live or die—two assassins who'd butchered his best friend's family and who intended to do the same to his family.

A surge of adrenaline rushed through his body. He stood there feeling as tall and strong as his father had always been.

Only the two men and his finger against the trigger existed at that moment. No need to take a deep breath and let it out slowly, as his father had instructed. Calm and in control, the task at hand came naturally to him. He smiled when the first shot fired and struck its mark.

And the shooting stopped only when all shots had been fired into the backs of Santana's men and they lay dead on the ground.

# CHAPTER 1

## Present Day

The Orleans Criminal District Court located on Tulane Avenue had original jurisdiction over all state criminal cases for crimes that occurred in Orleans Parish. The serious felony trials took place there. Twelve elected district judges shouldered the burden of an overcrowded criminal docket—everything from rape, robbery, assault, kidnapping and murder, and a seemingly endless inventory of drug cases.

Louisiana was home to some of the toughest drug laws in the nation. Getting caught with even a trace of cocaine could mean a minimum of five years behind bars. Possessing large amounts could result in a fine of up to six hundred thousand dollars and sixty years of hard labor in the state penitentiary; a life sentence awaited second offenders. Hard labor didn't mean what one might have thought—shattering rocks with a pickaxe—but it did mean incarceration at a very nasty place.

Detective Lieutenant Jo Crowder sat in a courtroom on the second floor, waiting for the bailiff to call the court to order. She was familiar with all of the courtrooms, but that one in particular was the preferred courtroom of Judge Allen, the court's president judge. Being the head honcho had its privileges—he could assign cases to the other judges. There was a downside—he was expected to handle the serial murders, mass shootings, and high-profile prosecutions of public figures.

A fourteen-year veteran of the New Orleans Police Department, Jo Crowder earned her reputation as the department's top homicide detective. With degrees in criminal justice and criminal forensics, her days as a patrol officer were predictably short-lived. The youngest patrol officer ever to earn a detective's gold shield, she found her niche in solving the most heinous crimes. She had the highest conviction rate in murder cases and the lowest number of *cold case* files—unsolved crimes. For other detectives, such files were like forgotten leftovers hidden behind something on the bottom shelf of the refrigerator.

But Jo Crowder wasn't like the others. She took cold cases personally. She couldn't get the victim's faces out of her head, no matter how hard she tried. For her, the cases had no shelf life or expiration date. She reviewed the files repeatedly, looking for something she'd missed or a new approach to the investigations—something … anything that might help her solve crimes that had been forgotten by everyone except the victim's loved ones … and her. Her perseverance occasionally paid off—she eventually solved some of them.

New Orleans needed someone like Jo Crowder. Famously known for music and merriment as it was for mayhem and murder, the city had one of the highest urban murder rates in the nation. Armed with state-of-the-art forensic skills and a keen intuitive sense, she had an uncanny knack for thinking like the violent offenders and cold-blooded murderers she pursued. She didn't just get under the skin of a suspect; she wore it like a cloak.

By all outward appearances, the pretty, five-foot-five, 125-pound woman didn't look the part of a no-nonsense, tough-as-nails cop. But she had chutzpah and a gutsy bravado that made her unflappable in the face of danger. It helped that she was a crack shot with her pistol, boxed, had black belts in the martial arts, and regularly cross-trained at the police academy gym.

But her ride to the top of her profession was not without its bumps and bruises—many of her own making. She disdained bureaucratic red tape and flouted the rules, even broke a law or two along the way for the greater good. She was impatient, could be intolerant, headstrong, and, on occasion, insubordinate. She was not one who suffered fools easily. She didn't just ruffle feathers; she plucked them out one by one until all were removed.

In short, she was a suspect's worst nightmare … and, sometimes, her captain's worst headache.

Still, you couldn't argue with the results. Her commendations for bravery were unmatched by anyone in the department. But her success was not without controversy. Her record-setting kills in the line of duty didn't just wrinkle a few brows of criminal justice reformists; they contorted their faces. For some she was a rogue cop and a vigilante with a badge. But for the victims, their families, and a mostly adoring public, she was an avenging angel.

The truth? She'd always been found to have acted within her legal right to use deadly force to protect her life or the lives of others.

So far, at least.

The bailiff entered the courtroom and took his customary post alongside the jury box—a sure sign the trial was about to resume. Jo turned to glance at the lawyers who had squared off during the trial.

A special prosecutor had been appointed by the governor. Zack Hitchens had left the Shreveport D.A.'s office ten years ago to join a private law firm representing clients accused of financial crimes and other white-collar offenses. But his legacy as a top prosecutor had been secure by the time he left government service. She knew, more than anyone, that Hitchens's selection was necessary to eliminate bias and any appearance of impropriety if the case had remained with the Orleans Parish District Attorney's Office headed by her brother, Tom Crowder.

Tom, a skilled prosecutor, had routinely recused himself from prosecuting cases in which his sister was the lead investigator. He'd assign the cases to one of his assistant D.A.s. It had been particularly important in high-profile cases when the lead investigator was expected to sit at the prosecution table during the trial, provide testimony about the investigation, and assist the prosecutor in presenting the evidence.

Andrew Schulman sat at the defense table. He'd come from Baton Rouge to handle the defense—because of the notoriety of the case. She knew Schulman well; one might say intimately well. They'd shared a personal relationship for a while, but like her other romantic trysts, it had ended when he expected more from her than she was willing to give.

Lucky in cards, unlucky in love.

Schulman's record representing defendants accused of serious crimes was well known in Louisiana. He had represented more than a dozen men at capital murder trials. In cases involving the worst of the worst, Schulman's foremost objective was to keep his clients from receiving a lethal injection. By picking apart the often-overwhelming evidence, he was able to achieve many mid-trial pleas to a lesser degree of homicide and get his clients a coveted get-out-of-death-row-free card that came with it. Although several clients ended up on death row, three walked out of the courtroom free men.

He was considered the best criminal defense lawyer in Louisiana.

The chatter in the gallery ceased when the bailiff boomed out his directive, "All rise. Court is now in session, Judge Allen presiding."

Allen, in his mid-sixties, was the most experienced trial judge on the court. A former prosecutor and public defender, he was respected by both sides and considered a fair-minded jurist in the opinion of most lawyers who practiced before him. He entered through a side door and moved swiftly to his chair behind the bench, his helmet of wavy white hair in stark contrast to his flowing black robe. He looked over wire-rimmed eyeglasses, his steely blue eyes shifting between Hitchens and Schulman.

"The jury has reached a verdict," he announced, his voice without inflection or emotion. A quarter of a century on the bench made receiving a verdict a ho-hum routine ... but not today. He nodded in the direction of the bailiff. "Bring in the jury.

The court official left through a door next to the jury box and returned a few minutes later with the jury. Six men and six women filed into the jury box and sat in the assigned seats they had throughout the trial. The foreperson, a middle-aged Asian American man, sat bolt upright in the first seat of the front row and held in his hand the verdict sheet that would determine the defendant's fate.

Jo studied the faces and behaviors of the jurors while preparations were made to announce the verdict. She'd prided herself in guessing right the jury's verdict in the many criminal trials in which she had participated. Yet she'd attributed little import to the facial expressions and body language of jurors.

To her, it didn't matter if jurors looked nervous, agitated, or upset, were weepy-eyed, smiled, or looked like the cat that had just eaten a cage full of canaries. Or if they leaned forward or back in their chairs, wiped sweaty palms and brows with a handkerchief, shook their head or nodded, or had looked at the prosecutor or defense counsel with a shit-eating grin on their face. Nor did it matter how long the jury had deliberated—one hour, two, five, or a day or more. She had juries return guilty verdicts in less than an hour and after deliberating for days.

Her only measure in predicting a verdict was the stuff of which verdicts were made—the facts as shown by credible evidence introduced at trial. If the witnesses for the prosecution were believable and held up on cross-examination, and if the state had some solid science-based evidence—a fingerprint, a strand of hair, a clothing fiber, a blood or DNA match that linked the defendant to the crime—a guilty verdict was as certain as winning at blackjack holding an ace and a king. If not, the state was likely to hit a face card on a pair of sixes.

In the case before the court, she didn't need to study the jury—only the evidence—and it was overwhelming. She recalled how the prosecutor had summed up the "indisputable facts" in his closing argument. He'd said, "The defendant was seen leaving the warehouse where the drugs and cash had been stashed. A security camera caught the defendant placing a large quantity of drugs and bundles of cash in a vehicle registered in the defendant's name. The drugs and some of the money were found at the defendant's home with the defendant's prints on them. Where the bulk of the cash remains hidden is known only to the defendant, who has refused to cooperate with law enforcement and reveal its location."

Facts don't lie. The jury's verdict was a forgone conclusion.

Judge Allen nodded at the court clerk. "Bring me the verdict sheet." The foreperson handed it to the clerk, who gave it to the judge, a formality in every case to be sure it had been properly completed. Protocol was protocol. Allen paused briefly to adjust his eyeglasses, scanned over the two-page document, and returned it to the clerk.

The judge looked over his reading glasses at the defendant. "The defendant will rise to hear the verdict." The defendant and Schulman both stood. "Madame Clerk, stand and read the jury's verdict."

The clerk, a slender, long-faced woman in her mid-forties with poker-straight hair pulled back tightly in a ballerina's bun, stood in front of the table where the trial exhibits lay and turned in the direction of the defendant. She had just enough of a southern drawl when she spoke to confirm her Louisiana roots. Without looking up, she read aloud from the verdict sheet in an emotionless monotone.

"On the charge of possession with the intent to distribute a Schedule One drug, to wit, heroin, in an amount greater than twenty-eight grams, a felony, the jury unanimously finds the defendant guilty.

"On the charge of theft in an amount having a value of twenty-five thousand dollars or more, a felony, the jury unanimously finds the defendant guilty."

Jo turned to look at the gallery as the jury was led out of

the courtroom by the bailiff. The first two rows on each side were reserved for the local beat and cable news reporters—their fingers pounding away at their laptops and cell phones like pianists playing an allegro. Outside, photographers and cameramen awaited the prosecutor, who would make the customary post-trial announcement to the newspeople and public that justice had been served by the jury's thoughtful review of the evidence and guilty verdict.

She reviewed in her mind what happened after a defendant had been found guilty of a felony. In this case, with a stash of money hidden away, the defendant would be considered an imminent flight risk—bail would be revoked. The newly convicted felon would be remanded into the custody of a sheriff's deputy and transported to the Orleans Parish Prison, pending sentencing.

Because it was a high-profile case, the sentencing hearing would be expedited. In seven to ten days, Judge Allen would reconvene and impose a prison sentence of not less than ten years, the mandatory minimum for conviction of a drug trafficking offense. Another ten years would be tacked on for the theft charge—but if the judge was merciful, it would run concurrently, not consecutively. In the end, the prisoner would be transported to prison in handcuffs and leg shackles and incarcerated there for a very long time.

After the jury left the courtroom, a deputy sheriff removed the handcuffs from his belt and walked over to Schulman, who grabbed hold of his client's arm. They turned to face the lawman.

The last thing that Jo Crowder remembered before she was handcuffed and led from the courtroom was her lawyer saying, "Jo, watch your back."

# CHAPTER 2

Jo Crowder sat in a crowded courtroom for the second time in a week. This time for her sentencing. Same courtroom. Same chair. Same cast of characters—Schulman, Hitchens, and Allen. Even the bailiff and court personnel were the same.

*Déjà vu.*

One thing did change. She wasn't wearing the modest, knee-length, black cotton dress she'd worn the day she was convicted. This time she was clad in a baggy, orange polyester jumpsuit, compliments of the Orleans Parish Prison. Not much of a fashion statement … but orange was the new black.

She looked behind her. Another sold-out performance. So many familiar faces. However, this time the press and national cable television reporters who had covered the trial were there to provide breaking news of her sentence and imprisonment and commentary on whether the sentence she received was unduly harsh or merely a slap on the wrist. The celebrity-trial groupies occupied the cheap seats in the back of the courtroom.

Two of Jo's younger brothers sat grim-faced behind her in the front row—the obligatory showing of familial solidarity. Both were in their police uniforms. Optics mattered—anything that might influence Judge Allen to show leniency.

Tom Crowder was there too. The oldest of her brothers wanted to speak on behalf of his sister. But she insisted he not make a spectacle of himself, not implore the judge to show mercy when in so many cases as a prosecutor he'd argued to Allen just the opposite. The hypocrisy would have been so thick you'd need a machete to hack through it.

What more could her brother say that wasn't already in the pre-sentence report: an exemplary record in law enforcement … that is, until now; the times she'd put her life on the line, was shot at, injured, and hospitalized; the commendations she'd received for bravery; and the role she played as a surrogate parent to her younger brothers after her mother died in a car crash when she was a teenager.

Jo remembered how Tom praised her as a role model at the press conference he gave when he became the District Attorney of Orleans Parish—how proud he was of her that day and how happy it made her feel. The only thing that made Jo happy at that moment in the courtroom was that her parents were not alive to witness her fall from grace. If a car crash and cancer hadn't killed her parents, the debacle that was taking place in the courtroom surely would have.

Jo hadn't helped her cause much the day she was arrested. She'd claimed the stolen money and drugs found at her home had been planted, perhaps by another cop or an ex-con she'd put away who had an ax to grind with her. It seemed believable at the time. She knew she had a target on her back. One felon she'd put away had taken a shot at her the day after he was paroled. Fortunately, the bullet into the windshield of her pickup truck hit the rear-view mirror, altering its trajectory just enough to miss her head.

When someone took a shot at you, inches ... and luck ... mattered.

The "I'm being framed" defense had its flaws, particularly after forensics determined that her prints were all over the fruits of her crime, and she'd been seen on a security camera putting the cash and drugs in her truck.

Zach Hitchens had just completed his argument to Allen. Its brevity came as no surprise to Jo. His main points were the obvious ones: the overwhelming evidence at trial, the coverup attempt, the refusal to return the rest of the money she'd stolen, and her lack of remorse all justified a lengthy sentence.

Hitchens argued for a sentence of twenty years.

Schulman didn't have much to say either. He simply rattled off the things Jo's brothers had said in the pre-sentence report.

Schulman argued for a sentence of ten years.

The judge sat there stone faced and interrupted not once. Jo knew he had made up his mind before the hearing.

She predicted the outcome—Allen showed no mercy and sentenced her to twenty years and a fine of one hundred thousand dollars. She winced. For all intents and purposes, she was financially ruined and had been given a life sentence.

~

She sat in a Department of Corrections van with another defendant sentenced that day. Like the stringy, mousy-haired convict in the seat in front of her, Jo had spent the past week in the women's section of the Orleans Parish Prison, sharing a cell with three other prisoners. Her steel-frame bunk bed had a thin, hard mattress and a small, spongy pillow. Jo suspected the gray pillowcase had once been white. Her sheet had urine, rust, and menstrual blood stains. The metallic sink and lidless toilet were visible from the gangway, and a reminder that the imprisoned had not only lost their freedom but also their privacy.

The jail was designed to house defendants awaiting trial and sentencing who couldn't post bail. With money hidden away, Jo was deemed a flight risk. Bail was revoked after her conviction.

As comfy as her quarters had been, the van was taking her to a different detention facility to begin serving her sentence. An hour's drive from New Orleans, the detention facility had once been a middle school with an asbestos problem and a long history of neglect. It had been closed five years before being converted into a dormitory-style prison to house inmates until the new women's prison was built. Construction problems, insufficient funding, and a pandemic had intervened to delay its completion. It would be another year before it could receive houseguests.

Not much thought or money went into securing the temporary detention facility. New locking mechanisms on the doors and windows, a twelve-foot-high chain-link fence, and some security cameras were the primary modifications. Reconfigured classrooms called pods accommodated twelve inmates each. The place was grossly understaffed—the guard to prisoner ratio was half that of other temporary facilities scattered throughout the state.

The place had a reputation for being the easiest Department of Corrections prison facility from which to escape. Or attempt escape, at least. In the two years it had operated, it had seen four escapes, most through doors left intentionally or unintentionally unlocked. No one knew for sure. No internal investigations were ever conducted. Wearing the bright orange scrubs with a DOC logo on the back and having no place to go, all escapees were captured within the hour and moved to more secure facilities afterwards.

*No harm, no foul.*

Jo knew about the facility's reputation for being lax on the rules. Guards were mostly men. Some traded drugs, alcohol, candy, or cosmetics for sex. For those who had transferred from the women's prison when it closed, the place was a country club by comparison.

Jo had joined a sundry group of African American, Latina, Caucasian, Creole, and Cajun women of all ages, some still in their teens, with one thing in common—all were convicted felons locked away for murder, manslaughter, assault, grand larceny, robbery, drug offenses, and other serious crimes.

Her handcuffs and leg shackles were removed when she arrived at the facility, and a body search was performed by a female guard. Afterwards, the new arrivals were placed in a locked room and taken separately for their orientation with the warden of the prison facility. Jo was taken second.

She was led by a stout, thin-haired, uniformed guard whose nameplate read Carver. A holstered pistol and canister of mace hung lazily from his belt. The guard had handcuffed her behind her back as soon as they left the room. Before they reached the warden's office, he stopped and told her he needed to search her for contraband.

When she saw Carver look up and down the corridor with the anxious look of a boy about to do something naughty, she knew what he said was bullshit. They were alone in the corridor. She didn't see any security cameras pointed in their direction. Carver took his time patting her down, being sure to linger in all the right places. She was half tempted to knee him in the balls, but she didn't want a demerit on her first day of school. He was the one with the hall pass, not her. And if she reported the jerk, he'd just deny it. It would be his word against the unsupported allegations of a convicted felon.

*Same old, same old.*

Warden Sylvia Green's office had previously been occupied by the school principal. Part of the word *Principal* was still visible in faded gold leaf on the door under a thin brass plate with the word *Warden* on it. Carver removed the handcuffs before they entered the office—he didn't want his boss to know about the foreplay.

"Take a seat, inmate Crowder," Green said, focused on information in the file on her desk. "Your handcuffs and leg restraints were removed when you arrived here, and they will remain off unless you give us a reason to use them."

*Handcuffs?* Jo forced herself not to laugh, but the grin was impossible to completely hide. She suspected Carver had been getting his rocks off handcuffing inmates and feeling them up during their orientations for quite some time. She got rid of the grin as soon as Green's eyes rose from the paperwork and zeroed in on her. The last thing she wanted was having her jailor think she was a smart ass.

"You will be housed here until the construction of the new women's prison is completed," she began. "So, let's get the rules straight right from the start." She reached for a pocket-sized handbook titled *Rules of DOC Women's Prisons*, handed it to Jo, and then recited shorter versions of the rules from memory.

"Do as you are told by the guards. Do not argue with the guards. Do not steal from the commissary or other inmates. Do not engage in any sexual acts with guards or other inmates. Do not curse at or make obscene or threatening gestures to the guards or other inmates." Green paused to cough and clear her throat. "Do not kick, slap, punch, or spit at the guards or other inmates. Do not report late to your workstation or leave early without a guard's permission. Shower at the times assigned to you. Use tampons or sanitary napkins when you menstruate. Do not possess any eating utensils, shivs, alcohol, illegal drugs, or contraband. Report to me or the deputy warden any threats or inappropriate acts against you by a guard or inmate."

Green popped a cough drop into her mouth. It clinked against her teeth when she moved it side to side with her tongue. Jo could smell the menthol.

She continued, "Meals are served in the cafeteria during two rotating shifts. You'll have twenty minutes to finish your meals and return your tray and eating utensils to the bins before you leave. Showers are in the evenings after dinner. You'll have ten minutes to shower and return to your pod. Your prison-issued robes must be tied when standing and walking in the corridors. There are five roll calls a day. Don't miss any.

"You are assigned to one of the two shifts in the cafeteria and will be paid forty cents an hour, which will be deposited into your commissary account on the first day of the month."

Green paused, looked down at Jo's file, and then back at her. "I see you were a cop. I'd think twice before sharing that information with other inmates. Do you have any questions, inmate Crowder?"

"No, ma'am," she replied respectfully. "I intend to obey the rules and do my time in peace."

"You've been assigned to pod four, bunk seven. Towels, toiletries, and institutional clothing are in your numbered box on the floor below the lower bunk. Your day begins at six a.m. Lockdown and lights out are at ten p.m."

Jo heard the door open, turned, and saw Carver standing

beside it. She knew to stand and leave the office without being told.

"Come with me. I'll show you your bunk, workstation, and give you a guided tour of the place," he said smugly once they were alone in the corridor. Jo felt a set of bulging eyes ogle her as she walked beside the plump, puffy-faced guard.

The pod was empty when they got there. Carver stood a few feet from her bunk. "Your prison scrubs are in your box. I'll need what you're wearing. They are not the institutional clothing of this facility."

She pulled the box from under the bunk, found the scrubs, and laid them on the bunk. When she realized he wasn't going to leave the pod or turn away, she turned her back to him, stepped out of her slip-ons, took off her jumpsuit, and began to put on her scrubs.

"I'll need all of your clothes," he smirked. "Everything you need is in the box, including shoes and socks."

The creep enjoyed watching her strip. He was close enough to her that she could smell his body odor. She kept her back to him when she removed her bra and put on the thin, flexible, prison-issued replacement. Most bras were made with spandex and difficult to tear apart. The prison-issued ones were cotton, and unlikely to be strong enough to strangle someone or strung together with others and used as a rope.

"Panties too," Carver barked. "Gotta be sure you don't have something hidden you shouldn't have."

*Really, Carver? The bra, I can understand. But my panties?* When was the last time someone was strangled with a pair of panties? She could discern an uptick in Carver's breathing as she removed them and put on a pair of prison underwear. Once again she shoved aside the impulse to put him in the hospital.

She doubted a male guard was supposed to watch her

undress. A female guard had done a body search when she arrived. And Carver's gratuitous frisk revealed nothing.

She was sure of one thing after Carver felt her up and made her strip in front of him—she'd need to watch out for him.

In prison, she'd have to watch out for a lot of things.

# CHAPTER 3

## Phoenix, Arizona

The twenty-five-kilogram box was delivered to the mailroom of the Phoenix Division of the Drug Enforcement Administration around noon. It had been shipped from a Federal Express shipping center in Nogales, Arizona. Nogales and its sister city of the same name in the Mexican state of Sonoma were border towns separated by a wall and razor wire and patrolled by armed agents on both sides. Other than being a port of entry between two nations, the cities had little else in common.

Nogales, Arizona, was a small, quaint, family-friendly town of twenty thousand. It sat on a high mountain pass. Trees and lush gardens filled the neighborhoods. The city enjoyed a bustling economy and had a reasonable standard of living. Healthwise, it had the lowest cancer rate in the nation. The air and water quality were good. The crime rate was low.

A nice place for Americans to live and visit.

By contrast, Nogales, Mexico, was a sprawling city of a quarter of a million people. Set deep in the dusty, sun-blasted lands of the Sonoran Desert, it was surrounded by cactus-covered hills and valleys of brittle bush. A third of the population lived in poverty. The water was unsafe to drink. Crime was rampant. It boasted one of the highest murder rates of cities in Mexico. For good reason—it was a favorite nesting place for the Sinaloa cartel, one of the largest traffickers of heroin and fentanyl in the world.

Not a nice place for *Americanos* to live and visit.

The package passed through the screening process without incident and ended up in a mail cart. It made its way to the third-floor office of Antonio Vega, Special Agent in charge of DEA's Phoenix Division. Its proximity to the border made the division one of the busiest in the United States for controlling drug trafficking.

Vega was promoted to his job five years ago following a successful sting operation that led to the capture of El Gordo—The Fat One—who headed the Candelária cartel, which operated in the Mexican state of Durango. The drug lord had been wanted for trafficking narcotics, money laundering, and murder for nearly five years but was able to avoid capture by constantly moving to sanctuaries in remote areas of Mexico.

At the time, El Gordo was the third largest drug trafficker in the world, responsible for tons of heroin, cocaine, and crystal meth making its way across the border on boats and airplanes, in hidden compartments of cars and trucks, and in condoms swallowed by or forced into the rectums of mules—humans paid to smuggle drugs across the border.

The sting operation had consumed the better part of two years. Vega had led the midnight raid that caught the drug lord and his detachment of bodyguards completely by surprise. The big break came when the Mexican American undercover agent Vega recruited infiltrated El Gordo's criminal organization and became one of his personal bodyguards. He'd learned that his boss intended to spend the night with one of his mistresses at a posh hotel in Guadalajara, the capital of the Mexican state of Jalisco.

El Gordo had rented every room on his floor and secretly secured access through a rear entrance. A half dozen of his men were deployed to cover the front and back of the hotel. Two men with assault rifles stood outside his room, one of whom was Vega's undercover agent. This man's identity was known only to Vega and a few others.

The men guarding the hotel were easily subdued by a detachment of male and female DEA Special Response Team members posing as American tourists. Of Mexican descent, Vega convincingly passed as a kitchen worker delivering a room service order. After the undercover agent took out the other guard with the butt end of his rifle, Vega used the master keycard he'd gotten from the main desk to open the lock and catch the big Mexican with his gun on a chair next to his clothes and his head between the thighs of his mistress. The drug kingpin realized he'd lose in a shootout and went quietly in handcuffs and a hotel bathrobe.

Alerted to its arrival by his administrative assistant, the box was waiting for Vega on his desk when he returned to his office after a meeting. The assistant was a matronly woman in her late fifties who had been with the Phoenix Division longer than anyone working there, including Vega. He inherited the efficient subordinate with his promotion. She remained in the room when Vega opened the box and removed a large cylindrical container wrapped in newspaper.

Vega chuckled. "What, the Maltese Falcon?"

His assistant laughed, but her merriment turned to horror when Vega pulled off the paper covering the glass container and she saw what was inside—a head floating in formaldehyde— eyes gouged out and tongue and ears cut off.

Though severely disfigured, Vega knew to whom the head had once belonged.

~

Vega's flight arrived at Reagan National Airport in Arlington, Virginia, at noon. A car and driver waited and drove him to DEA headquarters in Springfield for his one o'clock meeting with Monica Stallings, head of the agency. Appointed by the president and confirmed by unanimous consent of the Senate two weeks ago, Stallings was a fifty-year-old former United States Attorney with a reputation for being tough on drug traffickers. Vega was familiar with Stallings's prosecutorial skills. He'd been her chief investigator when she successfully prosecuted El Gordo, who was convicted of operating a criminal enterprise and sentenced to life in prison.

Vega was there to deliver some very bad news to his new boss—the fentanyl epidemic was about to get a lot worse, and he was no closer to capturing the person responsible now than he was a year ago.

When the infamous El Leon, head of the Chiapas cartel, was indicted for drug trafficking, money laundering, and murder, Vega spent an entire year investigating the cartel's operations in Mexico and the United States. He paid out hundreds of thousands of dollars for information on the location of the drug lord's labs and storage facilities; but when the raids were conducted, they found only empty buildings.

A bounty of two million dollars for information leading to the capture of El Leon sparked little interest. The risk was too great—the price of betrayal was a fatwa calling for an ignominious death.

Vega and Stallings met in her office and sat at a table across from each other. They had grown to be friends during the prosecution of El Gordo. He knew Stallings to be an unpretentious, no-nonsense, down-to-earth pragmatist, and someone you couldn't bullshit.

After an exchange of pleasantries and a vote of confidence in Vega, she asked, "What should be my priorities as administrator, Tony? I value your opinion."

*Priorities?* There was only one priority—capturing El Leon and shutting down his operations. Vega moved uneasily in his chair before opening his briefcase and pulling out a clear plastic bag.

Stallings picked up the bag and studied the pills inside. Each pill had an M inside a square on one side and the number 30 on the other.

"Synthetic opioids made to look like prescription oxycodone," Stallings deduced. "I've seen thousands of them in evidence lockers over the last five years."

Vega's brow furrowed when he raised his eyebrows. "Not quite like these."

Stallings eyes shifted from the bag to Vega. "What do you mean?"

"Our lab analyzed several of the pills in that bag. The pills are laced with fentanyl, probably sourced from China, that make them a hundred times more potent than prescription oxycodone and fifty times more powerful than heroin."

Stallings shifted her gaze back to the bag. "So, you are saying these are more potent than the ones we usually see?"

"No. They actually have less fentanyl than we typically see, which means the pills are cheaper to produce."

Stallings felt the pills with her fingers without opening the bag. "What makes these different, more dangerous?"

Vega opened his briefcase, pulled out a report, and handed it to her. He knew what the laboratory analysis of the pills showed, but he wanted his boss to read the two-page report before discussing it further.

Stallings put down the bag of pills and picked up the report. She spoke as she read what was in the pills. "Three point one milligrams fentanyl, which is still high enough to be a lethal dose, oxycodone hydrochloride, and …" She paused a moment to reflect on the other active ingredients found in the pills, and then spoke haltingly as if surprised by what she saw, "three, four methylenedioxy–methamphetamine and lysergic acid diethylamide."

What Stallings read aloud, Vega translated in everyday language: "Ecstasy and LSD have been added to the pills. Because those drugs cause increased activity in the dopamine and serotonin in the brain, users feel an immediate increase in energy, an elevated feeling of well-being and mood, and sexual arousal. They are uninhibited and euphoric."

Stallings shook her head slowly. "A bad combination for someone who doesn't know the pill contains a potentially lethal amount of fentanyl. The high one feels is hallucinogenic and so pleasurable that taking more than one pill will be irresistible to some."

Vega nodded. "And will lead to an almost certain overdose and death. Monica, this is the most dangerous drug to have ever been trafficked in the United States."

"How much is on the streets?"

"Enough of it ended up in Nevada and California to see

accidental drug overdose cases double in four months in those states. We had more than a hundred thousand drug overdose deaths nationally last year. Once these pills hit the distribution centers, they will be in every major city throughout the country. Drug-related deaths nationally could easily double. On the street, the pill is called the 'kite flier.'"

"How did you find out about it?"

Vega handed her a photo of a pretty, blue-eyed, blonde-haired, eighteen-year-old girl with a happy smile on her face standing in front of the University of Southern California sign etched in cement at the entrance to the school.

Stallings picked up the photo and studied it. "So, who's the all-American beauty?"

"Senator Conway's twenty-year-old daughter, a third-year scholarship student at Southern Cal. The photo was taken by her mother the day she moved into her dorm freshman year."

"And?" Stallings prodded.

"Overdosed in her boyfriend's apartment last year. The senator wanted the agency involved. I ended up with the toxicology report from her autopsy, which showed the drugs found in these pills." His eyes shifted to the bag of pills on the table and then back to Stallings. "The boyfriend thought he had purchased oxycodone and had no idea what was in them. He said it was the first time they had taken two pills. When she convulsed and stopped breathing, he called nine-one-one. He had a seizure when help arrived. The paramedics injected both with naloxone. He survived, she didn't."

"Who are the traffickers?"

"So far only one cartel has been able to produce this in the lab." Vega pulled out three photos of a man and put them on the table in front of Stallings. In two of the photos, he was standing beside a much younger woman. "His name is Diego

Garcia-Hernandez. They call him El Leon—The Lion— because of the brutality of the murders he's ordered. Before his men behead the victim, they gouge out his eyes and cut off his ears and tongue—the price you pay if you see, hear, or say something you shouldn't have."

"What about his personal life?"

"His parents emigrated from Guatemala to southeastern Mexico when he was seven. His father farmed poppies for El Lobo. Garcia killed two *sicarios* of a rival cartel when he was a kid. It pleased El Lobo so much, he took the boy under his wing. He was his youngest and most ruthless assassin, reportedly responsible for hundreds of deaths in the bloody war between El Lobo and the Santana cartel.

"It was only a matter of time before Garcia turned on El Lobo. He formed his own army of *sicarios*, who murdered all of El Lobo's lieutenants and *jefes*—the bosses—who worked for the cartel under El Lobo. Garcia personally took care of El Lobo. He slit his throat with the *cuchillo* he had from childhood, the knife the farmers use to scrape off the raw opium—a symbolic gesture to avenge his father's servitude under the drug lord."

"Where is he now?"

"He lives somewhere in the Sierra Madre mountains of southern Mexico. He has dozens of safe houses and moves from one to another so frequently that it's been impossible to find him."

"Why not send in one of our Mexican American agents to infiltrate the cartel like you did in capturing El Gordo?"

"I did. His head was delivered to my office last week. The disfigurement was quintessential El Leon."

Stallings grimaced. "What happened this time?"

"I was as careful as before. Only a few of us knew the

agent's identity. I personally recruited him when he applied to become an agent. I made sure he entered our training program under an alias. I falsified a criminal record for his new identity when he went undercover and listed him as a fugitive on our most-wanted list on charges of drug trafficking and murder—qualifications that would endear him to the cartel. It took months for him to work his way into Garcia's army of hitmen. Like before, he had a burner phone and wasn't to contact me until he had a definite time and place where we could capture Garcia. But someone figured him out."

"Do you suspect a mole?"

"We've had agents who've sold information to the cartels, particularly about our raids on distribution sites and storage facilities here in the states. For most agents, it's a one-and-done thing—the money they receive is that substantial. They leave us, they claim, to enter private sector security. Sometimes we can identify them by following the money trail."

"And this time?"

"This time, I suspect the mole was someone who had access to our personnel files and was able to determine that the agent's job assignments were bogus. It's been a priority of our division to capture Garcia for more than a year. For the mole, it was just a matter of selling the photo in our undercover agent's personnel file to one of Garcia's distributors here in the states, who sent it up the chain of command."

"How did you connect the pill to Garcia?"

"We got a break six months ago. Garcia's wife, Elena Sanchez-Gomez, was captured in Louisiana." Vega stopped to tap a finger on the image of the woman in the photos. "That's her with Garcia. She was here for a meeting with distributors in Texas to market the new drug they call *oro blanco*—white gold. We were tailing her and her bodyguard in their vehicle, hoping to catch the lot of them at the location of the meeting. We found the drugs in the trunk of the car."

"What happened?"

"While in Louisiana, near Baton Rouge, a state trooper pulled them over for speeding. The plate was phony, and the driver was a felon with an outstanding warrant. The trooper called for backup. There was a shootout. The driver, bodyguard, and a state trooper were killed."

"What about Garcia's wife?"

"She shot one of the state troopers with a derringer she had concealed in a holster strapped to her calf. He survived but had to retire on disability."

"Were you able to bring charges?"

"Only for the drugs found in the vehicle. Louisiana wanted its pound of flesh and prosecuted Garcia's wife on gun and drug charges and attempted murder. She was convicted and sentenced to twenty-five years on the state charges. She's incarcerated at one of Louisiana's temporary detention facilities until the construction of the new women's prison is completed."

"And Garcia? How do we stop him, Tony?"

"We find him and take him out—a full tactical assault. We'll need the cooperation of our Mexican counterparts, of course. You'll have to coordinate with the State Department."

"And how will you find Garcia?"

Vega's cheeks puffed out, and he let out a long sigh. "That is the million-dollar question."

# CHAPTER 4

She lay in her bunk, wondering how long it would take for the drudgery of prison life to break her spirit. For the past week, she got up with eleven other inmates as soon as the guard unlocked the door to the pod and, like an alarm clock, rang out loudly, "Inmates, out of your bunks—now." He delivered the command without an iota of humanity. Jo would have welcomed some sarcasm from him, like "Up and at 'em, ladies," or "Rise and whine," or "Wakey, wakey, eggs and bakey!"

*Prison life. Get into it.*

A guard was assigned to each pod and responsible for twelve inmates in each of three eight-hour shifts. He followed them to the cafeteria, their workstations, the exercise yard, and the community room for an occasional lecture, class, or movie.

The place lacked air conditioning and fans. Jo, like most inmates, slept in her underwear and a t-shirt. A few lay naked on their beds—she suspected one or two of them in order to lure a guard into an encounter for gifts and special treatment.

Letitia Hines, a waifish, twenty-five-year-old African American inmate, had already been assigned the top bunk. She'd been her boyfriend's getaway driver during a botched robbery that left a convenience store clerk dead. She was convicted of aiding and abetting and felony murder and, like Jo, was sentenced to twenty years. She was a year into her sentence.

Jo figured it was important to buddy up with an inmate who could advise her on the dos and don'ts of prison life. For her, Hines was a good fit. She had already told Jo which inmates were the violent offenders, the snitches, and the bullies and their victims. Hines counted herself among the rest—prisoners who wanted to be left alone and serve their time without drama or trauma.

Hines and Jo were assigned kitchen duty. Not a bad assignment, because their food portions were generous. Then again, eating too much crappy food could have its drawbacks—indigestion, diarrhea, or both. The scrambled eggs were so runny they had to be eaten with a spoon. The sides consisted of an unrecognizable meat and clumpy grits. Sunday special was creamed chipped beef on toast … that rightfully earned its other name—shit on a shingle. Lunch was mostly baloney sandwiches and hot dogs and over-baked beans. The soup was mushy noodles in a watered-down broth so salty it could pass as sea water. Dinner wasn't much better. Meat loaf made with more breadcrumbs than ground beef, stew heavy on potatoes and thin on meat, and pasta so starchy the noodles stuck together.

All in all, the food sucked.

*Prison life. Get used to it.*

During her third week, Jo's life took a sudden turn for the worse. One of the prisoners, a Russian woman by the name of Gantz, was a bully and a lesbian—not a good combination if she had someone targeted for her next punk. The woman was so brawny and butch she could easily have passed for an inmate in a men's prison. She was incarcerated for sexually assaulting a woman and beating her half to death afterwards.

Carver wasn't the only pervert Jo had to avoid.

Hines stood over Jo in the exercise yard while she knocked off fifty pushups in a minute. She had her uniform shirt off and was wearing a t-shirt that was sweat soaked from the mid-afternoon heat.

"Crowder, your girlfriend is smilin' at you," Hines snickered playfully.

Jo returned the volley. "Maybe it's you she's eyeballing, Hines. She looks like the type who likes the dark meat on the drumstick. And you know what they say?"

"What they say, white girl?"

Jo chuckled. "Once black …"

"No, you're more her type. It's your whisker biscuit she be wantin' to nibble on … and expectin' you to return the favor."

The big Russian with the crewcut was four or five inches taller and weighed a good forty pounds more than Jo, who rolled over on her back and banged out fifty sit-ups. Her well-defined biceps and lean but muscular physique were the reward for years of workouts and weight training. It helped that she was skilled in the martial arts, had kick-boxed competitively, rock climbed, and, until her arrest, regularly sparred with the men at the police academy gym.

Jo stood and put on her shirt. No need to tempt Gantz if her leers were directed at her, not Hines.

She'd soon find out.

At dinner, Hines and Jo took their usual places behind the counter to ladle out food as the inmates passed through the line with their plates.

Hines moved over and nudged an elbow into Jo's arm. "Here she come. She be wantin' more than a double helpin' of them potatoes you servin'."

Jo saw the moving mountain of gristle smiling in their direction through crooked, yellow-stained teeth. Gantz passed by Hines after receiving some food and held her plate out in front of Jo. When she opened her mouth to speak, Jo felt her skin crawl.

"Tonight, I visit you in your bunk," she smirked in a gravelly Slavic accent. "We have some fun together, you and me."

Jo wanted to bitch slap the supersized, shit-eating grin off her face. "I'll pass on the invitation, Gantz. You're not my type."

Gantz's grin twisted into a scowl. "Do not disappoint me. You may have heard. I do not take rejection well."

Jo had to be careful. To piss off Gantz could mean a shiv in her back while she was in the shower or exercise yard or lying asleep in her bunk. And to fight Gantz could mean a transfer to a more secure facility—something she had to avoid at all costs.

She needed a plan ... and fast.

Hines heard the exchange between Jo and Gantz. "She just speed dated you, girlfriend," she joked, moving her head from side to side for emphasis. "What's you going to do?"

"I have a plan, but I need your help."

"Sure. Anything—except being the one sleepin' in your bunk tonight?"

"I want you to distract the guard in the kitchen while we're washing dishes and cleaning up. Tell him you need to go to the infirmary for some Tylenol because you're having your period and have cramps. Make sure the guard's back is to me when you talk to him."

Hines did as she was asked, and with the guard's back to her, Jo slipped one of the kitchen's three carving knives into the waistband of her prison trousers.

That evening, when it was time to shower, Jo stayed back after Gantz and the other inmates had left the pod. She went quickly to Gantz's bunk, opened her locker, took out one of her extra-large t-shirts, wrapped the carving knife in it, and placed it under the mattress of her bunk.

On her way back from the showers, she dropped her bar of soap on the hallway floor. When she bent over to pick it up, she slipped the anonymous handprinted note ratting out Gantz under the door to the office of the deputy warden who worked the evening shift.

Just before lights out, two guards entered the pod and went directly to Gantz's bunk. Jo watched through happy eyes as one of them lifted the mattress and found the knife. The big Russky shouted one obscenity after another as the guards handcuffed her and led her to a room that served as solitary confinement. She'd be there until she was charged with theft and possession of a deadly weapon and relocated to a more secure facility.

Hines looked down at Crowder from her bunk. "White girl, you is one slick bitch. Remind me never to piss you off."

Jo smiled.

She had solved a problem that could have ended badly for her.

But her problems were just beginning.

Jo sat in her bunk reading a dog-eared paperback she'd gotten from a door-less broom closet that served as the prison library. She'd been through a book a week, only a month into her sentence. Prison boredom was so thick a chainsaw was needed to cut through it.

*Prison life. Get over it.*

She recognized the strikingly good-looking Latina as soon as she entered the pod and was led by Carver to the bunk Gantz had occupied. People were around this time. He didn't stay and watch her undress.

About Jo's height and weight, the woman was in her mid-twenties and, like Jo, looked younger. Thick, wavy, richly brunette hair draped her shoulders. She needed no makeup to enhance a blemish-free honey complexion. Her large, seductively penetrating eyes were the size and color of Kalamata olives. Full lips and high cheekbones gave her beauty-pageant good looks. The newspaper photos of the new arrival did not do justice. She remembered them well. One was of her coming into the East Baton Rouge courthouse for the start of her trial; the other was of her leaving the courthouse after her sentencing. Both times she was in handcuffs and leg shackles, with armed correctional officers on each side of her.

Flashbacks of the photos brought back memories of her own trial and sentencing and the unpleasant reality that she'd be required to serve two-thirds of her sentence before she was eligible for parole. The best-case scenario? She'd be fifty-one years old when she was released.

Jo Crowder couldn't fathom spending the best years of her life in prison.

She suspected that the wife of Diego Garcia felt the same way.

# CHAPTER 5

Inmate Elena Sanchez-Gomez lay in her bunk after lights out wide awake. For the past hour, she stared into the darkness, lamenting her predicament.

It was one of her own making.

Diego wanted to send Carlos, his boyhood friend and trusted lieutenant. He told her that because he was indicted, it was too dangerous for her to go to America. If the DEA was willing to pay millions for information leading to his arrest, they'd pay handsomely for information leading to his wife's capture.

Elena was as stubborn as she was fearless. Before her husband had become wanted in two countries for drug trafficking and murder, she had crossed the border many times, always in planes that landed at airstrips carved out of fields in sparsely populated areas of Florida, Arizona, and Texas. She'd met with distributors, set prices, and negotiated deals for weapons to be smuggled into Mexico. She also kept the records of the cartel's criminal operations. Elena was as important to the cartel as Carlos. Her husband called her his *reina guerrera*—warrior queen.

Things changed when warrants were issued for his arrest in both Mexico and the United States. He and Elena had to become invisible. Like most drug lords, Diego Garcia had many hideouts. They were protected by an army of loyalists, many of whom had been soldiers in the Mexican army. He had the local police and government officials of many cities on the payroll. The uncooperative ones risked a bullet in the brain or being blown up in a car bombing. In most of the villages in the immediate vicinity of their homes, there were no police—only the gangs, armed thugs, and assassins that Diego controlled like puppets on strings.

The villagers and peasant farmers looked to the cartel for work and provisions. In return, the cartel expected their absolute loyalty. Diego rewarded them by funding the building and renovation of schools, churches, and clinics. Elena encouraged the acts of benevolence and often oversaw the construction projects.

The local populations viewed the cartel as their government and Diego Garcia as their *presidente*. Rival cartels were treated like foreign adversaries. Strangers and outsiders who ventured into the towns and villages Garcia controlled were interrogated by his men and forced to leave unless the vetting process showed they could be useful in the operations of the cartel.

Diego owned many aircraft, which he learned to pilot. A quick getaway was the best defense. Fields were cleared near Diego's homes and used as airstrips. A fully fueled helicopter was always parked near his hideaways. An army of soldiers guarded him and Elena, who had at their disposal an arsenal of weapons—assault rifles, grenades, and anti-aircraft weapons.

Diego and Elena were confident that, if they were careful, the DEA and Mexican authorities would never find them. That had been the plan … until she was caught.

Elena knew someone had ratted her out. DEA agents were on the scene of the shootout within minutes—a response time too quick for them not to have been following her. She was right about the snitch. Her lawyers learned from her indictment in the federal drug trafficking case that an unidentified informant had forewarned the DEA of her arrival. Elena's arrest was inevitable, even if the state police had not made the traffic stop.

Diego's American lawyers had nefarious ways of determining the identity of informants, particularly when the cartel had an unlimited amount of laundered cash with which to bribe government officials. And when they found the snitch, Diego Garcia would have his eye-less, ear-less, tongue-less head on a pike.

Elena reflected on the day she'd convinced Diego to send her to America to introduce *oro blanco* to their distributors. She snorted cocaine regularly and smoked heroin occasionally—the drugs helped her forget the bad things that had happened to her and the bad things she'd done. It was she who suggested that their counterfeit oxycodone pills be redesigned—a pill that would earn the cartel tens of millions of dollars more in profits each year. It was only right that she be the one to make the trip as the cartel's emissary.

She knew the potential danger of the fentanyl in *oro blanco* but had to try it to be able to describe its effects to their American distributors. The euphoria she felt when the pill took effect was like nothing she had ever experienced with cocaine or heroin. Her body tingled as she soared through the air on what felt like a magic carpet ride. Her world was transformed into vivid colors, fragrant smells, and pleasant sounds. The flowers around their home sparkled like gemstones, the blooms gave off intoxicating scents, and the birds chirped in symphonic harmony. She felt sexually aroused. Her body quivered pleasantly when she touched herself. Afterwards, when the excitement of her mind-expanding adventure ebbed, she felt intensely relaxed and content. There were no unpleasant feelings when the effects of the super high wore off, only a desire to relive the experience again and more intensely. She had to fight the urge to enhance her hallucinogenic high by taking more than one pill.

Elena was concerned that the new pill could increase the number of accidental drug overdoses, already at a record high in America. But it wasn't out of concern for the innocent victims, it was the reality that the more deaths that occurred, the fewer regular customers there would be to buy the pills, and that could negatively impact the cartel's bottom line.

Diego was less concerned. He'd told Elena it didn't matter how many died—there would always be others to replace them, and the pills would be so much in demand, they'd always have the largest market share. In the end, it didn't matter to Elena either—the cartel wasn't a pharmaceutical company that needed to warn users not to exceed the recommended dosage.

Diego's plan had been for Elena to contact their distributors in the Pacific Southwest and then move from one region to another until the continental United States was fully covered. Carlos would traffic the other drugs the cartel produced. Elena's conviction and incarceration would not alter Diego's plan. For him, *negocio es negocio*. His words resounded in her mind as if he lay beside her, whispering them in her ear. "It isn't *personal*, Elena, it's strictly *negocio*."

As Elena lay there unable to sleep, she reflected on her troubled past and the unhappy circumstances that led her to Diego. When she was an infant, her parents emigrated from Venezuela to Tuxtla, Mexico, the capital of the state of Chiapas. Her father was a tailor and her mother a seamstress. They made and mended clothes from their home. When her parents refused to be extorted by one of the local gangs, they burned down their home with them in it. Had Elena not been in school, she too would have been among the charred remains.

She was eight years old.

With no family in Mexico to take her, Elena was placed in one of the more than seven hundred public and private orphanages in Mexico that housed over thirty thousand children. She'd been unluckier than most children—she was placed in a public orphanage, where she was physically and sexually abused by the men who ran it. When the abuse had become too much for her to bear and she was about to be sold to a sex trafficker, she escaped to the streets.

She was twelve years old.

Over the next two years, she became one of the multitudes of homeless children who roamed the streets of Mexico. She learned how to steal food, clothes, and other necessities from the local merchants. She slept in boxcars of trains until she found an abandoned building on the outskirts of town. She nested in the building and began a tolerable existence with a companion—a stray dog she'd named Chico.

One day when she and Chico were in the city foraging for food, she was confronted by several members of a local street gang. Her beauty could not be concealed even though she'd cut her hair short and wore boy's clothes to look more like the hundreds of runaways who roamed the streets without anyone's notice or concern. Many of the boys joined the gangs that terrorized the people who lived in the city.

The ruse was uncovered when one of the ruffians ripped open Elena's shirt and saw her developed breasts.

"Razzi," the young man cried out to the apparent leader of the squad, "we have a *chica* trying to look like a *chico*."

"Paco, take her into the alley and strip her," Razzi ordered.

Paco lifted Elena over his shoulder and hurried into the alley with her pounding the man's back with her fists. Razzi and two others followed them in.

"*Yo primero*," Paco huffed, announcing to the others he wanted first dibs.

When he laid Elena down and began to rip at her clothes, she punched him hard in the face and swung her feet wildly to get him to release his hold on her, but to no avail. When he began slapping her face, Chico growled and bit at the man's leg. Razzi pulled a knife from a sheath attached to his belt, approached the dog from behind, grabbed a handful of hair from the nape of its neck, and slit the canine's throat in one quick slice. He wiped the blood from the blade on the animal's coat and returned the knife to where it had been.

"You'll have to wait your turn," Razzi hissed, pulling Paco off the girl. Elena was on her hands and knees on the ground naked except for her socks when Razzi unzipped his pants and prepared to turn assault into rape.

Elena remembered it like it was yesterday. The way the pebbles and grit scratched the palms of her hands and kneecaps. How the salty smell of sweat and body stink of her attacker was so stomach churning she vomited. How the thick, humid air was like breathing in smoke. Yet she'd forced herself to scream for help as loud as she could.

And then she saw Diego for the first time.

He, Carlos, and two of Diego's men appeared in the alley.

She later learned they had been on their way to a nearby café to transact business when they heard her screams. They entered the alley just as Razzi was on his knees and ready to take her from behind.

Diego had told Elena afterwards that when he saw her kneeling in front of the thug with a terrified look on her face, he saw the face of his sister, Ceci.

When Razzi saw the men enter the alley, he stood and zipped his trousers.

"*Amigos*, you can have her when we're done. We found the little *puta callejero*. You wait your turn, *si*."

In Diego's mind, it was like Ceci was the one he had called a little "street whore." A head nod was all it took for Diego's men to stand beside him and Carlos, blocking the exit.

Razzi's men spread out too.

Knives were the weapons of choice of many gangs. It was a noiseless way of ending someone's life. Razzi and his men pulled out their knives.

Elena remembered the steely, confident look on Diego's face while she gulped in air to catch her breath. He stood his ground, unfazed by the acts of aggression.

Diego grinned. "You don't bring a *cuchilla* to a gunfight, *mi amigos*." His words were seared in Elena's brain … forever. "Kill all but the rapist," he ordered.

His men pulled out their pistols and shot three of them dead. The deafening sound of the blasts echoed in the alleyway and rang in Elena's ears like the peal of a tower bell.

Razzi stood alone, the knife still in his hand. He must have recognized Diego Garcia from photos of him in the newspaper.

"El Leon," he muttered dejectedly, dropping his knife to the ground.

Elena had a flashback of her watching Diego beat Razzi

with his fists until his face was covered with blood, and he didn't stop beating the man until he lay dead with the others. Elena Sanchez-Gomez smiled for the first time that day.

# CHAPTER 6

The more ethnically diverse a prison population was, the more likely gangs formed among inmates serving long sentences, almost always along racial lines. Jo recognized them during her time in the exercise yard, even without Hines pointing them out.

One such gang was a group of Latina prisoners who called themselves *Las Proscritas*—The Outlaws. Membership in the gang had its privileges—trading items purchased or stolen from the commissary and other inmates, sharing contraband smuggled into the prison, and providing protection from bullies and other gangs. Rival gangs frequently fought over racial slurs hurled at each other.

Jo had seen several such incidents in the month she'd been there. The pattern was always the same. A gang member would distract the guard posted in the yard, while inmates formed a wall between the guard and the combatants. The inmates then fought until one of them capitulated or the guard broke up the fight.

Jo wondered whether anyone else recognized the wife of Diego Garcia. She found out two days after her arrival when Elena showed up in the cafeteria and was assigned a job serving food alongside her.

Several members of *Las Proscritas* entered the food line and passed by Jo. One of them stopped in front of Elena, who was serving soup. She was in her mid-to-late twenties, a stocky woman with generous hips and tattoos on her neck, forearms, and knuckles. Jo recognized the woman as Moreno, the leader of the Latina gang and the one involved in most of the fights she'd witnessed in the exercise yard, each time with Moreno beating up the other inmate.

After Elena filled her cup with soup, Moreno spit in the cup and threw it in Sanchez's face. "You are the *puta* of Diego Garcia, whose men murdered my brothers," she growled.

Jo watched in silence. She knew it wasn't a good idea to call the wife of El Leon a whore.

Elena wiped the soup off her face with the sleeve of her shirt and glared at Moreno. "And his men will kill what remains of your family for your disrespect," Elena shot back.

Moreno returned Elena's angry scowl and warned, "*Eres una mujer muerta.*"

Jo translated the threat in her head: "You are a dead woman."

Jo had read about Elena's history of violent behavior. She was unique among the wives and mistresses of drug lords. When she was taken in by Diego Garcia, she became his teenage mistress before becoming his wife. It was widely rumored she had returned to the orphanage from which she escaped with several of Diego's soldiers, who abducted the two men who'd abused her the most. They brought the men to a field outside the city and hung them by the feet from trees. But it was the hand of Elena Sanchez-Gomez that held the *cuchilla* that slit their throats. She was fifteen years old at the time.

For Elena, Moreno was a clear and present danger. Inside the prison, she didn't have her husband's protection—none of his paid assassins were there to eliminate Moreno and others in her gang who might help Moreno exact revenge for her brothers' murders.

And all that Jo or anyone else could do about it was stand around and watch.

~

So far, Elena's transfer to a less secure prison facility had gone badly. Her first day there, her sneakers were stolen while she showered. The worn-out ones left under her bunk and her shower slippers would have to do until she could buy new ones at the commissary.

The cartel's American lawyers who had represented her in her criminal cases made sure she had the maximum allowable money in her commissary account—three hundred dollars. Except for new shoes, she'd need every penny of it … if she was going to buy some protection. She needed a bodyguard—someone who'd have her back if Moreno tried to put a shiv in it.

Elena had a premonition that things would get much worse than stolen shoes. Once Moreno put the word out that she was Diego Garcia's *puta,* and that her husband had Moreno's brothers killed, she'd be targeted. Moreno wasn't the only one she needed to worry about. Every member of *Las Proscritas* was a potential assassin.

Fear of reprisals from Moreno would lead other Latina

inmates to distance themselves from her, and the other inmates couldn't care less about what happened to a Latina. She'd be ostracized, alone, and a *dead woman walking*—an island in an angry sea with a category five hurricane coming directly at it.

Elena needed someone to protect her. But who?

She'd noticed that a white prisoner occasionally stared at her during their shifts in the cafeteria and in the exercise yard. The inmate was frequently in the company of an African American inmate. It appeared to Elena that this white woman harbored no racial prejudice.

The inmate was tomboyish and physically fit. For the last two days, she'd spent most of her time in the yard, exercising, shadow boxing, and occasionally practicing complicated martial arts techniques. Elena thought she might be ex-military.

The inmate had witnessed the incident in the food line but said nothing about it afterwards. She'd showed no emotional reaction to the death threats made in her presence. It was as if she had ice in her veins—a nonchalance that suggested to Elena she wasn't afraid of being around violent people and was a person quite capable of defending herself.

Elena needed to partner with someone who could protect her. And she needed to do it soon. None of Moreno's gang were in her pod or worked in the cafeteria, so they posed no threat to her when she was there. She was most vulnerable in the yard on days Moreno and her confederates were also there.

On the several days since the threats were exchanged, Elena stood or sat alone close to the guard. The problem was that the guard didn't always stay in the yard. He occasionally left and went behind a storage shed to smoke. Sometimes he had a female inmate accompany him.

It was the perfect time for Moreno to attack her.

Elena had a plan. She'd get to know the white inmate

with whom she bunked, worked, ate, and showered—and fast. She'd offer her two hundred dollars to keep her safe. That sum would buy a lot of things in the commissary, and a lot of drugs, alcohol, and cosmetics from the guards.

Yes—she'd get to know the inmate whose name was Jo Crowder.

# CHAPTER 7

The next day, after a half-hour workout, Jo sat alone on a bench at one of the tables in the exercise yard. Hines had been diagnosed with appendicitis and taken to a hospital in an ambulance, accompanied by an armed guard.

Only half of the inmates were allowed in the yard at one time. Moreno wasn't in the yard that day, but Jo knew it was just a matter of time before she'd be back to have it out with Diego Garcia's *puta*.

She'd felt Elena's watchful eyes on her the past couple of days, but more so that day in the yard when Elena walked over and sat on the bench opposite her. "You hear Moreno threaten to kill me, *si*?" the Latina muttered.

Jo, who was straddling the bench, turned to study Elena's face as she spoke. It was difficult for her to believe such an innocent-looking countenance belonged to the woman who worked alongside the infamous El Leon.

"And she intends to make good on that threat," she continued.

"And I heard you threaten to have the rest of Moreno's family killed," Jo replied nonchalantly.

Elena nodded slowly a couple of times. "For my people, nothing is more satisfying than *venganza*. My husband, he would never let her disrespect go unpunished."

Jo's Spanish was good enough to say, "*Ojo por ojo*."

"*Si*, an eye for an eye," Elena repeated in English. "And a life for a life. Anything less is a sign of weakness. You know of my husband, *si*?"

"I know he is a very rich and powerful man in Mexico, but of no use to you while you are in a Louisiana prison."

"Do you know why I am here?"

Jo brought her legs together under the table and leaned forward. "You shot a cop and are serving a twenty-five-year sentence."

"And you. Why are you here?" Elena queried.

Jo found the young woman engaging and continued the back and forth. "I stole some money and drugs from a distributor for the Medellín cartel."

"How can an American woman steal from the cartel and still be alive?"

"It was evidence taken in a raid. I'm a cop … was a cop." Jo stared off into the distance. She'd gone from cop to convict in a matter of months. The reality was slow to set in.

"A cop?" The Latina's face had a look of surprise.

Jo nodded. "Yes, a cop. The cartel didn't know I stole from them. My lawyer got the government to agree to keep the source of the drugs secret during my trial." She panned her gaze around the yard. "They realized if it got out and I was convicted, I wouldn't last long in any prison." Jo felt a sudden pang of anxiety. She'd remembered Warden Green cautioning her to keep to herself she had been a cop, and there she was, spilling her guts to Sanchez. In all her conversations with Hines, she'd never told her.

"How many years is your sentence?"

"Because I was a cop, I got twice the minimum sentence—twenty years."

"In Mexico, what you do goes on all the time. The *policia,* we pay them in pesos and drugs to look the other way. The ones that don't—we have ways to deal with them."

Jo didn't need the wife of one of the most notorious drug lords in Mexico to elaborate.

"So why do you do it?"

"Do what?"

"Go bad."

*Go bad.* The words hit like she'd just been punched in the face. Her brothers, stunned by her arrest and conviction, couldn't help but ask the same question: "Why, Jo? ...Why did you do it?" Sanchez, like her brothers, was probing for an explanation why someone in a position of authority and trust who had accomplished so much would throw it all away doing what she did. She was too pained to explain it to her brothers and simply dismissed it with the standard "I don't want to talk about it" response. But there, in a prison with another *bad* person, she felt unrestrained and could bare her soul to someone about what she had done ... and what she had become.

"Why?" she asked again.

"It's a long story, Sanchez," Jo replied gruffly, as if annoyed. But, in truth, she wanted to talk about it. She was pissed off at so many people, but most of all at herself—not for what she'd done, but for getting caught. Sanchez was probably the only one who'd understand how a culture of absolute corruption corrupts absolutely.

The words flowed like lava from the mouth of a volcano. "Other cops in the department had gotten away with it and a lot worse things," she explained. "Taking bribes, extorting suspects, planting evidence, lying on the witness stand. You have no idea how much of what we seize ends up in some cop's pockets. Shit, they sell the drugs back to the dealers." Jo shook her head in disgust. "Here I am, putting my life on the line every fucking day doing my job, while others are getting away with shit—buying new cars, paying off their mortgages and credit card debt, and padding their bank accounts. And me, I can barely afford the mortgage payment on the dump I call a home, have student loans to pay off, and still owe money on my truck."

Sanchez watched Jo in silence as she opened up to her. Jo couldn't explain it, but there was comfort in having the Latina's dark, friendly eyes fixed on her.

"When I learned that my captain was getting a cut of what those around me were taking, I snapped. I got shit-faced that night. Blackout drunk. I knew the corruption was so widespread things would never change. I was fed up being the odd cop out." She couldn't suppress some self-directed sarcasm. "And it was so easy to do and not get caught."

"But you got caught," Sanchez said without sarcasm or reproach in her words, only empathy.

Jo wasn't stupid. She sensed Sanchez's interest in her was premeditated—she needed a bodyguard and was interviewing her for the position.

"Bad luck," Jo lamented.

"What do you mean … bad luck?"

"The raid on the Medellín warehouse … I was there. I hid some of the drugs and cash and went back for it later. I had disabled the security cameras but didn't know there was one on a building across the street. It was all there in living color."

"What were you going to do with the drugs?"

Jo shrugged. "I have connections to know where to sell it. Had. *Had* connections. Most of us knew where to go. Who to see."

"And what you stole, the drugs and money? What happened to it?"

"They found the drugs and most of the money in my bedroom. Hidden under the floorboards. But I stashed some of the money away. It's safe. It'll be there when I find a way to get out of here."

Sanchez's eyes widened. "You mean escape from here?"

Jo raised her head and stared into space with determined eyes. "There's no way I'm sticking around until I'm eligible for parole. I have enough money to cross the border and start over." Just what she planned to do after getting into Canada or Mexico, she hadn't thought through. Escaping was foremost in her mind.

"Diego, he sent someone to bribe a guard and help me escape, but they find out. Now, they move me from one place to another until the new prison is built. I will be leaving this place in a couple of months."

Jo got cynical. "If Moreno makes good on her threat, you'll be leaving this one in a body bag."

Sanchez didn't appear to be put off by her dispassionate remarks. She smiled at Jo instead. "Call me Elena," she said, her voice soft and friendly.

Jo liked the familiarity. In prison, inmates referred to each other by their last names or nicknames prisoners had given them.

"It's Jo—Jo Crowder."

The smile left Elena's face and was replaced by a rigid stare.

"I have a proposition for you, Jo. You help me get out of here, and I will take you to my husband. He will reward you for bringing me to him, and he will give you his protection."

*Get out of here?* Jo turned her head and laughed, but only loud enough for herself to hear. That had been the only thing on her mind since she spread her cheeks and coughed for the prison matron during the cavity search. From day one, she began mapping out in her head every corridor, door, window, air vent, and security camera; and memorizing how, when, and where deliveries were made, and which gates were left open and for how long. She learned the guards' routines, bathroom habits, and smoke breaks. It wasn't a matter of whether she'd find a way to escape—it was only a question of how and when.

Jo had to admit—Elena's offer had merit. Jo would have to cross the country to get to Canada. She'd be caught before she got halfway there. Mexico was close by, and Elena would know how to get her across the border. Still, two people escaping more than doubled the things that could go wrong. She'd put an end to the discussion. "I'm not seeing it, Elena. It's twice as hard for two people to escape."

Elena's eyes stayed fixed on Jo's. "And it is more than twice as hard for an American woman to travel through Mexico alone. The cartels and street gangs look for women who have no one to protect them, dope them up, have their way with them, and sell them to sex traffickers. Believe me, I know of what I speak."

Jo had no doubt Elena knew what she was talking about. The cartels were notorious sex traffickers, including her husband's.

Jo had enough of Elena Sanchez for one day. She told her she'd think on it, then got up and walked away, found a place where she could be alone, and did some pushups and sit-ups. She perspired heavily. It helped wash away the rekindled memories of her arrest and conviction, if only for a short while.

When rational thought returned, she nixed the idea of escaping with Elena. The drug lord's wife was too dangerous a person to befriend. A third of the inmates at the facility were Hispanic—many incarcerated for drug convictions, some undoubtedly with connections to cartels that might have a beef with El Leon. Jo thought it odd they'd put a prisoner with a target on her back in a facility known to be understaffed. Once news of Elena's imprisonment spread, there could be others besides Moreno who might want to whack her.

Jo saw that Elena was still sitting by herself on the bench. She decided not to go sit with her and stood with her back against the fence instead. Befriending Elena would be dangerous, but ignoring her would be a sign of disrespect and could result in reprisals from her. Her history of violent behavior and reputation for getting even with her detractors had been extensively reported by the news outlets during her trial.

Jo had a fine line to walk—she'd limit her interactions with Elena as much as possible, but not completely ignore her.

~

Living in the same pod, working elbow-to-elbow in the same job, and being together in the yard placed the two inmates in each other's company most of the day. To create some distance between them, Jo requested a kitchen assignment that took her away from the serving line. When Elena walked toward her in the yard, she went into her exercise routine. When they were in the pod, she made sure to stay in bed as much as possible, reading a book or pretending to nap.

Elena got lucky—Moreno was sent to solitary confinement for two weeks for fighting. But it soon became apparent that Moreno had put the word out—Elena was to be shunned by all inmates or face consequences. Jo watched Elena approach inmates in the pod and yard to engage them in conversation, and each time they walked away. Two were Hispanic—one turned and gave her the finger; the other made the cut-throat gesture with her hand.

With Hines still in the hospital for complications from her surgery, Jo kept to herself and as far away from Elena as space permitted. She had one thing on her mind—*her* escape. But every time she envisioned herself an escapee on the run, she faced the reality that she didn't know where and how to cross the border into Mexico or where and how to find a safe haven when she got there. She had no identity papers, only a lot of American dollars that would draw attention to her. Maybe Elena was right—Jo's best chance of surviving her ordeal was to partner up with her, who knew how to speak the language, cross the border, and navigate her way through Mexico.

She had no choice—she'd let Elena Sanchez into her life.

Jo ended her usual workout in the yard early and fixed an inviting stare on Elena, who sat alone near the guard.

Elena seized the opportunity to connect. She walked over and asked, "Can we talk … Jo?" Her voice was soft and intimate.

Jo was receptive to the overture. They went and sat next to each other on a bench.

Elena's warm, unblinking eyes looked deep into Jo's face,

as if mapping out every minute detail of its features. "Moreno will be back next week," she said. "And you know what that means."

Jo's face formed slowly into a smile, as if amused. "Yeah, I can see how popular you are with the sisters."

"I won't last a week on my own, and you know it."

"Let's put it this way, Elena. The betting money is on Moreno."

As before, Elena apparently didn't take offense at the sarcasm and chuckled when she said, "I am, how you say, a long shot in the race."

"Let's hope you don't come up lame and have to be put down."

"My odds, they improve with your help. I see how fit you are. You have the skills to protect yourself …" She paused a moment before adding, "and defend me."

"I don't know, Elena. I counted four, plus Moreno. You do the math—five against two. Your odds improve, but mine definitely go down."

"Not if we escape before she comes back."

"We?"

The cartel baron's wife flashed a disarming smile. "You need to take me with you."

True. Jo needed Elena as much as she needed her. But what could Jo expect in return? "So, what do I get from you?"

"I know where to cross the border and how to travel through Mexico without getting caught, kidnapped, raped, or killed. You protect me, we get out … then I protect you."

"I'm still getting the lay of the land, Elena. If we are to escape, our best chance is from this place. If we end up in the new prison together, escape will be impossible. How much money do you have?"

"Two hundred fifty dollars."

"I have a couple hundred. Let's be frugal with our money. We'll need it if we are to get out of this place."

Elena reached over, gripped Jo's hand on the table, and squeezed it gently. Her touch was warm and tender—almost sensual. Like it or not, Jo felt a bond was forging between two convicted felons with more in common than they might ever have believed possible … until that moment.

Elena's face brightened into a smile, and Jo returned it.

Jo reflected on her decision. On one hand, she'd be joining forces with the wife of a notorious drug lord. On the other hand, serving her time meant she'd be in her fifties with the best years of her life behind her when she was released. There would be no life for her in America. A crooked cop who had brought dishonor to Louisiana law enforcement and disgrace to her family would not be welcomed back. There'd be nothing and no one to go back to.

Her only chance for a new start in life was to escape from prison with Elena, flee to Mexico, and come under the protection of El Leon.

# CHAPTER 8

Elena stayed glued to Jo after they agreed to partner up and escape. They ate, worked, and spent their free time together. Elena was as protective of Jo as she was of Elena. And she'd proved it. They caught an inmate trying to steal from Jo's box under her bunk. Before Jo could intervene, Elena pounced on the thief, grabbed her by the hair, and slammed her face against the floor, bloodying her nose. Jo had heard Elena say to the inmate, "Do this again, I slit your throat."

The young woman had only a granola bar in her hand.

That night in the showers, Jo couldn't help but notice Elena studying her naked body as she showered next to her. And she couldn't help but stare at Elena's near-perfect figure—narrow shoulders, full breasts, slim hips, and lithe but shapely legs. By comparison, Jo was broad shouldered, small-breasted and flat-bottomed—cute, but by no means gorgeous.

Yet Jo knew how to catch the eye of a man and reel him in—and always on her terms. When her libido got the best of her, she'd put on her push-up bra, don the mini-skirt she'd worn undercover pretending to be a teenage prostitute, and step into a pair of five-inch stilettos. She'd apply just enough makeup, dab some perfume in all the right places, and head over to nightclubs in neighboring towns. It was rare she left without the man of her choice, who was always willing to spring for the motel for their one-night stand.

Jo wasn't the passive one in her sexual adventures. Always the aggressor, she was the one who initiated foreplay and determined how the sexcapade would unfold. She rode her man like a rodeo bull rider, and she was the one who always climaxed first … and last. The handcuffs stayed in her purse, unless her partner wanted to experience subjugation by a dominatrix.

Looking over at her new partner, she couldn't help but notice how Elena lathered herself with the bar of soap, all the time fixing a seductive gaze on her. The way she touched herself made Jo uneasy. Jo understood her sexuality, but was Elena just discovering hers?

On Sunday, Jo and Elena made trips to the commissary to purchase lightweight sweatpants and shirts, baseball caps, and a wristwatch. They went separately a half hour apart so as not to draw attention to the similarity of their purchases. The clothing items were available in two colors—beige and grey. They chose different colors. The DOC prison logos would be hidden when the clothes were turned inside out.

To prove she was all in, Elena bought a hand-sized radio, the most expensive item at the commissary. They'd use it to barter with the inmate whose illegal lighter they needed to create a diversion.

That night after dinner, Jo sat cross-legged on her bunk, her pillow between her back and the bed railing. Elena sat opposite her, one leg draped over the edge of the bed, the other bent at the knee, a bare foot resting on the mattress.

By then Elena felt comfortable opening up about her personal life. She confided in Jo about being abused in the orphanage, her life as a street urchin, and the isolation she felt being married to a man with a bounty on his head.

"The money, it no longer buys me the freedom to do what I want, when and where I want to do it," she said, her voice heavy with discontent. "We go into hiding when Diego learn he would be arrested. Since then, he moves from one safe house to another. Always with armed guards ready to defend him from the police, military, and DEA. Most of the time, I stay in our home in the mountains. When I leave, I go in a vehicle of reinforced steel and bulletproof windows with many men guarding me. When we travel, Diego, he rents all rooms on our floor of the hotel. The restaurants, they close when we eat there." She ended her diatribe with a sigh.

Jo was curious about something. Was Elena given a way out, a chance to cut her ties with a man with whom her continued relationship could only end badly? She asked: "Did the Feds offer you a deal?"

"*Si*, they tell me the federal and state charges go away if I tell them where to find Diego and how we run things. They give me a new identity and let me live in America."

"Why didn't you take it?"

Elena shot a wide-eyed look of surprise in Jo's direction. "I not betray Diego. I say no, and because I do, they come down hard on me."

"How?"

"When I was sentenced in federal court, the judge, he give me another twenty-five years."

Jo understood the stark reality of back-to-back, twenty-five-year sentences—Elena would be sixty-three years old when she was eligible for parole. By then, the Latina beauty sitting next to her would be wrinkled and gray. Prison life meant an unhealthy diet, poor healthcare, and degradation of one's mental state. She'd be as broken as a junkyard jalopy, good only for the scrap heap.

Elena was close enough to Jo to tap her lightly on the hand. "And you, why not cooperate with the authorities and expose the corruption? It would have helped you, *si?*"

"You don't understand, Elena. Cops who rat out other cops have targets on their backs. Sure, I could have gotten a reduced sentence, but I'd have to testify about what others have done. I'd be trading ten years off my time for a death sentence when I got out." Jo hadn't been facing Elena, but she looked at her from the corners of her eyes. "You know, if by some miracle we make it out of here, we'll only have each other to depend on."

Elena smiled pleasantly at her. "*Si*, we look out for each other."

Jo shifted gears. "We'll wear our sweats under our prison uniforms and hide our hats in our pants. We'll ditch the prison clothes the first chance we get."

"How do we get to the money?" Elena asked excitedly.

"It's hidden in a locker at a storage facility in a small town about a two-hour drive from here."

"But how do we get there?"

"I'll hot-wire a car from an indoor parking lot near some office buildings. There's a good chance the car will be owned by someone who works in the area and won't know it's been stolen until the workday is over. I'll switch plates with another vehicle."

"And once we get the money?"

"We'll need new clothes. You'll cut your hair. I'll drive

us to the border. Then it'll be up to you to get us across and through Mexico to your husband."

Elena nodded her assent. "*Sí*, I cut my hair short. Hair comes back. Dead people do not."

"How will you get us into Mexico?"

"Do not worry. I know where and how to cross the border." Elena sounded completely confident. "But it will be dangerous for us in Mexico when they know I have escaped. Diego's enemies will look for me, and you will be a dead woman if you are found with me. Me, I can be held for ransom. You—you have no value to them."

"So how do we travel through Mexico without getting caught?"

"We travel like migrants do—on foot. We ride the trains. We have money. Maybe we take a bus to get to the train."

"Train?"

"*Sí*, in boxcars that are left open or on top if they are not. We do not look men in the eye. We stay with the women and children."

"Are there many women and children?"

"More than ever before. If they lose their men to violence, they travel to the border. If they have money, they pay a coyote. He takes them across."

Jo raised an eyebrow. "And if they don't have money?"

"They join a caravan with those who seek asylum or go home."

Jo folded her arms against her chest and closed her eyes. She let her mind wander, trying to picture Elena and her huddled up in a boxcar. After a few minutes of silence, she looked at Elena and asked: "Elena, where is your home in Mexico? Where do you and Diego live?"

"In the Sierra Madre mountains to the south. But Diego,

he could be anywhere."
"So how will we find him?"
"We won't. Diego, he will find us."

# CHAPTER 9

Elena lay in her bunk, unable to sleep. Unpleasant memories rattled her brain—the smoldering building, the burned, blackened bodies of her parents, and a few singed photographs the only proof they'd ever existed. She took the photos with her to the orphanage, hid them under her pillow, and held them over her heart every evening when the dormitory went dark, and they remained there until the break of dawn.

Her mind was a hornet's nest, all abuzz with remembrances that had broken her heart and darkened her soul. She was raped for the first time when she was ten years old by the spiritual advisor for the orphanage. She was his exclusive property for a year. After that, she was passed around to others as if they were friends sharing a bottle of tequila. She'd learned to shut out the physical and emotional pain. She stared not at the men who mounted her, but blankly into space. It was a life of emptiness in a world of nothingness.

The children at the orphanage were rarely adopted. The city was mostly poor people who could barely afford to take care of their own children. The usual course was for the children to remain there until they were old enough to be released to the streets or sold off to sex traffickers. Some, like Elena, mustered the courage to run away.

When Diego rescued her, he took her to live with him. He had sex with her the very first night. She felt nothing, even though he was gentle and kind to her. But she had once again become someone's property.

Diego was good to her. He brought in private tutors to educate her. He showered her with gifts. And when she turned sixteen, he married her in a church ceremony.

Diego Garcia didn't want his child to be born out of wedlock.

Elena would not come to know motherhood. She miscarried on the three occasions she became pregnant. By the time she was twenty-one, Diego stopped trying. Elena was relieved when he resumed lovemaking with his many mistresses.

Elena closed her eyes to force herself to think of the present. She had accomplished her goal of finding someone who could protect her and help her escape. It surprised her that she felt an instant kinship with the former cop. When her parents died and the abuse started, Elena forgot how to love someone. Her marriage to Diego was for their mutual convenience. She never had a romantic attachment to him … or any man. Feeling close to anyone—man or woman— was a luxury she couldn't afford. The wealth and respect the criminal enterprise had brought her kept Elena faithfully by Diego's side.

But she'd trade it all for someone she could confide in, be close to, and care about.

Someone she could trust not only with her life, but also

with her heart.

When she held the hand and looked into the eyes of the woman who agreed to help her, something clicked.

She may have found that someone.

~

Jo needed an escape plan, and she needed it soon. When Moreno learned that she'd allied herself with Elena, her life would also be in danger. Mexican revenge was directed against the person who caused the harm—and anyone who stood in the way of getting even.

Their best chance of escaping was from the storeroom behind the kitchen that led to a loading dock. Every Wednesday morning, a truck entered through an unsecured gate at the rear of the facility. The driver backed up to the loading platform and unloaded dry goods, canned foods, and kitchen supplies for the prison.

Crowder and Hines's duties had included unboxing the items and placing them on the shelves in the storeroom. With Hines still in the hospital, her duties would fall to Elena. They'd be together, working unsupervised in the storeroom while the guard outside the kitchen waited for them to finish.

The driver's routine was always the same. After he made the deliveries, he rolled down the aluminum door at the back of his truck. With no lock on the door, it could easily be opened just enough for them to crawl in while the driver was in the cab of his truck completing his paperwork for the delivery. There should be enough time to create the diversion they needed to make their getaway ... if all went as Jo had planned.

It was Tuesday morning.

She had one more day to keep Elena safe.

# CHAPTER 10

Moreno had been released into the general population on Saturday, and three very tense days passed while Jo and Elena waited for the other shoe to drop.

Elena had managed to avoid direct contact with Moreno by slipping into the kitchen whenever she showed up in the food line. In the yard, Jo and Elena huddled near the guard to mitigate the chances of a confrontation. But the angry glare from the gang leader was always present, and it was only a matter of time before she would have her chance.

That chance presented itself on Tuesday, the day before the planned escape.

Jo suspended her usual workout. It was best not to draw attention to her athleticism and self-defense skills.

One of the Latinas with Moreno approached the guard and engaged him in conversation. Jo wasn't close enough to hear what they were saying, but their body language spoke for them. They were negotiating a sex-for-money transaction. Five minutes later, the guard and inmate were behind the storage shed and out of sight.

"Torres, Delgado," Moreno called out to two of her confederates. The trio moved quickly toward Elena, while the other inmates in the yard stood behind them in a semi-circle to witness the action.

Jo stepped in front of Elena. "Back off, Moreno!"

Moreno stopped when she was about twenty feet from Jo. "I'll cut you, bitch, if you don't get the fuck out of my way." She pointed the shiv at Jo and waved it side to side as if she was slashing her.

Jo knew what to expect and how she'd respond. She'd trained for it in the dojo with other martial artists. Torres and Delgado would approach together. One would stop; one would continue on and initiate the action. If she wasn't subdued, the other stood ready to pounce. While these two engaged Jo in the scuffle, Moreno would rush forward and stab Elena, probably in the chest and throat. Because Jo had stood up for Elena and had witnessed her murder, Moreno would slit her throat too.

The other inmates would quickly disperse into small groups with their backs to Elena and Jo's dead bodies. Ratting out Moreno meant testifying in court and retribution from *Las Proscritas*. Those who watched would stand united and say nothing when questioned about what happened.

The murder weapon would be placed in Jo's hand. Moreno was wearing a latex glove and would conceal it in her shoe, then dispose of it later. The only forensic evidence at the scene would be Jo's prints on the shiv and Elena and Jo's blood on the blade.

An apparent murder-suicide.

*Venganza*, the Mexican way.

Jo shot a glance at Torres, who stood her ground about

ten feet from her. To Jo, it meant that Delgado would strike first. Delgado rushed forward, right fist cocked and ready to launch. Jo kept her hands by her side. She wanted Delgado to believe she'd have an unobstructed path to her and that her only reaction would be to turn her head and cover her face with an arm to minimize the damage from the blow.

But Jo had other ideas.

When Delgado's fist shot forward on a trajectory to her face, Jo, in one synchronized movement, parried the punch with her left hand while simultaneously stepping forward and delivering a palm strike to Delgado's nose. The momentum from Delgado's forward progress enhanced the power of the strike. She felt the crush of nasal bones and cartilage as her attacker's head whiplashed. Delgado fell back and hit the ground hard, blood spurting from her nose and mouth.

Torres hesitated, as Jo knew she would—in shock by what she'd seen. It was ample time for Jo to shuffle step forward into a karate stance and close the distance between them. Before Torres could move toward her … or back off … Jo, in the blink of an eye, delivered a spinning wheel kick to the side of Torres's head. She dropped like a felled Sequoia, knocked out.

Jo turned to face Moreno and resumed a karate stance—legs apart, knees bent, back erect, and hands extended forward one behind the other. She waved the fingers of her outstretched left hand in a gesture of engagement. She wanted to take the weapon away from Moreno and stick it up where the sun don't shine. She'd taken knives away from punks before and knew Moreno was holding the short end of the shiv.

Moreno won a reprieve by hesitating just long enough for the guard and his female companion to reappear from behind the shed. The crowd immediately dispersed into small groups. Moreno hid the shiv in the waistband of her pants under her shirt and stepped back to join her group.

Jo went to stand by Elena.

The guard was familiar with Moreno's reputation for violence. When his attention was drawn to the two inmates lying injured on the ground, he yelled, "Is this your doing, Moreno?"

The guard pulled out his baton and extended it to full length. "Who started it?" he demanded to know, now face-to-face with Moreno.

Moreno turned her head in the direction of Torres. "She did," pointing at the unconscious inmate on the ground. "She punched her," pointing at Delgado, who had mustered the strength to stagger to her feet and was trying to stop the flow of blood from her nose with a sleeve.

Jo nudged Elena's arm with an elbow as if to say, "I knew this would happen." Moreno had a very good reason to keep Jo out of the fracas. Jo wasn't afraid to tell the guard about the shiv she was concealing, an offense that would lead to criminal charges and her transfer to a more secure facility. Moreno needed to offer something to Jo to gain her cooperation and a second chance at Elena.

The guard must have had his suspicions about Moreno's story. He turned and looked at Jo and Elena. "Is that what happened?" he asked the closest witnesses.

They had a telepathic meeting of the minds on how they'd respond.

Jo nodded. "Like Moreno said," pointing at Torres, still motionless on the ground. "She started it."

"And that one," Elena said, looking at Delgado, blood still dripping from her nose. "She finish it."

After dinner, Elena took her usual place on Jo's bunk. They skipped showers. Moreno was still in full revenge mode. No sense chancing fate.

"You saved me out there today," Elena whispered. "*Gracias, mi amiga.*"

Jo poked Elena's leg with her foot. "Hey! I told you … we are in this together."

Elena had a curious look on her face. "Jo, have there been many men in your life?" she asked timidly.

There was a throatiness in Jo's laugh. "A few." She usually carried a couple of condoms with her in case her sex drive shifted into overdrive and the opportunity presented.

"Have you ever been in love?"

"I thought I might have been once, but things didn't work out. What about you, Elena? Have you ever been in love?"

"Diego … I am property to him. A possession he owns." She sighed and shook her head. "I have no feelings for him or any man … no feelings."

Jo understood why. Elena's only experiences with men resulted in maltreatment, sexual abuse, and servitude. The exchange of personal information piqued Jo's interest in knowing more about her Latina friend. "Do you have any children?" she pried.

Elena looked away. "Diego's babies, they die inside me. After that, he goes to his mistresses unless he is drunk or high, and then he has his way with me. Three have given him daughters but no sons. He takes care of them, and they tell no one who is the father. Too dangerous for them." She turned her gaze on Jo. "Do you want children someday?"

Jo shrugged. "I don't see it in my future. Not now. Not after all that's happened to me."

They were looking into each other's eyes when Elena

asked, "Have you ever been with … a woman?"

Jo knew where this was going. Sex had always been forced on Elena. She'd been victimized by so many men for so long that she was incapable of trusting a man with her heart. She'd been stripped of her youth and never allowed to develop normally from adolescence to womanhood. She'd never had a chance to come to terms with her sexuality. "No, Elena. I've never been with a woman," she replied uneasily.

Elena winced as if disappointed by her response. "Have you ever wanted to be?"

Jo was out of her comfort zone. She answered with a question of her own. "Have you?"

Just then Carver entered the pod and went to Jo's bunk. "Crowder, the warden wants to see you tomorrow morning in her office. I'll come get you at ten. Be ready."

Jo and Elena's eyes locked. Jo felt a rush of anxiety and sensed from the forlorn look on Elena's face that she did too. They needed to be together at ten that morning in the kitchen when the deliveries were made. There was a very narrow window of time and opportunity.

"Why?" she probed.

"You'll find out tomorrow," he bellowed over his shoulder as he walked away.

When Carver was out of earshot, Jo spoke somberly. "If we don't escape tomorrow, Moreno will have another week to get to you. The next time she's in the yard with us, she'll find a way to separate us or gang up on me. I may not be able to protect you."

Elena moved closer to Jo until they were side by side. She looked at Jo and spoke softly. "Whatever happens to us—to you and me tomorrow—you will always have my trust and gratitude. If we get back to Diego, you live there with us. Our house, it has many rooms. Our people will protect you, as they protect me. It will be a good life, I promise." She paused a moment, and then said, "We will be like … *hermanas*."

Elena's eyes glistened in the glow of fluorescent light as she reached for Jo's hand. This time she held it in both of her hands, raised it to her lips, and kissed it.

She let Elena hold her hand until her grip loosened.

"Yes, Elena … like *sisters*," Jo said as Elena's fingers slowly slipped away.

# CHAPTER 11

Jo glanced at the watch she'd purchased from the commissary the moment Carver entered the pod a couple of minutes late. Elena, accompanied by a guard, had headed to the kitchen at a quarter to ten. Jo had no more than twenty minutes before the delivery man, after unloading his truck, would complete his paperwork and drive off.

"Let's go," Carver snapped.

Jo didn't need his encouragement. She walked quickly out the door.

Every minute mattered.

She could only speculate about the reason for the meeting—a transfer to a different pod or to another facility, or maybe a different work assignment. If all went as planned, the reason wouldn't matter—she'd be long gone.

She wondered if Carver would be all touchy-feely again and frisk her before they went into Green's office. If he did, he'd surely discover the second set of clothes under her prison uniform. She'd have a hard time explaining that away. Carver could only conclude that she planned to escape from the kitchen storeroom, the least secure area of the prison. Elena would be a suspected collaborator in the escape, searched, and found to have the same paraphernalia on her, including the illegal lighter Jo had given her that morning. They'd have no choice but to remain silent and demand a lawyer when they were charged with attempted escape. They'd be separated and sent to more secure facilities, where they'd be closely guarded.

As they approached Green's office, Jo felt an uptick in her heart rate. Her mouth went dry. She felt warm, and it wasn't because she was wearing two sets of clothing. It was the rise in her blood pressure brought on by a tension-filled moment of reckoning.

She arrived at the door several steps ahead of Carver and reached for the door handle, hoping to snuff out the chances of him frisking her again.

"Hold up, Crowder," Carver yelled out. "What's the hurry?"

"I have kitchen duty at ten," she replied, hoping that Carver wouldn't detect the nervousness in her voice.

"I'll get the door," he said, stepping in front of her and opening it.

*What … no frisk?*

She'd avoided the fly in the ointment and the monkey in the wrench.

So far, at least.

When Carver put his hand on her back and pushed her into Green's office, she had a far bigger problem on her hands—Green was nowhere to be seen.

She heard the door close and the sound of the lock turning.

Alone with Carver in a locked office, she turned to face him. "Carver, where's Green?"

"At meetings all morning outside the prison," he responded smugly. "Now don't you think it's time we get acquainted?"

Jo thought about punching the creep in the face or kicking him between the legs. But he was still too far away.

She glanced at her watch. It was five minutes after ten. The driver had probably arrived and was beginning to unload his truck. She'd have maybe fifteen minutes before their chance of escaping that day would be lost.

She needed to confront the problem head on. She grinned at Carver and, trying to be promiscuous and agreeable, forced herself to say, "Let me see what you're offering."

She stepped back and stood by Green's desk.

He'd have to come to her.

Carver leered at her as he unbuckled his guard's belt and put it on the chair in front of Green's desk.

She did a quick survey of the objects on the desk. The typical stuff you'd expect a prison administrator to have—computer, telephone, pencil holder, a stack of files ... and a glass paperweight the size of an orange sitting on top of a pile of correspondence.

Carver moved toward her, undoing the button on his pants and pulling down the zipper. Jo decided to forgo the foreplay and dropped to her knees, looking up expectantly. He stood in front of her, grinning like the Cheshire cat, and lowered his pants and underwear to his knees, revealing himself fully.

The disgusting thought of touching this man gave way to the delight she'd have when she grabbed his testicles and squeezed them with all her might. The many hours she'd spent compressing her hand gripper at the highest tension setting gave her twice the grip strength of the average woman.

Jo looked up at Carver, a naughty grin on her face. The lecherous stare he gave her in return would soon be replaced by the wide-eyed, open-mouthed, contorted look of agony.

The last thing Carver saw before his world went dark was the smile on Jo's face when her right hand shot forward and gripped his testicles so tightly he collapsed to his knees. Before his scream could gain velocity, she jumped to her feet, grabbed hold of the paperweight and smashed it against Carver's temple, knocking him out.

Another glance at her watch. It was ten minutes after ten.

She rolled his flabby body over and handcuffed his right hand to his left leg. She ripped off a computer cable and used it to bind the other extremities in a similar way. Green's scarf hanging from a tree stand served a purpose too—she used it to gag him.

Jo unlocked the door and turned one last time to see Carver on his stomach, pants down and hogtied.

"This should put you in good with Green when she returns to her office," she said, laughing over her shoulder.

There was no time to waste.

She scurried out the door and rushed to the kitchen.

# CHAPTER 12

"You're late," the guard grumbled when she arrived at the cafeteria. "Sanchez is waiting for you."

"Sorry … that time of month," she replied demurely, moving quickly by him and through the cafeteria to the kitchen storeroom.

Elena rushed to her, an anxious look on her face. "He … he just returned to his truck," she stammered nervously.

Jo reached out a hand. "Give me the lighter. You know what to do."

Elena handed her the lighter and headed to the loading dock. Jo rushed into the kitchen and climbed on a countertop close to a sprinkler head on the ceiling.

The building was old. So was the sprinkler system. When one head was activated on the older systems, they all went off.

She placed the flame as close as possible to the head. Thirty seconds later water showered the kitchen and elsewhere in the facility. She jumped to the floor and pulled the fire alarm lever on the kitchen wall on her way out.

The alarm blared throughout the facility. Jo knew what to expect. She'd read about the fire drill in the prison handbook she'd been given during her orientation. The inmates were supposed to gather in single file wherever they were in the prison, wait for a guard to lead them to the exercise yard, and muster in four rows with the inmates from their pod.

The drill in which Jo had participated two weeks into her sentence gave her the idea of how she'd create the diversion. The slow, disorderly way the drill had been conducted when the alarm sounded convinced her there would be bedlam when the sprinklers went off and the evacuation was supposedly for real.

When she got to the loading dock, the truck had pulled away and was halfway to the exit. Elena had done her part— she had raised the rolling loading door about four feet and gotten in.

But would Jo be a minute late and a few steps short?

She jumped to the ground and ran as fast as she could to catch up to the truck. Elena was on her knees, holding the bottom of the door with one hand and reaching out with the other to help pull Jo in.

The truck slowed down just before leaving the facility. It gave Jo the chance to grab hold of Elena's outstretched hand. She lunged forward into the back of the truck but landed only partially the way in. The truck accelerated through the opened gate to an access road that merged with the highway up ahead. Jo's legs dangled from the truck and the toes of her sneakers dragged on the asphalt. When the truck picked up speed around a curve, her legs swung to the side and she felt her grip on the bed of the truck loosen.

She was falling out.

She'd never catch the truck once it was on the highway.

And then Jo felt her body slide forward into the truck. Elena had reached out and grabbed the seat of her pants with both hands and pulled her into the truck—just as it accelerated onto the highway.

Jo rolled over on her back, huffing and puffing from exhaustion, her arms extended like outstretched wings. When her breathing normalized, she sat up against the side of the truck. Elena went to sit next to her. Jo turned and looked at her confederate with appreciative eyes. "Thanks, my friend."

Elena nudged closer, squeezed Jo's hand, and smiled. "Like you say, Jo, we are in this together." The distant sound of sirens prompted her to blurt, "Police."

"No. Fire trucks on the way to the prison."

"What now?"

"We get out of our scrubs, ball up the shirt, put it in the pants and tie the legs together. Leave nothing behind."

There was enough light to see what was in the back of the truck. A dolly lay in front of boxes stacked evenly in rows. "He has more deliveries to make," Jo deduced. "We need to get out of the truck the first chance we get."

When the truck entered city limits, it turned down a one-way street. There was no traffic behind the truck when it stopped at an intersection.

"Out, now," Jo shouted. She threw her bundled uniform to the ground and jumped out first. Elena followed. Jo barely had enough time to lower the door before the truck pulled away.

They put on their ball caps and headed into the city, dropping their prison scrubs in a public trash receptacle the first chance they had.

"We have time," Jo said. "There will be an all-points bulletin out for us, but not for an hour. They'd want to avoid the embarrassment of another prison break. They'll think we are on foot and send guards out to look for us in the neighborhoods around the prison."

Elena asked, "The police, where will they go?"

"Here. It's the closest city. We need to get off the streets and out of here as quickly as possible."

They headed in the direction of the taller buildings in order to locate an indoor parking lot. They found a four-level garage fifteen minutes into their walk and used the stairwell to go to the second floor. Jo figured the lower levels were more likely occupied by people who arrived early and worked in the nearby office buildings. There was a good chance they'd be there all day.

She looked for an older model car. Newer vehicles were nearly impossible to hotwire. After checking the doors of a half-dozen cars, she came upon an unlocked, well-maintained, decade-old Toyota Camry. The car would blend well in traffic.

Five minutes later they were out of the garage, their exit made easier with the keycard found in the console.

They had no cash. Jo checked the fuel gauge—a quarter tank. Plenty of gas to get to where the money was hidden. After that, they'd stop and get some clothes for their trip through Mexico.

"So where are we headed, Elena?"

"Texas," she replied.

"Texas is a big state."

"To one of your national parks. It is in the Chisos Mountains and Chihuahuan Desert."

"Big Bend National Park," Jo said, as if answering a question her seventh-grade teacher had asked. She'd been to national parks to hike and rock climb, but never there. But she knew of it. "Why cross from the park?"

"There, the Rio Grande is narrow and shallow most of the

year. We wade or swim across to Boquillas. It was a mining town a long time ago. *Americanos*, they cross the border and visit."

"Border patrol?"

"No customs or border patrol on this side. Only a park ranger who checks passports when you leave and come back."

"So where do we cross?"

"Where our people sometimes cross—about five miles downriver from the port of entry. We park the car and walk there."

"And then?"

"We do not go to Boquillas. Immigration agents will want to check our passports there. We walk to the bus station in El Llano. There we can exchange dollars for pesos and take a bus to Chihuahua City. Then we ride the train like the migrants."

"Do the cartels operate in this part of Mexico?"

"*Sí*. When the Guadalajara cartel break up, other syndicates form and fight each other over territory and supply lines."

"What territory does Diego control?"

"Our poppy farms, labs, and storage facilities are in the states to the south. We go to Tuxtla, the capital of Chiapas."

"How far do we need to travel?"

"A very long way. More than a thousand miles. That is why we ride the trains. It is good we travel south. Migrants enter Mexico from Guatemala and travel north to the border."

"Who travels south?"

"Mostly migrants turned back at the border who have no place to go but to the place they come from."

Jo drove into a residential neighborhood. "Elena, look in the console for something I can use as a screwdriver."

Elena found some coins and held them out in her hand.

"That dime will do just fine," Jo said as she proceeded

down a quiet one-way street and parked in the middle of the block. She removed the license plate from their car and switched it with the out-of-state plate on the car behind her.

Five minutes later they were on their way to a storage facility in Prairieville, an hour's drive from New Orleans, where twenty-five thousand dollars was stuffed in a gym bag. After they picked up the money, they'd travel the state roads into Texas. Jo estimated that the eight-hundred-fifty-mile drive to Big Bend National Park would take about eighteen hours with a two-hour rest stop thrown in.

If all went well, they'd be crossing the border into Mexico the next morning.

# CHAPTER 13

Prairieville was a safe place to retrieve the money and buy clothes. A suburban bedroom community south of Baton Rouge, the township had little crime and was policed by a small sheriff's office.

Two hours after their escape, Jo pulled into the storage facility where she'd hidden the money. She'd gotten in by cozying up to the attendant on staff, paying double what it was worth, in cash, and giving a fake name.

A code punched into a keypad gave her access, and with the brim of her ball cap pulled down low, she went to the locker she had rented before her arrest.

She was back in the car with the gym bag five minutes later.

They stopped at a Walmart in a shopping center a few miles from the storage facility.

"Elena, it's safer that I shop for our clothes."

"*Si*, we are the same size, don't you think?"

Remembering Elena's curvaceous body from the shower, Jo chuckled. "Sure, Elena, we'd fit into each other's clothes.

So, what will we need for our trip through Mexico?"

Elena rattled off a list of things. "Trousers that are denim—they are durable. A couple of t-shirts each, jackets with hoods, underwear, socks, hats with brims, something to eat, bottles of water, and bags to carry our things in." She paused momentarily, as if reflecting on what else they might need. "Sunscreen and scissors to cut my hair."

"And sunglasses," Jo added.

"*Si.* Big, dark ones."

Elena put on her ball cap and slouched low in her seat while Jo shopped. When she returned, they drove to a remote area of the parking lot, where they changed into the clothes Jo had purchased with money from the gym bag. The Panama-style hats, hooded sweatshirts, scarves, and thick-framed, dark-lens sunglasses would help hide their hair and some of their faces.

Jo split the money with Elena. They hid the bundles of fifty-and-one-hundred-dollar bills in socks and buried them in their backpacks under their clothes, snacks, and bottles of water. They stuffed some fifties in the pockets of their trousers.

When Elena began to cut her own hair, Jo stopped her. "Let me do it," she offered. She couldn't bear to see Elena do a hack job on her lovely locks. "Only enough to fit your hair better under your hat. I bought some hair clips for you to pull your hair together."

When she finished, they dumped what remained of their prison clothes and the gym bag in a trash receptacle on the way out and drove southwest past Lafayette and Lake Charles to Texas. They listened to a local radio station, waiting for news of their escape.

It came an hour from the Texas state line.

Jo raised the volume. "In a daring escape from a women's

prison facility outside New Orleans, twenty-five-year-old Elena Sanchez-Gomez escaped with another prisoner. Sanchez is the wife of Diego Garcia-Hernandez, the infamous El Leon and the head of the Chiapas cartel. Garcia is wanted in Mexico and the United States for drug trafficking, money laundering, and murder.

"Garcia's wife was serving a twenty-five-year sentence for shooting a Louisiana state trooper, severely injuring him. The other escapee is Jo Crowder, a former New Orleans Police Department homicide detective, serving a twenty-year sentence for drug trafficking. It is believed the two prisoners escaped in the back of a delivery truck after setting off a fire alarm and the prison's sprinkler system. Federal, state and local police agencies in Louisiana and neighboring states have launched a manhunt for their capture. Border patrol agents have also been alerted."

Jo looked over at Elena and laughed. "That's us, all right—*Thelma and Louise*."

"These women? Who are they?" Elena asked, an inquisitive look on her face.

"Like us, two women who took a road trip to Mexico to avoid being caught by the police."

Elena didn't ask how their trip ended … and Jo didn't feel the need to tell her.

~

It had been five hours since they left Prairieville. They had stopped a couple of hours from San Antonio for gas, a restroom break, and some takeout food. They ate in the car.

Jo had done all the driving and was sleepy eyed. It was too risky to have Elena behind the wheel. If they were pulled over, she, not Elena, had the better chance of talking their way out of it. If Elena was in the driver's seat, she just might put the long blades of the scissors on the seat next to her through the cop's Adam's apple.

Elena Sanchez-Gomez was a very dangerous woman. Jo wondered how many people she'd shot and throats she'd slit. Anyone who disrespected or threatened her could end up dead—the threat to kill Moreno's parents for what their daughter tried to do to Elena in prison seemed very real. And now that she had escaped, Elena might want the pleasure of killing them herself.

Elena dozed off as soon as Jo lowered the volume on the music station that was playing, but she needed some nap time too. A truck stop was better than a mall to get some sleep. Malls were patrolled by security guards. Truck stops were intended to provide a place for drivers to eat and sleep in their cabs. But such places were havens for drug and sex transactions. Not the safest place for two women to catch some sleep, but it would have to do. She pulled into a truck stop that had diesel gas and a no-name diner and found a dimly lit spot to park some fifty yards from the closest semi.

The noise from unlatching her seatbelt and lowering the back of her seat was enough to awaken Elena, who offered to drive while she slept. Jo explained why that wasn't a good idea but left out the part about the scissors and Adam's apple.

"Go back to sleep, Elena," she said softly. "It may be the last time we rest before you get us across the border."

Elena stretched out her arms and yawned lazily. "In Mexico, we must be careful where we rest and sleep," she cautioned. "The safest places are the churches. Some of them have shelters where migrants can get a meal and stay the night."

"You risk being recognized."

"It is more a risk to sleep in the parks and alleys. The gangs, they look for young women and girls on the streets, kidnap and rape them, and then sell them to sex traffickers. If they find the money, we will be taken somewhere in the desert and killed after they have their way with us."

Jo would have no choice but to rely on Elena once they got to Mexico. Who better than someone who had once lived on the streets?

They lay back in their seats for some much-needed rest. Jo had always been a light sleeper. It came with being a homicide detective. Her dreams were slideshows of crime scenes and faces of men, women, and children who had been beaten, shot, stabbed, and strangled. She'd awakened in a cold sweat on many a night, her heart racing and her body shaking.

But it was the painful memories of the victims that motivated her to pursue violent offenders with the nose of a bloodhound. And when the scent led her to them, she had to suppress the urge to put a bullet in their brains and end their killing sprees right then and there.

She sat back on the edge of sleep and reflected on her circumstances. On the lam with the most wanted fugitive in America, she could only speculate what her life with Elena would be like if she were reunited with her husband. Would she be conscripted to work for the cartel? Her background as a convicted drug trafficker qualified her for a job with a criminal enterprise that profited from the sale of narcotics. But would Diego Garcia let her into his inner circle of trusted confidantes?

Jo had many questions.

When they resumed their dash to the border, she'd probe Elena for some answers.

# CHAPTER 14

Tapping on the window startled Jo and Elena out of their hour-long naps. In the darkness, Jo couldn't get a good look at the face of the man who was doing the tapping.

Before she'd dozed off, she lowered the window a few inches to let in some diesel-laced air on the sultry night. She conversed with the stranger through the opening. "What do you want?" She didn't try to mask the irritation in her voice.

The man bent over and spoke into the opening. "Looks like y'all won't be going anywhere anytime soon," he replied in a dense southern drawl.

She turned on the dome light to get a better look at his face. He was so close she could smell the alcohol in his breath. His thick neck and bulbous jowls suggested he was a large-framed man. A scruffy beard covered his face from his ears to the middle of his neck. His rough, unkempt appearance suggested he was a local.

She breathed a sigh of relief—he wasn't local law enforcement. "What do you mean?" she asked the meddlesome redneck.

"Unless you got yourself two spare tires in your trunk, y'all be driving on rims."

Jo had no choice but to unlock her door and leave the safety of the vehicle to see what he was talking about. She turned and whispered to Elena, "Put on your sweatshirt, pull up your hoodie, stay in the car, and don't speak."

Jo unlocked the door and got out of the car. Nearly a foot taller, the man towered over her.

She looked at the front tire.

"Nope. They be the ones in the back."

She walked behind the car and saw two flat tires in the illumination of the parking lights of a pickup truck.

*His truck.*

The chances of having two flat tires while parked were infinitesimally small. Someone had either deflated them or punctured them with a sharp object while they slept.

*Probably him.*

"You know it's not too smart for women to park here," he huffed. "The boys over there driving them rigs hook up with the local women for some recreation, if you know what I mean. Sometimes the gals need a little convincing."

The quick assessment she did of their circumstances gave Jo only one option—they'd have to abandon the car. "How far is the next town?" she asked.

"Sellersville, seven miles that way," he said, pointing into the darkness. "But it's not safe to walk the highway at night."

Jo had her reservations about getting into a stranger's truck, but they had no choice. Otherwise, they'd be walking a dual-lane highway for a couple of hours in the dark. If a local cop passed by and stopped, they'd have no IDs to prove they weren't vagrants, or worse—that they weren't the two convicted felons who'd escaped from a Louisiana prison that morning. "Fifty bucks for a lift into town," she grudgingly proposed.

The big man's breathing was raspy, and the air around him reeked of booze and tobacco. "Sure, but first I need the money."

Jo returned to the car. The man loitered nearby but was out of earshot. "Elena, we have no choice," she whispered. "The creep probably deflated our tires, but he's our only way of getting to the next town. It's too risky to walk there."

She reached into her pocket for a fifty-dollar bill. "Let me do the talking."

Elena slid the scissors on her seat up the sleeve of her sweatshirt. They grabbed their backpacks, got out, and followed the stranger to his truck. Jo gave him the fifty, opened the passenger door, and pushed down the back of the front seat so that Elena would know where to sit. She wanted to be up front and within arm's reach of the stranger.

"Where are you ladies headed?" he asked.

Jo caught him adjusting the rear-view mirror and watched as he shifted his eyes back and forth from the road to the mirror, probably to get a good look at Elena. Like most men, he wouldn't be disappointed.

"San Antonio," Jo lied, hoping the chitchat would end quickly.

"Why there?"

"Visiting a sick relative."

"Yours or hers?"

"Mine. An aunt I haven't seen in a while."

"San Antone's a hundred miles from here. You're going to need to fix them flats if you intendin' to get there in your car. There's a garage in town that can fix them for you tomorrow."

"What's the name of the garage?" Jo asked, not wanting

him to think they had abandoned their vehicle.

"Jessup's Garage, on Fifth and Main. Tell the owner Hoss sent you." The bull-necked stranger turned and looked at her. "You be needing a place to stay the night," he continued. "There's a motel off the highway within walking distance of town that only takes cash. A no-questions-asked kind of place, if you get my meaning."

His meaning was perfectly clear to Jo. And it was the perfect place to hide out. "Good. Drop us off there."

They drove down the highway about five miles and turned onto a narrow, two-lane road.

"Sellersville is this way," he advised.

The announcement was as sudden as the turn was abrupt, causing Jo's body to jerk to the side. The road was unlit. The houses she saw in the illumination of the headlights were shabby-looking cabins and mobile homes. She saw no signs for Sellersville.

When she felt they had traveled at least seven miles, she asked, "How much farther to the motel?"

"Not too far now," he replied, a sudden gruffness in his tone of voice. He turned onto a single-lane dirt road and proceeded into the woodlands to a small cabin, where he stopped and turned off the engine.

"What's going on?" Jo demanded to know, fighting the urge to back-knuckle him even before she heard his answer.

The red flags had all been there. Two flat tires. A stranger offering to help. Two defenseless women taken to a cabin in the woods.

He was surprisingly agile for such a burly man. He was out of the truck before she could deliver the strike.

Her mind predicted what would happen next.

# CHAPTER 15

They walked to the front door of a solitary cabin in the isolation of lonely woodlands with a gun pointed at them. The stale air reeked with the smell of diesel fuel and spoiled meat. The source of the foul odor—a rusty, old generator and a lidless barrel of garbage that graced the front of the run-down structure the stranger called home.

Jo stopped short of the door and stood on spongy floorboards of a rickety porch. She hoped their abductor would come closer and give her the opportunity to strike. She'd taken guns away from perpetrators before. But they had to be within arm's reach and pointing the gun at her to do it.

He didn't take the bait.

"It's open. Go in, put your packs on the table, and sit on the couch."

The lights were on in the main living area, revealing a habitat of squalor. They had no choice but to do as they were told. They watched as he opened one of the backpacks.

"What the fuck!" he exclaimed, as he flipped through a

stack of hundred-dollar bills. "Did you rob a freaking bank? Where'd you get this kind of money?" Not waiting for a response, he opened the other backpack, rummaged through it, and found more money, his eyes wide open with excitement.

He went to a box on a table, reached for a roll of duct tape, and tossed it on the couch between Elena and Jo. He aimed the gun at Elena. "You—tape your girlfriend's hands behind her back, and then her feet. Be real generous with the tape."

When she was finished, Jo and Elena's eyes met just long enough to exchange subtle head nods.

Jo sat bound on the sofa, her eyes riveted on Elena. The stranger wanted the alpha female out of the way so that he could prey on the quiet one who looked weak and defenseless.

Looks can be deceiving.

"In the bedroom," he demanded, waving his gun in the direction of a room without a door.

Jo scooted over to the edge of the sofa to get a better view of what was happening inside.

Elena went submissively into the room and faced the side of the bed. Her soon-to-be rapist was right behind her. He nudged her in the back with the barrel of his revolver. "Now, take off your clothes, all of them."

Elena didn't hesitate. In one swift movement, she removed the scissors from her sleeve, turned, and plunged them into her attacker's eye.

The gun dropped to the floor when his hands went instinctively to where the pain was most acutely felt. He shrieked, blood streaming between his fingers. "You bitch, you fucking bitch … you blinded me," he screamed.

While his hands still covered his wounded eye, Elena stabbed him again, this time deep into his chest. She left the scissors embedded in him. The man collapsed to the floor and howled like a wounded animal.

Elena then calmly walked over and picked up the gun. She went to where he lay in a fetal position on the floor and stood over him. When she pointed the gun at him, the man recoiled in fear, looked up at her with his one good eye, and begged her not to shoot him.

Jo sat paralyzed and watched Elena fire a bullet into the stranger's forehead. His head snapped back and bounced off the floor; and he begged no more.

The funereal silence in the cabin was deafening when the shockwaves from the blast settled. No one moved an inch, least of all the stranger. Jo's eyes remained fixed on Elena. The sulfurous smell from the gun's discharge lingered in the thick, stagnant air. Elena turned and looked at Jo, her arm still outstretched, the gun still pointed at the man's head, as if she wanted … needed … some sign of approval from Jo for what she had done.

Jo nodded.

Elena smiled.

After Elena removed the duct tape, they worked like experienced gravediggers to dispose of the body. Each grabbed a foot and dragged the body out the door into the woods to a clearing where the soil was soft and tree roots did not impede their digging. Elena had found two pots in the kitchen that they used to dig a hole. An hour later, the grave was deep enough to partially hide the corpse. They rolled the body into the hole and covered it with leaves and branches.

They returned to the cabin, removed the blood-splattered sheet from the bed, and wiped the blood from the floor with it.

Elena washed the blood from the scissors and put them in her backpack with bullets she'd found on a shelf in the kitchen. She used one of them to replace the bullet that was lodged in the brain of their abductor and put his gun in the pocket of her sweatshirt.

Jo looked around the cabin. There was only the one bed and no framed photos of family or friends. The dump showed no evidence of a woman's touch. He lived alone in apparent seclusion.

The body wouldn't be found for a while.

Their work completed, Elena turned out the light and left the cabin; and Jo followed her out with a neatly folded bloodstained sheet in one hand and the keys to a pickup truck in the other.

The fugitives traveled through the night in a beat-up old pickup. The clank of the engine and the smell of exhaust strongly suggested the need for an oil change and tune-up. Jo figured it was best to stay off the highways and travel the back roads even though it would add an hour to their road trip. This time there would be no stops other than to buy necessary provisions and gas up a dead man's truck.

She looked over at Elena and wondered if she had any misgivings about what she'd done. The images of how she snuffed out the life of their one-eyed abductor were still vivid in her mind—how he cowered on the floor with the scissors still in his chest, and looked up at his executioner, blood leaking out his eye socket and pleading with her to show mercy. Elena showed no emotional reaction when she pulled the trigger and said nothing about it afterwards, as if blowing a man's brains out was as normal as smacking the backside of a misbehaving child.

Jo had no qualms about how Elena handled things. Not

then, when they'd exchanged nods after Elena bound her with duct tape and she silently agreed to her plan to use the scissors in a way that would end badly for her attacker. Although the cold, calculated way Elena had used his gun to kill him sent shivers down Jo's spine, she'd given her tacit approval. She could have yelled out for Elena not to shoot him. She'd sat back and watched instead.

If their roles were reversed, and Jo was the one in the bedroom with him, how would she have handled things? Her police training and martial arts skills undoubtedly would have been sufficient to neutralize the threat of being sexually assaulted. She'd subdued her share of perpetrators after a scuffle. In this case, however, she'd have beaten him more badly than was necessary. But he would have survived the whooping, and like a boxer who'd gone down for the count, he'd eventually have gotten up to fight another day.

Jo wouldn't have shot him. With his gun in her hand and pointed at him, she'd have Elena bind and gag him with the duct tape. He'd have been alive when they left with his cellphone, gun and truck. It would've been unlikely he'd find a way out of his bondage or that someone would find him for at least a day or two. By then, they'd be in Mexico—the man no longer a threat.

Yet the stranger had every intention of killing them. He'd have no choice if he wanted to keep the money—more money than he'd ever seen in his pathetic life. After raping them, he would have strangled them. Strangulation was a rapist's preferred manner of death. Quiet and neat, not loud and messy like shooting someone. No need to remove bloodstains and spatter.

Afterwards, he'd have put their bodies in the bed of his truck, covered them with the sheet from his bed, driven deep into the woodlands, and dumped their bodies. In time, their naked, unburied corpses would become fodder for wildlife and decompose, leaving only skeletal remains.

As for him, he would have bought a newer truck and not lost one minute's sleep over what he'd done. For all Jo knew, he may have done this kind of thing before or, emboldened by having raped and murdered two women so easily, he might have raped and murdered again.

Elena had no regrets about what she'd done.

Thinking it over again, neither did Jo.

Like telepathy, Elena also had killing on her mind. She asked, "Have you ever killed anyone, Jo?"

Jo paused before answering, as if she needed the time to calculate the number. But she didn't need the time—she remembered every man whose life she'd ended. She hesitated only because her mind made screenshots of their faces in rapid order. "Yes, Elena, five men … all in the line of duty."

With inquiring eyes, Elena queried, "Like I do today?"

"Yes, like me, you had no choice," Jo said supportively. "He surely would have killed us to keep the money."

"This may not be the last time we have to kill," Elena advised matter-of-factly. She pulled out the dead man's revolver from the pocket of her jacket, opened the barrel and spun it, as if she was checking to be certain it was fully loaded. "You are good with your fists and fight like a *soldado*. But our enemies will be many once we cross the border. A soldier's fists will not stop a bullet." She returned the gun to her pocket. "It is best I keep the gun."

Elena had always been dangerous, but now she was armed and dangerous. She wondered how many men Elena had killed and the circumstances. So little provocation was needed for her to use deadly force. The way she'd handled the gun in the cabin proved she was experienced in using firearms—standing upright with her feet shoulder width apart, fully extending her arms, firmly gripping the revolver in both hands, and aiming it confidently at the target. The bullet hole was right in the middle of his forehead.

*Aim small, miss small.*

Elena was right. They may have to kill again to stay alive. And Jo knew who would be the one doing the killing.

# CHAPTER 16

"Your Spanish, how good is it?" Elena asked at daybreak, rubbing the sleep from her eyes with the back of a hand.

Elena had slept the last two hours while Jo fought drowsiness driving through the night, aided by the adrenaline rush from their encounter with the stranger. Elena renewed her offer to relieve Jo at the wheel, but she declined. Elena was now armed with scissors and a loaded gun. God help the cop who might stop them along the way. "Four years in high school. Another year in college. I'm better at listening than speaking, but I get by."

"I do the talking … you speak in my language if anyone ask you questions. Keep it to *si* and *no* and mumble everything else as if you are slow of mind. I will say you and your husband are from Venezuela." Elena paused intermittently to construct the narrative. "He got sick … and he die … and now you go back there. I … I am your husband's sister. We go together."

Curious, Jo asked, "Do you and Diego speak to each other in Spanish?"

Elena laughed deep down her throat. "Only when we are angry at each other." Jo found Elena's attempt at humor endearing. "When he grow up," she explained in her unpolished English, "his mama make him speak like *Americanos*. She want the family to end up here, away from the cartel his papa grow the poppies for. Diego, he was only twelve years old when he kill the assassins sent to murder his family. He hate the cartels, and he want to come to America to escape the corruption … the violence. Strange how things work out for him. He become one of those he hate so much."

"And his family, what became of them?

"They live in America. Too dangerous for them to stay in Mexico. Diego, he become very wealthy. He give them new names and smuggle them across the border many years ago. He give them money to start a business and send his sister to school. He hire lawyers, and they make sure his family become citizens. Ceci, his sister, she become a doctor, a wife, and a mother three times. *Solo en America, si.*"

Jo shook her head in amazement at the lengths Diego had gone for his family. "Only in America." It was the dream of many undocumented immigrants who crossed the border.

Jo thought how paradoxical it was that Diego Garcia was able to buy the American dream for his family but not for himself. Now, the only things he had to look forward to living in Mexico were being captured and imprisoned or dying by unnatural causes.

Jo changed the subject and asked, "What will you want me to do when you are back with Diego? I can't just live with you and do nothing."

"We work together on the inventory, shipments, offshore banking. We make sure our friends are paid."

*Friends?* More like collaborators being paid bribes and

hush money.

"What does Diego do?" Jo thought but didn't say: *other than traffic heroin, cocaine, crystal meth, and fentanyl pills that kill thousands of people every year, and order his men to extort, kidnap, and kill politicians, police, journalists, and anyone else who got in his way?*

"Diego, he handles production, our supply lines, and how we clean the money. Carlos, he manages distribution, and Raul, he makes sure we are protected and punishes those who break the rules."

Jo had her doubts about Elena's plans for her. To allow an *Americana* so close to Diego Garcia's inner circle would be risky for him. She'd have access to so much information about the cartel's operations. Did Elena have that much influence over the infamous Leon?

"Will Diego trust an American woman he doesn't know?"

"He trusts me. He knows you can never go back to America and needs his protection. And one more thing."

"What, Elena?"

"He slit your throat if you ever betray him."

~

They arrived at Big Bend National Park shortly before eight in the morning. The last hour's drive was through desert wasteland. The air conditioning in the pickup was as dead as its owner. They traveled in the rising heat of an early west Texas morning with the windows down and their hoodies in their backpacks.

The park had not yet opened. No one manned the entrance station. As Jo passed by, she put her hand to her face in case there was a security camera monitoring visitors.

A dirt and gravel road led them to the Boquillas del Carmen port of entry. There was no need to stop at the passport-scanning kiosks. They found a place to park the truck. Using the dime in her pocket, she removed the license plate from the truck, emptied the glove compartment of anything that might identify the owner, and put everything in her backpack to be disposed of later.

They gathered their things and walked into the desert.

# CHAPTER 17

Larger than the state of Rhode Island, Big Bend National Park was in a remote, uninhabited area of west Texas. The closest American settlement was a town ten miles away. They'd stopped there and bought provisions at a convenience store.

It could have proved to have been their undoing.

Jo worried they might have been recognized there. While she shopped, the clerk changed the channel on a wall-mounted television. Elena and Jo's faces were plastered on the screen. The volume was turned up enough for her to hear snippets of the story: "Authorities believe the fugitives are likely to try to cross the border from Texas … State and local law enforcement are monitoring all roads to border towns … Additional border patrol agents have been deployed to facilitate their capture."

Jo had already placed her goods on the counter. Leaving them there and walking out of the store would draw attention to herself. She had no choice but to pay for them.

The clerk, a short, small-framed man with a comb over and thick eyeglasses, was familiar with the escape from earlier news stories. "It was all over the news last night," he said to the woman wearing the Panama hat and dark sunglasses while ringing up her order.

The clerk studied Jo as he bagged the food and bottles of water. She didn't have enough change from the fifties she'd used at Walmart to buy everything with small bills. She had no choice but to lay a fifty on the counter.

"So, what do you think?" the clerk asked, staring into her face with eyes that looked twice their size.

"About what?" she replied, an edginess in her tone she couldn't control as hard as she tried.

"Do you think they'll make it across the border?"

Jo pushed the fifty nearer to her interrogator, hoping he'd quickly complete the transaction. "Not my circus, not my monkeys."

"Just making conversation is all," he whined. Before opening the cash register, he took the fifty in both hands and stretched it out a couple of times as if he suspected it might be counterfeit. He brought the bill within inches of his coke-bottle lenses for a better look. "Are you in a hurry or something?" he asked, opening the till and putting the bill under the cash tray.

She held out a hand for her change. "I'm on my way to see a sick relative."

The pest narrowed his eyes into a squint. "This is the last town in Texas before you get to the border," he declared suspiciously.

Jo wanted to grab the runt by the collar, pull him over the counter, and slap some sense into him. Instead, she remained calm and said, "She lives in El Paso." She remembered from the map that the city was west of Big Bend.

"Out of the way, being on this road, don't you think?

Interstate would have been faster."

"Wanted to pass by the park on my way." Jo had always been a convincing liar. She had to be with suspects, lying to them about having an eyewitness or finding fingerprints and DNA at the scene of the crime, in order to pry loose a confession. But she was worried the jerk behind the counter was starting to see through her bullshit.

She needed to end the interrogation. "Change," she demanded, bending the fingers of her outstretched hand back and forth a couple of times.

With change in hand, she turned and hurried out the door.

The problem came when she saw the clerk look out the window at their truck as she got in. He had a clear, unobstructed view of Elena in the front seat, who wasn't wearing her hat and sunglasses. No one could forget such a pretty face.

No one.

Jo wasn't sure if the clerk got the license number of the truck before she floored it and left the store in a cloud of sand and dust. They still had a ten-mile drive to the park. If he called the local cops, they might try to make names for themselves and race down the deserted desert road in pursuit. She increased her speed and arrived at the park ten minutes later, her spirits bolstered by the absence of sirens.

~

A half hour into their hike, Jo understood why people visited the park. It was a majestic assemblage of golden hills, rugged rock formations, dramatic canyons, and a lunar-like landscape that defied logic—the parched, scorched dirt they walked on sported natural beds of lushly green vegetation with vibrant blossoms of vivid colors. The herbaceous sage brush, cactus flowers, and desert willow combined to produce a floral, woodsy fragrance that sweetened the earthy scent of desert soil.

She took an occasional deep inhale as she walked slightly behind her tour guide. "Desert is beautiful, *si?*" Elena said, as if reading Jo's mind.

"What's it like in the mountains where you live?"

"A different kind of beauty … you will see."

Jo reflected on the reality of what to expect, living with Elena and working for the cartel. Once there, she'd never be allowed to leave, unless Elena was with her surrounded by armed guards. It would mean a different sort of prison.

But her voluntary servitude did present an opportunity to potentially gain her freedom, if she could somehow find a way to escape. Working with Elena meant she'd have access to information that could bring down the wanted drug lord and his criminal enterprise. Unlike Elena, she'd spill her guts to the DEA in exchange for a new identity in a witness protection program.

But if she ran off, she'd have to travel alone through Mexico to the border more than a thousand miles away. On foot, she'd be caught within the hour. Her only chance was to steal a vehicle and hope to get enough of a head start to outrun the posse Diego Garcia would send to bring her back. It would be a race to the border. And there was no trophy for a second-place finish. The consolation prize? She'd be hung upside down from a tree, and Diego would slit her throat from ear to ear. Elena, feeling betrayed, might want the pleasure of doing it herself.

The unpleasant reality was they hadn't yet crossed into Mexico, and she was already plotting to betray Elena *someday*. Then again, a man had kidnapped and planned to rape and murder them—and that was in America. If Mexico was as dangerous a place as Elena had said more than once to her, they might not ever make it to Diego Garcia … and that *someday* might not ever come.

# CHAPTER 18

They walked directly into a rising sun. The brims of their hats and sunglasses did little to cool them. To avoid sunburn, Jo had applied a healthy amount of sunscreen to her arms, neck and face. Elena required a lesser amount to protect her honey-toned skin.

Though it was still early morning, it was summer, and the average temperature was more than a hundred degrees. Jo had caught a glimpse of the temperature on the wall-mounted thermometer at the port of entry when they passed by. It had registered 101 degrees, and that was more than an hour ago. The sign above it flashed *Heat Stroke Warning* and then *Stay Hydrated.*

The terrain was uneven and rocky for most of their five-mile trek. They were greeted by the musky smell of the riverbed and placid waters of the Rio Grande. Perspiration had soaked through their shirts and beads of sweat dripped from their faces.

Elena laid her backpack on the ground, stepped out of

her shoes and socks, and peeled off her trousers and shirt. Jo followed her lead, but slowly, and waited to see if Elena would remove her bra and panties.

They watched each other strip down to their underwear, Jo still in awe of the shapeliness of her companion's body. She was what the men Jo knew called a "knockout." If the Venezuelan belle didn't loathe men so much, she'd be a fine catch for some lucky man … as long as he didn't mind sleeping next to a woman who kept a *cuchilla* under her pillow at night and a derringer strapped to her calf during the day.

They stuffed their clothes and sunglasses in their backpacks and tied the chinstraps of their hats to their bags.

"You follow me," Elena instructed, resting her backpack on her head like a peasant girl taking a basket of clothes to the river to wash. "I feel the bottom for rocks that are sharp, so you are not cut. We go slow."

Elena's concern for Jo did not go unnoticed or unappreciated. Her faithful companion wanted to protect her. Jo had had two partners while a homicide detective, and both had been devoted to her safety, and she to theirs. A partner's first duty was to protect the other and never put that person in harm's way, even if it meant putting your life on the line. Elena was no less her partner than they had been. If necessary, she'd do the same for Elena.

Jo genuinely had feelings … perhaps affection … for Elena. In many respects, Elena was like her—independent-minded, confident, irrepressible, bold, and not afraid to express herself … not for who she was supposed to be … but for who she was.

Jo followed Elena as instructed. The water was cool enough to make the wade across the natural border between the two countries a welcome relief. The water was neither crystal clear nor terribly murky, and deep enough in which to swim.

Where they had crossed was desolate on both sides of the border. They could see several miles into Mexico clearly—not a building or road in sight, just hot sandy soil, cactus plants, clumps of desert sagebrush, and a collection of irregularly shaped rock formations. An impressive vista to enjoy, if it hadn't been so damn hot.

They were alone … and it was so very warm.

"We are safe here," Elena said. "Our undergarments, we let them dry on the rock." She removed her bra and panties and rung them out without a hint of shame. "It will not take long. We cool off in the water, *si*."

Before Jo could do likewise, her bathing beauty was midway across the narrow waterway, wading at its deepest point, and waving for her to come in.

Jo felt Elena's watchful eyes as she removed her own sodden underwear. No woman had ever looked at her the way Elena had. Only the men did. Horny guys wanting to get laid, Jo sometimes agreeing, but only on her terms.

She was unsure how she felt about a woman coming on to her. In the showers at the police academy gym, the women showered without even a glance at one another. Jo had usually been focused on the next part of her job rather than on the naked bodies of her female colleagues.

The salacious way Elena's eyes examined her body and the look of prurient curiosity on her face made Jo feel like she'd just removed pasties and a G-string after completing a striptease. She swam out to Elena and bobbed with her in the water. Elena's breasts bounced above the water line like balloons floating in the air, her nipples erect and pointed at her, beckoning.

She took a deep breath and exhaled slowly … very slowly. *Stay focused,* she screamed to herself … *stay focused.*

"Unless we find a shelter with a shower, this may be the last time *we* bathe for a while." The pronoun was pronounced seductively.

Elena reached out both hands—an invitation to physically connect. Jo instinctively returned the gesture, not sure why … maybe because she needed Elena to get her through Mexico alive, or maybe because her Latina belle was the most beguiling woman she had ever known.

Elena held her hands for what Jo felt was a very long time and didn't release her grip until she had raised one of them and gently brushed the back of Jo's hand against her cheek.

Elena smiled affectionately at her, and Jo couldn't help but smile back.

Jo was now sure of one thing—Elena wanted them to be more than *hermanas*.

# CHAPTER 19

"Which way?" Jo asked as they dressed and gathered their things.

Elena looked skyward at the sun before answering. Jo suspected it was to orientate herself for their journey.

"That way," she pointed. "We go south until we see the road to Boquillas, but we go the other way."

"How long will we be in the desert?" Jo wasn't looking forward to another long hike, this time under an unforgiving afternoon sun.

"We stay in the desert away from the road until we get to El Llano. With the uneven ground and heat, four hours, maybe more." They'd used three of their six bottles of water walking to the river. "We be careful with our water."

Jo understood the importance of staying hydrated … and rationing their water. It wasn't unusual for her to drink a half gallon of water or more during her workouts in the gym. "We drink a half bottle of water every hour," she said. Her eyes diverted to the Rio Grande. "What about the river water?"

"No. It will make you sick."

They left the relative coolness of the waterway and walked south into the stifling desert heat. An hour later they stopped for a water break. They'd each had their own bottle for the first two hours. They shared the last bottle three hours into their hike.

Out of water, they walked in silence. Talking wasted energy and dried out the mouth. Jo's mouth felt like it was stuffed with cotton balls by the time the road came into view. They were far enough away from the road that anyone passing in a vehicle who saw them wouldn't know if they were men or women.

Elena set the pace, which was consistently brisk. Jo glanced at her watch. They'd been walking for almost four hours and were covered in sweat. They had stopped to rest only as long as it took to sip their ration of water.

The sporadic buildings they saw along the road became small subdivisions of one-story buildings that were similar in size and construction. When El Llano came into view, they walked to the road and into the city of twenty thousand scattered about in two-story apartment buildings and single-story cement and adobe bungalows.

They walked the back streets to the center of town, stopping at a fountain in a park. They cupped their hands and splashed their faces.

"Do not drink," Elena cautioned. "Fountain water, it is not chlorinated. The bacteria will make you sick. We drink only bottled water."

Two women sat on a bench in the park, with their children kicking a ball back and forth in front of them. "Wait by the fountain," she told Jo, and then walked over to the women and conversed with them. One stood and pointed in two directions.

"Well?" Jo asked when Elena returned.

"The bus station, it is a twenty-minute walk from here. The church is on the other side of town. They help migrants and homeless people. We go there, but first we get pesos, water, and bus tickets."

Elena navigated their way to a building with a sign over the door that read "*Estación de Autobuses*." The bus station was a one-story cement structure with an uneven roof and peeling paint. Two empty buses lay still in a lot next to the building.

About a dozen people were seated on benches when they entered. Elena folded five hundred dollars in fifties in the palm of her hand and went to the currency exchange kiosk. She fed the machine and Jo collected the pesos and put them in her backpack.

"What's the exchange rate?" Jo asked.

"One dollar gets us almost twenty pesos."

"How much are you getting?"

"Ten thousand pesos in one hundreds and two hundreds. Bills larger than that will draw attention to us." Standing at the kiosk for too long would also draw attention to them, so five hundred dollars would have to do.

Elena pointed to the lavatory. They went in, used the washroom, split the pesos in half, and stuffed the bills in a front pocket of their trousers.

"We buy our tickets to Chihuahua City today," Elena said when they left the lavatory. She studied a chalkboard by the ticket agent's desk. The bus was scheduled to leave at nine-thirty the next morning.

Elena paid for two tickets and handed one to Jo. They put them in their pocket and left to find the church.

~

Elena led the way in the direction she'd been given. They stopped for bottled water at a grocery store. Two bottles went into their bellies right away, and two they saved for their bus trip.

Elena occasionally reversed the way they were walking when she saw men coming toward them. Gang members usually walked in pairs—others joined them when they had some mission to accomplish.

Street gangs extorted the merchants in return for protection, and rival gangs often preyed on the same businesses. And when one gang demanded more pesos, the other one did as well. When a third gang emerged in their territory, the other gangs joined forces to eliminate the competition. Elena told Jo that was how they maintained peace. Jo wasn't sure *peace* was the right word for it.

Children roamed the streets as they walked to the church— usually in groups of two or more. Elena remembered how it was when she was a street urchin. How they would gather in the parks to barter things they'd stolen. Many, like Elena, were skilled pickpockets, purse snatchers, and shoplifters. Some ended up recruited by adults to steal for them in return for money, food, cigarettes, or a place to stay—away from the gangs and police, who stole any money found on them.

A descending sun darkened their way to the church where they hoped to find shelter. Once there, they found a building across the street from *Iglesia de San Pedro*—Saint Peter's Church. A gathering of mostly women and children sat or stood on the sidewalk in a crooked line that ran the entire length of the block and around the corner. The women held the hands of the children—some of them nestled together in groups. All kept their bags of belongings close to their side. The men in line were mostly elderly and, by their tattered clothing, looked to be chronically homeless. They stood separate and alone. Still, the women kept their distance from them.

Jo translated the Spanish-written sign on the door: *Opens evenings at 6. Must leave by 8 in the morning. 24 sleeping places.*

Elena counted the people as she and Jo took their places at the back of the line. Twenty-six. But there were five or six children small enough to share a cot or bedroll. There just might be room for them.

Having to stay the night in a shelter rekindled memories of her years on the streets. After she ran away from the orphanage, but before she found the abandoned building that would become her home, Elena had stayed in shelters in the city whenever a door of an empty boxcar was not left open. There, they were provided cots with a thin, stained mattress and no pillow—a blanket the only amenity. The less fortunate ones ended up on the floor with a blanket.

As the line moved slowly forward, a young man queued up behind them. He looked fit and carried no bag of possessions. He seemed out of place among the women, children, and the elderly.

Elena recalled how some men and women would enter shelters with the intention of stealing from others while they slept. She had done it a couple of times herself—a pair of shoes and a hat she later sold.

Others joined the line behind the man. They'd probably be turned away. But would the loner behind them make it in?

They were warmly greeted by the nuns who operated the shelter. With the cots already taken, they were led to a room where bedrolls and blankets were laid out on the floor in rows and spaced about six feet apart. They took two of the three that remained. The loner gained entry and took the last one. A grab of the arm from Elena kept Jo from taking the bedroll next to him.

They unraveled their bedding and unfolded their blankets. Their backpacks hung from a shoulder when they went for their meal. Cardinal rule—*Leave no possessions unattended.* The chairs and benches in the meal room were all taken, so they found some open space against a wall and sat on the floor.

They drank soup from a cup and ate vegetable and meat stew from a wooden bowl with a plastic spoon. Famished from their arduous journey through the desert, the weary travelers devoured every morsel of meat, potato, pea, and carrot. They sopped up the liquid at the bottom of their bowls with the bread they'd been given. A second helping would have been welcomed. They watched with still hungry eyes as what was left in the pots was taken away.

When they returned to their bedrolls, Elena moved hers closer to Jo's. With their blankets rolled up for pillows, they lay on their sides facing each other, their backpacks held tight to their chest. Elena watched Jo fall right to sleep. She thought about moving close enough to Jo to hear her breathe and touch her cheek with her fingertips. But protecting her companion was her first priority.

She rolled over to keep an eye on the man lying on the bedroll ten feet away. Sleep would not come quickly, or at all. She kept the pistol in her backpack, but the scissors remained firmly in her grip.

# CHAPTER 20

Elena awoke shortly before daybreak and was surprised to see the bedroll next to her empty. She looked over at Jo, who was asleep and still clutching her backpack. The scissors were now loosely in Elena's hand, and her backpack was no longer in her grasp—it lay a few feet from her.

Could the loner have taken it while she slept and found the money and gun inside? She had been so tired fighting to stay awake that her sleep was deep when it came.

She opened her backpack in the twilight of dawn and inventoried its contents—her rolled up sweatshirt was at the top, and under it two bottles of water, another t-shirt, and a pair of underwear. She dug deeper and felt her scarf, sunglasses, and some uneaten beef jerky. And then she felt what was at the bottom—the gun she'd used to kill the stranger and the sock with Jo's money.

She breathed a sigh of relief and put the scissors in her pack and the gun in the waistband of her trousers under her shirt. Exhaustion claimed her yet again, and she dozed off. An hour later, a burst of sunlight through a window awakened her. She blinked the sleep out of her eyes and saw Jo sitting up on her bedroll, doing an inventory of the things in her backpack.

"He's gone," Jo announced, shooting a glance at the unoccupied bedroll.

Elena sat up and stretched her arms. "He was gone when I woke up an hour ago."

Jo looked at her watch. "Seven thirty." Breakfast wasn't offered, only a bottle of water on their way out. "Let's wash up and get the bottle of water they promised. Where do we hide until the bus leaves?"

"We stay in the church for an hour. Then we make our way to the bus station on side streets like yesterday. We buy some food along the way."

"And in Chihuahua City?"

"We look for an empty boxcar or flatbed and ride south to Saltillo."

"And if there aren't any?"

"We hide and wait for another train."

~

Twenty minutes later, they were seated in a pew in the middle of the church. Most of the women and children at the shelter attended the mass, and there were only a few empty seats in the small church. With their husbands dead or missing, the women had only their faith in God to guide them.

Jo had never attended a Catholic mass. She'd grown up a Methodist, but her father lost his faith and stopped going to church after her mother was killed in a car crash.

So did she.

It wasn't that she denied the possibility of a supreme

being, she just didn't accept the probability of there being one—not the brand organized religions marketed and sold to consumers. For Jo, it wasn't enough for clergymen to expect her to take their word for it. Like the many criminal cases she'd solved as a homicide detective, she needed proof.

She looked over at Elena, who had removed her hat and, like most women there, wore her scarf as a head cover. There were times during the mass that Jo's companion appeared to be silently praying—but probably not. And when communion was offered, Elena joined the others in consuming a thin circular wafer placed on her tongue by the priest.

Jo wondered if it was possible after all that had happened to Elena in her life—the abuse she'd endured as a child and the many crimes she'd committed over the years—that she believed in a God who would forgive her sins and salvage her soul?

Jo wanted to blend in with the congregation, so she followed the traditions of the church and stood, knelt, and sat whenever Elena and the others did. She also followed Elena in the communion line, scarf over her head and hands pressed together in prayer.

On the way back to their pew, Jo saw him in the back of the church—the man who'd slept in the bedroll next to Elena. He stood by the door with two other men.

If she saw them, Elena did too. It was impossible to miss three pairs of glaring eyes fixed only on them.

⁓

They remained in the pew when most of the others left the church. Several older women stayed longer to pray. "Kneel, like you are praying," Elena whispered to Jo. Jo had looked over her shoulder a couple of times when the mass ended to see what the men were doing. They were among the last to leave, and the man from the shelter stared them down one last time as he walked out.

Elena nudged Jo out of the pew. "Follow me," she said, and then walked to where the priest was busying himself extinguishing candles on the altar.

"*Padre, por favor ayudanos,*" she said to the clergyman. Jo translated Elena's words as she spoke. "Father, please help us," she began. "We, my brother's widow and me, are on our way home to Venezuela. Three men follow us, we believe with evil intentions. Will you allow us to leave through the back of the church?"

Elena reached in her pocket and pulled out a folded pile of pesos and offered the money to the priest, who didn't hesitate to take it. She'd given him the equivalent of a hundred dollars in pesos, an enormous sum, just to let them out the back door.

The priest motioned to them with a hand to follow him into a room that served as the sacristy, the place where he kept his vestments and prepared for mass. He opened a door that led to an alley. They moved quickly down the passageway to the street and walked in the direction of the bus station.

When they were a couple of blocks from the church, they slowed their pace. Jo felt the need to look over her shoulder from time to time. "Do you think they recognized you?" she asked when no one was around.

"Maybe," Elena replied. "But it could be they saw two young women at the shelter they could kidnap, dope up for a couple of days, have their way with them, and then sell to a *burdel.*"

"What do you think they will do?"

"When we not come out, they go to the priest, and he tells

them what he did. They may have to get physical with him, but he will tell them."

They were about halfway to the bus station when they approached a small grocery store.

Elena touched Jo's arm with a hand. "I buy something for us to eat later."

Jo waited outside. When Elena returned, they split up the tortillas and apples she'd bought and put them in their backpacks.

A glance at her watch led Jo to caution, "The bus leaves in twenty minutes, Elena."

"We will be there in ten minutes … no more than that."

When Elena picked up the pace, Jo wondered if she doubted her estimated time of arrival. One thing was certain. They needed to be on that bus. El Llano had suddenly become a very dangerous place to be walking the streets.

They were about to learn how dangerous.

~

They were halfway down the block when Jo heard a man yell, "*Deténgase donde estás!*" They stopped as ordered and turned to see the man from the shelter rushing toward them with a gun in his hand.

It was a quiet, narrow street with the backs of buildings on both sides. He'd probably been following them for several blocks until he found them on a street where they'd be alone. He spoke in Spanish. "Into the alley—now," he demanded, waving his gun in the direction of a passageway that dead-ended at a brick wall. "I thought you might be going to the bus station and use side streets to get there. No one stays in a shelter with that much money on them."

They not only had roughed up the priest but stole the money Elena had given him.

"How much more do you have?"

"A lot," Elena replied, showing not a semblance of fear. "You let us go, and we give it to you." She pulled out the pesos from her pocket and threw them on the ground in front of him. The bills separated when they hit the ground. He squatted to collect them, then stood and stuffed them in his pocket after giving the pile a quick look to estimate how much was there.

"And you, your money." He pointed the gun at Jo, who reached into her pocket and, as Elena had done, threw her pesos on the ground. "You have all of our money," she said in imperfect Spanish. "Now, let us go."

"*Americana*," he grunted. "We get as much for you as we get for the beautiful *señorita*," he said in broken English.

This time Jo spoke in English. "If you do, I'll tell the others you have our money, and you'll have to share it with them," she threatened, hoping to appeal to his selfish greed.

The man laughed mockingly. "You tell them, and then I beat you later. Maybe I do not stop until you are dead."

Jo realized she hadn't gone far enough in the negotiations. "What if I told you I have access to more money than you have ever seen in your … life?" She controlled the urge to say, "sick and pathetic life." "I'm an American and can give you U.S. dollars that you won't have to share with anyone."

He grinned excitedly. "How much money?"

"More than twelve thousand dollars."

"How did you get that kind of money?"

"I stole it, which is why I'm in Mexico. You give us our pesos back and let us go and the money is yours." She twisted her wrist and looked down at her watch—they had five minutes to get to the bus station. Maybe it wasn't a good idea to waste time negotiating for the pesos. Every minute mattered. But they'd need some money.

"You take me to the money, and I let you go," he promised unconvincingly.

"Both of us."

"*Si*. I would not want your friend to tell the others about our little agreement." His face contorted into a wicked scowl. "Now take me to it."

"I don't have to. The money's in my backpack. Let me show you."

He snapped the barrel of his gun up and down twice to signal his consent. Jo took off her backpack, opened it, and pulled out the sock full of money. She tossed it at his feet. He picked it up and removed the pile of money. He couldn't resist the urge to flip through the fifty-and-one-hundred-dollar bills, smiling broadly as he did.

When he realized he'd hit the jackpot, he cried out with exuberance, "*Jesucristo*!"

The name of God's son was the last thing Jo heard the man say before Elena pulled the gun from the waistband of her trousers and fired three shots into his chest.

The man backpedaled, flapping his arms like the wings of a bird, until his body slammed into the wall of the alley. The pistol dropped from his hand. He had just enough time to cover the bloody holes in his shirt with his hands, look at his executioner with a face full of confusion, and fall over dead.

"Get the money," Elena shouted, still pointing the gun at their attacker as if he might still be alive and in need of more lead to finish him off.

Jo rushed to stuff the pesos from his pocket and the sock full of money in her backpack. She looked at her watch and then turned to face Elena, an anxious look on her face. "We need to run to have any chance of catching the bus."

Elena studied the man's lifeless body one last time, smiled slightly, and put the gun to her backpack. A nod of her head to Jo was the sound of the bell.

The foot race was on.

# CHAPTER 21

The bus was leaving the parking lot when they turned the corner.

Elena was out of breath and gasping for air. She stopped, bent over, and grabbed her knees. "I … I can't breathe," she stammered.

"Catch your breath," Jo yelled over her shoulder. "I'll stop the bus."

Jo's tank of air was close to empty, but she took off after the bus, now a half block away. She ran into the street, her arms uppercutting through the air and in sync with her breathing. Her cheeks puffed with each exhale. The bus slowed at the intersection and started to turn just as she came alongside it.

She banged at the door and yelled, "*Deje de! Por favor deje de!*" The driver braked and pulled a lever on the console to open the door. Jo's heart heaved in her chest. "*Tengo … un … boleto,*" she gasped. She pulled the ticket from her pocket and waved it to him.

When Jo saw Elena jogging wearily toward her, she cried

out to the driver in Spanish, "*Y mi amiga también,*" and then in English, "And so does my friend."

Elena lumbered to the door with her ticket in one hand and her sunglasses and hat in the other. She stepped up, gave the driver the ticket, and followed Jo into the bus.

~

They took seats at the back of the half-full bus. The cat was out of the bag when Jo told the bus driver that the other woman was with her—a Latina and an American traveling together. But it was either catch the bus or stay behind in an unfriendly city.

They sat together with their backpacks on their laps. Elena discreetly held Jo's hand until her breathing normalized, hoping that in the ruckus the bus driver hadn't recognized them. It excited Elena that she would be sitting shoulder to shoulder with her friend on a long bus ride, and that they'd have to bring their heads … and faces … close together and speak to each other in whispers.

Elena took a sip from a bottle of water she got from her backpack. "You do good back there," she said in a hushed voice. Jo started to get a bottle of water for herself. "No, we share," Elena said, handing it to her and watching her sip from it. She liked sharing things with Jo, and she liked it when they touched. "The money, it distracts him," she recounted, smiling at Jo, who smiled back.

It prompted a bittersweet memory.

At the orphanage, there was another girl about Elena's age who was also being abused. Her name was Izzy. She was shy and withdrawn and cried herself to sleep whenever the men had taken her to a bedroom and raped and sodomized her.

But Elena never cried when it happened to her. Not once. Not ever. She was able to leave her inner self during the debasement and return to her humanity afterwards, only incrementally more emotionally damaged than before.

One evening, Elena went to Izzy to console her, something she had wanted to do for a long time. She sat on her bed and stroked her hair and cheek gently with her hand. Izzy stopped her sobbing and reached up with her hand, and touched Elena's cheek and lips with her fingers. Elena took Izzy's hand in hers and kissed it. Sitting there next to Jo, Elena remembered how good it felt touching someone tenderly and being touched back the same way.

When Izzy pulled her blanket to the side, Elena lay beside her and put her arms around her friend. Izzy nestled in her arms. They kissed on the cheek … and then on the lips, and they didn't stop kissing until they both fell asleep.

The next day, Izzy was sold to a sex trafficker. Elena went to Izzy's bed that night and brought Izzy's pillow back to her bed. She hugged and kissed it and cried herself to sleep.

The next day, Elena ran away from the orphanage with a change of clothes, her toothbrush, and Izzy's pillow stuffed in a laundry bag.

When her reverie ended, Elena realized that she felt the same connection to her friend Jo that she felt that night with Izzy.

~

"How many stops will the bus make?" Jo asked.

"It stops in four cities before we get to Chihuahua City," Elena replied. "Some get on, some get off. We leave the bus only to use the lavatory … but never together."

"How long will it take to get there?"

"Four and a half, five hours."

At the first stop an hour into their trip, more passengers boarded the bus than got off. The same was true an hour and a half later at the next stop, where Elena left the bus to use the lavatory. She wore her sunglasses and kept the brim of her hat down low.

Jo had her scarf covering her head and tied at the chin. With more people on the bus to notice her, she kept her sunglasses on.

The day was warm and sunny, and the bus had no air conditioning. Many of the windows were opened, allowing the air to circulate when the bus was moving. But it quickly turned sultry when the bus was parked. Beads of perspiration dotted Jo's forehead.

To avoid drawing attention to themselves, they decided to separate. But it risked having someone sit next to them who might want to engage in conversation. They took the window seats across from each other. That way, they could look out the window and avoid eye contact with the passenger next to them.

Jo left the bus to use the lavatory when they stopped the third time. She took her backpack with her, so her seat was left open. When she returned, it was taken by a woman and child, and an elderly man occupied the seat next to Elena. She looked for an open seat. Only three remained in the middle of the bus. She took the window seat by a middle-aged woman with a bag on her lap.

They had only one stop left. Jo figured that Elena wouldn't leave the bus again. Nor would she. They'd sit tight until they got to Chihuahua City, two hundred miles into the first leg of their journey to Tuxtla, another eleven hundred miles away.

Jo wondered what trials and tribulations lay ahead. They came close to being kidnapped in El Llano. If they couldn't get on a train, they'd need to find a place to sleep in Chihuahua City. Another shelter? The first time staying in one almost ended very badly for them.

It made Jo recall the events of that morning, when one of their would-be kidnappers confronted them on the street. They were two days on the run and Elena had already killed two men. She laughed to herself—two for two was a hell of a batting average. Part of Jo wanted to be horrified at the carnage Elena left in her wake. The more practical, new Jo saw both killings as necessary.

Elena had no choice. The men she'd shot dead were evil men who wanted to harm them. They deserved what they got. Both of them.

*You didn't fuck with Elena Sanchez and expect to walk away in one piece, or at all.*

Jo and Elena were much alike. The five men Jo had killed in the line of duty were evil men who had harmed others and wanted to harm her. Like Elena, she had no choice. They too deserved what they got. All five of them.

*You didn't fuck with Jo Crowder and expect her to turn the other cheek and walk away.*

From the day she was arrested and the world she'd known came crashing down on her, Jo had to force herself to focus not on what she had been, but on what she had become. She was now a dirty cop who'd stolen drugs and money. She had planned on trafficking the drugs for profit. Some of those who eventually bought the drugs might have overdosed and died because of her criminal acts. She knew that but suppressed the thought that such would occur. Self-interest … yes— and greed … intervened to dispel her concerns. Jo was as imperfect and capable of bad acts just as those she'd spent a career trying to capture, convict and put away.

In principle, Jo's propensity for wrongdoing was much like Elena's. The only difference was that Elena's life of crime had begun much earlier and Jo's was just beginning. Jo was joined at the hip with a very dangerous woman involved in a very dangerous business in a very dangerous country. To survive in Jo's upside-down world, she not only had to think like Elena but had to act like her too.

Jo closed her eyes, rested her head against the window frame, and succumbed to a dreamless nap.

# CHAPTER 22

Jo was jarred out of her catnap when the bus screeched to a stop at the last station on their way to Chihuahua City. The lady next to her got off the bus with a half dozen other passengers, who were replaced by an equal number of travelers. Jo had hoped one of the women who boarded would take the seat next to her. Instead, a young Latino man with a backpack like the one under her seat sat beside her. He held it on his lap tight to his chest.

The driver left the bus and returned to his seat with a newspaper. The rest stops were usually about ten minutes long. He spent his respite reading the lead story on the front page.

Jo was close enough to see the headlines in bold print: **_Elena Sanchez-Gomez Ha Escapado._** A photo of Elena covered the upper half of the page. Jo's photo below it, with a caption too small to read, got second billing.

Jo felt an uptick in her heart rate and the facial flush that came with a sudden rise in blood pressure. She adjusted her sunglasses and scarf as if to do so would improve her camouflage. While covering their eyes and hair may have worked as disguises for passengers who had seen their photos, the driver had eyed them without their sunglasses and hats when they boarded the bus in El Llano. How could he forget the woman banging on the door to let her and her *amiga* get on the bus? And Elena's exceptional beauty was impossible for any man to forget.

The minute he'd spent reading the cover story felt like ten. *Turn the page,* her mind screamed. *Go to the sports page. Read the obituaries.*

The driver glanced at his watch and then turned around to look at the passengers. His dark, suspicious eyes shifted side to side as they worked their way up the rows of seats. Jo slumped in her seat and tried to find cover behind the head of the passenger who sat in front of her. Elena was too far back to see the newspaper the driver had been reading. She was dead meat if for some reason she had removed her sunglasses.

Jo speculated on what the driver might do if he connected them to the photos. If he remembered their tickets were to Chihuahua City, he'd know they were still on the bus. He might get off the bus and tell the ticket agent to call the police. If he did, the police would either stop the bus on the way to Chihuahua City or arrest them when they got there.

The driver folded the newspaper and put it behind his seat. He pulled out a cellphone, made a call, and spoke into it for a very long minute. He took a last look at the passengers when the call ended, closed the door, and drove off on the last leg of their journey.

For Jo, a nagging question remained.

*Who did the bus driver call?*

~

Jo avoided eye contact with the man who sat beside her. To discourage conversation, she looked out the window for a while, then rested her head on the back of the seat and pretended to be asleep. It gave her time to reflect on what might happen when they got to Chihuahua City.

If they were greeted by the police, there would undoubtedly be many of them. A few would stand back, holding assault rifles with itchy fingers on the triggers. Others would wait at the door for each passenger to leave. Knowing who they were looking for, they'd have no trouble identifying them.

Two scenarios played out in her mind.

In the first, they'd be arrested, their hands tightly cuffed behind their backs. They'd be taken to separate vehicles and locked in a back seat with a metal grate between it and the front seat. They'd be transported in their mobile cages to an *estación de policia*, where they'd be strip searched, cavity checked, photographed, and fingerprinted.

The money and Elena's gun would be found in her backpack. More money would be found in Jo's. The money would not find its way into an evidence locker. Checking the gun, they'd see that three bullets were missing. Someone would sniff the barrel and realize it had been recently fired. When the report of the man's death in El Llano reached Chihuahua City, and the three bullets removed from his chest had been matched with Elena's gun, both of them would be charged with murder.

They'd be led to separate, small, windowless rooms still handcuffed behind the back, made to sit on a stool, and interrogated under a bright fluorescent light—maybe slapped around a little in the process. They'd be denied food and water. The grilling would go on intermittently for hours. Neither Jo nor Elena would break.

They'd be transported to a maximum-security prison, where they'd hibernate in cells with lidless, stained ceramic toilets and sinks with warm, dirty water until court proceedings resulted in their trial, conviction, and sentence of life imprisonment. Diego would hire the best criminal lawyers who could do nothing more than sit there and watch. As before, nothing would come of the bribes he was willing to pay.

Mexico would not agree to extradite them to the United States, which might not even petition for it. What would have been the point? Elena Sanchez and Jo Crowder would spend the rest of their lives rotting away in the inhospitable conditions of a Mexican prison.

*Good riddance.*

American justice, the Mexican way.

The second scenario, however, was much more likely to occur—Elena would open fire and kill as many policemen as she could before they riddled her body with bullets. Caught in the crossfire, Jo too would lie dead in a pool of blood.

Mexican justice, the Mexican way.

# CHAPTER 23

Twenty minutes after they left the last rest stop, Elena heard the siren in the distance. Less than a minute later, a police car stopped the bus and parked in front of it, flashers going.

Elena reached for her backpack under the seat, unzipped it, and felt for her revolver. She would not be taken alive—not this time, not ever again.

Two policemen got out of the vehicle and walked to the door of the bus. The driver turned off the engine and opened the door.

From where she was seated in the back, Elena could see the policemen out the side windows at the front of the bus. One of them waved for the driver to get out. They entered afterwards, one behind the other.

*"Permanecer sentada y no moverse,"* the one in front shouted.

Elena intended to *stay seated and not move*. Fidgeting in her seat was a suspicious sign of nervousness, likely to draw their attention.

She was surprised they hadn't pulled out their weapons, a

mistake that could prove fatal for one or both of them. They had to know about her history of violence and that she'd shot a cop in America. Were they that sure she didn't have a weapon? Possibly. After all, they wouldn't know she had already killed two men with the gun she held in her hand.

She had a flashback to earlier that morning when she stood over the man she'd shot and had told Jo to take back their money, but not his weapon. She thought that leaving the gun would suggest to the police the man was involved in a gang-related shootout. Now she wished Jo had taken it. If she had, she'd be holding it in her hand with her finger on the trigger. And, like Elena, she'd open fire as soon as they were close enough to gun down. An ex-cop who'd killed five men when her life was on the line wouldn't hesitate to shoot two men dead when her freedom hung in the balance.

Now it was left to Elena to do the shooting … for both of them. But when? Should she wait until they found her companion and attempted to arrest her?

Or should she do it … now?

The policeman in front inched forward, looking into the faces of the passengers. There were many young women on the bus. His progress would be understandably slow. She'd have time to see what the other cop would do.

*Good.* He was following a few steps behind, double checking the faces of the people his partner had examined. She'd have a good shot at both as soon as they found Jo. Then again, they were looking for a Latina and one in particular—the wife of El Leon. They just might pass by Jo and come closer to their executioner, making her job a lot easier.

There was a problem—three bullets were in the chest of a dead man in El Llano and she hadn't had time to reload with the ammo taken from the stranger's cabin.

Two men.

Three shots.

*Decision time.*

She'd put a single bullet into the head of the one in front. His partner would get two in the chest before he could pull out his gun.

*Decision made.*

Elena watched as the two of them moved forward until they stopped where Jo was seated. There was no way she'd let them take her—not this time. Izzy was taken from her, but never Jo. She discreetly pulled the revolver from her backpack and kept it by her side, but out of the sight of the passenger next to her, who was focused on what was unfolding in front of him.

"*Tu mochila,*" the policeman in front demanded.

He wanted the backpack. Elena saw Jo bend over slightly, as if she was about to reach for the bag under her seat. She knew that when the cop opened it and found the money, he'd know they'd found the woman who escaped with her. They'd also know that Elena was on the bus. He'd quickly unholster his weapon and keep it at the ready. So would his partner, but he'd aim it at Jo while the one in front made his way down the aisle to look for her.

Elena moved up in her seat, gripped her left hand on the back of the one in front of her, and put pressure on the balls of her feet. She readied herself to stand and shoot as soon as the policemen reached over for the backpack. He'd be occupied with what he was doing and partially blocking his partner's view of her when she stood, aimed, and fired.

Elena wasn't nervous. Her gun hand was dry, her heartbeat was regular, and her breathing was normal.

She tightened her finger on the trigger.

Just as Elena had begun to rise, the man next to Jo handed his backpack to the policeman. Elena dropped back in her seat and watched what happened next through stunned eyes. After he opened and rifled through it, he pulled out a large, clear plastic bag of white powder. He unsealed it, put two fingers in and pinched some of the powder. Elena knew all too well what heroin looked, smelled, and tasted like. The cop sniffed and then tasted it, grimacing in reaction to its bitter taste.

The man was quickly handcuffed and removed from the bus. The driver returned to his seat and didn't wait for the policemen to leave the scene. He pulled out onto the roadway and continued on to his final destination.

When the man beside her became distracted, Elena deftly returned the gun to her backpack. She rested her head against the back of the seat and thought how lucky *they* had been.

The *they* she was thinking about weren't two fugitives who had just avoided capture, they were two men who had come within a hair's breadth of making their wives widows.

# CHAPTER 24

They arrived in Chihuahua City mid-afternoon, leaving the bus separately and joining up in front of the bus station building.

"What now?" Jo asked.

"I go in," Elena replied. "I buy some more water, a newspaper, and get a map of the city. You wait up the street for me."

They were both wearing scarves to cover their hair. For Elena, the most wanted woman in Mexico, it wasn't a burka, but it would have to do.

Five minutes later, they began their hour-long journey through the city in the usual way, using side streets to avoid as many pedestrians and policemen as possible. Elena had the map to navigate their way to the depot and the warehouses where materials and goods were stored. When the train arrived, the process of unloading and loading would occur, and when it was completed, they'd have their chance to sneak into an empty boxcar or climb on a flatbed.

They passed by the warehouses and walked up the tracks to where a group of migrants had gathered at the bottom of a hill that led to several vacant, windowless buildings, the likely temporary homes of some who waited the night. The vagabond group was scattered in a depression between grassy knolls. The topography kept them out of the sight of the warehousemen, forklift drivers, and engineers.

There were nine of them—two men, five women of various ages, and two children—a girl in her early teens holding the hand of a boy about five years old. Elena and Jo passed by the men and sat by two young women, who looked to be about the same age. They later learned from them that they were sisters trying to get home to relatives in Guatemala. They had been traveling in a caravan with their mother and were rejected at the border. On their way back, the mother had a heart attack and died. What money they had was used to bury her. The others in the group had shared stories with the sisters with a common theme—without money to pay a coyote to sneak them across the border, they were turned back by border patrol and forced to go home to their countries of origin.

The travelers kept their bags close to them. No one talked. No one smiled. They just waited there for the train.

Elena nodded at Jo, then stood and resettled far enough away from everyone to not be heard talking. She pulled the newspaper from her backpack. It was a different tabloid from the one Jo had seen the bus driver reading, but with the same photos of them on the front page, this time side by side. The headline in Spanish read **El Leon's Wife Escapes from American Prison**.

Elena summarized what was written.

"The man, the one at the store, he tells the police he sees us. They find the truck in the park and know we cross the border there." She paused to let out a breath of relief. "We do good to buy the tickets and leave when we did. The police, they look for us between Boquillas and Chihuahua City and watch the bus station there."

Elena continued to read, this time without commenting. Jo sensed there was more to tell her. "What else, Elena? What else does it say?"

"They pay two hundred fifty thousand dollars to anyone who finds us and tells the police."

"We've become lottery tickets," Jo said sarcastically. "Everyone will be looking for us and trying to cash in. Are we safe riding the train?"

"The police, they know we need to travel like migrants, and the immigration agents look for migrants on the trains, arrest them, steal their money and valuables, and put them in jail until they can be deported. If we are caught with them, we will be recognized, and it will be over for us."

"So how do migrants avoid getting caught?"

"The healthy ones … like us … jump off the train when it slows down, but before it gets to where it stops. We hide until it leaves. Then we run and jump back on the train before it moves too fast."

Elena folded the paper and put it in her backpack.

They ate a tortilla and shared a bottle of water. Jo stretched out on the ground with her head on her backpack and feet crossed. Elena sat with her knees up, her arms around her legs, and stared at Jo.

"Elena, were you scared on the bus when the police got on?"

"No. I was thankful."

"Thankful?" Jo looked at Elena with startled eyes.

"*Si*. The guns, they stay in their holsters."

"But they would have pulled them out and arrested us if they recognized me."

Elena's eyes darkened with intensity. "I never let them take you from *me*." She said "never" again, this time in Spanish—"*nunca*."

Her words and passion caught Jo off guard. They were spoken with such conviction, as if she would never let anyone come between them—no one … not ever. Jo suspected she'd have opened fire if it was Jo's backpack they'd taken. And knowing how proficient Elena was with a gun, two cops would probably be dead.

Their conversation prompted Elena to find three bullets in her backpack and reload her revolver without taking it out. "I keep it loaded from now on," she said, closing her bag.

Jo gave a long, deep sigh of relief. It would have gotten ugly had they been recognized. It played out in her mind— two dead or dying cops on the floor of the bus, Elena pointing the gun at the passengers and bus driver as if it was loaded and telling them to stay in their seats. She'd have taken the cop's guns and given one to her. With Elena holding everyone at bay, Jo would have confiscated the cell phones of the bus driver and passengers and the keys to the bus.

They'd have fled in the patrol car. Jo would have driven, leaving Elena to ride shotgun. One or two passengers would have lied about not having a phone and used it to call for help. Patrol cars would be swarming the area within minutes, roadblocks would soon be in place on all main and secondary roads, and a police helicopter would be dispatched to look for them if they were on foot. They'd be found within the hour. Elena would not want to be taken alive. The shootout would be just like Butch Cassidy and the Sundance Kid's last stand, only in Mexico instead of Bolivia.

Jo sighed when the reality of their circumstances smacked her in the face. Their only chance of survival was for them to find Diego Garcia before the police found them. No one played the zero-sum game better than Elena—there were only winners and losers. For the wife of El Leon, there were no alternatives, no middle ground, and no room for compromise. For her, it was a simple matter of life *or* death.

# CHAPTER 25

Night had fallen. The shrill sound of a whistle in the distance announced the imminent arrival of hope for eleven weary travelers—hope for a journey to somewhere other than where they had been.

It rumbled down the tracks like a bull on the run—a big, black beast pulling thirty-five boxcars and tons of cargo. The headlights eerily resembled eyes—narrow and dim as the train approached and wide and bright as it closed in and chugged by. The brakes hissed like a hole full of rattlesnakes when it slowed and screeched to a halt in the darkness of night.

It was too late to load and unload boxcars.

The bull would rest there until morning.

It was safe to sleep the night in an empty boxcar when the warehouses closed and the engineers went into the city to find a place to sleep. There usually were a few doors whose rusty hinges and rollers made completely closing them no longer possible.

When the engineers left the area, the men in their group

led the way down the tracks to a partially opened boxcar. Jo and Elena stayed at the back of the pack, whose members scurried in the dark like mice spooked by a tomcat's growl.

The men climbed in first and helped the children and those who had difficulty lifting themselves in. Jo and Elena declined help and climbed in on their own.

The migrants staked out spots against the sides of the boxcar. With the door half open on a moonless night, there was only enough ambient light to see that the faceless, shadowy figures inside were humans.

The temperature had cooled by the time they boarded. Jo and Elena put on their sweatshirts and pulled up their hoods. The stagnant air inside had an underlying scent of sulfur and urine, proof that the car had carried migrants before … and would again. Whether other itinerants joined them along the way remained to be seen. Space was already at a minimum, more so when everyone stretched out to sleep.

A couple of hours later, the sounds of sleep had overtaken the whispers, coughs, and grunts. One woman sobbed intermittently for an hour, followed by another hour of sniffles.

Jo and Elena lay side by side facing each other and resting their heads on their backpacks until sleep silenced the snores and moans.

At daybreak, the men jumped from the boxcar and, as before, helped others out. It was unsafe to remain on the train when the cargo was being loaded. The engineers who drove the train checked for migrants and reported them to the police, who detained them until immigration agents arrived and took them to detention centers.

The ragtag group of strangers gathered where they'd been before. Most ate the food and drank the bottled water they'd brought, but only in small quantities.

From their time in the desert, Jo and Elena understood the need to ration.

Two young women appeared on top of the hill. One was holding a small child in her arms. They came down and sat next to Elena. One appeared only slightly older than the other, who sat with her arms around the child, a girl about four years old. The older one spoke to Elena in Spanish and wanted to know if they too were separated from their husbands.

Elena told them the story she'd made up earlier about Jo being her widowed sister-in-law.

The older one then proceeded to tell the unhappy story of their pilgrimage from Nicaragua to the border city of Nogales, Mexico. The younger woman hugged the child and wept as she did.

The women were sisters in their early twenties whose husbands had crossed the border illegally four years ago to find work, leaving their wives behind, the younger of whom had been pregnant. The men faithfully sent money back to them until the sisters had enough saved to travel and pay a coyote to help them cross the border.

They had traveled by bus and train until they were halfway through Mexico when misfortune struck—the younger sister's travel bag was stolen one night while she slept. With half their money gone, the siblings continued on, and tried to negotiate down the coyote's fee. He'd baited them into giving him most of their money under the false pretense he would take them across the border. He'd driven them into the desert, stolen their remaining money, and left them there without any water.

Lost, they wandered for two days, taking turns carrying a sick, dehydrated child on their back. On the third day, they came upon a road that led to a village, where they found food and shelter at a church. They couldn't travel for a week because of the child's poor health. And when they did leave, the child was so weak she had to be carried.

Their journey home had been long and arduous. They'd hitchhiked from city to city, staying at shelters whenever they could. Their method of travel came with unhappy consequences. One Samaritan proved to be a predator—he raped the childless sister in front of the other and her child.

When the child's health continued to decline, they had no choice but to ride the trains with other migrants. It was the fastest way for them to travel home but came with great danger to themselves and the child. They lived in constant fear.

The narrative was interrupted from time to time by the child's occasional fits of coughing and crying. When the story ended, Elena spoke to the older sister, while Jo translated in her head.

"Do you have anything in your bag to write a note on?" she asked.

"Yes," the woman replied meekly.

"Give it to me."

The woman rummaged through her bag for a pencil and a pack of letters secured by a string. She removed the last page of one of the letters, the back of which was blank. She handed the pencil and piece of paper to Elena.

Jo watched as she wrote a note in Spanish on the last page of a letter that had been written by the woman's husband. She wrote an address on it, and then the note:

*Hector Gonzales-Mendes,*

*The sisters and child travel under the protection of Diego Garcia-Hernandez. Get them safely across the border.*

*Elena Sanchez-Gomez*

Elena looked at the young woman and said, "Give me your bag." When she handed it over, Elena opened her backpack and removed the sock that lay at the bottom. She removed fifteen hundred dollars from it and pushed what remained in the sock deep into the young woman's bag.

"Show this note to no one but the person whose name is on it." She handed the note to the woman. "Return to Nogales on a bus from Chihuahua City." She removed a folded pile of pesos and the map of the city from the pockets of her trousers and handed them and the cash to her. "Use the map to find the bus station and the pesos to buy the tickets. Go to the address in the note and give the sock to Hector Gonzales-Mendes. He will know what to do. The American dollars are for you when you cross the border."

The young woman read the note and began to cry. "*Eres un angel,*" she said through her tears. Her deep sobs were not out of fear or sadness, but of hope and happiness. She moved closer to Elena, reached for her hand, held it in both of hers, and kissed it over and over again.

Jo heard the woman say again as she rose to leave, "You are an angel."

At that moment, Jo buried all the illegal, immoral, and evil things Elena Sanchez-Gomez had ever done in the deep recesses of her unconscious mind and felt a special kinship with Elena that warmed her heart.

If she'd been asked to describe her friend at that moment in time, only one word would come to mind ... *remarkable.*

# CHAPTER 26

Three hopeful itinerants were on their way to be united with loved ones. They'd surely make it—they were under the protection of Diego Garcia-Hernandez.

But what of Elena and Jo? They didn't have the protection of El Leon. With more than a thousand miles of Mexican soil still to cross, they were two convicts on the run: fair game for police and immigration agents, who would be patrolling the freight train railway stops looking for migrants.

The whistle blew a few seconds before the bull's iron head moved southward. Its pace was slow at first, but quickly gained momentum. Meanwhile, nine desperate journeymen raced to the boxcar that had been their home and would be again.

Jo and Elena put their sunglasses in their pockets and secured their hats to their backpacks, which they carried by hand. No sense losing the only disguises they had in their mad dash to the boxcar.

The men climbed in first. One stayed by the opening and helped others aboard. Jo and Elena stayed back with the teenage girl and boy, who stumbled and fell as the train sped up.

"Help the girl," Jo yelled to Elena, who grabbed the girl's hand and ran with her to the boxcar, where the man pulled them in.

Jo quickly shouldered her backpack, lifted the boy into her arms, and ran as fast as she could down the tracks. She was still a boxcar behind when the train picked up speed.

The boy cried out for his sister when Jo reached the opened door. The man waited by the door and yelled to the boy to grab hold of him. Jo used her remaining strength to lift the boy into his outstretched arms.

The rescue was like a shot of adrenaline and gave Jo a second wind. It was reminiscent of her time boxing, when, dead tired in the final round, she'd be energized after landing a solid punch and go on to slug it out until the bell sounded, win or lose.

It was the extra effort that counted.

Jo removed her backpack and swung it to Elena, who stood beside the man. She then stepped aside to allow him to reach out his hand and pull Jo aboard.

The scream of the whistle coincided with another burst of speed. Before she could grab hold of the man's hand, the bull and its herd of boxcars and flatbeds stampeded ahead.

Jo quickly fell behind.

Elena stood by the door, her face a portrait of impending doom. *Run faster, Jo … run faster*, her eyes pleaded.

Jo was running on fumes. Her shoes felt like lead boots. Her heart thumped irregularly in her chest, and her lungs deflated. Air was suddenly absent. Still, she had managed to catch up to the opening. In one last try, she extended her arm as far as she could and felt the touch of the man's fingers on the palm of her hand … just as she stumbled and fell to the ground.

She lay face down in the rubble, out of breath. Her stomach heaved. She looked up and watched Elena get smaller and smaller as the train roared ahead. When the last boxcar rounded a curve a quarter of a mile ahead and was out of sight, she stood and brushed the dirt and gravel from her denim trousers with the back of a scraped palm.

Crestfallen, her mind asked, *What now?*

She was on her own in a foreign country with only some pesos and a pair of sunglasses in her pockets. Her backpack was gone. She had no cash for bribes. Her only option was to return and wait for another train. By then, Elena would be long gone and well into her journey home. She was brave, resolute … and armed. Jo had no doubt she'd succeed in her quest to be reunited with her husband. The thought made her smile, but only briefly.

Her moment of solace vanished when a hot flash of loneliness seared her inner self. She had been with Elena for only a short while, but it felt like she'd known her for her entire life. She marveled at her resourcefulness, admired her fearlessness, commended her courage, and valued her loyalty. She had never known such an enigmatic woman. Elena had the dispassion to shoot and kill someone one day and the compassion to help desperate people she didn't know the next.

Jo's *amiga* was a paradox.

She looked down the tracks one last time, as if she might see Elena walking toward her, arms outstretched and welcoming, a sweet smile on her pretty face. She sighed, turned around, and started back. As she walked heavy-footed down the lonely rails, her reflections of the time she'd spent with Elena and the things they'd done together weighed heavily on her mind …

and in her heart. And for the first time, Jo realized that when it came to the person who had become her one true friend in her crazy, new world … she had grown accustomed to her face.

~

Aghast, Elena stood by the opened door when the man lost his grip on Jo's hand, and she'd fallen to the ground. Her mind screamed at Jo, *Get up! Get up and run to me. I need you in my life … mi amiga, mi querida, querida amiga.*

Her eyes were like lasers fixed on where her dear, dear friend lay, who was on the ground looking back at her with eyes that cried out for Elena not to leave her. The scene quickly faded away, like the last seconds of a setting golden sun that inevitably descended into a black hole of darkness. As the boxcar approached the curve, the thought that she might never see Jo again made Elena's heart sink.

Like Izzy, Jo had been taken from her in a cruel twist of fate. If only she had run away with Izzy that night, they would have been together. If only the boy hadn't fallen, Jo would have been safely with her on the train. If only her parents had paid the extortion money, they'd have lived to raise their daughter, and she'd have grown up normal with the capacity to love and be loved. She had so many "if only's" in her life it brought on a tidal wave of sadness that overwhelmed her. Her parents, Izzy, and Jo had broken her heart into so many pieces that she feared it could never be patched up enough to ever give it to someone again.

They had been through so much together and had so much to look forward to. The finality of losing Jo and her last chance at happiness was like a stake had been driven into her heart. The weight of the disappointment collapsed Elena to her knees. Yet, as she knelt there like a humble penitent praying for a last chance at redemption, the sweet remembrances raced through her mind in tandem with the increasing speed of the train. The way she had felt that day in the exercise yard when she held Jo's hand for the first time—it was as if she had finally found that someone she'd been looking for since she'd lost Izzy—the someone who could make her feel good about herself and complete her as a person.

Why hadn't she touched Jo more? She'd yearned to do so ever since they frolicked naked in the Rio Grande. She wanted so badly to hold her in her arms and kiss her like she'd hugged and kissed Izzy that night in the orphanage.

She forced herself not to blink as the boxcar rounded the curve—her one last moment to see the person she had come to love with all her heart. She rose and stood unsteadily on her feet, shaking under a blanket of despair and desperation. She stepped closer to the opening. The rush of passing air blew Elena's hair like a flag on a windy day and dried the tears that ran down her cheeks. She held Jo's backpack tight to her breasts, just as she had held Izzy's pillow in her arms so many years ago.

"Come away from the door," she heard a woman say. "You might fall out."

Elena looked down and watched the railbed dirt and gravel race by. It was hypnotizing and made her unable to think clearly about what she should do.

But she knew she had to do something ... for *someone* dear to her heart.

The train's whistle whined loudly as it approached a crossing. It cleared the mist that had clouded her mind like a London fog. And as if a light switch had turned on, she saw clearly what she needed to do.

She closed her eyes and saw only the face of that *someone* when she stood by the door … and jumped from the train.

# CHAPTER 27

Migrants had not yet gathered when Jo returned to where she and Elena had waited with the others. She was alone. Her plan was to wait for a train until late afternoon. If one stopped and had an open boxcar she could ride the next day, she'd head back into the city and buy another backpack and some food and water with the pesos in her pocket. She'd return and spend the night in the boxcar, leave it at daybreak, and return to jump back in when the train departed.

She knew the routine on to how to survive. Elena had taught her well. Still, she regretted not having her backpack. She could have used the money to bribe policemen and immigration agents if she was caught.

But she regretted more not having Elena by her side.

She lay back on the ground, closed her eyes, and for ten minutes tried not to think about her predicament. But when she opened them, things had gone from bad to worse. Two men had come around one of the warehouses and stopped to smoke cigarettes. They passed a bottle back and forth that she suspected was liquor.

Jo had a bad feeling about what was unfolding.

She decided to walk back into the city before the men saw her sitting there alone. She would stay the night in a shelter and get a fresh start tomorrow. By then, migrants will have gathered there. There was strength in numbers. It would reduce the chances of her being the one singled out for abduction, or the one chased and arrested by the authorities. Then again, Elena had cautioned her about women traveling alone in Mexico—they were prime meat and every predator's prey.

Elena was right … as usual.

The men noticed her and walked toward her. She stood, put on her sunglasses, and hurriedly walked away.

One man, unsteady on his feet, staggered in the direction she was going to a point where he blocked her path. The other quickly approached from behind, passed by her, and joined his friend. With both men in front of her, she stepped back to gain some distance from them.

One asked her if she was alone. She lied and said her brothers were in the city and supposed to meet her there. They laughed and told her they didn't believe her. They offered her the bottle to drink from. She shook her head no.

She quickly concluded from the smell of liquor and their slurred speech and unsteady gait that they were drunk. Fighting someone intoxicated had its advantages. A drunk had impaired cognitive abilities and slower reaction times. But she had to contend with two of them, and drunks were wildly unpredictable.

She calculated the odds of subduing her abductors—she had no better than a fifty-fifty chance, and probably less. She wished she'd taken the pistol from the man Elena had shot. But she never thought she'd need it. Elena had always been with her and had proven her worth in using a gun.

Unless both men jumped her at once, she'd contend with the one holding the bottle first. The bottle was a weapon that could be used against her. She stepped back again when the two came closer to her. When the last drop was drained, the one who drank it dropped the bottle on the ground.

*He no longer could use it as a weapon.*

It wouldn't matter.

The bottle dropper pulled out a switchblade knife and released the blade. Jo understood enough of his Spanish to know that he wanted her to come with them up the hill to a shabby-looking, abandoned building surrounded by weeds and littered with trash.

Jo was left without options.

She turned, started up the hill, and prepared herself for the worst.

~

Jo recognized her voice before she turned and saw Elena walking toward them. Their backpacks lay on the ground behind her as she hobbled up the hill. She had shouted to the men to leave the woman alone and go, her voice cold and shrill.

It didn't bode well … for the *Méxicanos.*

The men hesitated at first, then laughed mockingly. One said they'd each have a *muchacha* and wouldn't have to share one.

Elena stopped a few feet from Jo, pulled out her revolver, and pointed it at the one who last spoke. "The only thing you get today are bullets in the chest unless you leave now," she threatened gruffly in her native tongue.

The smiles left their faces. One mustered the bravado to suggest she didn't know how to use a pistol and wouldn't shoot them.

Elena had no problem showing him how wrong he was.

She pointed the gun at the bottle that lay on the ground between them, a good twenty feet away from her, and fired a shot that shattered it. Startled, they both jumped back. The one with the knife turned and ran for his life. The other followed but stumbled and fell.

Elena went to stand over him and pointed the gun at his face. He groveled in the dirt, a raised arm his only protection, and pleaded with her not to shoot him.

Jo had seen this scene before—a subdued combatant who'd unsuccessfully challenged Elena Sanchez-Gomez, and then thought she'd show him mercy. The last two learned the hard way that the wife of El Leon showed no mercy.

Not ever.

Jo braced for the inevitable.

Surprisingly, she heard Elena say, "*Vamos.*"

The coward did as he was told—he rose shakily to his feet and staggered away.

Elena had saved her again, but this time did not exact *venganza* for the trespass. Nothing would ever surprise her about this extraordinary woman. She'd been her one true ally, who had planned from the start of their relationship to always be her protector.

Elena returned the gun to the pocket of her sweatshirt and turned to face Jo for the first time since she'd fallen to the ground and had faded out of sight. Their eyes locked.

"You came back for me," Jo said, her voice thick with gratitude.

"You knew I would," Elena said, her words spoken with

sincere tenderness.

This time it was Jo whose outstretched arms beckoned for Elena's embrace. Soon they were gently caressing one another. She felt the warmth of Elena's breath and the softness of her cheek on her face.

She sensed that Elena had wanted to kiss her for quite some time. She had longed for someone's affection—someone she could love and who could love her.

How could she say no?

"I could never leave you," Elena whispered in Jo's ear.

Jo felt the moisture of Elena's kiss on her cheek … and then on her lips.

# CHAPTER 28

Jo retrieved the backpacks. "We leave now," Elena said, as she limped in the direction of the city. "Not safe here, not today. The men, they come back when they sober up, this time with a gun."

Jo saw her companion struggle to walk. "Wait, Elena, hold on to me." Elena held Jo's arm close and gripped it with her hand. "You know, you could have been killed jumping off the train."

"My ankle, it twist when I hit the ground. It will be better tomorrow. We sleep in a shelter tonight and come back tomorrow."

Jo knew that Elena was downplaying her injuries. The tears in her clothing and abrasions on the palms of her hands suggested she had brush burns and lacerations elsewhere on her body, and her shallow breathing indicated she'd probably bruised a rib or two.

With some difficulty, they made their way back into the city to a church with no shelter. A priest directed them to one close by that did.

They spent the afternoon moving between the parks and plazas in the city and sat among the women and children whenever they could. When no one was looking, Jo put half of the cash she had in another sock and gave it to Elena.

When the shelter opened, they were given a supper of soup, meat, and bread. Afterwards, they settled into their beds. There were four beds in the room they were assigned. The other two were shared by a mother and her children, who spoke only in Spanish.

It was safe for them to speak in English. Jo went to sit at the end of Elena's bed. "Let me see your ankle," she said, unlacing her shoe and removing it and her sock. Elena winced as she did. "There's some swelling. I'll see if the kitchen has ice."

Jo left and returned with a plastic bag full of ice cubes. She raised Elena's leg and rested her foot on her lap. "This should help with the swelling and some of the pain."

"*Gracias*," Elena said, smiling sweetly at Jo. "You are very gentle when you touch me. If you are ever hurt or sick, I take good care of you."

The sincerity of Elena's pledge was apparent from the warmth of her smile.

When the ice had melted and the water warmed, she emptied the bag in a sink and returned to Elena's bed with a wet cloth. She raised the denim pant leg with the slit at the knee and dabbed away the dirt and dried blood from a laceration.

She wrapped Elena's ankle with her scarf to compress the swelling. "It's not a compression bandage, but it will have to do." She put her backpack on the bed under Elena's foot. "Keep it elevated until we leave tomorrow."

"You make a very good doctor or nurse."

Jo shook her head. "In another life, Elena, in another life."

The suggestion of a different career path resurrected memories of her time as a homicide detective tending to victims at crime scenes—pressing on gunshot and stab wounds to slow the bleeding, administering CPR to pulseless people to restore their vitals, and holding women and children in her arms who'd been raped and beaten to keep them from going catatonic. The lucky ones left the scene in an ambulance, with a paramedic by their side. The unlucky ones were taken away in a body bag to the office of the parish coroner.

Elena's ankle injury concerned Jo. She could tell from Elena's facial expressions and guarded movements when she walked that she was in a lot of pain. How could she be expected to run and jump on a moving train tomorrow? "Should I see if they'll let us stay here another night?" she asked. "It will give you time to heal."

"No. To stay in the city is too dangerous. We are lucky today. The Sinaloa and Juarez cartels are in Chihuahua City. We could have been taken by their men, who look for women on the streets."

When she finished wrapping Elena's ankle, Jo went to lie in her bed. Compared to the bedroll, the mattress was soft and comfortable. They rolled up their blankets and used them as pillows, and slept in their clothes.

Jo lay there, reflecting on what misadventures lay ahead. When they awoke, they'd be embarking on the fourth day of an odyssey that had been fraught with danger, and they still had most of Mexico to cross before they reached the part of Chiapas where Diego Garcia could rescue them.

Elena was right.

Getting on a train tomorrow was their only option.

~

Elena's ankle was a lot better when they left the shelter the next morning. The swelling had gone down when Jo unwrapped the scarf, and Elena's grimaces of pain were less frequent when she walked.

When they returned, a train was already waiting, with warehousemen loading and unloading cargo. Four men loitered in the area where they had waited the day before. Three huddled in a group. One elbowed the arm of another to get his attention. The three men turned to face Elena and Jo when they walked by.

Elena knew when a man's stare meant more than harmless admiration. She'd seen the look of lust on the faces of the men who'd raped and sodomized her. She'd seen it in the eyes of Diego and his faithful lieutenants. But Carlos and Raul stayed away from her out of fear of what Diego might do to them … and what Elena *would* do to them.

A fourth man stood alone, smoking a cigarette. A bandana hung loose around his neck, and he wore a faded olive drab shirt of the Mexican military and a soldier's beret. His beard was scraggly and uneven. He dropped his half-smoked cigarette to the ground and crushed it with the toe of his boot.

He glared at Elena when she approached.

The man took off his kerchief and used it to wipe the sweat from his face and neck. Elena hurried her pace, but his dark, inquisitive eyes remained fixed on her.

And then she saw it—the tattoo on his neck.

Elena found a place to sit as far away from the men as the space permitted and where she and Jo could talk privately.

Elena spoke first. "We do not ride in the same boxcar with them. Many women and girls are raped who travel without men to protect them."

"The one who stood by himself looked surprised when he

saw you pass by," Jo said. "I think he recognized you."

"It is possible. He wears the mark of the Juarez Cartel. He will know of Diego and me. This man, he must be on the run from his cartel. Like us, his best chance is to head south, riding the trains to Chiapas."

"If he knows who you are, he might use the knowledge to bargain with the cartel. Should we wait for another train?"

"No. We wait until the men are on the train, and we find another boxcar and climb in. It will take us to Saltillo, four hundred miles from here."

"And then what?"

"We jump off and hide until the next morning, and then we get back on."

"How far will the train take us?"

"To Tuxtla, another four hundred miles away. Then we go to San Cristóbal."

"Why there?"

"We go to a church and convent in the city. Diego and I marry in the church when I was sixteen years old and with his child inside me. He gives money to the priest and nuns and builds them a school. Diego knows I go there because I am safe with them."

"How do we get to San Cristóbal?"

"We walk."

"How far?"

"Forty miles."

Elena knew the truth about their dilemma once the train ride was over. Tuxtla would be swarming with police waiting to arrest them, rival cartels wanting to kidnap them, and gangs hoping to capture them for the reward money.

They would all be there—every one of them looking for the pot of gold at the end of the rainbow.

The train jarred forward when the whistle sounded. The men ran to the first empty boxcar and climbed in. Elena and Jo stayed back, jogging alongside the train until the next open boxcar approached. They ran parallel to it, threw their backpacks inside, and just before they climbed in, Jo saw the loner standing by the door of his boxcar, watching them.

Empty bottles, broken glass, and trash littered the boxcar, proof that it had been a mode of transport for other migrants. They sat with their backs against the side of the car opposite the opening and watched the desert landscape whiz by.

Jo suspected that Elena's dash to the train had aggravated her ankle sprain, and when Elena unlaced her shoe and started to take it off, the painful winces returned.

"Let me do that," Jo offered. When she removed the shoe, the puffiness had returned. "Keep the shoe off for a while."

Jo compressed the swollen ankle with her scarf like before, rested Elena's foot on her backpack, and went to sit beside her traveling companion. "How long before we get to the next stop?" she asked.

"Ten, maybe eleven hours," Elena replied. "It will be dark when we get there. That is good because the men will not see us get off the train and where we hide."

"The loner watched us climb into the boxcar."

"I see him too. We do not sleep here tonight. Too dangerous. The men, they know where to find us."

"So where do we sleep?"

"In the desert. If they come for us and not see us here, they think we no longer ride the train."

They sat in silence for hours at a time with intermittent chatter in between. Elena shared stories about the elaborate galas Diego arranged, the foreign dignitaries they entertained, and the celebrities they knew. Jo talked about interesting cases she'd solved. It didn't surprise her that Elena wanted to know about the men she'd killed.

There came a time when Elena asked, "Did you like being a cop, Jo?"

Jo hung her head. "For a while I did … but over time it broke me, seeing guilty men walk because liberal judges threw out evidence and confessions on technicalities. It was like the truth didn't matter. High-priced, slick-tongued lawyers got their rich clients off or sweetheart deals while the ones with the public defenders ended up with lengthy sentences in the big house. Where was the justice in that?" She shook her head in disgust. "And I got tired of going before the review board when I shot someone defending myself or roughed up some punk resisting arrest. I had a bad case of burnout, which is why it was so easy for me to cross the line."

"Why not walk away … do something else?"

"I was planning on quitting when I had enough money stashed away and go private. There are a lot of people willing to pay for some personal justice, particularly when they can't get it from the courts."

Elena's chuckle was barely audible. "We do the same thing—we are … how you say … the judge and jury."

Jo stretched out and rested her head on her backpack.

Elena did the same and asked, "What family do you have in America?"

Night had fallen and it had become chilly inside the boxcar. Jo zipped up her sweatshirt to the top. "My mother was killed in a car crash when I was thirteen. My father died ten years later from cancer. He lived just long enough to pin the badge on my uniform shirt when I graduated from the police academy. I have three younger brothers—all involved in law enforcement. You? Family somewhere in Mexico?"

Elena's face was visible in the glow of a hunter's moon that lay low in the horizon. She moved closer to Jo until their shoulders touched and sighed when she said, "My parents, they die when I was young."

Jo had read about Elena's troubled childhood, but curiosity made her ask, "How did you get along after they died?"

"I was eight years old with no place to go. The authorities put me in an orphanage. I run away when I was twelve. Two years later, Diego find me on the streets and he take me to live with him."

Jo felt the warmth of Elena's breath on her cheek when Elena turned her head and asked, "Did you have many friends in America?"

"Most of my friends were cops."

"What about women … women friends?" The timidity in her tone of voice couldn't fully disguise her excitement.

Jo muffled a laugh. "I grew up a tomboy and hung around with boys more than girls. When I was a cop, there weren't many women in the department, and only a few were homicide detectives. So, I buddied up with the men. What about you, Elena? Do you have many friends?" Considering her propensity for violence and her career path, Jo suspected not. Most men and women probably feared Elena as much as her husband.

"I had a friend once," Elena replied, a doleful expression on her face. "But she was taken from me. I was sad for a very long time." Jo turned her head in time to see Elena's face brighten into a smile and hear her whisper, "And then I met you."

# CHAPTER 29

The train slowed as it approached and passed by Saltillo. The lights of the city glittered like a thousand stars on a moonless night.

They sat side by side at the opening of the boxcar's door, their legs dangling over the edge with their backpacks on their laps. Perspiration had kept their skin moist since they frolicked naked in the river days ago. Yet, when the coolness of the evening dried their skin, their bodies gave off a surprisingly sweet scent.

When the whistle announced its impending arrival, the train slowed enough for them to toss their backpacks to the ground and safely jump off. They scurried into the desert, and under the cover of darkness, walked a quarter of a mile to find shelter in a cave-like hollow of a rock formation. They ate a tortilla, some nuts, and drank a bottle of water. The desert heat of the afternoon had turned to chill by the time of their arrival in the late evening.

With hoods up, they sat shivering in their sweatshirts. Jo

rubbed her arms to increase circulation and warm her body. Elena hugged her bent legs and rocked back and forth. They stared into the darkness until they were tired enough to stretch out and try to sleep. Jo lay beside Elena with her back to her. She heard Elena move closer to her.

"Are … are you … c-cold, Jo?" Elena asked, her body trembling.

"I didn't realize it got this freaking cold at night in the desert," Jo complained.

Elena spoke softly. "You will be warmer if I come closer and put my arms around you."

Jo sensed that Elena wanted to seize the opportunity to hold her and experience the intimate physical contact she'd been deprived of for so long. A lot of mental calculus went into her next words: safety once they reached Diego, chief among her racing thoughts. She also wondered just how far this might end up going.

"Yes," she whispered. "We'll both be warmer that way."

Elena wriggled nearer until her body followed the contour of Jo's figure. She wrapped one arm around Jo's waist, the other under her arm until her hand rested on Jo's breasts and nestled her face in the nape of her neck.

As Elena had promised, Jo's body warmed from her embrace. She lay fascinated, feeling Elena's breathing slow with the onset of her sleep, and they lay tethered until sleep claimed her too.

~

Dawn broke with a bright sun and the warmth that desert mornings bring. They stretched out and decided to ration their remaining food and water, sharing a tortilla and another bottle of water.

They walked to the train, keeping a careful lookout for the men. The offloading was underway and completed within a couple of hours. They hid behind a cluster of large rocks. Jo occasionally peeked around them to see what the men were doing while they waited for the train to leave.

The three men sat together like before, while the other stood nearby. Jo noticed the loner glance behind him from time to time, as if waiting for them to return to the train. When the whistle signaled the train's departure, the three men stood and raced to the train. But the other stayed behind for one last look around. Elena and Jo had just moved into the open and were in plain view when he did.

When the man turned and ran to catch up with the others, Jo said, "Keep your pack on your back and stay to my left. I'll climb in first and then pull you in. Your backpack will give me something to grab hold of."

Jo didn't want the train to get too much of a head start. They ran as fast as Elena's sprained ankle allowed. The men were already in their boxcar when they got to the train, and the loner stood by the door and watched them like before. By then, the boxcar they had occupied earlier had passed by.

But they had seen another boxcar at the end of the train with its door partially opened. It would be their last chance to ride the train. Not getting on meant spending another day and night in the desert or in the city and risk being recognized and arrested.

They slowed to a fast walk to allow the boxcar to get close enough for them to run with it and climb in. But as each second passed, the train gained speed. When it came into view, Jo shouted, "Stay close to me!" She began to run, carrying her pack in her left hand and looking over her right shoulder. When she was side by side with the opening, she tossed her pack in, stretched out her arms, gripped the floor of the car with her fingers, and pulled herself in.

She turned to face Elena, who was running behind her. "Run faster," she yelled, seeing that Elena was gulping in air and falling behind. Jo had a vision of her stumbling and falling to the ground, an eerie repeat of Jo's misfortune the day before. She knelt with one hand gripping the door and the other extended in Elena's direction. "Grab my hand, Elena, and hold it tight," she implored.

Jo saw Elena take a deep breath, quickly exhale, and muster the strength for one last burst of speed. When she was close enough, Jo gripped Elena's outstretched hand and pulled her close enough for Elena to lean into the opening. She then released her hold on the door and used that hand to grab the strap of Elena's backpack and pull her in.

A déjà vu moment for Jo—the time Elena grabbed her by the seat of her pants and pulled her into the delivery truck during their escape from prison. They lay panting on the boxcar's grimy floor until Elena began laughing. Soon enough Jo joined in, the two physically and mentally exhausted. But alive. Lucky to be alive.

Was it destiny, or dumb luck, that they continued to save each other?

But luck, even dumb luck, can change.

~

They settled in for another day's journey, this time to Tuxtla, where they'd part ways with the bull that will have carried them more than eleven hundred miles through Mexico.

But it was the last part of their trek that worried Elena

the most. They had no means of traveling to San Cristóbal, forty miles away. Once they were in Tuxtla, the police, cartels, and gangs would be looking for them on the roads and in the streets. The dragnet would be so dense, it would be impossible for them to penetrate it. Someone would catch them, and all their hard work would have been for naught. They'd be captured, kidnapped, or killed.

"It is very dangerous for us in Tuxtla," Elena said, an uncharacteristically worried look on her usually confident face. "They know we go there. We have no choice but to find a church and pay the priest to hide us until we find a way to leave the city. The priest is our only chance. For enough money, he find us a vehicle and driver to take us to San Cristóbal."

"And if the priest doesn't help us?" Jo asked soberly.

Elena didn't have a good answer to Jo's question. The priest or driver could just as easily go to the police and turn them in. There would be a quarter of a million dollars waiting for him if he did.

For two weary travelers on the run, the next ten hours on the train to Tuxtla would feel like an eternity, and just what they'd find when they got there would, for the time being, remain a mystery.

# CHAPTER 30

They arrived in Tuxtla in the inky blackness of night.

Jumping from a moving train chanced suffering a serious injury, or worse. But police and immigration agents waited for them at the end of the line. Jo looked out and saw the headlights of their vehicles at the depot a half mile ahead. They had no choice—jump then or risk being captured.

"Elena, we need to jump now," she said urgently. "I know you can't see the ground in the dark. I want you to crouch down close to the edge next to me, hold your backpack tight against your chest, keep your knees bent after you jump, and roll over on your shoulder when you hit the ground. We jump together."

"*Si*, we jump together. I do it right this time," Elena vowed.

Jo wasn't so sure Elena would make good on her promise. Her friend almost ended up lame after her first try.

"Now," Jo yelled as she sprang forward into the darkness, Elena by her side. Jo hit the ground hard and rolled over twice before her body came to rest on her stomach in the dirt and gravel of the rail bed. She looked up and saw a shadowy figure lying face down and motionless about twenty feet from her. "Elena, are you all right?" she shouted, her voice quivering with uncertainty.

Had she just caused her only friend in life to be seriously injured, or worse? Jumping from a moving vehicle was risky. Professional stuntmen had suffered head and spinal injuries that crippled them. A few had died. It depended on how hard you landed and what you landed on. Jo remembered that when a suicide victim died jumping off the roof of a building, someone at the scene almost always cynically joked, "It wasn't the fall that killed him."

Suddenly the gallows humor wasn't so funny, not when the jumper was someone who was connected to her in so many ways that were deeply personal.

Jo sprang to her feet and hurried to Elena. She dropped to her knees, turned Elena over, sat back on her heels and cradled her limp, lifeless body in her arms. She brushed her hand gently against Elena's cheeks and wiped away tiny pieces of gravel loosely embedded in her skin. She placed two fingers on her carotid artery and felt for a pulse. If there was one, it was too faint for her to detect.

She tightened her hold on Elena and drew her closer until they were face to face. She placed her cheek against Elena's mouth and nose, hoping to feel her breath. She thought she felt something … but maybe not. Could she have hit her chest on the ground hard enough to cause a traumatic cardiac arrest? If so, the chances of reviving her with CPR were in the single digits.

Regardless of the cause, Elena needed oxygen … and quickly. Jo didn't delay any further—she'd be Elena's ventilator until she could breathe on her own. She laid her on her back, opened her mouth, pressed her lips to Elena's lips, and breathed into her all the air that her lungs could produce … and she didn't stop breathing until she felt Elena's hand on the nape of her neck and the sweetness of her breath in her mouth.

She visualized Elena's exceptionally captivating eyes staring at her when she asked, "Did I do good, Jo?"

Jo breathed a sigh of relief. "Yes, Elena, you did good, you did very good."

As soon as Elena's breathing stabilized, they spent the next hour walking into the city and roaming the streets until they found a church in which to hide. They planned to sleep in the pews.

They found a small, unlocked church in a residential area of the city. Before she entered it, Elena caught a glimpse of a man standing at the corner of the street they had been walking on. He turned around and walked away when she looked in his direction. She couldn't see him clearly enough to describe him.

Her sixth sense told her that he had followed them to the church.

As she lay in a pew with the revolver in a pocket of her sweatshirt, Elena conjured up the memory of Jo's lips pressed firmly against her lips when she awoke after jumping from the train. Jo had explained the reason to her, but she preferred to recall it as an intimate moment between them … and the memory happily lingered until she drifted off to sleep.

She awoke the next morning to a man standing in the aisle pointing a gun at her.

This time the bandana covered his tattoo.

"Who are you, and what do you want?" Elena demanded to know. The harshness in the tone of her voice awakened Jo.

"You are the wife of El Leon," he exclaimed in English, his accent proof that he was a Latino.

"And you are on the run from the Juarez Cartel, *si*?"

"*Si, señora*. But I leave the cartel for a good reason. I have business with your husband, Diego Garcia."

"What business can you possibly have with him?"

"We know about the *oro blanco* … and will soon know how to produce it in our labs."

Diego Garcia had guarded the process of making his designer drug as if it were the code for a nuclear missile launch. Only Diego, Elena, Carlos, and Raul knew what was in *oro blanco* and how it was produced. But Diego worried that one of the chemists might secretly analyze the composition of the pills in the lab and sell the information to a rival cartel. It made every chemist and technician at every lab that produced the pills a potential traitor.

"And how do you know so much?" Elena asked.

"I heard your man discuss it with us. I know that we will be paying him a lot of American dollars for it."

"This man, what is his name?"

"His name I do not know—but I will know him when I am with him again. I know his voice."

Elena nodded. "What you know is valuable to my husband … and to an *hombre* like you."

"*Si*, this is why I help you get back to your husband. When they know I am gone, they will look for me and kill me if they find me. I seek the protection of El Leon."

"To prove the sincerity of your pledge, put your pistol away."

The man smiled and put the pistol in a pocket of his

jacket. "*Señora*, my name is Miguel Galindez," he said, and with a slight nod, added, "and I am in your service."

Elena kept her finger on the trigger of the gun in her pocket that had been pointed at Galindez's chest the entire time he spoke. She looked at him with suspicious eyes. "You were waiting for us, *si?*"

"*Si.*"

"How did you know we would be there?"

If his answer wasn't convincing, he could expect a chest full of lead. But his answer made sense to Elena. "The newspapers and news stations, they report that you cross the border in Boquillas," he explained. "You had no choice but to travel with migrants on the trains. How else could you travel as far as you need to go and not be recognized? The migrants, they do not know or care who you are. So, I wait where I know you must pass."

Elena took her finger off the trigger. She might need to shoot him later, but for now, he might be useful to them. If they could trust him—and perhaps even if they couldn't—just being with him would suffice. The authorities were looking for two women traveling alone, not a trio of itinerants traveling together.

"The authorities, they wait for you at the depot," he continued. "I knew you would jump off the train early, so I jump off early too and follow you here."

Galindez's appearance was the stroke of luck they needed—he'd be the bull they'd ride to get them to San Cristóbal. Elena pointed a finger instead of the gun at Galindez. "Can you find a way to get us to San Cristóbal?"

"*Si.* But it is too dangerous for you to be here," he warned. "I take you to the home of my brother. We go now before the priest finds you here. This priest, he is loyal to the Mendoza

Cartel and cannot be trusted."

Trust was in short supply. At that moment Elena trusted no one but Jo.

Elena and Jo got up, put on their backpacks, sunglasses, and hats, and followed Galindez out of the church. They took side streets to a three-story apartment building in another residential section of the city. The third-floor apartment was unoccupied when they entered. "My brother works at the textile plant," he said when he closed and locked the door. "I don't want us here when he returns tonight."

"How will you get us to San Cristóbal?" Elena demanded.

He smiled. "Do not worry. I leave you now and find different clothes for you to wear." He turned to Jo. "You, *Americana* woman, the newspapers say you stole money. Do you have any of it with you? We need a vehicle."

Jo flinched. Elena sensed it was because Jo was unsure if she should tell him about the money in her backpack.

Elena knew it was dangerous to trust a soldier from another cartel. But they had no other options. Besides, there was more money in it for him if he could identify the individual who intended to betray her husband.

Elena answered for Jo. "*Si*, we have more than twelve thousand dollars in our backpacks. We give it to you, and you take us to San Cristóbal. But we keep our pesos."

Elena's nod to Jo was enough to get her to retrieve the sock full of money in her bag. They handed their money to Galindez, who flipped through the piles, as if to be sure it was as substantial a sum as promised.

He put the money in a pocket of his jacket. "You can shower while I am away. There are towels in the bathroom." He opened the door and turned to face them. "What are your shoe sizes?"

They looked at each other and chuckled after they answered his question in unison with the same shoe size.

Galindez opened the door, turned, and cautioned, "Lock the door, and do not leave the apartment."

Jo locked the door when he left and turned to ask, "Can we trust him?"

"No," Elena replied bluntly. "I would never trust a *sicario* of another cartel. This man, he could have been sent to kill my husband, or he might want to find out where he is to collect the reward. Diego, he will not trust this man. If he doesn't believe his story, he will not be with us long."

"So why didn't you shoot him when you had the chance?"

"We need him to get us out of here. He knows the city and how to get the things we need. And if what he tells me is true, Diego will need to deal with him later."

They settled in and could do nothing other than shower, put on some clean clothes, wait for him to return … and hope they hadn't been fleeced.

# CHAPTER 31

Three hours later, there was a clammer at the door and the rattle of a key in the lock. When the door creaked open, Galindez stood in the doorway holding two large bags and one smaller one in his hands.

Jo almost didn't recognize him.

He smiled broadly to reveal for the first time a full set of teeth whiter and straighter than any man's she'd seen since crossing the border. The scraggly beard was gone. He was clean shaven except for a thin, well-trimmed mustache. Not wearing his beret allowed her to see a full head of brushed, curly black hair. Hair gel gave it sheen. He wore tan slacks, a collarless, pale blue shirt, and a thin-lapeled, leather sports jacket a shade darker than his shirt that fit perfectly and showed off a slim but chiseled physique. Low-cut, brown leather boots and a multicolored ascot neatly tied around his neck gave him the unconventional, sophisticated look of a bohemian.

He was as handsome as Elena was beautiful. He could have passed as her older brother. A thought flashed in Jo's head—if she had been a tourist in Mexico on holiday instead of an escaped convict evading capture, and he wasn't a paid assassin on the run from his cartel, a tryst with him would have been more than a distinct possibility.

Returning his smile came as naturally as taking a breath.

Galindez handed a bag to each of them. "One for the *señora*. One for the *señorita*. Now change in the bedroom, *por favor*."

When they emerged from the bedroom, they were dressed in disguises that covered their legs, arms, hair, and much of their faces.

"How did you get these clothes?" Jo asked. The smile on her face again came easily.

"My sister is a nun of the Order of *Santo Benedicto*. After I buy our vehicle, some clothes for me to wear, and go to a men's salon to bathe and shave, I drive to the convent where she is cloistered. The sisters, they give me the habits and shoes you are wearing. Of course, I make a generous donation of your money for their help."

The habits were the perfect disguises. The black tunics covered their bodies—Elena's shapely figure was hidden from view. The coifs and veils covered their head and hair. Only a small part of their faces was visible. The tinted, wire-rimmed eyeglasses he'd purchased for them dulled the color of their eyes.

"We throw away your clothes, your backpacks, and everything in them," he said. "And put these in the bags I buy for you." He reached into the smaller bag and handed them well-worn leather bibles, prayer beads, and two plain-looking handbags large enough to hold them. "There is a church with a convent in San Cristóbal where we will say you are going if we are stopped by the police on our way there."

Elena shot Galindez a quick, approving smile. "I know of it. It is where we need to go."

Nodding his head at Elena, he said, "You, *señora*, will be Sister Mariana, my sister's name. She even looks like you."

Jo figured as much. It didn't surprise her that his good looks ran in the family.

"And you, the pretty *señorita*," he said, turning to face Jo. "You are Sister Gabriela."

*Pretty?* Jo felt an uptick in her libido meter. But his flirting with her in front of Elena could earn him a pair of scissors in an eye or three bullets in the chest, or both.

There was precedent for this.

"One more thing," he said, reaching into a pocket of his jacket for two phones and handing one to each of them. "I buy cellphones with prepaid minutes for us. We have the same four-digit password—1980—the year of my birth. We use them if we get separated. I added our phone numbers to your contacts list. *Señora*, are you able to contact your husband with it?"

"No," Elena replied. "We also use these phones and change them every month with new phone numbers."

It made sense to use burner phones, Jo thought. They were often used by drug dealers, criminal conspirators, and for fraudulent purposes. They were untraceable. No cell phone records to disclose who's been called and when. If the GPS locator was turned off, the phone was impossible to track.

"Carry the phone in a pocket of your habit at all times," he instructed.

The pockets of their habits were deep and easily concealed the phones, their remaining pesos … and Elena's pistol.

"And now we wait and leave when the sun sets. It is safer we travel in darkness. I go out again, this time for food and drink."

Galindez returned with enchiladas, rice and beans, fruit drinks, and beer. They ate in silence, Jo savoring the first good, hearty meal they'd had in days. Then they waited. The beer made Galindez sleepy, and he dozed off in a chair for a while. For a time, Elena and Jo's eyes locked in a silent conversation that covered everything: no, they didn't have better choices; no, they still didn't trust Galindez; yes, they would keep a close eye on him; and finally, yes, they actually had a path through the dragnet encircling the city. Elena's eyes shone with hope and excitement.

When the grayness of dusk replaced the light of day, Galindez announced it was time to go. He opened the door for them to leave.

Jo turned to Elena, smiled, and with a nod of her head and a wave of her hand, said, "After you, Sister Mariana."

~

The nuns sat in the back seat of the old but functional sedan Galindez had purchased with the money they'd given him and listened to Latin pop music on the radio. In addition to being good looking, Galindez was blessed with an excellent tenor voice, as he proved from time to time by lowering the volume on the radio and serenading his travelers in a powerful, piercing falsetto.

Jo noticed Galindez adjust the rear-view mirror so that he could look at her whenever he sang a love ballad. With Elena napping beside her, she could risk smiling at him, and even giggled into her hand once when he stared at her with eyes that were lustful, but also sweet.

She had a hard time believing her admirer was a hitman

for a cartel. Could someone with such a sweet, innocent-looking face kill someone for no reason other than because he was told to do it?

But under his ascot, he wore the mark of an assassin. The Juarez Cartel was notorious for having its men decapitate and mutilate their enemies and dump their corpses in public places to intimidate local law enforcement, other cartels, and the general public.

Could he be so ruthless, violent, and cruel?

Jo had her answer when she turned and saw the same sweet, innocent look on the face of Sister Mariana. If Elena Sanchez-Gomez could kill someone for the least bit of provocation, so could the dashing, debonair Miguel Galindez.

Jo and Elena were both asleep when Galindez startled them out of their slumber. "Roadblock." The word was uttered sharply. "Let me do the talking. You, *señora*, speak for both of you and only in Spanish. Say that Sister Gabriela was born unable to speak or hear."

Jo moved forward in her seat and tapped Galindez on the shoulder. "Is it meant for us?" she asked, her heart thumping in her chest.

"Possibly, or it could be they suspect a shipment of drugs from one of the cartels will be passing on the road. Quickly, give me your phones. They may search you and question why nuns have them."

Jo saw Elena hand over her pistol too. She was right to do so. If the police searched her and found it, the ruse would quickly unravel. But could she trust Galindez to return it to her?

Galindez laughed when Elena gave him the gun. "Something tells me, *señora*, that you have no fear of me when I point my gun at you."

Elena laughed back. "Not when a loaded gun in my pocket is pointed at your chest, *señor*."

Galindez put the phones in the glove compartment and the revolver in the console with his pistol. The police would not be surprised to find guns on a man who worked as a driver in such a dangerous country as Mexico.

There were three police cars and a half dozen policemen. Both lanes of the road were blocked. On each side, two policemen inspected the vehicle while a third questioned the driver.

When it was their turn, a policeman questioned Galindez in Spanish. Jo translated their words in her head as they spoke.

"License and vehicle registration," he demanded, beaming his flashlight in Galindez's face.

Galindez handed him what appeared to be a driver's license. "The car, I buy it recently," he said. "It is not yet registered. But I have proof of ownership." He handed over the paperwork. Galindez spoke in a casual, easy voice.

"Open the hood," the policeman grunted, after taking a cursory glance at the papers and handing them back to Galindez, who pulled a latch from inside the vehicle that opened the hood. They used flashlights to check the engine compartment and trunk of the car and felt under the wheel wells and bumpers.

"Where are you going, *señor?*"

"I take the sisters to San Cristóbal," he replied calmly.

Jo admired his composure.

The policeman shone his flashlight on Elena's face, and then Jo's.

Galindez watched in the rear-view mirror.

"You," he said while the light was still on Jo's face. "Why are you traveling this road?"

Jo wondered whether there was enough of her American-looking face visible to arouse his suspicions. She remained silent, and patted her chest with her hand, then touched her mouth and ear with a finger, and shook her head. She had no idea how to do sign language, but figured he didn't know either.

Elena spoke up. "Sister Gabriela, she cannot speak or hear. She only communicates in sign language. We are nuns of the Order of Saint Benedict from Tuxtla on our way to our convent in San Cristóbal."

Jo sensed that Elena used the glare of the flashlight beam as a reason to cover her face with a hand as she spoke.

He saw the handbags on their laps. "What do you have in the bags?"

"Only what is important to us," Elena replied, bowing her head.

"We shall see," he snickered. "Maybe you are mules disguised as holy women carrying drugs for the cartel?"

"We serve only one master," she answered reverently, making the sign of the cross, "and he is *Jesucristo,* the son of God." She bowed her head when she said the name of Jesus Christ.

Elena's bravado in the face of danger had no limits, Jo thought. She spoke with such conviction, she convincingly passed for a nun.

The policeman opened the rear passenger door and grabbed Elena's handbag off her lap. He put the flashlight under his arm at an angle that allowed him to rifle through it. He felt around and pulled out the Bible, and then the prayer beads. He returned the items to the bag and gave it back to Elena, who handed him Jo's bag without him having to ask for it. This time, he didn't remove what he saw in it.

Satisfied, he told Galindez he was free to go.

When the lights from the police cars faded away, Galindez laughed heartily and said over his shoulder, "Bravo! Outstanding performances from both of you. I now see how you are able to escape an American prison, cross the border, and travel through Mexico without getting caught."

Jo and Elena exchanged smiles. Jo thought but didn't say, *And if we told you the whole story, you'd never believe us.*

# CHAPTER 32

It was late evening when they arrived in San Cristóbal. Elena directed Galindez past the church where Diego Garcia and his young bride were married. The convent, whose nuns had sung in the choir during their wedding ceremony, was a short distance from the church.

The horseshoe-shaped two-story stucco building had a courtyard in front and gardens in back. It was walled and gated. A tower extended from a terracotta roof with a statue of Saint Benedict recessed in an alcove.

The gate was locked when Galindez tried to open it. He rang a bell that sat on a pedestal several times and waited. No one came.

It was late. Elena suspected the nuns had all retired to their beds for the evening. "Try again," Elena urged him through her opened window.

Galindez rang the bell several times more. This time it produced the desired result. A woman appeared, wearing a robe over her nightgown and the head cover of a Benedictine nun.

"Good evening, Sister," Galindez said, when she approached the gate with a lantern in her hand. "I have two sisters of your order who need sanctuary. Will you be so kind as to provide it?" The Benedictine nuns in Mexico were bilingual. Jo was thankful he spoke in English. She could more easily follow what was being said.

"Let me speak to them," the nun replied.

Elena heard the exchange, got out of the car, and walked to stand beside Galindez. Jo followed and stood slightly behind her.

"I am Sister Camila. Who are you?"

"I am Sister Mariana," Elena responded. "This is Sister Gabriela. She cannot speak or hear, but she reads lips and will understand you if you raise the light to your face." The nun moved the lantern closer to her face. "We come from our monastery in Tuxtla," she continued, "and need the help of the priest at the church. Is Father Arturo Allende still pastor?"

"No. He passed away two years ago. God bless his soul. Father Luca Bastillo is pastor." Elena's sigh of disappointment was audible to everyone. She and Diego could count on the allegiance of the priest who had married them. But the cartels bought the loyalty of police, politicians … and priests with bribes. Could this Father Bastillo be trusted?

"Why do you need his help?" she asked.

"I can explain why to your Mother Superior. It's important that I speak directly to her."

"Reverend Mother is elderly. She sleeps now."

"Elderly? How long has she been here, at this monastery?"

"Many years before I came here, and that was eight years ago."

"Then she will know me and why I come here."

Sister Camila nodded. "We will provide you shelter. You

speak to her tomorrow after morning prayers, chores, and mass." The nun unlocked the gate.

Galindez stood beside the car.

Elena turned to face him. "*Señor*, come back for us tomorrow at noon."

He nodded his assent, got in the car, and drove off.

They followed Sister Camila into the convent to a room with three single beds, lamps and bibles on nightstands, a dresser, and a closet. "You sleep in this cell tonight," she said.

Cell? Jo chuckled deep down in her throat.

"You will find nightgowns and towels in the drawers of the dresser. Robes and slippers are in the closet. Do you wish for me to bring you some food and drink?"

"No, Sister Camila. You have been more than kind to us. God bless you," Elena replied, making the sign of the cross and simulating a silent prayer. "We pray now and then go to sleep."

Jo hid the smile on her face with a hand. More fine acting from her traveling companion. Galindez, already a fan, would have given her a round of applause.

When she opened the door to leave, the nun turned and smiled. "Sleep well, Sisters. May God keep you safe."

Elena and Jo sat on their beds across from each other. They removed their veils and head covers. Elena shook out her mane of chocolate locks that fell gently to her shoulders and smiled at Jo. Jo ran the fingers of a hand through her shorter, raven-black hair and giggled naughtily, as if the two of them had just pulled off the perfect con.

They were kindred spirits on an adventure that no two women could ever have believed possible. Escaped convicts on the run, who'd made it all the way through Mexico without being caught, kidnapped, or assaulted.

They reached out and held hands, and laughed so heartily they worried other nuns would hear them and come to investigate. And then, grinning from ear to ear, they exclaimed in unison, "We did it!"

~

The ringing of a bell in the hallway woke them, and early. The previous day, like the other four, had been long, intense, and perilous. Although Jo's body craved more rest, she forced full alertness on herself. Unsure of what to expect, they got out of bed, splashed some water on their faces from a basin on a table, and quickly dressed.

The sun had not yet risen. Jo had discarded her prison watch with her clothes in Tuxtla and there were no clocks in the room. Unsure of the time, she opened the door a crack to hear better what would happen next.

When they heard the shuffle of footsteps outside the room, Elena whispered for Jo to follow her into the hallway, where they took their places at the end of a procession of nuns on their way to the chapel for morning prayers.

The last ones to enter the chapel, they sat together in a pew in the back, where their awkwardness was less likely to be noticed. Whenever the sisters in the pews in front of them sat, stood, or knelt, so did they. Fortunately, the other nuns in their pew kept their heads rigidly bowed and their eyes focused on their hymnals.

Jo was thankful she was presumed deaf and unable to speak—she wasn't expected to pray out loud or sing.

A half hour later, the nuns filed out of the chapel. One of them tapped Elena and Jo on the shoulder while they were still in the pew and motioned for them to follow her. The nun found a broom, dustpan, cloths, and furniture polish in a closet, and distributed the cleaning materials among them. It was obvious that morning chores took priority over meals. Elena and Jo polished some of the pews, while the nun swept the floor and dusted the altar.

When another half hour had passed, the nun collected the cleaning materials and returned them to the closet. She took a seat in the front row. Elena and Jo stayed back and sat in the last row like before.

Soon thereafter, the other sisters returned to the chapel, led by an elderly nun, who walked with a cane to the front row pew. Elena nudged Jo, who nodded.

*Reverend Mother.*

A priest appeared and celebrated mass. Jo understood the exercise from before and mimicked the actions of the other nuns. She figured that the squat, middle-aged, bald-headed man was Father Bastillo. Toward the end of the service, the priest faced the nuns for the final prayers and blessings. When he did, his eyes fixed on Elena and Jo. If Jo noticed him staring, Elena must have too.

Was he curious about nuns he didn't recognize, or did he recognize the faces of escaped convicts from their photos on television and in newspapers?

When the mass concluded and the priest had left the chapel, the nuns followed their leader to the dining room, where they assembled around a large table with Reverend Mother at the head. The visiting sisters were directed to the chairs closest to her. After a short prayer, they ate in silence. Jo saw the old nun occasionally turn her head and look at Elena with bright eyes that lit up her wrinkled face.

When they finished their meal, the nun rose with some effort, placed a hand on Elena's shoulder, and nodded to her.

She shuffled out of the dining room to her office.

When they were all in the room, she indicated for them to have a seat with a wave of her hand.

She sat in the chair behind her desk, Elena in the chair in front of it, and Jo on a sofa. "We speak in English so that your companion can hear what we say."

Jo learned two things about the nun when she spoke—she knew Elena and, although cloistered in a convent, that they were two escaped convicts on the run.

"Do you remember me, Reverend Mother?" Elena asked.

"Of course I do, Elena," she replied softly. A sweet smile lit her face.

"Then you know why we come here?"

"You've done well to come to me before seeing the priest. He cannot be trusted. He warned me that you might reach out to us and that I was to inform him of it if you did."

"This priest, why can he not be trusted?"

Unlike Elena, the nun spoke in proper English. "He told me they went to all the churches and shelters in the city and threatened to burn down the buildings of anyone who rendered aid to you."

The nun didn't need to explain who *they* referred to.

Elena moved up in her chair. "The convent, it is in great danger if we stay here. We leave as soon as our driver returns at noon."

"You need not worry about that," she countered. "One of your husband's men came to the convent yesterday and forewarned me you might seek refuge here. He said he would contact me again tomorrow, and if you were here, your husband will send men for you."

"Diego will reward your kindness, Reverend Mother."

"My reward is helping a wife reunite with her husband."

Jo sat in silent awe of the respect this religious woman had for El Leon, knowing that his cartel was no less a criminal enterprise and malevolent than the others. In Mexico, a cartel was its own government. It expected the allegiance of those within its sphere of influence. A cartel made and enforced the rules, and punished harshly those who broke them. And those who were loyal to it, and at its beck and call, were provided with provisions and protection.

"It's best you remain in your room until your husband's men come for you. Sister Camila will bring your meals to you. When your driver comes at noon, we will direct him to the rear gate, which will be unlocked. You tell him you will be staying here."

Elena spoke for both of them. "We do as you say, Reverend Mother."

With a warm smile still on her face, she waved a hand for them to return to their room.

# CHAPTER 33

The text from Galindez went to Jo, not Elena. *Señorita, I am in a garden full of pretty flowers, but none as pretty as you. Please come to me.* Jo smiled silently at the innuendo so that Elena wouldn't see that her pursuer was not only a knight in shining armor, but a romantic one.

She had to be careful, very careful. If Elena got wind of Miguel's interest in her, it could end very badly for him, and any hint of reciprocity on Jo's part could doom her one chance of surviving her ordeal, and she wasn't thinking figuratively.

"The city crawls with *sicarios*," Galindez said, when all had gathered in the garden. "Like me, they hide the mark of their cartel with a bandana. But they walk the streets and drive in vehicles looking at the women—they look for you."

Jo didn't see their car on the street when she passed by the gate. "Where's the car?"

"They watch the church and convent. I park four blocks from here and walk."

Elena said, "My husband's men come and talk to the

reverend mother. When they learn I am here, we will be taken to Diego."

"Your husband, will he trust me … or slit my throat?"

"Have no fear. I tell him what you do for us, what you can do for him, and that you have earned my trust."

Jo wasn't so sure about the sincerity of her companion's promise.

"Will you permit me to call you Elena?" he asked with premeditated timidity.

To Jo, Elena's smile seemed forced.

"*Si*, call me Elena."

"And you, Elena, call me Miguel."

Jo sensed that Galindez wanted to personalize his relationship with Elena before meeting her husband. Being on a first-name basis with the woman Diego Garcia trusted most would help mitigate his natural disinclination to trust a former soldier of a rival cartel. But the infamous drug lord wasn't foolish or careless. Even if he believed Galindez's story that he was about to be betrayed, he might suspect the intruder was a *sicario* still loyal to his cartel and sent on a mission to assassinate him.

What did they really know about Galindez? He was brash and clever, and not at all afraid of coming face-to-face with one of the most notorious criminals in Mexico. Such bravado from a soldier of a rival cartel typically ended badly for him. Once a cartel's soldier, always *that* cartel's soldier. And the reason was simple—if you betrayed one cartel, you might betray another.

For all they knew, Galindez could be an undercover DEA agent on a mission to infiltrate the cartel and learn Garcia's whereabouts and the location of his labs and storage facilities.

The pieces of a puzzle began falling into place for Jo.

The DEA knew about the *oro blanco*—the white gold—Garcia was trafficking. It was found in Elena's car when she was arrested and would have been analyzed in a lab by the DEA's forensic pharmacologists when she was prosecuted for the federal drug crimes. What better way for an undercover agent to gain access to El Leon than to claim he could expose the rat who intended to sell his top-secret designer drug to another cartel?

The DEA could have tattooed the mark of the Juarez Cartel on Galindez's neck to prove he had been one of them. The DEA would know that their agent's best chance of getting close to Garcia was to intercept his wife on her way to him, and that she would be traveling with migrants on the trains. He'd know the getting-on-and-off routine she'd follow. He'd know she'd be traveling with an American woman. He'd know they'd have to spend some time in Tuxtla, where everyone would be looking for them. It was the perfect time and place for him to confront them, sell his bullshit story to Elena, and offer his help.

More puzzle pieces seemed to fit.

When they were hiding in the apartment of the alleged brother, he was gone for three hours. Was that enough time to buy a car, a fashionable wardrobe and the cellphones, go to a spa for a makeover, and then make the trip to the alleged sister's convent for the clothes? She had her doubts. But it was more than enough time to walk to a nearby apartment of a collaborator, where he could clean up at his leisure and have everything waiting for him there, including the car.

Jo thought back to her time in the apartment before Galindez returned with their disguises. While Elena showered, she snooped around. It was in her nature as a homicide detective to search the homes of suspects, frequently exceeding the parameters of a search warrant—sometimes even without one.

There were clothes in the closets and drawers, but they appeared too new for someone who supposedly had lived there for a while. The pants and jackets seemed to be for a larger man than the underwear in the drawers and shirts in the closet would fit. There were no socks. The two pairs of shoes that lay on the floor below the shirts appeared to be different sizes.

She'd checked the refrigerator. It was sparsely filled with unopened food products. There were no leftovers in the Tupperware containers at the back of a shelf. No butter, margarine or milk. She didn't recall seeing a coffee pot. No detergent sat under the sink with which to wash dishes. She spied a few bottles of beer in the fridge, but no bottle opener in the kitchen drawers. The trash receptacle was empty. And thinking back—*no framed photos of the brother, his sister, Galindez, or anyone else in the apartment.*

Jo had seen enough staged crime scenes in her career in law enforcement to know a poorly staged one that was put together in a hurry.

On the other hand, the brother might exist and have eccentricities that explained his wardrobe and eating habits. He might like wearing baggy pants. A lot of people in Mexico didn't wear socks. He might eat out a lot or bring home takeout. He might have taken the trash out on his way to work. The beer might have twist caps. He might not be the sentimental type who keeps photos of his family around.

The evidence against Galindez wasn't compelling. In a court of law, he'd be acquitted of falsely impersonating a *sicario*.

But Diego Garcia didn't need evidence. Suspicion was enough to convict Galindez. If the drug lord had a scintilla of doubt about Galindez, he was as good as dead.

Galindez posed a danger to Jo if he was a DEA agent. If the DEA learned Garcia's whereabouts, the raid that followed would lead to her capture … or, much more likely, her death in the collateral damage of a shootout.

Her musings were interrupted by Galindez, who asked, "And you, *señorita*, will you allow me to call you Jo?"

With the doubts about him still fresh in her mind, she stuttered a guarded reply, "Y-Yes, Miguel, call me … Jo."

Her concerns over how she and Galindez would be received by the infamous El Leon did not abate when they all agreed to buddy up and call each other by their first names.

And when she saw Father Bastillo staring at them from the window of Reverend Mother's office, what the drug lord would do to Jo Crowder and Miguel Galindez when they met him was the least of their worries.

~

"You are in grave danger," she began. They had been in their room less than an hour when  Reverend Mother called them to her office.

Elena knew why it was suddenly very dangerous for them to be there. She also had seen Father Bastillo looking at them in the garden.

"He saw you sitting together at mass," she explained. "He knows all of the nuns. I told him what you told Sister Camila, but he didn't believe your story. I acted like I hadn't spoken to you and that Sister Camila had been responsible for you during your visit with us."

"*Si*, Reverend Mother," Elena said. "We see him looking at us from your window and worry that he recognize us."

"He's intending to call the convent in Tuxtla and inquire

about you. I offered to do it and delay him finding out who you are, but he insisted."

"This priest, what will he do when he learns the truth about us?"

"He will call the local police, and they will come here and arrest you."

Elena moved uneasily in her chair, then stood. "We must go now. But the clothes we wear are useless to us if we leave in them."

The old nun raised a hand. "Do not worry, Elena. I've gathered some of the sisters' street clothes, the ones they wore when they came here as novices." She nodded her head in the direction of a bag on the sofa next to where Jo was seated. "There wasn't much to select from, but they should do."

"*Gracias*, Reverend Mother, we go to the hotel room of our driver and hide there."

"No, Elena. It is too dangerous for you to stay in the city. When the police don't find you here, they will block the streets and search for you. There is a village in the mountains called Rosa de la Montaña, a two-hour drive from here on the old road into the mountains to the south. It is a small hamlet and the place of my birth. There, an abandoned chapel sits on the outskirts. I made a map for you to find it." She gave the hand-drawn map to Elena. "You hide there until your husband comes for you."

"How will he know where to find us?"

"When his man comes back tomorrow to see if you are here, I will tell him where you are."

"Reverend Mother, what you do for us is very dangerous for you and the sisters if they find out you help us."

The nun's face brightened into a smile. "That, Elena, has been, and will always be, in the hands of God. Go now, get dressed, and leave through the rear gate that will remain unlocked until your driver comes to take you away."

When they returned to their room, Elena texted Miguel. Jo watched over her shoulder and read the message as she wrote it. *It is no longer safe for us here or in the city. Come at once to the garden gate. We wait for you there.*

Jo knew how dangerous it was for Miguel to continue to help them, whether or not he was a DEA agent. If the *sicarios* saw him when he came for them, he was as good as dead.

They all were.

# CHAPTER 34

**W**hen they returned to their room, they quickly changed into their new clothes.

Elena filled out her short-sleeve, floral-design casual dress in all the right places. Jo's dress was similar in design and size, but it showed off muscular biceps and calves and little else. The bodices were high to the neck and the hems below the knee. The garb was the plain, modest style of clothing one would expect of young women hoping to someday wear the habit of a nun.

The cotton button-up sweaters were of a similar design but of different colors and would provide ample protection from the night's chill. When they put on the eyeglasses and the berets the reverend mother had provided, they had the serious, studious look of schoolgirls.

They folded their habits and placed them in drawers of the dresser with their bibles and prayer beads. Before leaving the room, Elena wrote a brief note of gratitude to the only mother she'd known since her mother was murdered. She smiled as she did, Jo suspecting that she was remembering how kind she was when she'd put the veil over her head at her wedding and led her to the altar, and afterwards returned to lead the choir in spiritual prayer and song.

They found an inconspicuous place in the garden, where they had a view of the gate. Five minutes later, they heard the distant sound of sirens.

"The police, they come for us," Elena declared worriedly.

"And more than one vehicle is on the way," Jo added. The sirens got louder with each passing second. "Elena, shouldn't we take our chances on the streets?"

"*Si*. We leave now."

They moved quickly to the gate and out to the street. The cartel's men, hearing the impending arrival of the police, were likely to back off, watch from a safe distance, and bide their time.

They walked to the corner and waited for Miguel behind the convent.

"We're screwed if Miguel's not here—like now," Jo huffed. They had no idea where he was. Impatient, she pulled out her phone and called him. It rang, but he didn't answer. She called again. This time a familiar voice answered. "Pretty flower, how can I be of service?"

Uninterested in foreplay, she was gruff in responding, "Miguel, where the fuck are you?"

"A few minutes from the convent, but for me, it will feel like an eternity. You are eager to see me, *si*?" His flippant tone only served to piss her off more, and the chuckle that came after.

"Those sirens you hear are the police coming to arrest us. We are on the street behind the convent in street clothes. So put your dick in an ice bag and get here damn quick."

"Jo, it excites me when you talk dirty. But do not worry. I am almost there."

When the sirens ceased, Jo knew the police had arrived at the convent. "Hurry, Miguel," she screamed into the phone and ended the call.

Elena paced back and forth, checking up and down the street every few seconds. "We go now and find a place to hide. Not safe for us so close to the convent."

Elena was right. They were sitting ducks there on the street. Elena began to walk in the direction of an alley. "Wait," Jo shouted, grabbing her arm.

A car had turned onto their street a couple of blocks away. When it got closer, she recognized it as Miguel's. The car screeched to a stop. Miguel reached behind him and opened the rear passenger door. "Get in and get down," he commanded in a muffled voice, even though no one else was there to hear him.

They scrambled into the back seat, Jo on her back on the floor looking up and Elena stretched out on her stomach on the seat, staring down at her partner.

Miguel drove away, but at a speed that would not draw attention to his vehicle. "Elena, a police car comes in our direction. Get on the floor with Jo … now. Cover yourselves with the blanket. And be still."

Elena slid easily onto Jo and pulled the blanket on the seat over them. Jo could hear and feel her heart thumping in her chest.

Or was it Elena's?

They lay cheek to cheek, breathing into each other's ear.

And then, the lively sound of Calypso music pierced the suffocating silence. Miguel had turned on the radio and had it blaring. Jo could see his head bobbing to the beat of the music with an uncovered eye.

When he slowed to a stop, he opened his window to speak to a policeman. Jo didn't hear the opening of a door and figured that the cop stayed in his vehicle. Miguel lowered the volume on the radio enough for Jo to hear their conversation. Although they spoke in Spanish, it was an easy translation for Jo.

The cop asked, "Sir, did you see two women walking together on the streets on your way here?"

There was no hesitation in Miguel's response. "Only a couple of nuns about four blocks from here, maybe five minutes ago," he replied with the nonchalance of someone who had no interest in knowing the reason for the inquiry.

Jo heard the cop say to his partner before the roar of the engine signaled their departure, "Call it in—we are looking for two women dressed as nuns walking north into the city."

As soon as the police car pulled away, Miguel turned up the music and finished singing the song that played on the radio. "They are gone. You can get up," he said when the song ended.

Elena darted a quick kiss of triumph on Jo's lips before sitting up and throwing off the blanket. The two sat back, let out a collective sigh of relief and smiled at Miguel, who intermittently glanced at them in the rear-view mirror with a prankish grin on his face.

"Bravo, Miguel!" Jo exclaimed. "They'll be looking for us walking the streets in nuns' habits while we drive in the opposite direction out of the city."

Jo envisioned how things would play out at the convent, a cocky smile still on her face. When the police questioned Reverend Mother, she could hear her say:

"When Father Bastillo told me who they were, I couldn't

believe they would be so brazen as to pretend to be nuns. I asked Sister Camila to bring them to me, but when she looked for them, they were gone. Do not worry. They will not be too difficult to find. They were on foot when they came to us wearing the habits of nuns of our order—the Order of Saint Benedict. They have no means of transportation, money, or street clothes. At this moment they are walking the streets of San Cristóbal in their disguises. We, the sisters and I, will pray that you find these criminals and arrest them. Now go with God's blessing."

Jo chuckled when she heard Miguel say, "So where do you schoolgirls want me to take you?"

~

Vega sat in an office at the Drug Enforcement Directorate's field office in Tuxtla, picked up the handset of his landline phone to call Monica Stallings, and had second thoughts. He cradled it, pulled out his cell phone, and texted her instead.

Antonio Vega
*Arrived yesterday. Not sure who I can trust.*
Monica Stallings
*Understood.*
Antonio Vega
*We're close.*
Monica Stallings
*How close?*
Antonio Vega
*Our asset is in San Cristóbal. I'm headed there now.*
Monica Stallings
*Are you prepared to engage?*
Antonio Vega

*Gunship and SWAT team are camped outside the city, waiting.*
Monica Stallings
*And you?*
Antonio Vega
*Will follow asset to target's location and do a reconnaissance.*
Monica Stallings
*Good luck and Godspeed.*

Vega was wary of his agency's collaboration with the DED, Mexico's intelligence agency and secret police force. The DED was created five years ago. Like its predecessor, the Federal Security Directorate, the DED had a history of illegal detentions, torture, assassinations, and forced disappearances. Many agents moonlighted as informants for the cartels, providing information about the identity of DEA and DED undercover agents and planned raids on labs and storage facilities. Many left the DED to work full time for the cartels, which paid handsomely for their services as hitmen and in the security forces that guarded the cartel's labs and storage facilities and protected its drug lords and lieutenants.

Vega worried that the DED could not be trusted. Only a select few knew the identity of Vega's undercover informant, whose mission was to locate El Leon and compromise his operations. But the same was true before, and the DEA agent's head ended up on his desk, floating in formaldehyde. The rest of him was never recovered. The funeral had been a closed casket affair and attending it had haunted Vega. Only the head in a sack lay in the casket when his remains were buried. His young widow sobbed uncontrollably during the service, and she fainted into the arms of her brother at the cemetery when his casket was lowered into the ground.

Even now, weeks later, the flashbacks kept him up at night. It was a tough decision to try again. But he had no choice.

The body count from accidental overdoses continued to rise as *white gold* hit the streets of more American cities. The only way to slow the emerging fentanyl epidemic was to stop the manufacture of Garcia's drug. The best way of doing that was to cut off the head of the venomous snake responsible for producing it, and that meant catching the reptile.

The success of Operation Snowfall was dependent on finding Diego Garcia. When he was located, the plan was for a DEA gunship and SWAT team led by Vega to attack from the air, while the ground forces, composed of DED special agents, set up a perimeter defense, cutting off escape routes. After the gunship destroyed any aircraft and vehicles, the team would deploy from the gunship, neutralize Garcia's security forces, triangulate his location, and move in. With the DED agents providing additional coverage, Garcia would be surrounded and give up.

Fine in theory, unlikely in reality.

So many things could go wrong. At the top of the list was his operative being discovered, tortured, and eliminated before Garcia was located and the raid could be executed. After all, they had a grim precedent.

Vega was certain of one thing—when threatened, a pride male and its lioness would fight back. Garcia, his wife, and their army of assassins placed little value on human life. Killing was in their blood. They were likely to fight to the death.

Vega was a realist—his perfect plan might not end perfectly. There would be bloodshed and lives would be lost … on both sides.

The only uncertainty was the final death toll and which side would need more body bags.

# CHAPTER 35

Rosa de la Montaña was a typical pastoral hamlet in the Sierra Madre Mountain range of Chiapas. Sparsely populated, its inhabitants were mostly poor farmers. The village served as the marketplace where crops were sold and then transported by truck to San Cristóbal, and little more.

Over time, the commerce became barely enough to support the farming community and residents of the village. The merchant shops had dwindled to a few. The school and medical clinic closed years ago. The closest city was a two-hour drive away.

Reverend Mother's map led them to the chapel, a small cement building with broken windows. A cross was etched into the concrete above an ordinary-looking door with rusty hinges that kept it from fully closing. Inside, the statues and altar had been removed. Only pews made of cypress remained, and they were water stained because of holes in the roof.

It appeared that God too had abandoned the village.

But for three itinerants on the run, a deserted chapel in

an isolated village few visited was the perfect place to hide.

Elena and Jo rested in the chapel, while Miguel looked for a street merchant to purchase food and drinks. When he returned, they ate a simple meal of tortillas, tomatoes, and prickly pear cactus. They drank from a large bottle of fruit juice.

When the meal was finished and the sun began to set, Miguel left to smoke a cigarette. Jo welcomed her privacy with Elena. She went to sit next to her, who was seated in a pew by a window. "Does Diego have a house close by?" she asked.

"*Si.* The reason I come to San Cristóbal. Diego's home is hidden in the mountains to the south, not far from here. It is where I go when he rescue me from the streets."

"Why can't we drive there from here?"

"The way up the mountain and through the forest take us on narrow, dirt roads difficult to find."

"Will Miguel be allowed to drive us there?"

"No. We will be taken there."

Changing the subject, Jo asked, "How will Diego find the person Miguel can identify?"

"Raul, he take him to the labs where we make *oro blanco*. He find the traitor there."

Jo still had her doubts about Miguel's story. If he was working undercover, it could be a ruse to locate the cartel's labs. "And if he finds the person?" she inquired, knowing the answer beforehand.

"Like any traitor, he will be executed and made an example of." The consequences for betraying El Leon, especially selling the formula for *oro blanco*, would be severe and swift.

Even before Elena responded, Jo had a vision of a decapitated man hanging by the feet from a tree, blood dripping from the neck of the carcass.

"And if he doesn't find him?"

"Miguel, he is of no use to Diego."

Same vision, but this dead man she'd known.

It made Jo reflect on what would happen to her if she was no longer of use to Diego … or Elena. What if she refused to do what Diego wanted her to do? Submit to his urges? Take drugs? Kill someone? And Elena, she clearly wanted them to be more than sisters. What would Elena do if she refused?

*Stay focused, Jo. Think like the disgraced, convicted felon you are. What would that person do?* That person had already sold her soul to the devil. She'd have no choice.

She'd do whatever was necessary to survive.

The coldness of Elena's words about Miguel was disturbing. He had twice saved them from being arrested—when they were stopped by the police on their way to San Cristóbal with the disguises he provided, and again when he cleverly deceived the police at the convent. Once he had taken Elena's gun, only to return it afterwards. How often did he have to prove his loyalty to her?

It made Jo question Elena's loyalty to her.

She felt the need to move away from Elena. She stood and looked out the window. What she saw, she could not explain.

Miguel stood by his car, cellphone in his hand.

Even in the shadows of dusk, Jo had a good view of him from the window. He had his back against the driver's door of his car, head down, double thumbing the keyboard on his phone. He stopped several times to read what was being texted back. It was very clearly a back-and-forth chat with someone.

But who and why?

The possibilities streaked through her mind like flashes of lightning.

Maybe he was texting the alleged brother that he was in

danger. If Miguel was someone who had betrayed a cartel, his brother might also be targeted, and it would be a good idea to warn him.

But why not leave a note for him in his apartment? Why not call or message him sooner? It would have been the first thing a good brother would have done … unless he had no brother to contact.

The other possibilities seemed more likely to her—he was an undercover agent, reporting to his superior that Elena had bought his story, and he'd soon be infiltrating Diego Garcia's inner circle and learning the locations of his labs and storage facilities; or he was a loyal member of the Juarez cartel, updating his lieutenant on his mission to learn Garcia's whereabouts and assassinate him; or he was part of a criminal conspiracy, contacting his confederates to come that night to kidnap Elena and hold her for ransom.

Her musings abruptly ended when Miguel stopped messaging, put his phone in the pocket of his jacket, and lit a cigarette. She moved away from the window so he wouldn't see her watching him and returned to Elena's side.

Unsure of how Elena wound react to knowing what Miguel had done, she kept it to herself. But they'd both need to be vigilant when it came to someone whose actions could be nefarious. Jo needed to express her reservations. "Elena, what do we really know about him?"

"We know nothing, but so far, what he does brings us closer to Diego. I keep my gun close to me and will use it if he does anything suspicious."

Miguel messaging someone on his phone was likely to be behavior suspicious enough for Elena to consider shooting him the next time he walked through the door.

"We are near the end of the line," Elena continued.

"Diego's men will soon be here, and we will be safe. But until they are here, we do not let him out of our sight."

"Tonight, we sleep in shifts," Jo said. "Let me have the gun. I'll give it back to you when I wake you up. He'll think you have the gun. If he tries to take it from you, I'll know what to do."

Elena smiled her approval, reached in the pocket of her dress for the gun, and handed it to Jo.

When Miguel returned to the chapel, he sat slouched in the pew in front of Jo. When night fell and it was dark inside the chapel, Elena stretched out in the pew across from Jo and eventually fell asleep.

It was a good time for Jo to inquire about the brother. "Miguel, aren't you worried your brother may be in danger?"

He turned his head and answered with a question, "Why?"

"Because the cartel might go to him for information about you or harm him because of what you've done."

"They do not know I have a brother."

"Still, don't you think you should contact him in case they find out you do? You know, just to be safe."

"My brother, he does not know I work for the cartel. It is better he does not know."

Jo laid down in her pew and pretended to fall asleep. It gave her time to mull over who Miguel might have contacted. Texting his brother was no longer a possibility. She reflected on the other possibilities again.

When she felt she might doze off midway through the night, Miguel sat up in his pew and startled her out of her drowsiness. In the shadow of moonlight beaming into the chapel from the windows and holes in the roof, she saw him stand and walk stealthily to where Elena was sleeping and look down at her.

His back was to Jo, who quietly reached for the gun in her pocket and gripped it with her finger on the trigger. Was this the opportunity he needed to take Elena's gun from her? If he had contacted a confederate earlier to arrange Elena's kidnapping that night, he'd surely want to take the gun from her first.

When Miguel reached into the pocket of his jacket, Jo pulled out her gun and pointed it at the center of his back. In the pin-drop silent stillness of the dead of night, she heard her heartbeat loud in her chest. She couldn't see if he was holding his pistol, but if he had Elena at gunpoint, he was a dead man. Jo knew at that moment that her transformation was complete. She had become Elena's alter ego, willing to do whatever was necessary to protect her … even kill for her.

She'd never let anyone take Elena from her … *nunca*.

And then Miguel turned in the direction of the front of the chapel and she saw what he held in his hand—a pack of cigarettes. She took her finger off the trigger and rested the gun on her chest under her sweatshirt.

When he left the chapel, she awakened Elena, handed the gun to her, returned to her pew, and was soon asleep.

She awoke at the break of dawn to see Elena sitting upright in her pew. Miguel was gone—maybe to relieve himself, or smoke … or do some more messaging.

She was thankful she hadn't told Elena that Miguel had messaged someone. She'd have demanded an explanation, and if she didn't like what she heard, she'd have shot him dead the first chance she had.

The uneventful night meant that Jo could rule out another possibility—Miguel wasn't part of a plot to kidnap Elena. The more she thought about it, the only possibility that remained was that the man who claimed to be Miguel Galindez was sent to take out Diego Garcia and destroy his criminal enterprise.

As far as she was concerned, whether he was sent by the good guys or the bad guys was the only unanswered question.

# CHAPTER 36

Vega left San Cristóbal a half hour after Galindez fled the city and followed him to Rosa de la Montaña using his state-of-the-art GPS.

He parked his vehicle on a side street a safe distance from the abandoned chapel. As he waited, he reflected on the latest statistics. Drug overdose deaths had more than doubled over the past four months in the dozen states where Garcia was trafficking the white gold. He did the math in his head. When the thirty-milligram, light blue pill, made to look like prescription oxycodone, hit the streets in the remaining states, the lives lost from overdoses nationally could rise from a hundred thousand annually to as many as a quarter of a million.

Only God knew how many more would die when other cartels figured out how to make *oro blanco* and competition in the marketplace made it more affordable.

Vega's thoughts turned to his asset, whose mission was to find Garcia, locate records of the cartel's operations, and safeguard them during the raid. Most drug lords relied on paper records as backup and kept them close by at all times. Computers could be hacked and infected with data-eating viruses—the paper records were there if that happened.

Vega salivated when he thought what the records might show—the location of labs and storage facilities, the identity of suppliers, distributors, people on the take, the names of the shell companies involved in money-laundering schemes, and an accounting of the vast wealth Garcia had accumulated over the years with his ill-gotten gains.

If his asset could get close to Diego Garcia, the records of his criminal organization could be there for the taking.

~

The caravan of vehicles arrived around noon. Two jeeps in front of a Cadillac Escalade with oversized wheels and a bull bar, and two more behind it. Each jeep carried two men with assault rifles resting on their laps. The drivers were most likely armed with handguns.

Vega watched from his vehicle as the motorcade drove through the village. Such shows of force were intended to intimidate those who lived in the cities, towns, and villages within a cartel's sphere of influence.

Did Garcia make the trip himself, or did he send a trusted lieutenant? The bulletproof windows of the heavily guarded vehicle were darkly tinted and didn't allow Vega to see who was inside.

He did a quick calculation in his head. If Garcia had sent twelve soldiers to guard his wife, he certainly had as many at his home guarding him. That would be a lot of firepower to overcome during the raid, which is why Vega needed the support of the DED special agents.

When the caravan had passed by, Vega got out of his vehicle and moved stealthily to a position where he had a view of the front of the chapel. Several villagers walking the street ran down the nearest side alley to avoid being caught up in the fracas if the cartel was there on official business with a score to settle.

The men in the jeeps fanned out in front of the chapel, weapons at the ready. The driver of the Escalade exited the vehicle with a pistol in his hand. Vega was close enough to hear him shout, "Elena, are you in there?"

"*Si*, I come out now and speak to you about the others," a voice called out.

Vega saw Elena Sanchez-Gomez for the first time since her sentencing on the federal drug trafficking charge. Even with her shorter hair and plain-looking clothes, she looked stunning.

The driver holstered his weapon only after she left the chapel and closed the door behind her. They conversed in voices just loud enough for Vega to hear the gist of what they were saying. A few minutes later, Elena returned to the church and accompanied her companions out.

One of the soldiers shouldered his weapon, bound Miguel's hands in front of him with zip ties, blindfolded him, and led him to the rear seat of the Escalade. When the soldier went to do the same to Jo, Elena objected, "Not the woman."

The soldier looked to the man in charge for direction. "Are you sure, Elena?" he asked.

"*Si*, she poses no threat to us."

Jo took the seat next to Miguel, and Elena got in the front passenger seat.

When the motorcade was out of sight, Vega returned to his vehicle and waited ten minutes before driving away. The wife of Diego Garcia was on the last leg of her journey home. Where that was would be revealed to Vega when the blip on the screen of his mobile GPS no longer moved and came to rest in the den of the lion.

# CHAPTER 37

The Escalade rocked and bounced on dirt roads up and down hills and through valleys and woodlands. The engine strained loudly on steep upgrades, purred on the straight and level sections, and the brakes squealed on the sharp downslopes.

At first, Jo studied the changing terrain, trying to memorize the route they had taken, but an hour into their journey, she realized she'd never be able to remember it. The roads became barely discernible trails, were sometimes across fields with no identifiable pathways, and they turned so frequently she had no idea the direction they were going.

They traveled in silence. It allowed Jo the time to reflect on what lay ahead. She had a hard time believing Diego Garcia would be waiting at the door to greet Elena's new friends with open arms. He was careful enough to blindfold Miguel. Elena could vouch for her. Miguel claimed to have worked for a rival cartel, but only had its sign tattooed on his neck as proof. It would be reckless to not interrogate him before letting him anywhere near the infamous drug lord.

"Raul, will Diego be there when we arrive?" Elena asked, breaking the silence.

The driver had a name that was familiar to Jo—he was Garcia's enforcer.

"No, Elena. He is away on business. He returns tomorrow."

Jo could imagine Elena rolling her eyes. Elena had told her that such trips were more about monkey business than cartel business. But she didn't care who he slept with. For her, sex with Diego was a household chore.

Three hours into their trip, the Escalade slowed to parking-lot speed for several minutes before coming to a stop.

"I want to question them, Elena," Raul said, keeping his hands on the wheel and the engine running.

It made sense that Diego's capo would personally handle their interrogations. If he didn't like their answers, they might not be seen or heard from again.

"The man, Miguel Galindez, he goes with you. Question him, but return him in the same condition he is in today. We avoid capture because of him, and he has business with Diego. He stays in the guesthouse. Food will be brought to him. From this moment, the man is under the protection of my husband."

"And the woman?"

"She stays with me." Elena was emphatic. Her tone of voice made it clear who had the final say about her companions. "Diego, if he has concerns about them, he comes to me."

Jo was relieved to know that Elena was true to her word about protecting both of them. Elena made Miguel give her his gun before Raul arrived but let him keep his cellphone. Only the texts between them would be found when Raul checked it—Jo was sure of that. It was a burner, and therefore untraceable, but Jo was sure Raul would want to see the messages he'd sent out. Still unsure about Miguel's allegiances, she knew it wasn't a good idea to allow him access to a phone. But it was too late to tell Elena what she'd seen him do. She'd be angry with her for keeping the information to herself and letting her bring a potential undercover agent or assassin to the home of her husband.

That said, Raul and Diego had been in this business for decades, and not by making a lot of mistakes.

Elena got out of the vehicle and opened Jo's door. "Jo, come with me. Miguel, you stay in the car." In contrast to Raul, Elena spoke to them in a pleasant, conversational tone.

When Elena closed the door, Raul beeped his horn twice, and the procession of vehicles drove away.

Jo turned in a slow circle to see where she had been taken. They stood in front of a magnificent estate on the top of a hill that overlooked a mountain valley. At lower elevations, one-story buildings that resembled barracks and other buildings of various sizes and shapes were carved out of the woodlands, all interconnected by a series of unpaved roads and passageways. Men walked the dirt lanes, some carrying rifles over their shoulders.

Jo focused her attention on what looked like a military settlement. A water tower and parking lot with jeeps and pickup trucks sat off to the east, along with an open area next to it the size of a football field. The presence of gas pumps and a macadam square in the center had all the appearances of a helipad. To the west was a pasture with livestock and a farm. Several people tended to the animals and crops.

"Diego, he does this for his men," Elena explained. "The people who work in the fields and take care of the animals and our home also live here."

Jo noticed two men in fatigues milling around a two-story

building in the center of the hamlet. They were talking to four young women in short dresses and teased hair, who stood on the porch of a building that resembled a small rooming house.

When Jo figured out what was going on, she quipped, "Does Diego also provide his men with the entertainment?"

Elena's laugh was throaty. "The women, they come here to service the men."

"Are your other homes like this?"

"No. They have villages nearby."

Jo turned to study the large three-story white stucco house with a terracotta roof, large windows with canary yellow wooden shutters, and a dark-stained oak double-door entrance. The columned portico that graciously protruded from the front of the house gave the residence a stately elegance.

The perfect home for a rich and famous celebrity … and for a wealthy and infamous drug lord. Jo could almost forget she was secluded in the middle of nowhere and surrounded by an army of trained killers.

Elena drew closer to Jo and put an arm around her waist. She smiled sweetly at her and said, "We go in. I show you the house and your suite. We bathe. I bring you clothes. Tonight, we eat, drink, laugh. We are safe now."

Jo smiled back. In a reflexive response to Elena's friendly cuddle, she put her arm around Elena's waist. Joined at the hip, they walked side by side into her new home. As they did, Jo reflected on the strangeness of the moment. They had traveled like vagabonds for almost a week, having no one but each other to depend on. During their odyssey, they protected each other, took care of each other, and grew fond of each other.

Their journey having ended, Elena's way of life was about to be restored … and a new chapter in Jo's life was about to begin.

~

They entered the house through a spacious foyer. Midway through, a Latina, who appeared to be in her early sixties, approached, embraced Elena, and began to cry. Elena's eyes appeared to moisten, and she murmured words into the woman's ear while they hugged. Jo surmised she was a longtime member of the house staff who had a fondness for her mistress.

Elena's affectionate interaction with the servant surprised Jo. She had expected her to be dismissive of such displays of affection. The woman must have been important in some way in Elena's life. Jo had some idea how important when Elena looked at the woman, smiled, and called her "*persona amable.*" The words meant "kind person."

When her crying ebbed, Elena looked at the woman and said in Spanish, "Martina, this is Jo. She is my … friend. Treat her as kindly as you have always treated me, and she will return your kindness. Please prepare the guest suite for her. Later, we pick out nice clothes for her to wear."

The old woman's fealty to Elena was deep and sincere. Jo sensed that she was the one person in her life who had shown her compassion and understood the life she had endured before and since she became one of Diego Garcia's possessions. Jo found herself pleasantly surprised when Martina came open-armed to her and embraced her, as if to say, *"Thank you for being Elena's friend. She has never had a friend, and you will bring her happiness by being one to her."* Jo looked into the face of the glossy-eyed servant and said in Spanish, "Elena is fortunate to have someone like you in her life."

When Martina walked away, Elena explained her relationship with the woman and her family. "She care for me when Diego bring me here. Her two daughters work with her in the house. They live in small but comfortable houses near the fields, where their husbands farm the land and care for the animals."

Jo was moved by Elena's sensitivity. This warm and accepting side of Elena felt as welcomed as it was unexpected. She may have been frigid in her relationships with men, but it was not of her making. She had been close to only a handful of people since her parents were murdered. Jo had counted three: the friend she spoke affectionately of when she was a child, an elderly nun, and Martina, the woman who had nurtured her through her adolescence.

And now four, including Jo.

Elena gave her the grand tour of the house. They began with the first room, a massive parlor. The cavernous room featured plush antique furniture, original artwork and tapestries on the walls, and Mayan sculptures on pedestals. Its museum elegance seemed oddly out of place in the secluded mountain home of the son of a peasant farmer.

The lavish décor continued: a formal living room, a games room with a pool table and tables for poker and roulette, a library, and a room with comfortable furniture and a wall-mounted big-screen television that served as a den. The dining room had a table large enough to accommodate sixteen people. Crystal chandeliers hung from the ceiling. Below them, gold-plated candelabra rested on an embroidered white linen tablecloth. Jo ran her fingers over slick marble countertops as she followed Elena into the kitchen, where an island served as a workstation, with modern-day appliances. The room had ample space for an eight-chair round table by floor-to-ceiling windows nestled in its own rotunda. The room was an architectural marvel.

Jo couldn't help growing curious to know how they could entertain without revealing where they lived. "Did you entertain much in your beautiful home?" She asked in the past tense, knowing that it would be foolhardy for them to continue to socialize at a home that was now their secret hideaway.

"Before Diego was indicted, we entertain business associates, politicians, celebrities, and many high-ranking government officials from many countries to the south."

"Isn't Diego worried one of them might tell the authorities where he can be found?"

"Diego, he is very careful. His helicopter, it carries twelve people. He has Carlos or Raul fly our guests here. They make sure to fly low and fast and in the wrong direction for a while to confuse them."

There were several other rooms on the first floor. Elena stopped at one. "This is where we work, you and me," she said. "A desk and chair will be brought in for you tomorrow." She pointed to a room across from hers. "Diego, his office is there." Like Elena's office, its door was closed. Jo suspected they were kept locked when they were not in them, maybe even when they were.

A terrace with lush gardens, a guesthouse, and a pool sprawled out at the house's rear. A pond lay in the distance. Two cottages occupied a grove not far from the house. "The cottages are for Carlos and Raul," she explained. The place had all the accoutrements of a home fit for a CEO of a successful Silicon Valley company … or a drug kingpin whose net worth was estimated to be half of a billion dollars.

They proceeded to the third floor, where Jo's suite was located. It had a large bedroom with a four-poster, king-size bed and furniture with Aztec carvings etched into the wood. She now had access to a walk-in closet, a sitting room with a sofa, a desk and chair, and a wall-mounted television. The adjoining bathroom had a large porcelain tub. She'd soon be enjoying a bath for the first time since her bail was revoked at sentencing and she was imprisoned.

When Elena left, Jo slipped out of her clothes when the water was deep and warm. She added some lavender herbal bath oil she found on the sink, stepped in, and soaked until the water cooled.

When she returned to her bed chamber, clothes were on the bed and in the drawers of her dressers. Two Versace dresses hung in the closet. They nicely complimented the floral Valentino mini dress with the plunging neckline that lay on the bed—a skimpy, sexy costume handpicked by Elena for their evening together.

The full-length mirror reflected the smirk on her face. She had worn slacks, collared shirts, and two-button blazers to work during her years as a homicide detective—the mini-skirts and tank tops in her closet were reserved for dates or when she prowled like a feline in heat. Most other times, she'd worn gym shorts, sweatpants, and t-shirts with N.O.P.D. logos on them. Jo from before owned two dresses she'd bought on sale at Target. The last time she'd worn one before her trial was at an uncle's funeral five years ago.

Rummaging through the drawers, she found undergarments, casual slacks, and shirts, but no bras. Elena had seen her breasts and knew she'd never fill one of hers.

She slipped into her dress, stepped into a pair of five-inch stilettos, combed out her hair, and spritzed with a perfume left on the dresser. The full-length mirror reflected the end product and the smile on her face. Out loud, she said, "Not bad for a thirty-six-year-old, tough-as-nails, former homicide detective and convicted felon on the lam."

She'd seldom worn makeup and, like Elena, didn't need to. Her thick, dark eyebrows, jet black hair, generous lips, and hazel eyes went well with a mostly wrinkle-free complexion. Her youthful appearance surprised the men she'd dated when she revealed her age. Still, she applied some blush, eyeliner and lip gloss—just enough accent to make her noticeable, desirable, and scintillating. But why? She wasn't trying to nab some doctor, lawyer, or bartender. She was having a date with a woman—a very enchanting one at that—who had tapped into all her nerve endings in a way that was intoxicating.

She had a flashback to their handholding at the prison and in the Rio Grande, and their kiss when Elena had saved her from her attackers at the depot, and when her lips pressed tightly to Elena's, breathing life into her when she lay unconscious on the rail bed. She suddenly felt emotionally overwhelmed. For the first time in a long time, perhaps ever, she felt … vulnerable.

Elena was nestled in an armchair, sipping from a glass of red wine, when she entered the parlor. Two open bottles of wine in buckets of ice and an extra glass lay on a granite-top table.

Jo felt Elena's lustful eyes study her as she walked in and sat in a matching chair on the other side of the table from Elena. They redirected to Jo's partially exposed breasts when she bent forward to pour herself a glass of wine.

Jo, too, stared pruriently at Elena, who wore a sleeveless, mid-thigh dress with a plunging neckline and sequins that glittered in the glow of a late afternoon sun. The garment highlighted Elena's assets—shapely starlet legs, and firm, well-endowed breasts. Unlike Jo, whose small, perky ones were revealed because of the looseness of the bodice of her dress, most of Elena's were exposed because of the fullness of her ample bosoms.

"I was too excited to wait," Elena admitted, a salacious smile on her face. She raised her glass. "Now we toast to our friendship and all that we have accomplished together."

Jo smiled back, raised her glass, and heard herself say, "To the most remarkable woman I have ever known."

# CHAPTER 38

Miguel Galindez sat nervously in a hardwood, cushion-less chair in a one-room building with unpainted pine oak walls, a plank floor, and a beam ceiling. He suspected that countless others had been interrogated by Diego Garcia's security chieftain sitting in that chair. He could only speculate as to what happened to them afterwards.

The spartan appearance of the room's interior made it a perfect place to beat the truth out of someone suspected of breaking the rules. There were a couple of fluorescent ceiling lights without covers to provide the appropriate Gitmo ambience. The only other pieces of furniture were a large wooden trunk the size of a hope chest and a chifforobe next to it. Miguel figured that they contained the tools of the trade—a cat-o'-nine-tails to flog some sense into someone, a hammer and baseball bat to crush knuckles and kneecaps, a vise to squeeze out the truth, assorted *cuchillos* with which to cut, gouge, and sever body parts, and thirty feet of rope to hang the really unlucky ones, perhaps mercifully.

Raul sat in a chair behind a plain-looking metal desk. The top was dented—Miguel suspected by foreheads being slammed into it. Stains marred the floor around the chair—likely the remnants of wounds inflicted.

Raul had told the two men with him to wait outside. He didn't need their protection. The loaded gun on his desk was enough.

"Do you possess a cellphone?" Raul asked.

"*Si*," he replied.

"The phone, put it on the desk."

Miguel did as he was told.

Raul picked it up. "Passcode, *por favor*."

"1980, the year of my birth. I have nothing to hide."

"We shall see about that, *mi amigo*."

Miguel watched as Raul used the phone to search for contacts, text messages, and voicemails.

He found nothing incriminating, as Miguel knew he would.

"You send messages to Elena and the woman. Why?"

"I buy the phones for us to communicate and evade the police on our way here."

"Give me the phone number of a relative or friend. I call this person to see if you are who you say you are. They describe you to me."

"My parents are dead. My sister, you cannot call her … she is a cloistered nun. My friends all work for the Juarez Cartel, who look for me and want me dead." Miguel vetoed telling him about the brother. Once he was in Garcia's good graces, it wouldn't matter that he withheld the information from Raul. He'd say he only wanted to protect him.

"A convenient answer," he snickered, curling his lip. "You no longer have a reason to contact Elena or the woman—or anyone else." He put the phone on the table and smashed the screen with the handle of his gun. "How can you prove you work for the Juarez Cartel?"

Miguel loosened his scarf and turned his head to reveal the cartel's mark on his neck.

Raul snickered and grunted. "Why does the cartel want you dead?"

"I leave because they suspect I have important information for Diego Garcia. When they find out I am gone, they will know I betray them and come for me."

"What information?"

"My words are only for the ears of El Leon."

Raul glared at him through half-closed lids. "And the tongue in the mouth that speaks them can easily be removed. I have many ways to convince you to share your knowledge with me." He paused to look at the furniture in the room as if to suggest what was in them. "You will talk. They all talk."

He was playing with fire, but he possessed the Elena card. He stared at Raul through resolute eyes. "I do only what *he* wants me to do," he asserted confidently.

Raul coughed a scornful laugh. "How can you know what he wants you to do? You have never met him."

It was time for Miguel to pull the ace up his sleeve. "Elena, she told me to tell no one but him. She said that is what he would want me to do."

Raul responded with a startled look. The lioness had spoken for the lion. It was risky for Raul to probe further. To defy Elena was to disrespect her husband.

Raul's saggy cheeks tightened into a sarcastic smile. "How do you know I won't kill you when your business with Diego Garcia is over? My memory is long, like the tail of an *apache Méxicano*."

Point made—Mexican raccoons were famous for the length of their tails. It was dangerous to be on the wrong side of a man who had probably killed with impunity working for Garcia. But Miguel had no choice. He let out an inconspicuous deep breath when his interrogator looked away.

"Tell me, how did you find Elena?"

"She needed to travel thirteen hundred miles and not be recognized. Her only way was to ride the trains with the migrants, who would not know or care who she was. So I wait and watch for her in Chihuahua City, where the train stops. I follow her like a migrant on the train to Tuxtla and to where she hides in the city."

"Your clothes, they are the clothes of a *niño bonito,* you know, a 'pretty boy,'" he mocked. "You do not look or talk like the men who work for the cartels." He tapped the desk with sausage-like fingers and snorted. "So, tell me, how many men have you killed working for the cartel?"

Miguel conjured up a devilish grin, leaned forward in his chair, and said, "With a gun, a *cuchillo*, and my hands—too many to count." He studied the face of the serial executioner sitting across from him and hoped his anxiousness didn't show while he waited for Raul's reaction.

The stocky-built, thick-necked enforcer sat back in his chair, rested his folded hands on his chest, and laughed so heartily through a grin his belly shook. "I know what you mean, *mi amigo*. I know what you mean."

Miguel wasn't the least bit surprised by Raul's response.

# CHAPTER 39

Jo lay naked and foggy-headed in bed. She rested on her side, staring at lit candles on the dresser that flickered and danced like shadow figures on the wall and provided the only light in the room.

She didn't remember lighting the candles, and wondered why she wasn't wearing the silk nightgown that hung on a hanger in the closet next to her high-end dresses. In fact, she had a difficult time remembering much of anything that had happened after she and Elena ate the fine candlelight dinner Martina had prepared.

When the mist cleared, she remembered more about what had happened that night. They drank two, maybe three, glasses of wine before dinner, and another glass while they dined. In the still quiet that blanketed the house, they sat at opposite ends of the long dining-room table, ogling each other while the food kept coming. Elena started by eating her food with her fingers and licking the sauce and juice from them, like a kid capturing the last drips of a melting ice cream cone with a snakelike snap of the tongue—all the time with her eyes riveted on her dinner guest. Jo followed along, mimicking the action, and soon both were teasing one another. They wiped the residue of the mini banquet from their chins, not with a napkin, but with the back of a hand. It was earthy, animalistic, and sensual.

Elena told Martina that she and her daughter could return early to their homes in the hamlet, which meant that Jo and Elena were alone in the secluded mansion in the mountains.

When they returned to the parlor, Elena played music— soft, relaxing orchestral arrangements. She turned the lights off in the room. The moon was full, and its light beamed through the windows, creating a warm and soothing glow.

The atmosphere was intimate and romantic.

Jo remembered more. Elena had stepped out of her shoes, and she did as well. They stood for a moment facing each other in the middle of the parlor. Like magnets to metal, they quickly closed the distance between them, and ended up so close Jo could smell the sweet scent of a fine merlot on Elena's breath. She remembered being incredibly aroused. She tingled down under—she always did during foreplay.

Their arms locked in an embrace. Jo wasn't sure who initiated it, but it was simultaneous and mutual … and felt natural. In the reflections from a mirror on the wall, their faces appeared as silhouettes in the pale shimmer of moonlight. They bent their heads slightly to the side and looked deep into each other's eyes.

She remembered how their eyelids slowly fluttered shut until their lips met in a gentle kiss. The kisses were soft and brief—at first. But as Jo's heart raced, they became moist, long, and passionate.

She couldn't remember if she had pulled the straps of

Elena's dress off her shoulders, or if Elena had. It didn't matter; they were soon naked in each other's arms.

The fogginess returned, leaving her with the unanswered question about what had happened after that.

Jo had her answer when she rolled over and saw in the glint of candlelight—Elena's perfectly sculpted, naked body next to her under the sheet.

⁓

The sound of a helicopter circling the house awakened her from a slumber that had been long and dense. Still tired, she lay on her side with her head on a pillow and blinked away the sleepiness.

She stared at the dresser where the candles had been.

*No candles.*

Her cheeks puffed when she exhaled a deep breath. She rolled over and wasn't sure if what she saw … or didn't see … made her happy or sad.

*No Elena.*

She felt the smoothness of silk on her body, raised the sheet and saw that she was wearing the nightgown from the closet.

*It had all been a dream.*

Flashbacks of the past evening came quickly, like turning the pages of a photo album. They drank wine and laughed about their prison adventures, their daring escape, and the perils that befell them on their journey there. Images of licking sauce off her fingertips didn't come this time. After dinner, they returned to the parlor, listened to music, and had more wine. This time they sat close to each other on the sofa. Jo felt a pleasant buzz and sensed that Elena did too.

They held hands, frequently smiling at each other—

intimate moments that came so naturally to Jo that she had begun to doubt her sexuality.

Elena rubbed Jo's hand against her cheek and kissed it. "Jo, I know you not be with a woman before," she said warmly. "And me, only one night with someone, a long time ago. I feel close to you, as I did that night with her. Do you feel close to me?"

Jo remembered how she felt at that moment. She had never felt so close to anyone, man or woman, as she had felt with Elena. The wine helped her ignore the faint alarm bells ringing in the back of her mind. "Yes, Elena. I feel close to you," she confessed, raising Elena's hand to her lips and kissing it.

She knew Elena wanted to kiss her passionately on the lips, and she had to resist the urge to let her. "Elena, we go slow. We will always be friends ... sisters, and in time will grow closer. Can you give me some time? Will you do that for me?"

Elena looked intensely into Jo's eyes. "*Si*. I do that for you ... *mi* Jo."

And for the first time since she had met the most enchanting woman she had ever known, Jo felt guilt ... and shame. She would soon do things that would diminish herself as a friend, a sister, and a person.

# CHAPTER 40

The blip on the screen of Vega's GPS hadn't moved for a half hour. As soon as he noticed it stopped, he drove into the woodlands and found cover behind a rock formation fifty yards from the dirt road he'd been traveling on. To be sure they'd reached their final destination, he waited another fifteen minutes before going to the cargo area of his vehicle for the drone.

He knew his operative's location but didn't know the terrain or the location of Diego Garcia's home, other buildings, guard stations, vehicles, and anything else they might encounter during the raid.

Vega couldn't risk going closer and getting caught. He'd be tortured until he spilled his guts about Operation Snowfall. It made him wonder whether he'd rat out his asset. Everyone had a breaking point. Why not him? He was only human.

The drone would be Vega's eyes.

He found an open area and set the drone on the ground. Using the joystick on the controls, he flew the drone to the location mapped on his GPS. Traveling fifty miles an hour at a height of four hundred feet, the drone reached its destination in less than twenty minutes. It followed the dirt road the motorcade had just taken, and that Vega's ground forces would take in transport vehicles to get to Garcia's hideaway.

When the drone arrived at its destination, Vega had it ascend to eight hundred feet and hover above Garcia's secluded estate in the mountains. He focused on open areas where the gunship could land and he could deploy his men. The camera located the guard posts, vehicles, and helipad. The gunship's missiles would take out Garcia's helicopter, the vehicles, and the barracks, and its 50-caliber machine gun would take out those standing guard. The overwhelming firepower would leave Garcia with a greatly diminished fighting force that the SWAT team would eliminate.

He watched the screen on his control panel as it hovered above the drug lord's house and scanned the terrain in all directions. Later, he'd study the reconnaissance film and formulate a plan of attack.

The drone completed its mission in ten minutes. To stay longer risked being discovered. Vega pressed the home button on the controls to initiate its flight back to him. When it landed, he packed up and returned to Tuxtla.

On the drive back, he reflected on how far he'd come in his pursuit of the infamous El Leon. So far, everything had gone according to plan. But he had doubts about the success of the mission, more so than at any time before. Finding Garcia's house didn't necessarily mean they would find him in it. The drone recorded an empty helipad. Garcia piloted his own aircraft. If his helicopter wasn't there, he probably wasn't either.

The longer he had to wait to conduct the raid, the more

time there was for Garcia to find out from his snitches at the DED, and perhaps at the DEA, the identity of his infiltrator and that a raid to capture him was imminent. Garcia, his men, and the records of his operations would be gone in a matter of hours. When Vega and his calvary rode in, they'd find an empty house and the dead body of his operative.

The infiltrator knew what to do and the timetable—seventy-two hours to locate the records of Garcia's criminal enterprise, safeguard them during the raid, and prevent Garcia from escaping at all costs, even if he had to be eliminated.

Vega spent the evening devising a plan for the tactical assault. Tomorrow, he'd explain it to his men and to the DED special agent who would be leading the ground forces. After that, all he could do was wait and hope that Diego Garcia was home when they paid him a visit.

~

The sealed plain envelope with his name on it lay on the desk when he returned to his temporary office at the DED.

When he opened it and saw what was inside, he was overwhelmed by a sense of impending doom.

# CHAPTER 41

Jo's bedroom windows overlooked the front of the house. She stood at one and saw Elena on the lawn, casually dressed and looking as radiant as ever. She figured Elena had heard the helicopter fly over the house and was waiting for her husband to come to her.

Diego Garcia arrived in a military-style Jeep driven by one of his men. He got out and stood his ground while the vehicle made a U-turn and drove away. He stared at Elena for a long moment before walking to her.

The media photos Jo had seen of him understated his native good looks. He defined the phrase "tall, dark, and handsome." If his vast wealth had been earned legitimately, she could see him gracing the magazine covers of *Forbes* and *Esquire*.

He was dressed in a tailored, sand-colored suit with a soft luster that matched the sheen from a full head of neatly combed, thick black hair. On exiting the vehicle, he buttoned the form-fitting suit jacket that showcased broad shoulders and tapered to a slender waist. Close-fitted pants outlined long, muscular legs that nicely complemented a sturdy torso. His shirt was opened at the top, revealing a gold necklace that glittered in the morning sun. He had the three-day unshaven face that many women found sexy.

Jo was one of those women who did. Then again, she liked the mostly shaven ones too, and one in particular, who adorned his upper lip with a tailored mustache. But, in the end, she was more interested in the hardware than the stubbles.

He walked briskly to Elena and stopped, facing her. There were no hugs and kisses, only the blank, expressionless look on faces of people who were emotionally estranged. As Elena lamented to Jo in their heart-to-heart conversations on the train, her frigidity trumped any displays of affection with men, including Diego. Physical contact between them was limited to when Diego was drunk on liquor or high on drugs, and his lust for her made her lack of affection for him irrelevant.

Jo wondered what their first words to each other might be. They certainly wouldn't be the tender words spoken at a long-awaited reunion of star-crossed lovers. Elena's words would more likely be about how much profit they'd made while she was away.

*It isn't personal, Diego, it's strictly business.*

When the exchange of words ended, Elena accompanied Diego into the house, no doubt to her office or his, to tell him the amazing story of her escape and journey home.

~

They sat in wingback chairs in Diego's office on opposite sides of a coffee table. A block of cocaine sat on a mirror on the tabletop between them. Using a razor blade, he separated enough for four lines, and snorted two of them through a glass tube, one in each nostril.

Elena sensed that by day's end, the combination of drugs and whiskey would lead to a sexual encounter with Diego. Like so many times before, she'd submit to his desires. She'd go to his bedroom. The foreplay would be hurried—the quicker she got him to climax, the better. As soon as he fell asleep or lost interest, she'd go to her bedroom.

He pushed the mirror closer to her. "Elena, we share, *si?*"

She waved the back of her hand at the white powder. "Later, perhaps," she replied dismissively, leaving open the option for the stimulant if Diego was determined to have his way with her that night.

"This woman, how useful was she to you?" Diego asked, pulling the mirror back, inhaling another line of coke, and squeezing the residue from his nostril with a finger and thumb.

"She save my life in prison and plan our escape. The money she stole, we use it to get here. She is smart, clever, and brave. I want her to stay and work with me."

He raised his eyebrows, which furrowed his brow. "You trust this woman that much?"

"*Si*, I trust her with my life, and she did not fail me." Elena had never trusted anyone before … not ever. It was an entirely new experience for her. But her mind—and heart—convinced her she could trust Jo.

Diego relaxed in his chair, closed his eyes, and waited for the high to kick in. "Then she is your responsibility," he said sluggishly. "This woman, does she know she can never leave us?"

Elena glared at Diego. "I slit her throat if she ever try to leave," she blurted reflexively.

She instantly regretted these words. The thought of harming Jo evoked a pang of despair not unlike the one she felt when she was alone on the train and thought she would never see her again. But Diego's words made her reflect on the possibility that Jo might want to leave her someday. Elena's heart skipped a beat at the thought.

Her mind pivoted to a sweeter remembrance—when they sat on the sofa holding and kissing each other's hand, tender moments she relived over and over again in bed that night, fighting sleep so that the blissful memory would linger.

Elena knew in her heart she could never harm Jo, even if she tried to leave her. In the end, it wouldn't matter. Diego would send his men to hunt her down and bring her mutilated head back to him in a sack as a trophy.

The unhappy reality was—if Jo was determined to leave, she was destined to die.

Unless … they fled together.

Elena would never let Jo leave without her—*nunca*. She'd betray Diego and leave him instead. Elena's mind worked out the details at lightning speed. They'd take as much money as they could lay their hands on. She had access to millions in the safe. And her jewelry was worth at least a million more. This time Elena would plan the escape. They'd leave when Diego was away on one of his *business* trips. He'd be gone a couple of days. They'd have a vehicle, an enormous amount of money, and a substantial head start. But more importantly, they'd have each other. Together, they had been a formidable force to be reckoned with before … and could be again.

They'd cross the border into Guatemala and settle in a Central American country, probably Panama, a hub for money laundering, with the strictest confidential banking laws in the world. They'd have plenty of money to obtain new identity papers, bribe government officials, bankers, and law enforcement, and pay lawyers. They'd blend with the population. They'd never be found, not by the American or Mexican authorities … or by a revenge-seeking, ruthless drug lord, no matter how hard he looked for them.

Elena's bittersweet reflections were interrupted by Diego, who said, "This man, Miguel Galindez, how did he help you?"

"Without him, we would not make it out of Tuxtla. He tells me he can identify the man who betrays you."

"Betrays me? How?"

"He knows how we make *oro blanco* and plans to sell what he knows to the Juarez Cartel."

"Someone who works in the labs?"

"*Si*. A chemist or one of the technicians."

Diego tapped his lower lip with a finger, staring out the window. "I will have Raul bring this Miguel Galindez to me. I offer him money and safe passage into Central America for helping you and for finding this traitor. If he wants more than I offer, I agree to what he wants, and when he is no longer of use to me, he will no longer be among the living."

"He will not anger you, Diego. His people want him dead. He has no choice but to accept your help. And while he is here with us, we treat him good. I am in his debt for what he has done for me and the woman."

Diego had a quizzical look on his face. "This woman, why is she so important to you?"

Elena bowed her head and stared into the tabletop like someone deep in thought. When she replied, her words were spoken slowly, softly, and affectionately, "We understand each other … we trust each other … we protect each other … we care about each other."

Diego couldn't hide his discontent. "I have always provided for you, protected you, Elena. Why have I not earned your affection?"

Elena's head snapped up to look into Diego's disillusioned eyes. "My gratitude and loyalty you have always had, but not my heart, Diego … not my heart."

Diego recoiled, his mouth dropped open, and his eyes fixed on Elena's in disbelief. "But I have truly loved no one but you, Elena … no one but you."

"Love, Diego, it is more than the act of making love. It is respecting someone you care about who cares about you the same way. It is about feeling good about who you are on the inside whenever you are with that someone. When that someone completes you as a person, is that not love, Diego, is that not love?"

Diego hung his head and looked at the floor. "I suppose you are right, Elena. I suppose you are right."

They sat in silence for a while. Elena spoke next. "Carlos, where is he?"

Elena found Carlos repulsive. He had an uncontrollable addiction to cocaine and heroin. When he combined it with liquor, he became violent. She was surprised and disappointed he hadn't died from an overdose. He carried naloxone with him on business trips and trained his bodyguards on how to administer the injection; his many mistresses kept Narcan nasal spray with the condoms in their apartments. At least a half dozen times, the lifesaving drugs had to be used to counteract a suspected overdose.

Carlos also had an insatiable lust for women and girls of any age. He'd have the prostitutes in the compound come to his cottage two at a time whenever he felt the need to indulge, which was frequently. The sex was often rough, sometimes brutal. Elena had heard the screams of women in bondage more than once. On one occasion, the cries of pain ceased only when a last breath was taken.

His lechery extended to the one woman he could never have. She had seen the lustfulness in his eyes from the first time they met. Elena made sure he'd never have his way with her. He had Diego teach her how to shoot both a pistol and a rifle, as well as how to use a switchblade knife. She soon became proficient in her use of the weapons, which she kept close whenever Diego was away from the compound and her only protection was an elderly housekeeper.

"He returns from meetings with our distributors in America, but tonight he spends it relaxing in Mexico City," Diego replied. "He will be back tomorrow."

Elena put the unpleasant thought of Carlos's return out of her mind and asked, "*Oro blanco*, do we have enough of it to supply our distributors?"

"We opened two more labs since you were arrested. Our production has increased fourfold."

"And our profits?"

He grinned. "You will see it in the books."

"Who paid our people while I was away?"

"Carlos, I have him do it."

*Carlos had access to the money in the safe.* She suspected that Diego's boyhood friend had been stealing from him for some time to finance a gambling habit. Elena put aside her suspicions, at least for the moment. Her thoughts returned to the money Diego had made in her absence. "Will I be pleased?" she asked.

"You will be pleased, Elena … very much pleased." Diego smiled at Elena. "You come to me tonight, *si*."

Elena flinched. "I have never denied you when you must satisfy those urges," she replied coolly, reminding him that any desire to have sex was one-sided.

Whenever he forewarned her of his intentions to have

his way with her, she buried her servitude in white powder. She pulled the mirror toward her and snorted the last line of cocaine.

Diego removed his suit jacket and rolled up the sleeves of his silk shirt. "And now, Elena, tell me about your adventure, and then I meet the woman—the disgraced cop who calls herself Jo Crowder."

# CHAPTER 42

Vega sat in his office at the DED and disconnected the USB cable from the drone to his laptop. He had spent the last two hours reviewing the reconnaissance video on his computer and preparing a sketch of his attack plan.

He pinched the bridge of his nose, squinted, and reviewed the drawing one more time through tired eyes. The buildings, guard stations, barracks, and heliport were designated by rectangles and squares of various sizes, and the roads by parallel lines. A square in the center of the sketch with the initials "DG" showed the location of Garcia's home. X marked the spot where the gunship would touch down and deploy the SWAT team. Curvy lines and arrows signified how the SWAT team would disburse, return enemy fire, and close in on the target. Inked dots showed where the ground forces would deploy to set up a perimeter defense. Lastly, he positioned where he and his twelve men would surround Garcia's home, with him at the front of the house to call out for Garcia and anyone else with him to lay down their weapons and come out with their hands raised high. The drawing had all the features of a military action against a hostile adversary.

He sat back in his chair, clenched the nape of his neck with his hands, and twisted his torso side to side to relieve his upper body stiffness. His plan was complete. All that remained was to execute it.

But what he couldn't plan for was how Garcia's men would respond to the attack, where they'd take cover, and what weapons they'd use against him. For all he knew, they could have anti-aircraft weapons and use them to take out the gunship and his SWAT team before they could be deployed.

Vega's empty stomach knotted. The cost in lives and limbs could make winning the battle a pyrrhic victory … or a catastrophic defeat.

It was late. He'd call it a night, return to his hotel, have a drink or two in the bar, get something to eat, and maybe have a drink or two more. He'd then stagger to his room, try to go to sleep, and hope the mission and the fate of so many men hanging in the balance didn't contribute to another night's insomnia.

~

When he returned to his hotel, he went to the front desk and requested a wake-up call. The clerk handed him an envelope with his name on it. He waited until he was in his room to open it.

The booze and a full stomach had their intended effect—he was dead tired, the predicate for several hours of uninterrupted sleep. The hope vanished when he opened the envelope and saw through half-closed eyes what was inside— two photographs and an unsigned handwritten note that read:

"Café San Marco. 9am." He called the front desk and learned the café was a block away from the hotel.

He quickly undressed to his briefs and lay in bed with his head propped on two pillows, wide awake from an unexpected surge of adrenaline. He studied the photos again, this time allowing his analytical mind to provide the relevant context about their significance.

Vega felt a connection to what he saw in the first photo—the grainy newspaper photo of a decapitated man hanging by his feet from a tree. He strongly suspected that his head was in a casket buried in a cemetery outside Nogales, Arizona. The other photo was a gut punch for the second time that day—it was the person in the photo in the envelope left on his desk.

Vega was sure of one thing—whoever sent those photos was about to become very rich.

~

Vega walked briskly down the street to Café San Marco. He was about to meet the person who wanted to be compensated for keeping what he knew to himself—a *pay-up to shut-up* transaction.

How much was Vega willing to pay to keep Operation Snowfall and his operative alive? One million dollars? Two? So much taxpayer money had already been spent on finding Garcia, and millions more were still to be spent on capturing him. Was it worth a million dollars to not have to start over again?

The economics favored it. Pay a million dollars to save twenty. Vega was being asked to put a value on someone's life—the person he'd recruited and sent undercover to locate Garcia and help take down his criminal enterprise. If the roles were reversed and Vega was the asset, he wondered just how much the United States government might pay to keep him from being tortured, decapitated, and hung from a tree like a piñata.

One thing was certain—he needed to know the bottom line about what he was willing to pay before he walked into Café San Marco. He did a quick analysis in his head. The DEA was willing to pay two million dollars for information that led to the arrest and conviction of one of the most dangerous men on the planet—so it made sense to pay that amount. The extortionist would know about the bounty on Garcia's head. He'd be foolish to ask for anything less and, boldly, might demand a million more.

As Vega entered the coffeehouse, he concluded that all he could do was listen … and agree to pay.

He noted about a dozen patrons seated at tables when he entered, some eating biscuits, muffins, and pastries. The sweet and spicy aroma of Mexican coffee permeated the airspace. A nice place to stop in the morning before going to work.

If only his purpose was so benign.

Vega panned his gaze left and right, focusing on the men. Three were seated alone, drinking coffee, two of them reading newspapers. The third wore the uniform of the *Guardia Nacional*—the National Guard—Mexico's federal police force since 2019. He sat typing on his laptop. None of the men raised an eyebrow in his direction when he passed by.

He chose a table in a corner at the rear of the cafe so that he had a good view of the single men and anyone who might enter. A waitress came over to take his order—black coffee and a bottle of water. His jacket covered his shoulder holster and pistol.

The silencer was in his pocket.

You never know—he could need it. If the person's goals were unattainable, Vega's only course of action might be to agree to them, follow him when he left the café, and put a bullet in the back of his head the first opportunity he had.

*Dead men don't talk.*

Unless the dead man had a partner or two waiting in the wings to speak for him and sell his information to Garcia instead of the DEA.

But Vega knew—*shooting the messenger wasn't an ideal solution.*

One of the men reading a newspaper laid his pesos on the table and left the café. The other one departed shortly after the waitress brought Vega his drinks.

Only the military man remained.

Vega had entered the café at five minutes to nine. He looked at his watch. He had been there for twenty minutes. Would mystery man be a no-show, perhaps spooked by fear of being captured and imprisoned for extortion?

The guardsmen closed his laptop, put it in his leather valise, paid the bill, and got up to leave. Or so Vega thought—until he walked over to Vega and said, "Special Agent Vega, may I join you?" He didn't wait for a reply and sat in the other chair at the table.

Corruption in the military was commonplace since the cartels took control of the country decades ago, making Vega wonder whether the man seated across from him was just another one who'd sold his soul to the devil. The double-dealing and deceit had spread to government agencies and law enforcement like a cancer. The *Policia Federal*—Federal Police—were "as crooked as the spine of a hunchback," according to one journalist, who disappeared the day after his op-ed appeared in the newspaper. The Mexican National

Guard was formed for the specific purpose of confronting the cartels and combating the widespread unscrupulousness of Mexican law enforcement … but with dubious success.

"Colonel Rafael Ortega-Ramirez," he announced. "My men, they call me 'El Cazador,' I like to believe with the utmost affection."

The words meant "The Hunter." The soldier's tongue-in-cheek comment had a calming effect on Vega. "And what does the colonel do for the National Guard?" Vega asked, all the time studying the face of the interloper. The colonel's military bearing and youthful appearance suggested he had been promoted much faster than most, and his near-perfect English proved he was an educated man.

"I lead a special unit of the National Guard devoted to ending drug trafficking, gun smuggling, kidnapping, and gang violence … a noble mission, I'm sure you will agree." The serious look on Ortega's face transformed into an affiliative smile.

Vega relaxed for the first time since he'd entered the café. He had fully expected to be meeting with an extortionist. Perplexed, he asked, "Why send the photos, Colonel?"

"Because we have a common purpose in the work we do— to bring down the cartels. My people, we concentrate our efforts on the three that operate in the southeastern states. For the past year, our focus has been on Diego Garcia and the Chiapas cartel. Tell me, does the name Morales-Mendoza mean anything to you?"

Vega recognized the name. Luis Morales-Mendoza was his creation, and the asset who went undercover for him, whose wife became a widow under his watch. He suppressed a shudder at the thought of the head in the jar. "How did you know the dead man in the photo was mine?"

"A year ago, we apprehended a lieutenant for one of the cartels during a raid. Normally, like you, we collaborate with the DED on the raids we conduct. I became suspicious when our last two with them were busts. So, we went solo on this one. Finally, success. This lieutenant we apprehended, he wanted to deal. He gave us the name of a DED agent who was being paid by the cartels to forewarn them about our joint operations."

Vega wasn't surprised. He had raids go south working with the DED. "Did the snitch confess when you arrested him?"

"He wasn't arrested," the colonel replied matter-of-factly.

"I don't understand." Now Vega was surprised and also confused.

"When we learned his identity, we wired his apartment and listened to his cellphone calls. Even though we could only hear his end of the calls, he was clearly reporting to his contacts at the cartels about his knowledge of raids that were about to take place. The informant had quite an operation going. He usually demanded a ten-thousand-dollar cash payment for the information. Occasionally he provided the cartels with the names of operatives in their organizations who were getting paid by the DED for information about the location of storage facilities and labs. For that information, he charged double. When we searched his apartment while he was at work, we found one hundred fifty thousand dollars in a suitcase in his closet."

Vega now understood why the agent wasn't arrested. He continued the narrative for the colonel. "So you were able to learn what operations he was aware of over the past year and conduct the raid before the cartels had the chance to react?"

"No. To do that would have compromised the reliability of the DED agent's information. Instead, we went forward with the raids as scheduled, knowing we'd find nothing there. But before the raids, we did stakeouts and followed the men who'd removed the equipment from the labs and the drugs, guns, and money from the warehouses. We followed them to their new locations, waited a while, and then raided those places."

"A clever ploy, Colonel, to be sure. But how did you connect the dots between the photos and me?"

"We learned yesterday the identity of another of your undercover agents." The informant, now an unwitting double agent, was feeding information to the colonel. Vega was impressed. "In a call we listened in on, we heard the informant say to a confederate that he'd ask for forty thousand dollars again, like they did with … Morales-Mendoza. I suppose he asked for so much money because he had to split it with the collaborator who gave him the name of the undercover agent."

Vega moved up in his chair. "This collaborator—have you been able to identify him?" he asked, his voice heavy with anticipation.

"No. But he is one of your people."

A man in the DED who was on the take Vega could understand, but someone at the DEA ratting out one of his own, knowing he was sentencing him to death? Still, he suspected as much after what happened to Morales-Mendoza. "How can you be so sure?"

"I went back and listened to the conversation the informant had with the collaborator when he was given Morales-Mendoza's name." He paused a moment, as if he wanted to build to a suspenseful denouement.

"And?" Vega prodded eagerly.

"Of all the calls we recorded, it was the only *other* time the conversation was in English."

Vega had his answer and now had to face the grim reality

that someone at the Nogales field office was likely responsible for Morales-Mendoza's death and would soon be responsible for the death of another person he'd sent to work undercover for him.

"Colonel, I must keep Garcia from receiving this information."

"I know. We both work to the same end—to capture and smite a monster. But I cannot allow you to reveal the identity of the DED informant, who unknowingly provides us with information about the other cartels in this region."

"Then help me intercept the information before it reaches Garcia."

"I intend to help you, but we must act quickly. The way these transactions go down is for the informant to call his contact person for the cartel and describe what he is selling in broad terms, for example, a planned raid of a lab, and the fee he expects to receive. The contact person has Garcia approve the deal and provide the money. He then contacts the informant, who sets the time and place for the exchange.

"How did you find out the information the informant was selling if he didn't say what it was over the phone?"

"He enters the information in a ledger he keeps in his apartment, along with the phone number of the contact person and the amount of the payment. We found the ledger when we bugged his place. He always schedules the meeting on a weekend, so that he doesn't have to leave work or make the exchange at night. This gives us a window of opportunity to enter his apartment when he's at work and look at the ledger before the exchange is made."

"Where do the exchanges take place?"

"He's careful to choose public places, usually one of the parks in the city or the bus station. The one who brings the money wears something that will identify him. They also agree on a secret question and answer between them. It's what you Americans call 'cloak and dagger.'"

His last comment elicited a chuckle from Vega. "Do you know when and where this exchange will take place?"

"Saturday."

"Do you have a plan?"

The colonel moved his chair closer to Vega and, in a hushed tone, revealed his plan.

# CHAPTER 43

"The books, we keep them in our office," Elena said, using one of the keys on her ring to open the door.

*Our office?* She was rapidly assimilating into the operations of the cartel. She'd soon know where the labs and storage facilities were located, who supplied the cartel its fentanyl, the identities of the distributors, the dummy corporations and businesses that laundered the money, and the investments and assets accumulated with Diego Garcia's illicit wealth. Jo recalled that when the drug kingpin Joaquin "El Chapo" Guzman was sentenced to life in prison for trafficking narcotics, the court ordered the forfeiture of $1.6 billion of his assets.

Jo followed Elena into the office, which would now be *their* workplace.

The office was a large room with barred windows that faced the side and rear of the house. There were upholstered chairs, a sofa, assorted tables, and a credenza. Two desks and chairs were by windows. The larger desk was cluttered with paperwork, and a closed laptop computer lay at the center.

The slightly smaller one's desktop was bare.

Jo knew which desk was hers.

Elena walked to her desk and felt for something under the desktop. She must have pressed a control button, because a painted mural on one of the walls retracted to reveal a safe. To Jo, it looked to be about four feet square—extremely large for a residential wall safe. Elena walked over to it, rotated the dial of the combination lock clockwise, counterclockwise, and clockwise again, and depressed the door handle that opened the safe. Jo strained her eyes to zero in on the numbers she dialed but wasn't close enough to see them—this time.

Looking over Elena's left shoulder into the safe, she saw three identical metal briefcases on the bottom shelf, stacks of neatly bundled pesos in various denominations, and a pile of what looked like bearer bonds on the middle shelf, and a book, ledger, and  a box full of what looked like credit cards on the top shelf.

"The ledger shows what we take in and what we pay out. The book has the products in our inventory, what we receive from our suppliers, and what we give to our distributors."

Jo was looking at a treasure trove of evidence for anyone wanting to shut down Diego's criminal operations. A memory flashed in her mind when, even before they'd crossed the border, she considered betraying Elena *someday* and finding a way to bargain for her freedom in exchange for the information contained in the book and ledger in the safe.

But Elena—what about her?

Maybe she'd be able to convince Elena to escape with her. She'd be part of any negotiations Jo had with the DEA. They had partnered up before when they escaped from prison and made their way through Mexico. They could do it again on their way back to the United States.

Jo moved to Elena's other side, where the door of the safe angled open. She caught a glimpse of the lock and was able to see the last number of the combination.

*One down, two to go.*

Jo's eyes drifted to the briefcases. "What are in those?" she asked, pointing at them.

"Money. Diego, he takes it with us if we need to leave here. Two million dollars in two of the cases. The third one, it has identity papers and passports, and room for my laptop and what is in the safe."

Jo smiled. A well-thought-out escape plan. With hundreds of millions of dollars of wealth—and your freedom—on the line, a drug lord can never be too careful … or prepared.

"When do we start?" Jo asked eagerly. It was her first day on the job. Elena was her boss and mentor. She had only the one chance to make a good first impression.

She thought she'd made a good impression with Diego when she met him for the first time earlier in the day. The three of them sat in the parlor before breakfast, sipping from cups of coffee and brandy. She told him about the crimes she'd committed, their escape from prison, and anecdotes of their perilous journey there. From time to time, Elena interrupted to exaggerate Jo's role in her narrative, and Diego smiled approvingly at Jo when she did. He'd been polite, attentive, and asked several questions that showed a sharp mind.

"Now," Elena replied. "Today, we count the money in the cases, the pesos, and everything in the safe and see if they match the balances in the books."

"Why wouldn't they match?" Jo asked.

"I have been away for many months. Someone I do not trust has had access to what is in the safe."

"Who, Elena? Who don't you trust?"

Elena didn't answer her question, perhaps because she didn't want to accuse someone of stealing from Diego before she had her proof. Coming from Elena, the mere accusation could have unpleasant consequences for the suspected embezzler, whether or not he was guilty. Or maybe because she wanted to know if the person she suspected had sinister intentions, worse than skimming off the top.

Either way, Jo was sure of one thing—if that person was willing to steal from Diego Garcia, he was willing to betray him for the right price.

And that was something Elena would never let happen.

~

Before counting the money, Elena spent an hour going over some of their regular record-keeping duties. Principal among them was documenting every kilogram of heroin, block of cocaine, bag of crystal meth, and fentanyl-laced counterfeit prescription pill produced and packaged at the labs and stored in the warehouses. A trusted manager at each lab and warehouse transmitted the information to Elena in encrypted messages to her laptop computer, which had state-of-the-art anti-hacking and anti-virus software. The totals were then entered in ledgers, providing Diego an ongoing accounting of the cartel's inventory.

Elena sat at her desk with her laptop opened. Jo stood by her, looking over her shoulder at the screen. "The labs and warehouses and the packaged products have numerical codes that identify them," Elena explained. "We know who is responsible if what is produced does not match what has been delivered. The money is also packaged with codes that show how much and where it is kept. Diego, if he finds out someone is stealing, he has Raul deal with it … but sometimes he takes care of it himself."

Elena opened the hardback journal. "This book, it has all the people we pay—politicians, government officials, police, prison administrators, priests, and businessmen—people who have influence and can make things happen … or not happen." She turned the pages slowly. Jo saw at least a hundred names with the date and amount of the payments that ranged between one thousand to fifteen thousand U.S. dollars in pesos.

"And the ones who receive these payments, how are they paid? That's a lot of pesos to stuff in an envelope."

"We mail or deliver to them anonymous prepaid debit cards in the amount of the payment. I keep a constant supply of them in the safe."

Jo had an "aha!" moment. "So, with a debit card, there's no way of tracing the source of the funds or who is using the card."

"It is one way we clean money in America and bring it here. The cards, they are like cash. We count the cards later. But first we see if all of the money is in the cases."

Elena picked up one of the cases and walked over to a money-counting machine that lay on the top of a table. She put the case on the table next to it. The case had a combination lock. She entered the combination and opened the lid to reveal two rows of five bundles of one-hundred-dollar bills.

"Hand me the bundles, and we see if each one contains one hundred bills."

Jo took off the paper band and handed the first bundle to Elena, who ran it through the machine. It spun rapidly, and within seconds, the counter stopped at one hundred. Jo gave Elena another bundle. It too contained one hundred bills.

They followed the same routine with four more bundles until Jo put a hand on Elena's shoulder and gently squeezed it. "Elena, you're assuming that a thief would skim one-hundred-dollar bills from the stacks in equal numbers so that the bundles appeared to the naked eye to be the same thickness." Jo paused to study the catlike look of curiosity growing on Elena's face. "How do we know that the bills in the bundles are all one-hundred-dollar bills?"

Elena raised her eyebrows that wrinkled a tight-skin brow ever so slightly. "Because I counted them myself."

Jo knew that skimming a few bills off the top wasn't the only way to clandestinely steal from bundled bills of the same denomination. The analytical mind of a detective kicked in. "Who knows the combination to the safe?"

"Diego and me. But he gave it to Carlos so that he can keep the books and pay the men."

"And the cases?"

"Only Diego and me." She was emphatic. "Diego, he would never give anyone else the combination."

"Do you know how easy it is to get into a case like this one?" Jo quizzed Elena.

Elena inspected the case. "But there are no marks that show it was forced open."

"Lock the case, Elena, and scramble the numbers for me." After Elena complied, Jo put the case on her desk, sat in her chair, and narrated what she was doing. "There are one thousand different combination settings on three-dial combination locks. But the thief wants to get to the combination as quickly as possible.

"I set the numbers to zero–zero–zero and apply pressure to the button as if I'm opening the case. But I keep pressure on it whenever I rotate the tumbler rings, starting with zero–

zero–one, and spin the tumblers right to left as I go through the numbers sequentially." Jo felt Elena's eyes beam over her shoulder like lasers as she set the tumblers to zero–zero–one. Elena was wearing a diamond-studded Rolex watch. Always up to a challenge, Jo gave in to her competitive urges. "Time me, Elena." Using her thumb, she rotated the tumblers, moving from right to left until the number was reached and the lock snapped open.

Jo turned and smiled at Elena. She didn't have to ask. "Just under four minutes," Elena announced, as if she'd timed someone who'd just run a sub-four-minute mile. Surprised, she asked, "Jo, you know that from your training as a cop?"

"I know that from learning how to think like a criminal who wants to steal what's inside a locked briefcase."

"You open the case, but the piles, they have the correct number of bills."

Jo walked back to the six bundles the machine had counted that lay on the table. Elena followed in her footsteps. She removed the paper band from one of the bundles and spread the pile out on the table so that the denominations of the bills in the middle could be seen—every other bill of the fifty bills in the middle was a ten-dollar bill.

"They're called filler bills. It's a common trick when trying to scam someone who's thinking all the bills are the same. And by mixing the tens in this way, someone flipping through the piles is less likely to notice what's been substituted. I bet when we go through the piles one by one, we'll see the same pattern of deception."

They each took a case and went through the bundles. When they finished, they found fifty thousand dollars in ten-dollar bills had been substituted for five hundred thousand dollars in one-hundred-dollar bills—four hundred fifty thousand dollars had been stolen from the cases.

When the audit was completed, they bundled the ten-dollar bills—the proof Elena needed to make her case to Diego.

They counted the pesos. Fifty thousand dollars in pesos was gone. And the debit cards should have totaled a million dollars—another two hundred fifty thousand dollars had found its way into the pockets of the thief.

Jo knew that Elena didn't need to make a list of suspects. The thief was Carlos.

"We do not tell Diego," Elena cautioned. "Not until we see what else he has done."

*What else?* Carlos's coffin was nailed shut when he pocketed the first Benjamin. Jo could visualize Elena confronting Carlos with the evidence just before Diego pulled out his pistol and shot him dead. "It's not personal, Carlos," she could hear Diego say, standing over his bloody corpse. "It's strictly business."

# CHAPTER 44

After a sudsy bath, Jo lay on the bed in her bathrobe and reflected on the events of the day.

Her introduction to Diego that morning had gone well. She had expected he'd treat her coolly, like an uninvited guest. But he was warm, welcoming, and grateful. She remembered how penetrating his large dark eyes were when he fixed them on her face and said with heartfelt sincerity, "You keep Elena safe in prison, help her escape, and bring her safely to me. I am in your debt."

Her hours with Elena that afternoon also proved fruitful. It solidified their working relationship. She'd helped Elena uncover Carlos's embezzlement, something that would keep her in good standing with Diego, even if it did not bode well for his boyhood friend.

Jo glanced at the clock. It was time to dress for dinner. This time she'd pick out the dress she would wear. Elena was true to her word that by day's end she'd have a full wardrobe of formal and casual clothes. When she returned to her room, the dressers were well stocked with undergarments, mostly made of silk. She was surprised to find several push-up bras. Elena certainly didn't need them, but Jo could sure use the help.

One closet in her room was filled with casual clothes—slacks, skirts, blouses, jackets, and scarves. The shoe bins provided her with a variety of footwear—pumps, wedges, espadrilles, kitten heels, slip-on sneakers, and ankle boots.

But it was in the closet where three formal dresses had hung when she left that morning that she found three additional dresses—all top-of-the-line garments by famous designers. Below each dress lay a color-coordinated pair of high heels.

She selected another Valentino—this time a brown, green, and gold polka-dot party dress that worked well with the emerald five-inch-high heels assigned to it.

The final touches were a multi-colored gemstone necklace, matching bracelet, and a pair of diamond stud earrings.

She combed out her hair and spritzed with a mildly sweet Chanel *Eau de Parfume*.

She took a moment to look at herself in the mirror. She stood three inches taller and pirouetted, the twirling motion causing her dress to rise high above her knees. The dress and jewelry were as bright, vibrant, and multi-colored as her large hazel eyes.

The sudden rush of excitement she felt quickly dissipated. She sat on the bed and reflected on the unpleasant reality of Elena's world since she and Diego went into hiding.

Elena had explained what their lives had been like before Diego was indicted. Diego had always insisted that their dinners be formal. When Diego took her from the streets, he bought clothes for her to wear. She was a fourteen-year-old girl in a young woman's body. He purchased dresses that revealed more of her body than covered it—clothing that no responsible adult would ever allow an adolescent Elena's age to wear. He insisted she wear them at dinner when he returned from his frequent business trips. On most evenings, he'd have sex with her afterwards.

After he married her, he showcased his young beauty at galas and lavish parties for important people from whom he expected favors, where celebrity performers provided the entertainment. They were seen as a couple at stage productions, the opera, and sporting events—always with an entourage of influential people who were beholden to him.

Elena soon became a celebrity herself, appearing in fashion magazines dressed to the nines in the clothing of famous designers. She received offers to model for high-end clothiers, but she turned them down.

She was admired for her beauty throughout Mexico, but also praised for her charitable works. With cartel money, she funded the construction of clinics and schools and provided food and clothing to the poor. She was responsible for the closure of some of the worst orphanages in Mexico and the arrest and prosecution of the child abusers who ran them.

Elena confided in Jo that on occasion she avoided police intervention and arranged for the pedophiles to be abducted, tortured, and buried alive. She didn't say whether she stayed around to watch.

She didn't need to.

Jo's reverie ended with a heavy sigh. Before their notoriety caught up with them, Elena and Diego enjoyed the life of the rich and famous as respected public figures. Now, with two countries looking to arrest and imprison Diego for the most heinous crimes, they were exiled to their home secluded in the mountains. Diego's only refuge was in heavily guarded safe houses scattered throughout southeastern Mexico, where he'd conduct business and consort with his mistresses.

And now, since her arrest and conviction, Elena also had to remain out of the public's eye. Elena now faced the stark reality that she was no less a prisoner in her home than she had been in the American prison from which she had escaped.

~

They had planned on meeting in the parlor at six, but Jo arrived to find the room empty. She roamed the house in the direction of the kitchen, being led there by the pleasant aroma of citrus and spices. The thought of another meal cooked by Martina made Jo's stomach rumble with hunger.

The sound of the television drew Jo in its direction. Elena was nestled on a sofa watching the screen when she entered.

She greeted Jo with a warm smile and the wave of a hand. "Come, have some wine and sit with me. We watch the evening news and see if they talk about us." She spoke excitedly, as if she expected to receive an accolade.

Elena looked stunning in her blue pastel, A-line, chiffon and lace cocktail dress. Jo's attention was immediately drawn to Elena's breasts, where a peach pit-size sapphire dangled from a silver necklace in her cleavage. The gem was nicely complimented by vivid blue-diamond earrings and a ring that showcased a diamond in a cathedral setting that sparkled whenever she moved her hand.

Elena had natural good looks. But when she dressed up and added the slightest bit of makeup, she was breathtakingly beautiful.

Miguel stood at the bar with a drink in his hand, looking suave in a gray linen suit and milky-white silk shirt he'd left unbuttoned at the top. He gave Jo a welcoming smile, showing off teeth as bright white as his blouse. He bowed slightly, as if to say that he approved of how she looked. Then, after glancing at Elena to be sure she wasn't watching, he cocked an eyebrow at Jo.

Miguel's interest in her was surprisingly welcome. She hadn't been on the receiving end of attention from a guy looking this good in a long time. She found herself aroused. It blunted some of Elena's allure that had been building as each day with her brought them closer together in ways she never thought possible. She had a fleeting naughty thought of sneaking out of the house and meeting up with Miguel in the guest house for an hour or two of uninhibited sex.

But she knew that was foolhardy. Like Elena's relationship with Diego, she had become Elena's property, her sole possession. No one would be allowed to share her.

But could she live with that?

Perhaps not.

Probably not.

Definitely not.

She sashayed over to the bar. Her calf muscles tightened and filled out as she walked. They always did when she wore high heels or did squats in the gym. But she only wore heels when she prowled the bars and never felt comfortable walking in them. She had to practice in her room last night before her tryst with Elena.

Miguel's beckoning puppy-dog eyes surveyed her body from head to toe as she walked over to him. "Allow me," he said through wet lips.

"Chardonnay, please," she replied cheekily.

"I hope you do not think me too forward if I tell you how lovely you look tonight," he purred quietly, pouring a glass of wine and handing it to her.

If looks could undress, Miguel was staring at a naked woman. Jo allowed her grin to twist into a wry smile.

"How many men's hearts have you broken, pretty flower?" he sighed lazily as he whispered.

Jo liked men to flirt with her, and she liked to flirt with them. She sipped from her drink and moistened her lips with the tip of her tongue afterwards. "Too many to count," she boasted playfully.

Jo turned and went to sit with Elena, still locked in on a news story. A wall clock ticked its way to six o'clock and the start of the evening news.

The lead story was an on-the-scene reporting of a car bombing that killed a local politician. He had promoted legislation that would have doubled the penalties for carjackings when occupants were held captive in the vehicle and imposed a life sentence if they were injured in any way. The reporter spoke in Spanish, but Jo got the gist of what he said.

It was the third car bombing in a month. This time the victim was lucky—his family wasn't with him. Jo wondered which cartel ordered the hit. It was just as likely Diego's had as any of the others. A chunk of a cartel's business was kidnapping wealthy people and holding them for ransom. The easiest way to kidnap them was to carjack their vehicles with them inside.

The reporter turned and pointed at a heap of blackened metal still smoldering from the fire. He concluded with an interview of a witness, who recounted how the blast blew apart the rear of the vehicle, which quickly became engulfed in flames. "Horrific" was how he described the man's screams as he slowly burned to a crisp like a forgotten T-bone on a backyard grill.

The anchor in the newsroom broke for commercials. "At

least we weren't the lead story," Jo said wryly. "Maybe we're old news."

No such luck.

After commercials promoting a Mexican beer, a weight-loss medication, and women's cosmetics, the newscaster updated viewers on the week-long manhunt for the wife of El Leon.

Miguel was still ogling her. If she had to be honest with herself, the danger of being caught was turning her on. She teased him by pulling up the hemline of her dress and slowly uncrossing and crossing her legs, pausing midway to give his wanton eyes a peek into her inner sanctum.

Miguel moved quickly to a chair across from the sofa that gave him a better view in the event of an encore. He unbuttoned his suit jacket before he sat. His tight-fitting shirt outlined a muscular chest and hardened abs.

Elena raised the volume on the television and ended the vision of dancing sugar plums in Jo's head.

Three sets of eyes widened when the photo montage began.

There were photos of Elena looking glamorous at a red-carpet awards ceremony; one shaking hands with a Venezuelan dignitary; and one of her in a hard hat, standing with a local politician at the construction site of a clinic. Those complimentary photos were followed by the mugshot the police took when she was arrested and video footage of her leaving the courthouse in an orange jumpsuit, cuffed and shackled.

For the umpteenth time that week, the newscaster went over Elena's crimes, arrests, convictions, and sentencings.

Jo took a deep breath, pursed her lips, and let her exhalation slowly release like air from a leaky balloon. The news story had focused on Elena. *Good*—maybe Jo was no longer a news item.

It was not to be.

Her photos appeared chronologically—her police academy graduation photo when she was twenty-three, a photo of her with the governor when she was awarded a medal for heroism in the line of duty, and her personal favorite—the police photo when she was arrested and booked.

There was a similar narration of her criminal past.

The newscast included a live interview of a law enforcement spokesman, who complained about the hundreds of sightings of Elena and Jo that turned out to be wild goose chases. He reminded the viewers of the reward for their capture and ended the segment with a hotline phone number to call.

Elena reached for the remote and turned off the television. She looked at Jo with a satisfied look on her face. "The reward, it makes people see us everywhere," she laughed while she spoke.

His words came from the doorway in a voice that was attentive and authoritative. "You are correct, Elena. They see what they want to see."

Diego Garcia cut an imposing figure, standing tall, clean shaven, in a different suit from the one he had worn that morning. Raul, looking disheveled, loitered a few feet behind him.

"Come, my friends," he said, shooting glances with a slight nod at Jo and Miguel. "We eat. We drink. And afterwards, we talk."

~

They ate without speaking. Elena had explained to Jo that Diego grew up eating his meals in silence.

The dining room table could seat sixteen, but only six

chairs surrounded it. Jo assumed it was because the dinner parties had to end when Diego went into hiding. Elena and Diego sat at the ends of the long table. Jo sat near Elena and across from Miguel, and Raul by Diego.

The absence of chatter sharpened the sound of silverware cutting, scraping, and banging on ceramic and porcelain bowls and dishes, and magnified the sound of their chewing, swallowing, slurping, and sipping. Clearing one's throat drew the attention of the others like a sudden clap of thunder.

Jo casually watched the diners as they ate. Diego, Elena, and Miguel consumed ample portions of Martina's offerings, the men stopping for an occasional sip of whiskey and Elena a taste of wine. Raul ravished two platefuls of food and refilled his glass of tequila until the bottle he'd opened was mostly gone. All but Miguel looked down at their plates while they ate. His penetrating stare was fixed on Jo and gave him the opportunity to flirt with her.

Jo had always been a risk taker. When danger lurked, she boldly pushed forward. She was the first one to enter after the door was kicked in.

She'd let him flirt with her … and she'd flirt back.

No matter how dangerous it was, she couldn't help herself.

It was in her nature.

They looked at each other in the way men and women did when sexual interest was spontaneous and mutual, like from across a bar or dance floor. He winked at her, and she winked back, but with an eye out of Elena's field of vision. Their dirty thoughts passed between them like telepathy.

Jo knew how to tease a man into seduction. She took a sip of wine and allowed some to moisten her lips. Staring into Miguel's lustful eyes, she ran the tip of her tongue slowly around her upper lip, keeping her mouth open as if she was about to lock tongues with him in an intimate kiss. Her fish was hooked when Miguel did the same thing after taking a sip of whiskey from his glass. The foreplay ended when their facial muscles contracted into subtle smiles only they could discern.

Setting the time for them to meet was all that remained.

At the meal's conclusion, Diego rose and said, "We relax now in the parlor, digest Martina's fine meal, and enjoy some brandy and cognac."

They filed out of the dining room and reconvened in the parlor. Diego poured cognac for Miguel and himself, and brandy for Elena and Jo. A sluggish Raul, sleepy-eyed from food and drink, was content to finish off his bottle of tequila.

Diego opened a wooden case on a table and offered Miguel a cigar. "Cuban—the very best," he boasted, handing him the cigar cutter. Miguel snipped off the end of his cigar, lit it, sat back, and puffed away.

"Very smooth," Miguel affirmed. "How do you avoid the counterfeits?"

Diego smiled. "I have Montecristos flown in from Havana."

Diego lit up his cigar and blew out a plume of sweet-smelling smoke that lingered in the air like a lazy, low-lying cloud on a windless day.

Jo and Elena sat together on a sofa far enough away from the smokers to avoid the hazy mist, but close enough to enjoy the pleasant aroma of tobacco leaf that was bold and spicy.

Raul declined a cigar and chain-smoked his cigarettes that invaded the air space like a cheap cologne.

Diego exhaled some smoke in Miguel's direction. "So, tell me, what does this man who wants to betray me look like?"

"I did not see him, but I hear his voice clearly and will recognize it when I do again."

Diego looked at Raul. "You and this man go to the labs tomorrow. You interrogate the workers one by one. He will watch from behind and listen. When the traitor is found, bring only his head to me."

Jo watched Miguel as Diego spoke and looked for his reaction. He nodded at Diego to indicate he understood the mission.

"And what do we do with the body?" Raul asked nonchalantly.

"Dump it where he lives. I want the police and newspapers to report his death. Let others know what happens to the Judas who betrays his master."

"And now I have something important to say. A DEA agent has infiltrated our operations and walks among us as I speak. He is probably one of the soldiers here in the compound. We caught the first one they sent before he could harm us. I will soon know this man's identity."

Jo glanced at Miguel, who was looking at her with a deer-in-the-headlights expression. Both took inconspicuous sips from their glasses and turned to stare blankly at a wall.

When the evening concluded, Miguel left to go to the guest house and Elena and Jo to their bedrooms, but not before Jo cornered Miguel and had whispered in his ear.

As they left the room, Jo heard Diego say to Elena, "Raul and I have some matters to discuss. You come to me later, *si?*"

"*Si*, Diego. I come to you," she replied, a blank expression on her face.

For Elena, it would be another night of involuntary servitude.

For Jo, it was time to consider her options and formulate a plan of action.

# CHAPTER 45

She looked at her watch, one of two timepieces Elena had left on her dresser. She chose the stainless-steel Cartier with the sapphire-studded bezel. It was a step up from the forty-dollar Timex she'd worn during her eight years as a homicide detective.

They agreed to meet at two, the time of night when only sleepwalkers and insomniacs were up and about. The booze and drugs would keep Diego and Elena asleep in beds in separate suites on the second floor.

The circumstances were more dire than ever before. Their secret rendezvous wouldn't be the steamy, two-hour romp in the sack Jo had contemplated when she and Miguel were making goo-goo eyes at dinner.

It was about survival.

When Diego announced the imminent revelation of the undercover DEA agent who had infiltrated his organization, Jo had to confront Miguel and get him to lay his cards on the table.

She had changed into casual clothes when she returned to her room—khaki slacks and a button-down blouse—and lay in bed, fighting sleep whenever she felt she might doze off.

She stepped into a pair of soft-soled walking shoes and closed the drapes to darken the moonlit room. A pillow under the sheet and ruffled bedcovers gave the bed the appearance of being occupied. Before she turned off the light, she slipped her phone into her back pocket.

Her shoes absorbed the squeaky floorboards like sponges as she tiptoed through the dusky hallway. A back staircase took her to a landing by the kitchen. She made her way to the back of the house, left through a door to the terrace, and hurried down a walkway that led to the guesthouse a short distance away.

Waiting for her in the shadowy darkness was Miguel. She entered the cottage and waited until he closed the door and turned on a light before sitting in one of two chairs that were separated by a small table. The window blinds had been lowered and closed tight.

Miguel went to a minibar and poured himself a whiskey. He smiled warmly at Jo. "Do you want a drink?" he asked. "Whiskey, rum, or tequila are your choices."

"I'll take a pass," she replied, returning his smile with a quick, no-nonsense one. She was there to talk turkey with Miguel. "So, what will you do when you come back tomorrow and tell him you were unable to identify the snitch?"

Jo was on to him. His story was made up so that he could get close to Garcia.

Miguel grinned and went to sit in the chair across from her. He swirled the whiskey in his glass before taking a sip. "How do you know I won't finger someone just to give him what he wants?"

The corners of Jo's mouth turned down and her eyes narrowed. "You'd do that only if you worked for the Juarez cartel and were on a mission to locate his labs or assassinate him." She was willing to play along with Miguel's cat-and-mouse game. "I saw you texting someone when we were in the village."

Miguel sat in the chair opposite her and took another slow sip from his glass of whiskey. "Were you a good detective, Jo Crowder?" he asked glibly.

"A very good one," she replied bluntly.

"Then tell me—who do you think I contacted?"

"You ruled out the brother you don't have … remember?"

"Maybe I called a friend—a girlfriend, perhaps—to tell her goodbye for the last time. After all, I did meet you."

Miguel's trademark bad-boy grin returned and hung around long enough for Jo's eyes to divert to the opened bedroom door. He had his shirt untucked and unbuttoned at the top, and his sleeves rolled up. She looked through his shirt with x-ray eyes and saw the firm, muscular torso of her past reveries. Had Diego not spoiled it by mentioning the infiltrator, they'd be frolicking in bed, not verbally jousting.

When she returned to earth, she said, "You can do better than that, Miguel. If you were running from the cartel, the only thing on your mind would be saving your life, not improving your love life. By the way, what's your other name—you know, the real one?" Sarcasm dripped off every word.

He took another sip of whiskey. "If I were not him, how do I know I can trust you if I tell you who I really am?"

"And, if I am wrong about who I believe you are, how do I know I can trust you with a plan that just might save both of us?"

Miguel's voice deepened, and he spoke emphatically.

"Jo, I must have your phone. Mine was taken from me and destroyed."

Jo figured Raul had taken Miguel's phone during the interrogation. She knew he'd need her phone to text whomever he had messaged before.

But to what end? He was blindfolded on their way there and wouldn't be able to tell his rescuer how to get to Garcia's military compound even if he hadn't been.

She pulled out her phone and put it on the table. "You'll have to do your messaging here and now. I need the phone back. Elena might contact me, and I'd have a hard time explaining why I don't have it."

"I will do it now while you are here." He picked up the phone and double-thumbed a short message. The ping from her phone seconds later signaled to Jo that the person he called was by the phone.

For five minutes they texted back and forth at a feverish pace. Miguel's face was tight and tense preparing the messages he sent, and his eyes were eager and hungry reading the messages he received. Some were read through a penetrating stare as if he were deciphering a secret code. When the texting ended, Miguel handed the phone back to Jo, who tapped the messages to see the exchanges between them. But she knew she'd find nothing—he had deleted them soon after they were sent and received.

Jo's mind raced. She couldn't stay there with Elena. Life with Diego walked a tightrope, where one wrong move this way or that would mean plummeting to her death. Against all odds, she had survived the escape and perilous journey there, but she could no longer count on Diego's protection, or Elena's.

Miguel looked down into his empty glass. "We have two

days, no more than that," he said soberly. He put the glass on the table and leaned forward to close the distance between them. He spoke in a hushed voice as if to prevent others from listening in on their tête-à-tête. "So, Jo, what plan do you have that will save both of us?"

Jo moved to the edge of her chair, leaned forward and, although no one was around to hear, whispered in Miguel's ear.

# CHAPTER 46

Jo's eyes opened sleepily to the glare of an early morning sun. She rubbed the blurriness away with clenched fists and stretched out before reaching for her watch on the night table. It was just after nine—late for her getting up in the morning.

Her interest in the man who called himself Miguel Galindez did not wane when their clandestine meeting ended. She had to resist the urge to stay, have a whiskey with him, and let their prurient interest in each other overcome their resolve to be chaste. In retrospect, an hour in bed together would have been a delightful respite from the stress brought on by their precarious circumstances.

The ping on her phone alerted Jo to Elena's text: *if you are up, come have breakfast with me.* Jo smiled and messaged back she'd be down in ten minutes. She washed up and put on the same clothes she'd worn to her meeting with Miguel.

Elena was sipping coffee when Jo entered the dining room and sat in her usual chair next to her compadre. Martina soon appeared, poured Jo a cup of coffee, and brought out breakfast.

Unlike Diego, Elena spoke while she ate.

"We check the inventory today. We have many months to go over. We see if someone has been stealing from us."

"Does it happen a lot—someone stealing drugs or money from the labs and warehouses?"

"No, because when it happens—Diego—he deals with it harshly. The men know what he does to those who steal."

Jo was reading between the lines and saw this as an opportunity. "Carlos stole from the safe while you were away," she said, blowing on the hot coffee and looking up from her cup with eager eyes as she spoke. "Do you suspect he may also have been stealing drugs too?"

The scowl on Elena's face hinted at her answer. "*Sí*. He believes that I will be locked up for a long time and no one will be checking the inventory."

"Where's Diego?"

"He meets with our suppliers. He left this morning in the helicopter with four of his men. He will be gone the night."

"And Carlos? When does he return?"

"He gambles at the casinos and stays with prostitutes tonight in Mexico City. He will fly here tomorrow."

"I saw only the helipad. Where does he land the plane?"

Elena gestured in a vague direction. "Diego, he uses a field a mile from here as an airstrip. There is a building there where he hides the plane, a gas pump, and a vehicle to drive him here."

"How many planes does Diego own?"

"Three that fly to America with our products. The Lear jet is kept at a private airport he owns."

"Isn't he worried the Mexican authorities will seize his assets?"

"Everything is in the names of shell companies. The

money and precious metals are in offshore banks or hidden in warehouses." Elena reached for Jo's hand, squeezed it gently and smiled happily. "Tonight, we dress up for dinner like the last time."

Jo understood the routine. When Diego was away, Elena and Jo could enjoy their evenings together alone. They'd hold hands and snuggle on the sofa, rub their hands against each other's cheek and kiss now and then. Elena had never had an intimate friend. After a night of unemotional sex with Diego, she needed to be with someone she cared about.

It pained Jo that her relationship with Elena would soon end, and when it did, Elena's life would be forever changed.

~

They spent the entire afternoon reconciling the inventory of drugs. In the months following Elena's conviction, there were weekly discrepancies between the bricks of cocaine that left the labs and the ones that were received at the warehouses.

"One hundred and thirty bricks in all," Jo announced after adding them up, shipment by shipment. "What's a brick worth in the United States?"

"Fifty thousand dollars each," Elena replied.

Jo did the calculation in her head. "Six and a half million dollars, Elena."

"*Bastardo*," she cursed. "Our profit from fentanyl increases four times, so when he steals the cocaine, it goes unnoticed."

"You were the only one standing in his way. You know what that means, Elena?"

"*Si*. Carlos, he is the one who tells the DEA I am in America … and Diego, he would never suspect it was him."

Jo let out a deep breath slowly. "Money is thicker than

loyalty."

"When I tell Diego, it will not go well for Carlos."

Jo reflected on the plan she and Miguel agreed on last night. It was all falling into place.

Tonight, she and Elena would spend the evening together.

Tomorrow, Miguel and Raul would return with bad news, and Diego and Carlos would be reunited for the last time.

# CHAPTER 47

Jo couldn't sleep, no matter how hard she tried. Every time she closed her eyes, she visualized the look of disbelief, disappointment, and despair that would soon be on Elena's face when she realized Jo had betrayed her.

Her evening with Elena proved more difficult than she thought possible. Their first evening together after their odyssey returned Elena to Diego had been full of happiness and hope. Jo was able to forget who she was and become the companion and intimate friend Elena so desperately needed. When Elena sat on the sofa holding Jo's hand and told her about her friend Izzy, how much she loved her, and the sweet memory of their night together, Jo's warm attachment to Elena deepened. She wanted to put her arms around Elena and hold her as tight as Elena had held Izzy that night.

But last night was different. Jo's heart ached knowing that she was about to bring down the curtain on Elena's fairy-tale dream of finding happiness with someone—her. She hated herself for having been dishonest and deceptive in her relationship with Elena. She had no idea she could grow so fond of … so intimately close to … a woman so different from her in so many ways. But she did. It hurt her … a lot. More than a lot.

But for Elena, the evening was like the one before. She smiled, laughed, and touched Jo lovingly. However, Jo's smiles, laughs, and touches were the scripted acts of a seasoned stage actress. Jo knew it had to be that way. She was about to betray someone who had trusted her so completely with her heart.

She had to act with a coldhearted indifference to her wellbeing and a callous disregard for her feelings. She had to beat Elena unmercifully with a club, as if she were a rabid, foaming-at-the-mouth dog, and forget about when she was a puppy who cuddled with her on the sofa and affectionately licked her face.

Jo lay in bed and felt her heart pound in her chest, her puffy eyes moisten, and her mouth droop. She pulled the sheet up and covered her face, as if to hide from the shame and guilt, and she used it to wipe away her tears.

~

Jo was awakened by the familiar sound of Diego's helicopter. Her evening with Elena had consumed the remaining hours of Friday. It was after midnight when they'd hugged and kissed goodnight. Although Elena clearly wanted more, she respected Jo's wish to take things slow, and even that wrenched at Jo.

She wrestled her conscience for a couple of hours before the wine and weariness caused her to doze off, only to awaken an hour later. When sleep did come, it was deep and mercifully shut down her tired, achy brain.

It was after ten when she washed and dressed for the hike up a mountain Elena had promised they'd take. She wore denim slacks, a cotton button-down shirt, a vest, and walking boots. Elena was similarly dressed when she joined her and Diego in the dining room.

Jo declined Martina's invitation for breakfast, her stomach too nervous to eat. She sat in her usual spot next to Elena and poured herself a cup of coffee from the serving tray on the table.

When Diego had finished his meal and lit a cigar, it was time for Elena to speak.

"Diego, I need answers from you."

Diego turned his chair to the side so that when he puffed, the smoke swirled in the direction of an open window. "What are your questions, Elena? What do you want to know?"

"Did you or Carlos arrange my trip to America?"

"Carlos did. He contacted the distributors and arranged the meeting."

"Did he know how my driver would get me there?"

"He mapped out the route he should take—one that kept you off the main roads."

Jo studied the faces of Elena and Diego as the exchange between them grew more intense, and then heated.

"Who did you put in charge of finding the man who betrays us?"

"Carlos."

"Why not Raul?"

"Carlos, he felt responsible for your arrest. He told me he should have insisted on having another vehicle with more men to guard you."

"Did he find this man, the traitor?"

"No. The DEA learned about your trip to America on a phone call from someone who refused to identify himself.

Carlos thinks it was one of our distributors."

Elena's voice went up an octave. "A distributor? This traitor, he informs on us, and he does not ask for money? Diego, it makes no sense." Her tone grew angrier. "Carlos cannot be trusted. He is the one who betrays us."

Diego put down his cigar. "Carlos would never betray me, Elena. Like Raul, he has been with me from the beginning, through the wars with the cartels, and to this very day."

"If Carlos can steal from you, he can betray you."

"Steal? What do you mean?"

Diego's back straightened in his chair while he listened to Elena recount how they discovered the theft of money and drugs. When she finished, Diego glanced first at Elena and then at Jo and said, "Say nothing of this to anyone. I will deal with Carlos personally when the time is right."

Jo knew that the time would be right very soon.

~

Elena and Jo hiked two hours through the forest to a ridge that gave them a panoramic view of the southern Sierra Nevada Mountain Range. Elena's shoulder bag carried the lunch Martina had prepared for them—sandwiches of veal and cucumbers and a thermos of freshly squeezed fruit juice.

The sky was crystal blue, and the mountain air was cool and fresh. A breeze blew Elena's hair across her face. She pulled it back and tucked it behind her ear. It invited Jo to study the perfect harmony of Elena's face for the umpteenth time: smooth forehead; large, alert eyes; slender, symmetric nose; pronounced cheekbones; and full, heart-shaped lips—a face that commanded the attention and admiration of any man ... and of one woman in particular.

They sat on the ground, listening to the sounds of indigenous wildlife while they ate.

Elena broke the silence. "Jo, you and me, we travel to Venezuela, the country of my birth. It is a beautiful country of mountains, lakes, beaches, and rain forests. Diego and me, we travel there many times and stay at the finest hotels."

Jo washed down a bite of her sandwich with a sip of juice and frowned. "We can't travel there, Elena. We are wanted criminals."

Undaunted, Elena explained: "We fly to a private airfield in Diego's jet. No customs or airport security to pass through. Diego will get us passports with new identities. We travel freely while we are there. I cut my hair short, you grow yours long. We change the color. No one will know who we are."

Jo knew there would be no trip to Venezuela with Elena, and her enthusiasm in discussing it resurrected her anguish. But she played along, feigning excitement when Elena talked about all the things they would do together. She responded to Elena's heartfelt declarations with insincere comments like, "We'll have a wonderful time together," "Can't wait," and "I'm so excited." Unlike Elena's winsome smiles, Jo's were dull and forced. She pretended to listen, but her mind tangled itself into an anxious mess.

She should never have allowed herself to grow so fond of Elena. But her partner's sweet words, warm smiles, and gentle touches were too disarming to resist. Now those words, smiles, and touches were like a hundred tiny cuts that punished her for having to drive a stake into Elena's welcoming heart. It made her own heart ache.

During a lull in the conversation, Jo begged off with a headache and wanted to take a short nap before they walked back. She stretched out on the ground and started to put an arm under the back of her head to serve as a pillow. But Elena pulled Jo's arm back and scooted close to her. "No, Jo. You rest your head on my lap," she said sweetly. "I will stroke your forehead and hair, and you will quickly fall asleep; I promise."

Jo felt the soft touch of Elena's palm on her brow and the gentle stroke of her fingertips through her hair. It relaxed Jo, and her headache went away, along with the negative thoughts that had tormented her of late.

The last thing Jo saw before her eyelids fluttered shut was Elena's endearing smile and her loving eyes looking down at her. And, as Elena had promised, she soon succumbed to a restful sleep.

# CHAPTER 48

Vega was waiting outside the hotel when the colonel arrived in the white patrol car of the *Guardia Nacional*. Two more vehicles followed along behind, each with two guardsmen.

Vega was dressed in the National Guard uniform Ortega had given him the day before, with the standard-issue pistol in a holster on his hip.

When he got in the vehicle, he noted the two assault rifles on the back seat. The plan was for them to follow Garcia's men out of the city, pull them over, search their vehicle for drugs, and arrest them for possession of the block of cocaine covered in brown paper resting on the console.

The firepower was necessary if they resisted.

The men would be taken to a federal detention facility, where a routine search would uncover the envelope they were after. Under Mexican law, the suspects would be held for seventy-two hours and charged. Mexico required pretrial detention for drug offenses. There would be no bail for Garcia's men. It could take half a year before the case went to trial.

Unlike the United States, in Mexico, you were guilty until proven innocent. The men would be convicted on the planted evidence and given lengthy prison sentences.

Garcia's loyalty to his soldiers meant he would take care of them while they were in prison. He might even bribe a prison administrator and some guards to facilitate their escape.

"He usually leaves his apartment to meet Garcia's man around noon. If he's on foot, we have someone follow him. If he's in his vehicle, we tail him in an unmarked car. We stay a safe distance back until we are told the exchange has been made."

Vega had taken Ortega into his confidence and told him about Operation Snowfall. The colonel told Vega it explained the sudden rise of overdose deaths in southeastern Mexico, Garcia's territory.

Vega admired Ortega for taking on the cartels, an endless, thankless job that could get him assassinated at any time. Vega also admired him for fighting them on their terms and using their playbook to get what he wanted. Planting evidence that could lead to the lengthy imprisonment of one or more men was a necessary evil to commit in order to catch a monster responsible for the deaths of so many people.

"How many men does Garcia usually send?" Vega asked.

"One vehicle, two men," the colonel replied as the motorcade drove off to find a place to perch closer to where the informant lived.

"Have you considered following Garcia's men after the exchange is made and have them lead you to Garcia?"

"Of course. But the envelopes pass through multiple hands. It always ends the same way—they find a way to give us the slip."

Vega's watch told him it was just after eleven. The

detachment of guardsmen had just taken temporary refuge in an empty parking lot adjacent to a boarded-up building a couple of blocks from the informant's apartment.

The stakeout gave Vega and Ortega the chance to exchange information about their personal lives. They had much in common.

Vega's father and grandfather were both military men, his grandfather in the Mexican National Army and his father in the United States Army after he immigrated to America, where he married Vega's mother.

Ortega's grandfather served as a guerrilla in Poncho Villa's revolutionary army during the early part of the twentieth century, and his father as a soldier in the Mexican Army.

Both were the first in their families to go to college, Vega on a scholarship to the University of Arizona and Ortega on a visa to the University of Texas. Both had failed marriages and kids they didn't see a lot.

The talk down memory lane made Vega introspective. "Do you ever think about cashing in your chips and getting out?"

"Sometimes. But then I remember the labs we've shut down, the drugs we've seized, and the arrests we've made. My friend, what we do saves lives."

"Sure, in the short term," Vega countered cynically. "But there are always labs and drug dealers to replace them. No matter how many publicity campaigns warn that drug use can lead to death, it gets worse every year."

Ortega's expression held a great deal of sympathy for such an experienced and hardened man. "Someone has to lead the charge. If not us, then who?"

Vega let the colonel's question linger while he looked out the window at nothing in particular.

"He's on the move," a voice announced over the radio. "Walking east to his car at the end of the block."

It was an open line that connected everyone. "Santiago, you know what to do," Ortega said into his radio transmitter. Santiago was the guardsman in plain clothes in the unmarked car who was to follow the informant.

"I'm on it, Colonel," Santiago replied.

The motorcade proceeded through the city with the directions Santiago provided but stayed a good distance back so as not to be seen.

It was a short drive to the park where the exchange took place. Ortega and his men idled their vehicles a few blocks away until Santiago advised that the informant had driven away and that Garcia's men were in their vehicle on their way out of the city. He described the sports utility vehicle and gave the license plate number.

Fifteen minutes later, when the SUV was on a one-lane asphalt road on the outskirts of the city, Ortega radioed his men in the vehicles behind him. "Fall back a block or two and divert the traffic coming our way. We'll take it from here."

Vega reached for an assault rifle, released the safety, and set the stock on the floor between his legs, barrel pointed up.

Ortega activated his siren and flashers. The SUV slowed down and stopped on the gravel shoulder, and the patrol car stopped about thirty feet behind it.

"Cover me," Ortega said when he opened his door with the microphone of the vehicle's public address system in his hand.

Vega got out and stood behind his opened door with the assault rifle pointed at the back of the SUV. It bothered him that the tinted windows didn't allow him to see inside the vehicle.

Ortega spoke in Spanish, his words amplified by the patrol car's speaker. "National Guard. Turn off your engine." A few seconds passed and the engine turned off. "Exit your vehicle with your hands raised over your head and place them palms down on the roof of your vehicle."

The front doors of the SUV opened in unison. Two men emerged simultaneously and did as ordered. They looked over the roof of the car at each other and mouthed words that Vega couldn't hear. He kept his aim on the passenger, figuring he probably was the one who had handled the exchange and was in possession of the envelope with the information he wanted. There was no way he'd let him get away.

Ortega leaned into the front seat to return the microphone to its holder on the dashboard, grabbed two pairs of handcuffs from the console, and walked toward Garcia's men. And then, in one coordinated movement, the driver pulled a pistol from inside his jacket and dropped to the ground, while the passenger did a head-first dive into the front seat. The vehicle blocked Vega's view of the man with the gun.

Two shots ripped holes in the airspace on a trajectory to Ortega's chest. Out of the corner of his eye, Vega saw his partner jerk back and fall to the ground.

Vega moved quickly to the back of the SUV, firing one shot after another in rapid succession through the rear window. The reinforced glass shattered, but only after eight rounds were fired. It was enough time for the driver to start the engine.

Vega shot inside the window in the direction of the driver's seat until he was halfway through his thirty-round clip.

The SUV moved forward, albeit slowly, its horn blaring. Vega kept shooting into the window, taking alternating aim at the driver and passenger seats until his clip was empty. He dropped his rifle and pulled out his pistol, with his aim fixed through the shattered rear window, his only pathway to the men inside.

The vehicle continued to drift until it rolled lazily into a ditch on the other side of the road. The horn went silent and the engine stalled.

Vega knew that he must have killed or seriously injured the driver, but he worried about the passenger, who he couldn't see through the darkly tinted side windows. Was he bent over on the floor of the passenger seat, holding a gun and waiting for Vega to poke his head inside the vehicle?

Vega crouched down and hurried to the driver's side of the SUV. He crept forward below the window line. When he got to the driver's door, he opened it, and the driver slumped to his side and fell halfway out of the vehicle, blood oozing from wounds to the head, neck, and back.

Vega moved in front of the opened door, his pistol in both hands and pointed at the passenger, who was bent over and convulsing from a gunshot wound to the head.

The other vehicles quickly arrived at the scene, their sirens screaming and flashers rotating like disco strobe lights. When Vega turned to look at Ortega, he stood beside his men, holding his Kevlar vest in one hand and rubbing his chest with the other.

Vega made his way around the SUV to the passenger side. The man in the seat was no longer shaking and his head hung low, revealing blood-matted hair on the back of his head, where a couple of bullets had blasted a hole the size of a golf ball. The fresh blood had a distinctive metallic smell that was familiar to Vega from his wartime experiences.

He holstered his weapon and reached for a sealed envelope

from an inside pocket of the dead man's jacket. He tore open enough of a side of it to access the contents and found what he was looking for: the identity of his undercover agent presently enjoying Garcia's hospitality. He breathed a sigh of relief, returned what he held in his hand to the envelope, and stuffed it in his pocket.

Vega picked up his rifle, still hot from the thirty-round barrage, and walked back to Ortega.

"I'll drive," Vega said to Ortega with a wry smile.

Sirens announced the arrival of the ambulances at the scene.

"Wait," Ortega said, reaching into the vehicle for the wrapped brick of cocaine on the console. He walked over to the SUV, opened the hatch, and placed it in a storage compartment on the floor of the cargo area.

Vega was already behind the wheel when Ortega got into the vehicle. "Where to?" Vega asked.

Ortega laughed, still rubbing his chest. "To the first bar we find on the way back to your hotel."

# CHAPTER 49

When they returned from their mountain hike, Elena and Jo retired to their bedrooms to rest, bathe, and dress for dinner.

Elena and Miguel lounged in the parlor with colorful drinks when Jo joined them. She took her place next to Elena on the sofa. Her occasional smiles at Elena lacked their usual vitality. "I heard a plane circle the house an hour ago. Has Carlos returned?" she asked.

"*Si*, much to his regret," Elena replied smugly. "He will join us for dinner."

More like the *Last Supper*, Jo thought.

Miguel had stood and poured Jo a glass of wine as soon as she appeared. "The more the merrier," Miguel quipped, grinning at her conspiratorially when he handed her the glass.

"Miguel was unable to identify the one who betrays Diego," Elena announced, a scowl scarring her pretty face. "He will not be pleased."

Jo saw Miguel nod slightly, and she returned the gesture

with a subtle nod of her own.

All was going according to plan.

So far at least.

They spent the next several minutes listening to music and finishing their drinks. When Martina's daughter announced that dinner was about to be served, Jo and Miguel followed Elena into the dining room. Raul and Carlos were seated at Diego's end of the table. Miguel and Jo took seats near Elena.

The same ritual of eating in silence followed. Jo used the time to study Diego's boyhood friend. He looked to be about Miguel's age, as well as his height and weight, which explained why Miguel fit into his clothes so well. Carlos's goatee was trimmed tight to the chin. His thin, straight hair receded from his forehead and was combed back without a part. Pomade gave it an oily look. When he stared at her, she saw the glossy, dilated eyes of someone high on drugs and alcohol.

Diego had not yet confronted Carlos about Elena's accusations. Jo's proof—he was still among the living. Then again, maybe Carlos's friendship meant more to Diego than his wrongdoings. Diego might have accepted Carlos's belief that the snitch was one of their distributors and had felt that the money and drugs he'd stolen were a drop in the bucket of the vast fortune Diego had amassed with Carlos's help— factors that earned him a pardon. Maybe Diego's hard edges had softened. Elena had spared the life of the man who intended to rape her. Diego might show similar compassion for a lifelong friend.

Elena picked at her food, occasionally staring at Carlos with angry eyes. Jo's appetite was still lost—she nibbled at the small portions on her plate. Miguel's lustful stares at Jo the previous evening were replaced by an occasional anxious glance that Jo volleyed back.

Diego and Miguel were satisfied with a single plate of food. Not unexpectedly, Raul devoured two helpings and his gluttony only ended because Diego asked Martina's daughter to clear the table. He explained that dessert and coffee would be served later in the parlor.

Diego then stood and announced, "And now we talk."

Jo suspected that the moment of reckoning for Carlos and Miguel was imminent. Carlos's transgressions and Miguel's failure to make good on his promise to deliver the traitor meant neither man was useful to Diego any longer. And therefore expendable.

Miguel busied himself by going to the bar and bringing Elena and Jo goblets of wine and Diego and himself glasses of whiskey. He let Raul fend for himself. Carlos was content to sit in a chair by a distant window and snort cocaine from a tabletop.

Diego turned and looked at Carlos, who sat with his head back, waiting for the high to kick in. "Carlos, come sit by me," he said amiably. "We have a cigar and talk."

Energized by the narcotic, Carlos rose and crossed the spacious room with confidence. He sat in an armchair next to Diego, who opened a box of Montecristos and offered them to Miguel and Carlos. Both shook their heads no. Diego snipped and lit his cigar, and a few quick puffs ignited the tip. He was calm and collected when he spoke. "Carlos, why do you say the one who informed on Elena was one of our distributors?"

The rush of euphoria induced a boldly stated reply. His fingers drummed against his pant leg. "W–Who else could it be, Diego? S–So few of us knew about the meeting."

Jo and Miguel exchanged wide-eyed, dampened smiles.

"But this person, he would not know the route Elena was taking to get there."

"T–They have their ways of finding out, Diego," he replied dismissively.

"I'm not so sure, my friend. You give them undeserved credit. And why turn on us? This distributor, he had much to gain selling *oro blanco*." Diego paused a moment to puff on his cigar. "Carlos, it has gotten back to me that you have been unlucky at the roulette table and have debts you have not paid, is that true?"

"Luck can change," Carlos blurted.

"And if it doesn't, what will you do, my friend? What will you do?"

Carlos let the question linger and closed his eyes instead of responding, as if to reflect on more pleasant things.

Diego stood, walked to the bar, and put his empty glass on the countertop and his cigar in an ashtray. He opened a drawer for a piece of rope and wrapped the frayed ends tight around a pair of wide-knuckled hands. He snapped it once to tighten his grip.

Carlos's back was to Diego when he walked toward him with the rope dangling from his hands. All eyes were like fingers pointed at Carlos, who opened his eyes and stared blankly into space.

Jo quickly glanced at the others. Miguel had the astonished look of someone watching the second plane close in on the World Trade Center. Elena's expression was bright-eyed and excited, like someone expecting to receive some excellent news. Raul showed no emotion and watched disinterestedly.

Jo felt her jaw drop when Diego reached over Carlos's head, wrapped the rope around his neck and, in one swift move, yanked the rope taut. Carlos arched his back and clawed at the rope with his fingertips, but Diego's stranglehold was too powerful to allow him to work them under the rigid line of hemp and pull it loose.

Carlos's face turned a shade of blue, his cheeks puffed, his eyes bulged, and his tongue went flaccid over his lip. He wheezed and gurgled, and spittle dripped from the sides of his mouth. Diego pulled so hard on the rope that he lifted Carlos out of his seat. When the death rattle ceased and his arms fell limply to the side, Diego relaxed his grip on the rope, and Carlos's lifeless body collapsed into the chair.

Jo resisted the urge to cover her mouth with her hands while Diego squeezed the life out of Carlos. To hide her shock, she dug her fingertips deep into the fabric of the arms of her chair.

Diego let the rope dangle from Carlos's neck, walked over to the bar, and poured himself another glass of whiskey. He took a sip and turned to face Elena. "Are you pleased, Elena?" he asked in a voice that was calm but hopeful, as if he had just given her a new gemstone as a gift and anticipated a favorable reaction.

Elena smiled. "Yes, Diego. I am pleased … very pleased."

Diego went to sit in his chair. "Raul, have your men bury the body with the others who have betrayed me."

"*Si*, Diego," Raul replied dispassionately, crushing in an ashtray the cigarette he'd smoked down to the filter while watching one friend kill another. He stood, approached Carlos, and lifted his dead body over a massive shoulder, the ends of the noose still dangling from his neck as he carried him from the room.

Diego took a long draw of whiskey from his glass, turned his eyes on Miguel, and glared at him disdainfully. "And you, my friend, are not able to identify the traitor as promised."

Jo saw Miguel glance at a window to no purpose other than to give him time to think. Miguel's eyes slowly gravitated to Diego's. "Not true, *señor*. I have identified this man."

"How can that be? You came back without his head."

Miguel stretched out an arm and pointed his finger at the empty chair next to Diego. "There sat the man who betrayed you—the man who stutters his words—and the voice I knew I would never forget."

# CHAPTER 50

Vega stood in front of the helicopter at the airfield where his men had gathered for the final briefing. The DED agents had already been deployed and stood ready to advance into the Lion's Den on Vega's command.

Vega spoke to his men about the importance of the mission. "Today, we bring an end to El Leon and his evil empire," he said, his eyes moving from one man to another to personally deliver his message to every one of them. Remembering what Ortega had told him the first time they met, he concluded by saying, "What we do today will save lives."

Nice pep talk—strike up the band and bring out the cheerleaders and pompoms.

But Vega's brain refused to suppress his doubts about the success of the mission. He'd stopped Garcia's men from disclosing the identity of his undercover agent. One life saved—at least for the moment. But when Garcia learned his men were intercepted and killed, he might suspect a raid on his home was imminent. He'd know that his informant at the DED had been compromised. How else could the National Guard have known Garcia's men were in possession of information about the DEA infiltrator's identity?

For all Vega knew, Garcia had already cleared out, taking with him the records of his criminal enterprise. When Vega and his men got to Garcia's hideaway, they might find an empty helipad and an unoccupied home. It could end any chance of capturing the drug lord, who might decide to leave Mexico and run his operations from another country where the DEA did not have the cooperation of its government. Garcia's *white gold* would continue its spread through the United States like an untreatable, metastatic tumor, killing hundreds of thousands of unsuspecting victims.

Vega checked his watch one last time. "Let's roll," he shouted enthusiastically. The men boarded in single file in a predetermined order. When they landed, they would exit the aircraft the same way. Vega had worked out every detail in his mind and on paper. But success would depend on how well his men responded to the resistance they'd encounter.

Vega boarded the gunship last and took the seat closest to the cockpit. Before he sat, he tapped the pilot on the shoulder and gave him thumbs up to proceed. The aircraft's twin turbines roared to life, and seconds later the rotary blades lifted the fighting force off the ground. The pilot banked into a turn and proceeded in the direction of Garcia's hideaway.

The Black Hawk gunship Vega had chosen for the mission was a bird of deadly force—wings armed with four air-to-ground missiles, seven-shot rocket pods, and a 50-caliber machine gun. The smell of spent kerosene in the jet fuel hung heavy in the enclosed airspace of the cabin and meant that the last phase of Operation Snowfall had begun. It energized Vega and conjured up memories of his time in the Army Special

Forces in Iraq and Afghanistan before he joined the DEA. He had led many missions in gunships like this one, and the same sweet smell of petroleum pervaded the helicopter, just as he remembered. As he did then, he compartmentalized his fear of failure, injury, and death in the deepest recesses of his unconscious mind and focused only on the success of the mission.

~

When Diego learned that his men had been pulled over and killed on the morning after Carlos's execution, he sensed that a raid was in the offing. He convened a meeting of Elena, Raul, Jo, and Miguel in the parlor.

He stood calm and confident, with the military bearing of an officer delivering orders to his troops. "We are no longer safe here," he said. His eyes moved to the recipient of his instructions as he spoke. "Raul, prepare the men for a raid. We will take the helicopter and as many men that fill the remaining seats. The others will remain here until we are safely away. Elena, you and the woman empty the safe." His eyes shifted to Miguel. "You come with me. We collect the drugs we have stored here."

Jo's plan to have Miguel finger Carlos as the traitor had won him a pardon.

But was it only a stay of execution?

Elena hurried into her office, with Jo right behind. Jo watched as Elena packed up the books, bearer bonds, debit cards, pesos, and her laptop computer—a body of evidence that, in the hands of the DEA and Mexican authorities, would bring an end to Diego Garcia and his criminal enterprise.

"Let's collect the jewelry," Elena said, putting the case on the floor next to the ones with the cash.

They rushed to the staircase. It was then that Jo heard the thunder of the gunship's engines and the vibrating hum of its whirling rotary blades over the house.

# CHAPTER 51

Vega watched from behind as the pilot descended in the direction of a helicopter parked on the tarmac at Garcia's paramilitary compound.

Garcia's men scurried like rats through a sewer to predetermined positions, while the civilians in the buildings fled into the woodlands. The drug lord's soldiers were well trained, Vega thought. A couple of dozen men moved quickly to protect their leader's home, with a majority of them spread out across the front of the house. Others took cover inside buildings in the hamlet, presumably as snipers if Vega's men invaded the settlement.

When the nose of the gunship was in alignment with Garcia's helicopter and a rocket was aimed at the target, the pilot pulled the trigger, and a missile shot like a bullet, striking the aircraft dead center. The helicopter exploded in a cloud of fire and smoke. The pilot ascended and banked into a turn, then went into a dive in the direction of the rows of trucks and jeeps parked on a macadam lot adjacent to the barracks. The second and third missiles struck strategic locations and destroyed some vehicles, upended others, and disabled those that remained. The gas tanks of the vehicles set off a succession of explosions and fireballs that from the sky gave the appearance of an ongoing artillery barrage.

The sky was dense with smoke, cinder, and debris as the barracks quickly caught fire. The wooden structures were like tinder in the path of a raging fire and assured Vega that it would spread quickly through the compound.

The pilot circled and returned to discharge the rocket pods, destroying the communications and utility towers, the generators, and the ammo storage sheds, igniting the explosives inside. The compound was one massive inferno and a funeral pyre for anyone still in the hamlet. Garcia's men fired their assault weapons at the aircraft, but they were no match for the gunship's machine gun. Many soon lay on the ground, their bodies riddled with 50-caliber bullets.

So far Vega's wartime operation was working as planned— the vehicles and helicopter Garcia could have escaped in had been destroyed, and they'd set his military settlement ablaze. The gunship's artillery had thinned out Garcia's army of soldiers. Vega's men would take care of the rest.

And then Vega saw it, as the aircraft banked into another turn. Tarps had been pulled away to reveal anti-aircraft artillery guns east and west of Garcia's home. Their armor-piercing shells placed the gunship at risk when it was airborne and his men in jeopardy when it landed.

"Vega, it's your call," the pilot shouted over his shoulder. "They have two guns, and we have only one missile left." Vega sensed that the pilot was worried the aircraft could be destroyed the next time around.

Vega had made his decision even before the pilot spoke.

"Approach from the rear, hover over the house until you can target one of the weapons, and destroy it with the missile. The machine gun will have to take out the other one."

The pilot didn't delay. He banked into a turn and approached Garcia's home low to the ground, where he came under machine-gun fire from Garcia's men. Although the bullets would not penetrate the armored skin of the gunship, shots that struck near the fuel tank could spark an explosion and bring down the aircraft.

It was a chance Vega had to take.

The copilot fired into Garcia's men as the aircraft passed over, scattering them and mitigating their threat to the advancing DED agents, who were closing in. The pilot hovered over the house and fixed his aim on one of the weapons. The missile struck its target, destroyed the gun, and incinerated the two men who were operating it.

The aircraft immediately came under fire from the other gun. Several shells struck the fuselage and blew holes through the armored plates.

"Pull back," Vega cried out, not wanting the shelling to blast a hole in the cockpit windshield. Vega's order came seconds too late. Several bullets peppered the windshield and partially shattered the glass, one striking the pilot, who slumped over in his seat. "Take over," Vega yelled to the copilot, who promptly took control of the aircraft, ascended, and banked into a turn away from the house.

"We have to take out the other gun before we land," Vega told the copilot while he unbelted the pilot and manhandled him into his unoccupied seat. The pilot sat there unconscious, bleeding from a wound to his chest.

When one of Vega's men came to the pilot's assistance, Vega climbed into the pilot's seat. "You do the flying," he said to the copilot. "I'll do the shooting."

Vega was familiar with how to operate the machine gun. "Come in low around the house," he directed the copilot. "You must get close for me to have any chance of taking out Garcia's men."

The gunship circled, came around the side of the house, and closed in on the remaining piece of artillery. As soon as the men came into view, Vega opened fire, and he didn't stop shooting until Garcia's men lay dead and the weapon was rendered useless.

When the copilot climbed into a turn, the aircraft shuddered violently. "Vega, we were hit. I'm losing power, and we'll crash if I don't land … and I mean now."

The copilot nearly lost control as he banked into a turn and proceeded to the front of the house. The engines screeched angrily as the aircraft dropped from the sky, swaying side to side, gravity pulling it closer to the ground.

"There, over there," Vega yelled, pointing to a clearing a couple of a hundred yards from the house. The pilot steered unevenly to the open space and didn't need to shut down the engines when he got there—they went lifeless when the gunship crashed on its belly.

"Deploy," Vega shouted. Doors on both sides were pulled open, and the men filed out and quickly scattered in a predetermined formation for the assault on the house. Vega grabbed his assault rifle and joined his men.

What resistance they'd encounter on their way to Garcia's home would determine the success of the mission.

# CHAPTER 52

An explosion shook the house before Elena reached the top of the staircase. She returned to the foyer and stood by Jo, who had opened the door and was watching a jaw-dropping spectacle—a funnel of dense black smoke rose from the ground where the helicopter had been parked, the vehicles in the parking lot were a heap of burning metal, and the men's barracks was a raging bonfire.

"Close the door," Diego yelled as he rushed into the foyer with Miguel close behind, carrying a suitcase full of drugs in each hand.

Diego rushed to a front window and pulled back the drapes to assess the damage. Jo joined the group looking over his shoulder. By then, many of the buildings in the hamlet were on fire.

Raul arrived in a jeep with two men, skidding to a stop at the front of the house. The men, armed with assault rifles, jumped out and took positions behind trees on the lawn.

*The last line of defense*, Jo thought.

They watched as the gunship's machine gun fired randomly at first, but many of Garcia's house guards were soon among the casualties.

The end was near—very near.

Diego had the door open when Raul ran to it and stepped into the foyer, breathing hard. "The helicopter is destroyed, Diego," he huffed. "And many of the men are dead. We have only the artillery to stop them now."

Two of Garcia's men came from the back of the house with assault weapons in their hands. "They attack us from behind," one of the men nervously exclaimed. The men's eyes turned back and forth from Diego to Raul, crying out for instructions about what they should do.

"Is the machine gun in place?" Raul asked.

"Yes," the one who had spoken replied.

"Grenades?"

"A few."

Diego spoke up. "Use them if they get close to the house. Now return to the terrace and take up positions there."

The men turned and hurried out the back of the house.

Moments later, Jo heard explosions at the rear of the property and knew that the grenades had been used.

"They are here," Diego exclaimed.

When Raul glanced out the window, his bulky jowls sagged into a look of desperation. "The artillery is no longer of use to us."

Diego turned to face Elena. "We leave now and take the plane."

*Plane?* Jo's mind ran in overdrive. *How are we going to get to the plane a mile away?* The jeep was their only way, but they'd have to drive through a battlefield and a crossfire to get there. And the jeep out front had four seats. There were five of them.

Who would be the odd man … or woman … out?

~

The SWAT team moved stealthily to the house. Garcia's soldiers were not up to the challenge, and Vega's men picked them off one by one. One man was shot before he could throw his grenade, which then exploded in his hand, also killing a nearby confederate.

The four combatants who remained yelled out to stop shooting and that they would surrender. Vega called for a ceasefire, and for the combatants to put their weapons on the ground and move into the open with their hands raised.

Several of Vega's men rounded up the prisoners, zip tied their hands behind their back, and had them sit in a group on the ground.

The shooting had ceased from behind the house. Moments later, several of Garcia's men were led to the front by a squad of DED agents and made to join the other captives.

All was quiet when Vega walked to the front of the house. He was partially shielded by the jeep parked out front. Some of Vega's men had their weapons pointed at the doors and windows in case they came under fire. Vega rested his rifle against the vehicle.

Vega didn't need a megaphone. His voice was powerful enough to be heard from inside the house. "Garcia … Diego Garcia-Hernandez, I want you to come out slowly … and I mean slowly … with your hands raised over your head. Do not lower your hands as you walk toward me. Do you understand, and will you comply?"

An eerie silence followed. Only the crackling of burning wood in the distance could be heard above the hush.

Vega stood there inhaling air heavy with soot and sulphur and feeling uneasy about what was unfolding. His mind considered the possibilities.

Maybe Garcia had abandoned his home before the raid began. But why would Garcia's men put up a fight if only to protect an empty house? It made no sense. Maybe Garcia and his wife had taken the coward's way out—a Hitler-Braun-like double suicide. A life behind bars awaited them if they surrendered—it may have been too much for them to accept.

Beads of perspiration formed on Vega's forehead, and his mouth went dry. He checked his GPS locator—it hadn't moved. His asset was in the house and did not call out when he spoke.

*The dead can't speak.*

Vega's stomach knotted with apprehension. He'd come so close to having executed the perfect plan. Among his men, only the pilot had been injured. But now the person he recruited to locate Garcia and help bring down his criminal organization—the person most responsible for the success of Operation Snowfall—had been sacrificed in the process. The thought of what he might find when he entered the house repulsed him.

He raised his hand and waved forward a detachment of his men, who moved in a V-shaped formation to the house with Vega in the lead, his pistol drawn. When he reached the front doors, he opened one slowly, and he and two of his men entered the house.

It was quiet inside—dead quiet. They separated and searched for the bodies in silence. Vega took the first floor and directed the others to the upper floors with his eyes and a pointed finger. He went from room to room and worked his way to the back of the house. Finding no bodies on the first floor, he returned to the foyer where his men waited, and he learned the awful truth.

No one was there.

# CHAPTER 53

They proceeded through the tunnel like miners looking for a coal deposit. The shaft ran in a straight line, seven feet high and six feet wide, with plaster walls and a concrete floor. The overhead fluorescent lights provided enough illumination for them to proceed without having to slow down as they passed through.

They walked with strident purpose, breathing stagnant air without uttering a word. Freedom lay a mile away. At the pace they were moving, Jo figured they'd be there in twenty minutes.

She reflected on their narrow escape as she followed Elena through the tunnel. When she'd heard the call for Diego to come out, she believed his capture was imminent. But he responded to the crisis as if he had anticipated it. He told Miguel to leave the suitcases of drugs and Elena to forget the briefcases of money. "There's money on the plane," he said. "Bring only the case with our records and your computer."

They had been mustered in the kitchen when he gave his instructions. Jo was closest to the hallway that led to Elena's office, where the briefcases had been placed. "I'll get it," she shouted and quickly turned and dashed from the room.

When Jo returned, she handed the briefcase to Diego, who led them into a storage room near the kitchen at the rear of the house. He moved a can of beans on one of the shelves, behind which was an inconspicuous latch with a covert purpose. When he pulled it, the shelving loosened from the wall and opened like a door to reveal the entranceway to the tunnel. Diego returned the can to its place and led the way. Miguel and Raul followed him. Jo lagged behind Elena. When she hurried around the shelving, she bumped the wooden frame with her shoulder, hard enough to shake the shelves and upend a couple of the bottles, one crashing to the floor.

Elena stopped and turned. "Are you hurt, Jo?"

"No, just clumsy," she replied, rubbing her shoulder.

After they had descended the staircase, Diego pulled back the rack of provisions tight to the wall until it clicked shut.

The brisk pace of their march caused the portly Raul to lag behind the others, and he was breathing hard halfway through.

As they approached the end of the tunnel, daylight beamed into the shaft and signaled their impending arrival at the airstrip—a field of tamped down grass disguised as a pasture. A Quonset hut that served as the hangar for Diego's plane stood a couple of hundred yards away. They huddled near the makeshift runway.

Diego turned to address the group. "Elena, you come with me," he demanded. "The rest of you wait here. Raul will guard the tunnel in case they find it and follow us here. I will fuel the plane, taxi here, and you can join us then."

When Diego motioned to Elena to come with him, Jo saw Miguel looking at her and shaking his head. She sensed he had the same uneasy feeling about their circumstances.

Did Diego really intend to take Miguel and her with them? He had the records of his operations in the briefcase he was carrying, and he had Elena with him. There was no reason to come back, unless it was for his faithful lieutenant … and only for him.

Jo and Miguel's eyes met for a telepathic mind read. Why didn't Diego want them to walk to the hangar with Elena and board the plane under cover of the building? Raul had his pistol. Miguel and Jo were unarmed and of no use to him if DEA agents had followed them through the tunnel.

Elena moved closer to her friends. "No, Diego. I stay here with them." The inflection in her voice was forceful and resolute.

Jo's mind exploded into a whirlpool of suspicion. Did Elena suspect that Diego might not be true to his word? She and Miguel were no longer of use to him. He may have worked it out with Raul to shoot them dead the moment the plane left the hangar.

Diego glared at Elena. "Come with me, Elena," he commanded a second time. "We are wasting time. I may need your help." His tone had a noticeable edge to it that was purposeful.

Still Elena defied him. "Diego, you go and be quick," she insisted.

Diego's face tightened into a scowl. Once Elena had made up her mind about something important to her, no one could change it. Not even Diego.

Diego turned and ran in the direction of the hangar.

The only unanswered questions were—would Diego come back for Elena, and who would be alive if he did?

~

Vega did a quick assessment of the situation. Garcia's helicopter was there when the raid began, so he'd been at the compound and, most likely, in the house. If he was there, his wife was too. The GPS locator proved that his agent was at that location just minutes ago.

He checked his GPS locator again. The blip hadn't moved. But the body wasn't in the house, which sat on a concrete slab—no basement. He checked again, and the blip was at a new location. His device showed movement every three hundred yards. His asset was three football fields away. But where? How did they avoid detection? The perimeter defense cut off all escape routes.

A neuron sparked. "There's a tunnel," he announced to his men. "It would be accessible from the first floor. Spread out and check the floors and walls. Look for a trap door under the carpets and seams in the walls that might be a hidden entranceway."

Vega worked his way to the back of the house, concentrating on the closets—a good place to conceal a secret door. Finding none, he made his way into the kitchen with his men.

"We can exclude walls and floors with heavy furniture and appliances," Vega said. "There would be no way to push them back in place."

"What about a storage room?" one of his men asked when he opened the door to the room.

Vega hurried over to the agent. "Yes, a good place to put it. Near the back of the house in a windowless room. They'd have less tunneling to do under the concrete foundation."

The agents checked the floor and walls for seams and found none, nor anything else suspicious.

Garcia saw the shelving and tugged at the sides. It didn't budge.

Another dead end.

And then he noticed it—a bottle was upended on one of the shelves and another bottle lay broken on the floor below it, as if they had tipped over when the wall of shelves was opened or slammed shut.

"Empty the shelves," Vega said excitedly. "Look for a handle, lever, or button."

The men did as ordered and quickly located a lever that sprung open one side of the shelving when Vega pulled it. He descended the staircase to the tunnel entrance with his men close behind. "You, come with me," he ordered the agent closest to him. "And you," he said to the other, "Round up a half-dozen men and follow us through the tunnel."

Pistol in hand, Vega led the way, with his agent on his heels.

# CHAPTER 54

**"T**hat was a lot of money for Diego to leave behind," Jo said to Elena, who stood between Miguel and her.

Elena shook her head and waved a dismissive hand. "The money is of little importance. But the records—if the authorities had them, it would mean an end to our operations."

Jo had seen the records and knew Elena was right. The DEA and National Guard would move quickly to close down the drug labs and supply lines, confiscate money and drugs in warehouses in Mexico and the United States, arrest distributors, and seize assets.

But unless they captured Diego, she knew it wouldn't be the end of the road for El Leon. Arranging raids, making arrests, procuring an indictment, and seizing assets would take time. On the loose, Diego would move quickly to safeguard many of his assets by hiding them somewhere else. He'd have plenty of seed money to start over and would be back in business in a few months.

The records were important, but capturing Diego Garcia

was crucial—it was the only way to end his reign of terror … once and for all.

When Diego entered the hangar, Raul moved to a position about twenty feet from the group. He pulled out his pistol and pointed it at Miguel. "Elena, come and stand by me. The woman, you stay where you are."

Elena moved closer to Jo. "What are you doing, Raul?" she demanded to know.

"The man and this woman do not come with us. Diego, he wants it that way."

Jo's eyes shifted from Elena to Miguel, who moved his right foot back and his upper body forward just enough to suggest he would lunge at Raul the first chance he had. With the gun still pointed at him, Miguel had no hope of covering the distance between them. He'd be shot dead halfway there. Miguel needed Raul distracted long enough to give him a good head start.

When Raul redirected his aim and pointed the gun at Jo, Elena stepped in front of her. "You fool. Put the gun away. I talk to Diego, and he will change his mind."

Raul grunted. "He told me you would say that. That is why he wanted you to go with him to the plane, so you do not see what I have to do."

"What you have to do is put the gun away and let me talk to Diego," she repeated, her voice an octave higher.

Raul turned his attention back to Miguel. He glared at him with evil eyes. "My friend, I told you that when your business with Diego Garcia was over, I might have to take care of you. Now, walk to the tunnel. *Vamos!*"

The haunted expression Miguel directed at Jo told her it was for the last time. His fate seemingly sealed, he turned and walked in the direction of the tunnel.

The moment Raul turned his back on Elena, she pulled out a derringer from a holster strapped to her calf, hidden by the pant leg of her slacks. She stepped away from Jo and pointed the gun at Raul, who was then much closer to Miguel.

"Put the gun away, Raul, or I will shoot you. I only ask the one time."

The sound of propellers drew Jo's attention to the hangar. The airplane rolled out of the building onto the field, with Diego in the pilot's seat.

Elena walked toward Raul, closing the distance between them. It was the right thing to do. Jo sometimes carried a two-shot derringer as a backup weapon. It had saved her life once. But, even in the hands of an experienced shooter, a derringer was much less accurate than a pistol. Jo knew that Elena had at best a fifty-fifty chance of hitting Raul, even if she managed to get off both rounds before Raul's semiautomatic handgun blasted her off her feet.

Raul froze when Elena spoke and turned to face her. It gave Miguel the opportunity he needed. He covered the distance between them quickly and lunged at Raul just as he pointed his gun at Elena. He tackled the big man, who hit the ground face down on his belly with Miguel on top of him.

Raul outweighed Miguel by at least sixty pounds, and much of it was muscle. He managed to roll over just enough to raise his gun hand and elbow Miguel in the face. The strike was delivered by an arm twice the size of an average man.

The blow stunned Miguel and knocked him off Raul's back. While he lay on the ground, regaining his senses, Raul stood and pointed the gun at him. But Miguel was close enough to kick Raul's legs out from under him and cause him to tumble hard to the ground. The gun flew out of his hand and clattered away.

Miguel quickly straddled Raul, sat on his massive chest, and punched him repeatedly in the face. But Raul blocked a punch and delivered a powerful right cross to Miguel's face that knocked him on his back.

Jo watched, Elena by her side with the gun still in her hands and pointed in Raul's direction, but their scuffling made it just as likely she'd hit Miguel if she tried to shoot Raul.

Raul managed to get his arms around Miguel in a wrestler's hold and pin him to the ground, but Miguel squirmed and rocked and was able to muster the strength to break free.

Both lay on the ground out of breath from exhaustion—Raul on his back and Miguel on his hands and knees. They looked at each other and then at the gun, only a few feet from Raul. When he rolled over to grab it, Miguel, now in a sprinter's stance, dove for the gun.

Raul got to it first.

When Miguel hit the ground, he landed on Raul and grabbed his gun hand by the wrist. The gun moved wildly in Raul's hand in all directions. Inevitably, it fired with Raul's finger on the trigger.

The bullet struck Elena in the chest. She fell backwards to the ground, the derringer still in her hand. She bled profusely from the wound, and her white blouse was soon the color of deep scarlet.

Jo looked over and saw Raul pointing his pistol at Miguel, who lay helpless on the ground. She bent over and grabbed the gun from Elena's flaccid grip. Raul spun to shoot Jo when he saw her pointing the derringer at him.

The rounds fired simultaneously and sounded like a single shot. They both struck their targets—Jo's in Raul's belly and Raul's in Jo's shoulder.

The derringer dropped from Jo's hand when she fell to the

ground on her back. She felt her right arm go numb.

Raul, bleeding from his abdominal wound, still had the strength to turn his gun on Miguel.

There was a round left in the derringer, but her gun hand was useless to her. She reached over, put the gun in her left hand, and pointed it at Raul—the weapon shook in her hand.

One shot, one chance—and only dumb luck to rely on.

The shot Jo heard didn't come from the derringer, and it didn't come from Raul's gun. It came from a pistol in the hands of a Latino dressed in the SWAT uniform of the DEA.

Vega stood at the tunnel with his gun still pointed at Raul, who lowered his head, stared at the blood gushing from the hole in his shirt and, two blinks of his eyes later, fell dead to the ground.

# CHAPTER 55

Jo sat listlessly on the ground, cradled Elena in her one good arm, and with the only hand that worked, she applied pressure to the gunshot wound to her chest. Blood seeped through Jo's fingers and commingled with blood that dripped from her shoulder wound.

*Blood sisters … now and forevermore.*

Vega ran over to where the women were on the ground. Jo's glossy eyes fixed on Elena's face, whose normally vibrant tawny complexion paled a shade from the loss of blood. Without looking up, Jo said to Vega, "He's in the plane. Stop the bastard. End it now."

Vega turned to face his men and shouted to them to take positions near the runway and open fire on Garcia's plane, which was about to take off.

Miguel rushed over to Jo, who waved him off with a shake of her head. She needed to be alone with Elena while her life slipped away. He backed off to give her the privacy her tearful eyes so desperately screamed out for.

Jo had seen bullet wounds that had punctured the heart before—the blood loss was impossible to stop without immediate surgical intervention. The heart was no longer able to pump oxygenated blood to the brain. Blood pressure dropped to zero. The victim lasted only minutes.

Jo had never felt more helpless than she did at that moment. The Latina beauty, who had been her friend, companion, and protector, lay dying in front of her, and she could do nothing to stop it.

The sound of gunfire made it difficult for her to hear Elena's final words. The numbness in Jo's arm was gone; only the pain in her shoulder remained. She wrapped the limp arm around Elena to complete a warm embrace and pulled her closer until she could feel Elena's faint breath on her cheek.

Elena used her remaining strength to raise her hand and tenderly touch Jo's cheek and then her lips with her fingertips.

*"Mi Jo, te amo,"* were the last words Elena ever said, and "My Elena, I love you," were the last words she ever heard.

Jo blinked away her tears and looked lovingly into Elena's eyes one last time, and with her last breath about to be taken, Jo pressed her lips against Elena's for one last kiss.

When he shot and killed Garcia's man, Vega breathed a sigh of relief—the person he'd sent undercover to locate Garcia and bring down his criminal organization was still alive. But Garcia was about to get away.

His gunship sat grounded, useless to him, and his men were too far away to cause enough damage to Garcia's plane to disable it. All that they could do was create a diversion and buy Vega some time.

He pulled out his radio, dialed in a frequency, and called the only person left who could stop the infamous drug lord.

Garcia maneuvered his plane as far away from the gunfire as possible without making the runway too short for takeoff. He stopped and revved the twin engines until the propellers spun at maximum velocity.

Vega watched from his location behind his men as Garcia's plane taxied into position, sped down the field, and lifted off.

And then he saw it—the gunship he had in reserve. It approached and circled the airstrip and fired its machine gun at the plane, but without success. Garcia's plane banked into an ascending turn. Vega's mind screamed, *Use the rockets! End it now … once and for all.*

As if the pilot had just been given his orders, he fixed his sights on Garcia's plane and fired two rockets. A heartbeat later the plane—and Garcia—exploded into a dusty cloud of a million tiny pieces.

The gunship returned and landed in the field. The person in the pilot's seat opened his door and stepped onto the field. Vega and the pilot met midway and shook hands.

"It's over, Colonel," Vega said, a relaxed smile on his face.

"No, my friend, it's not over," Ortega responded. "It's just the beginning, a very good beginning."

~

Jo held Elena tightly until she regained her composure and then rested her sister's head on the ground with her arms by her side. Before she stood, she touched Elena's cheek and lips with her fingertips one last time.

Miguel had watched Jo from a distance. He walked over and put his arms around her. Oddly, Jo felt like it was Elena's arms holding her close. When the tenderness of the embrace had served its purpose, she looked up at Miguel and smiled gratefully at him for having comforted her.

"I want to take off your shirt," he said when they separated.

"I bet you do," she responded playfully, her mood only slightly improving.

He smiled. "I want to examine your wound."

She was wearing a long-sleeved cotton pullover. He removed the sleeve from her good arm first, worked the shirt slowly over her head, and pulled it gently off her injured shoulder. Jo was thankful she had a push-up bra to exaggerate her assets.

Miguel threw her shirt over his shoulder and palpated the bony structures in Jo's shoulder with experienced fingers. "Nothing's broken. There's an exit wound. The bullet passed through cleanly, and the bleeding has mostly stopped." He ripped off the sleeves from her bloodstained shirt, tied them together, and used the cloth to bandage her shoulder. He then removed his shirt and put it on her. "Once the wounds are cleaned and sutured, other than a sore shoulder, you'll be fine."

"So?" Jo asked, a curious look on her face.

"So … what?" he responded quizzically.

"So, what's your name and who are you?"

He grinned cockily. "Major Gabriel Navarro-Gutiérrez, Mexican National Guard, at your service. My friends call me Gabe. And I do have a brother, three of them in fact, and a sister who is a nun. How do you think I got the clothes you wore?"

Jo laughed. "Four brothers. No wonder your sister became a nun. I have three younger brothers who fought a lot growing up, which is why I became a cop. Someone had to keep the peace." Jo had an ulterior motive for her next question. "I bet your *wife* was an unhappy woman when you agreed to take this assignment."

"Which is why I'm not married," he replied—much to Jo's delight.

Ortega approached Navarro and embraced him like a brother. "Well done, Major."

"Not quite, sir," he replied. "When you blew up the plane, you destroyed the records we needed to shut down Garcia's operations."

Jo spoke up. "Not true … Gabe." She had hesitated before saying his name, but it felt good when she did.

"Why so?" Navarro asked.

"Remember? I rushed out to get the briefcase with the records?"

"Yes, and you brought it back and gave it to Garcia. It was on the plane with him."

"If you are inclined to comb the woods for debris from the plane, you just might find a C-note or two out there."

Navarro laughed heartily. "You brought back the briefcase with the money. Jesus, Jo, weren't you afraid he'd find out?"

"He was about to be caught and needed to get out of there. I figured he wouldn't take the time to open the lock and look in the briefcase. And if you're a betting man, I'll bet you dinner at a swanky restaurant that I can open the lock on that briefcase in under four minutes."

He laughed. "You're on. It's a bet I win even if I lose."

Vega stepped closer to Jo. "How's your wound?"

"I'll be all right," she replied stoically.

"I suppose it was you who upended the bottles on the shelf."

By then, Navarro knew how to read the look on Jo's face and answer for her. "Of course, she did, and she knew I wasn't who I claimed to be—almost from the beginning."

Jo turned a somber gaze on Elena's body. Still puffy-eyed, she made eye contact first with Vega and then Ortega. "You take good care of her. She was an extraordinary woman whose life was ruined by awful men. She had no one she could trust or love. But there was much good in her." She turned for one last, painful look at the wife of El Leon.

Vega addressed Jo. "You go with the colonel and major and get the treatment you need. We'll talk later."

Jo nodded.

"One last thing," Vega said. He pulled out the envelope he had taken from Garcia's man and handed it to Jo. "I thought you should have it."

Jo put the envelope in the waistband of her slacks.

⁓

Navarro sat next to Jo on the gunship. "Aren't you going to look in the envelope?" he asked.

Jo just shrugged. "I know what's in it."

"Can I see it?"

"Sure." She handed him the envelope.

He opened it and took out a photograph. He studied it like he was looking at a Picasso for the first time. "I know this person."

"That makes two of us," she quipped. "Striking resemblance, I know."

"How did you pull it off?" Navarro asked.

Jo closed her eyes and rested her head on the back of her seat. "It's a long story."

Navarro reached out for Jo's hand, patted it gently, and said, "And I intend to give you all the time you need to tell it."

# CHAPTER 56

After the raid on Garcia's hideaway, Vega and Ortega combined forces and moved quickly to shut down his labs, seize the drugs and money in his warehouses, strangle his supply lines, and arrest his distributors. They figured they had at most a week before news of the raid and Garcia's death leaked and went viral. Until then, Jo's involvement in Operation Snowfall had to remain secret.

She was still a convicted felon and an escaped convict on the loose in Mexico. Vega put her in a suite in his hotel under a different name, and he arranged for some clothes to be brought to her. He also provided her with a stipend for her expenses while she remained in Mexico.

Navarro was put in charge of her security. Ortega knew the assignment would please him.

And it pleased Jo too.

The next day, Gabe and Jo met at Café San Marco. He wore his military uniform, and Jo was casually dressed in slacks and a button-down blouse. With a new identity and under the protection of the Mexican National Guard, she didn't need a disguise.

They sat inconspicuously at a corner table in the back of the café and enjoyed biscuits and jam with coffee. Jo smiled and chuckled when the expressions on Gabe's face triggered memories of things he'd done she found amusing, like clandestinely singing love ballads to her in the car on their way to San Cristóbal and discreetly flirting with her the first night they dined with Diego.

Gabe finished his coffee and motioned to the waitress for a refill. When the server was out of earshot, he asked, "So tell me, how did you pull it off?"

Jo sat back in her chair, squeezed her eyes shut for a moment to clear her head, opened them wide again, and recounted how it all came about.

"I met Vega for the first time when he came to my house and explained who he was and that his mission was to find Diego Garcia and shut down his operations. I was aware of the drug lord's notoriety, and that his wife had been recently sentenced and incarcerated for shooting a Louisiana cop. Vega explained who we were dealing with—the kind of people Diego and Elena were."

The mention of Elena made Jo smile, but only for a moment. The bittersweet memories of her still hurt too much. "He told me he'd done his homework on me. That I met all of the criteria for a role in Operation Snowfall. Well-trained in the use of firearms and martial arts. Able to defend myself with and without a weapon. He'd reviewed newspaper accounts of my arrests and interviews I'd given, knew I'd gone undercover before …" She trailed off, still thinking of Elena. Gabe didn't press, instead giving her all the time she needed.

"Vega knew I'd bent the rules, even broke them to make

an arrest—a quality he prized as especially high. He needed someone who could not only think like a criminal, but act like one … be one. He was convinced it was the only way for Operation Snowfall to succeed and for me to survive.

"My mission was to locate Garcia's hideaway, assist in his capture, and safeguard any evidence of his criminal operations I found."

"What a coincidence," Gabe said, eyes twinkling. His smile  warmed her up, and she smiled back.

"Vega believed the best way to get to Garcia was through his wife. I had to earn her trust, help her escape from prison, and make sure she didn't get caught, kidnapped, or killed on her way to her husband." Jo paused to look down and smile, as if reflecting on a pleasant memory. "As things turned out, Elena was quite capable of taking care of herself … and me … on our journey through Mexico.

"I needed to be a lot like Elena if I had any chance of having a relationship with her. A disgraced cop convicted of drug trafficking, serving a lengthy prison term, and wanting to escape to Mexico were the common denominators that brought us together, Gabe. But to be convincing to Elena, I had to convince myself I was the person Elena thought I was. A CIA psychologist in special ops counseled me on how to think and act like the person I was supposed to be and have the mindset to do whatever was necessary to accomplish the mission—whether it was sleeping with my adversary or killing him … or her."

"A sort of brainwashing—to act without doubting yourself," Gabe concluded.

"Precisely. And you don't know how close you came to getting a bullet that night in the chapel when you got up during the night and stood over Elena. It didn't matter to me if you were a good guy or a bad guy. I was there to protect Elena. If you had reached for your gun instead of your cigarettes, I would have shot you for sure, not a lethal shot—one in your shoulder. It would have been Elena who finished you off as soon as I gave back her gun."

"So, you had Elena's gun and were awake watching me."

"Right. Elena and I had agreed to take shifts. When you came back after your smoke, she was the one awake with the gun."

"And your arrest and conviction? How did they come about?"

"Vega arranged for drugs and money he'd seized in a Medellín cartel drug bust to be stored in a warehouse in New Orleans. He made an anonymous tip to me about its location. That put me in charge of the raid and gave me the opportunity to steal the drugs and money, which I did for real." She laughed, bitterness and amusement coming through equally. "That led to my arrest and conviction. Vega made sure there was a security camera across the street from the warehouse to show me committing the crime. Hello, twenty-five-year prison sentence."

Gabe interrupted the narrative. "So, the judge, prosecutor, and your lawyer were in on the ruse."

"No. The more people who knew, the greater the chance of a leak. I went through the criminal justice system like any other defendant. But it played out like we knew it would. Vega and I engineered it that way."

Jo's breathing became shallow—remembrances of the criminal proceedings and the judgmental faces of her family had momentarily taken her breath away.

She continued. "Vega arranged through his connections to have Elena transferred to where I was imprisoned. The prison had a Latina inmate whose brothers were killed by Garcia's men. It was inevitable this prisoner would want to get even. I had to make sure Elena saw my boxing and martial arts skills in the exercise yard. With no one to protect her, Vega was sure she'd come to me.

"Still, I had my doubts. She could have refused to want my help and faced down Moreno on her own or have reached out to someone else to be her bodyguard. She had the money in her prison account to pay for protection."

"Did Vega help you escape from prison?"

"He told me I was on my own to figure out a way to escape, but he pulled strings to get me into the easiest prison facility to escape from. Our kitchen assignments together weren't a foregone conclusion, but it happened. Vega couldn't influence everything without our deal being discovered, you know? Kitchen and laundry were the two most common work details." She laughed. "We did get lucky, though."

"How?"

"The kitchen was in an area of the facility that wasn't well guarded. But I had an alternate plan if we were assigned to the laundry."

Gabe smiled his admiration at her. "I'm sure you did, Jo. I'm sure you did. But how was Vega able to find Garcia's hideout? When I messaged the colonel on your phone that night, I told him I couldn't tell him where we were. He laughed and said not to worry because the DEA had someone on the inside who would lead them to him."

Jo rolled up a sleeve to reveal a faded pea-sized red mark on her arm. "I had a GPS microchip implanted in my arm that allowed Vega to monitor my location, but it was useless to me if we encountered any problems on our way through Mexico. He sent agents to follow me, but they were miles away. They wouldn't know if I was in any trouble, and they wouldn't be any help."

"Were you ever in any serious trouble?"

Jo's half-suppressed laugh was a fitting prelude to her reply. "Only … all the time. But Elena, being the very resourceful woman she was, saved our lives on more than one occasion."

Jo went on to describe Elena's heroics when they were abducted by the stranger on their way to the border, confronted by the gang member in El Llana, and challenged by the drunken thugs who wanted to rape them in Chihuahua City.

When Jo got to their harrowing experiences riding the train, she became reflective and spoke with uninhibited emotion as she did to Elena on the night of their tryst. "I thought I had lost her when I fell running to the train. When it rounded a curve and was out of sight, I didn't just feel alone, I felt lonely. And then Elena risked her life by jumping off the train and came back to save me yet again." She paused to reflect on the moment. "I was overwhelmed. I had never been so happy to see someone in my life."

There was another pause in the narrative, this time longer than the last. She cleared her throat twice before she spoke again.

"You know, Gabe, Elena was more responsible for the success of our mission than anyone else. Killing those men who wanted to harm us kept us moving forward. And staying with us and threatening to shoot Raul with her derringer kept you and me alive."

"Jo, you risked your life doing what you did. If Garcia had learned you were working for the DEA, you would have ended up as dead as Carlos. And how would you have cleared your name?"

"Vega videotaped the meeting where he explained my role

in Operation Snowfall. He made sure I had a copy of the tape, which I put in an envelope and kept with my will. And Vega would have gone public to clear my name."

"But you wouldn't have heard everyone singing your praises or have been around when you were recognized for your bravery."

"No worries," she joked. "Louisiana would have named a school after me."

Gabe laughed, but the levity soon receded, as if he'd noticed the look on Jo's face turn glum. "You were quite fond of Elena, I know. I saw it in the way you looked at her. Your eyes, Jo, are like windows into your heart."

"It's strange. I never thought I could feel about a woman the way I felt about her." Her eyes saddened into a shade of pink. "She died not knowing I betrayed her." She paused to take a deep breath and let it out slowly. "But she left me knowing that I loved her as much as she loved me."

Silence took over for a while, giving Jo time to revisit some of the memories.

"If she'd lived, it would have been difficult for you," Gabe said, speaking softly and easing Jo out of her reverie. "She would have been sent back to prison for a very long time."

Jo shrugged. "If she had lived, I had already decided to tell her to go along with my story that she had agreed to work with me to bring down Diego and his criminal organization. I'd have said she was the one who switched the briefcases to preserve the information I was sent to protect, that she was the one who knocked over the bottles on the shelf to show Vega where the tunnel was located, and that she was the one who prevented Raul from killing you and me. I'd have gone to the Board of Pardons and the governor of Louisiana to plead her case for clemency, and, if necessary, to the news outlets to gain public support for her. And I would have pressured Vega to take whatever steps were necessary to have her sentence commuted on the federal charges." Jo choked up. "I would have stood by Elena all the way, Gabe … all the way."

Gabe smiled affectionately at her. "And I would have backed you up completely, Jo … completely."

Jo reached across the table to hold Gabe's hand and said through misty eyes, "I knew in my mind … and heart … you would."

# EPILOGUE

A week later Monica Stallings stood before a room full of reporters at a press conference held at the DEA's headquarters in Springfield, Virginia. Standing with her were the United States Attorney for the District of Columbia and Antonio Vega. She was there to report on the largest fentanyl drug bust in the history of the DEA.

She said:

"A week ago today, agents of the Drug Enforcement Administration and Mexico's National Drug Enforcement Directorate, in collaboration with the Mexican National Guard, conducted a raid on the hidden retreat and paramilitary settlement of Diego Garcia-Hernandez in the Sierra Nevada Mountains of Southeastern Mexico. Garcia, known as El Leon, was head of the Chiapas cartel and wanted for drug trafficking, gun smuggling, money laundering, and murder in the United States and Mexico. Garcia and his wife, Elena Sanchez-Gomez, were both killed during the raid.

"Records found at Garcia's home identified the locations

of his labs and storage facilities, where the DEA and Mexican authorities confiscated heroin, cocaine, methamphetamine, and fentanyl with a street value of more than a billion dollars. The quantity of fentanyl seized, had it been trafficked in the United States, represented millions of potentially deadly doses.

"These actions were taken because families and communities across our nation have been devastated by the fentanyl epidemic. During the last calendar year, more than one hundred thousand people died of drug overdoses in the United States. Two-thirds of those deaths involved synthetic opioids—primarily fentanyl. And over the past two years, fatal overdoses doubled, with an estimated two hundred Americans dying every day from fentanyl poisoning.

"I want to thank Special Agent Antonio Vega and the DEA agents of his SWAT team who led the raid and risked their lives to bring down Garcia and his criminal organization that had been responsible for killing tens of thousands of Americans during his reign of crime and corruption.

"I also want to thank Detective Lieutenant Jo Crowder, a member of the New Orleans Police Department, who volunteered to go undercover for the DEA and who led us to Garcia's hideaway. Lieutenant Crowder was injured during the raid but is expected to make a full recovery.

"What the DEA has accomplished this week is of historical importance—it is the largest seizure of illegal fentanyl in the history of this nation. What the DEA has done this week saved thousands of American lives.

"But, sadly, the war on illegal drugs will not be won by the valiant efforts of the DEA and federal, state, and local law enforcement. They can only win the battles ... battles they will continue to fight until the war on drug trafficking is won."

After the press conference, and Jo's role as an undercover

agent on special assignment to the DEA was revealed to the public, Vega flew to New Orleans and met with the governor of Louisiana. He provided him with a confidential report that described Jo's role in Operation Snowfall.

The governor congratulated Vega on the success of the DEA operation and assured him steps would be promptly taken to expunge Jo's conviction, exonerate her from all wrongdoing, and reinstate her to her position with the New Orleans Police Department.

~

Jo parked her truck in the same place where she'd parked the stranger's pickup.

She'd been back in New Orleans for a month. When the interviews ended and public interest in her story waned, she returned to work to a rousing welcome. She thought that immersing herself in her job of catching bad guys would help her forget.

It didn't.

She'd driven through the night and covered the nine-hundred-mile drive from New Orleans in just under fourteen hours. She had a sandwich and four bottles of water in her backpack and a thermos of hot coffee on the seat. She wanted to be at the park before it opened and, as before, no one was around when she arrived.

She put on her backpack and began her walk into the desert directly into a blinding sun. She had a vision of Elena walking ahead at an energetic pace and with deliberate purpose. Yet her companion's gait was graceful, stepping around rocks and ruts without looking down, as if she had traveled the route often.

Jo reveled in the desolate natural beauty of the sunbaked

landscape they'd shared that day. As it did before, the vegetation softened the harshness of a never-changing wilderness. The colors remained vivid—the lavender flowers of the needle-spiked branches of the chola tree were just as striking, and the orange and lemony blossoms of the desert cacti were just as vibrant.

The smells, ranging from a bouquet of sweet-smelling floral fragrances to the pleasant, musky, earthy scents of the creosote bushes, were familiar and evoked pleasant memories of Elena. The sun beat down, and she soon soaked through her shirt and the bandanna around her neck. But the scent of her perspiration was not unlike what Elena's had been and conjured up another sweet remembrance of that day with her.

Two bottles of water later, she arrived at her destination. She recognized the rock formation where they had placed their undergarments to dry. She dropped her backpack to the ground, shed her clothes, and stepped into a river that separated two countries with not much in common. To the south was one of the poorest nations in the world, where its citizens were not welcomed as friends by its vastly wealthier neighbor to the north, but as members of a necessary workforce to help fuel the greatest economy the world has ever known.

Maybe over time that would change.

Jo swam out to where the water was deep and cool, and where she and Elena had skinny-dipped, bounced up and down, and let the water drip from their heads and faces like two ice cream cones melting in the sun. Jo's body cooled and tingled with the same excitement as it did that day together. She remembered how they'd looked at each other's naked bodies with inquiring eyes and mischievous grins.

The thought of her that day made Jo smile, and that smile lasted a good long while.

She was tempted to swim across nature's border canal and stand beside the rock where they had dressed and begun their incredible journey—two women, opposites in so many ways, drawn together with a common purpose—survival. She knew that yielding to the temptation of reliving the excitement of that moment would only evoke more bittersweet memories and deepen her melancholy. But no matter how hard she tried, she could not forget the most remarkable woman she had ever known.

She swam ashore, put on her clothes, and walked back, thinking of Elena and wondering whether the memories of her would be enough to someday lighten the weight of a heavy heart.

# A NOTE FROM THE AUTHOR

If you enjoyed this book, I would be very grateful if you would write a review and publish it at your point of purchase. Your review, even a brief one, will help other readers to decide if they'll enjoy my novels.

And I invite you to read my other Jo Crowder books, *Identical Misfortune, The Easter Murders,* and *Double Indemnity,* available in hardback and paperback at richardzappa.com, amazon.com, and barnesandnoble.com.

# About Identical Misfortune

When Veronica, a heartless sociopath, learns that her good-hearted identical twin, Ann, has married into a wealthy family, she very cleverly manipulates family members and the police into believing she's Ann, then stages Ann's suicide and makes off with millions. In a duel of wits between a cold-blooded killer and a cop, each brilliant in her own way, Detective Jo Crowder pursues Veronica while she schemes, lies and murders her way in and out of families on both sides of the Atlantic. But can Crowder stop the killing without turning her back on the law she's sworn to uphold?

**Here's what the reviewers said about *Identical Misfortune*:**

"A grim and engrossing procedural with a stellar cast."

— *Kirkus Reviews*

"A winding roller-coaster ride of betrayal and intrigue … as harrowing as the journey is, it's worth the effort."

—*Charles Ray, author & Awesome Indies Book Awards assessor*

"Utterly spellbinding crime drama thriller … a well-imagined and outstanding work of fiction.

— *Online Book Club*

"Suspenseful battle of wits … that balances cerebral puzzle solving with vigorous action."

— *IndieReader*

# About The Easter Murders

A serial killer chooses Easter week to leave dead pregnant teens in front of Catholic churches in New Orleans. Homicide detective Jo Crowder doggedly pursues a trail of evidence that leads to the arrest of Miguel Diaz, a twenty-year-old Latino nursing student. Crowder's instincts tell her that the evidence against Diaz was planted by the actual murderer. Though directed by her superiors to close the investigation, Crowder suspects Monsignor Rossi, whose connections to the victims are too suspicious to overlook. But can she prove that the clergyman is a cold-blooded murderer in time to save Diaz?

**Here's what the reviewers said about *The Easter Murders*:**

"Zappa beautifully captures multifaceted tensions that keep the story moving along at an easy clip. A twisty and highly readable thriller."

— *Kirkus Reviews*

"Once you start reading *The Easter Murders*, you'll find yourself compelled to keep on, following clue after clue, red herring after red herring, until all that is left is the inevitable, but unpleasant, reality. Zappa has outdone himself on this one. I give this 5 stars."

—*Charles Ray, author & Awesome Indies Book Awards assessor*

"A thrilling crime/drama mystery ... engrossing and difficult to put down ... four out of four stars."

— *Online Book Club*

"Zappa's *The Easter Murders* keeps readers entertained with solid police procedural work, tense courtroom drama, and insidious backroom dealing."

— *IndieReader*

# About Double Indemnity

Heartland Insurance, the brainchild of multimillionaire Jared Finch, has a simple business model—buy people's life insurance policies and collect the proceeds when they die. New Orleans homicide detective Jo Crowder and FBI Special Agent Alex Hill suspect there is a sinister relationship between Finch's company and a research laboratory that is testing an experimental serum on animals. Hill and Crowder team up to investigate why so many people connected to Finch and his company are dying. But are they willing to break the law and risk their lives to uncover the horrifying truth?

**Here is what the reviewers said about *Double Indemnity*:**

"*Double Indemnity* is an extremely well written contemporary thriller. Blending maverick cops, hardboiled killers and rogue businessmen, author Richard Zappa has created an engrossing and entirely believable crime novel."

— *IndieReader*

"Zappa's novel is remarkably eventful, featuring lots of murder, intrigue, and criminal schemes, as well as sexual attraction between the two main heroes. The plot is briskly paced, and the author never skimps on action."

— *Kirkus Reviews*

"Zappa is a skilled storyteller, and fans of crime novels will find a lot to love here. Overall, this is a well-written and exciting novel that builds to a satisfying final conflict while also leaving room for another book in the series."

— *US Review*

"Author Richard Zappa is both a first-rate writer and storyteller. His plot is intricate and involving, yet easy to follow. His action sequences, of which there are many, resonate

with cinematic intensity. Zappa uses dialogue as it should be used, with spice and bite. He increases reader involvement by making his protagonists face moral as well as physical challenges. And he does it all while keeping the pace of his story roaring ahead."
— *Pacific Book Review*

# ABOUT THE AUTHOR

Richard Zappa is a trial lawyer and novelist. A graduate of the American University Washington College of Law in Washington, D.C., he was an editor of the *Law Review* and Dean's Fellow to Adjunct Professor and former Associate Justice of the U.S. Supreme Court, Arthur Goldberg. During the course of a distinguished career as a top personal injury and medical malpractice lawyer, Zappa has litigated and tried numerous cases in state and federal courts, many of which resulted in multimillion-dollar recoveries for his clients. He retired in 2018 to write novels full time. A black belt martial artist and self-taught pianist, he writes from his homes in Wilmington and Rehoboth Beach, Delaware, and St. Thomas, U.S. Virgin Islands.

www.ingramcontent.com/pod-product-compliance
Lightning Source LLC
Chambersburg PA
CBHW061619210726
48287CB00001B/200